Michelle Smart's love affair with books started when she was a baby and would cuddle them in her cot. A voracious reader of all genres, she found her love of romance established when she stumbled across her first Mills & Boon book at the age of twelve. She's been reading them—and writing them—ever since. Michelle lives in Northamptonshire, England, with her husband and two young Smarties.

Millie Adams has always loved books. She considers herself a mix of Anne Shirley—loquacious, but charming, and willing to break a slate over a boy's head if need be—and Charlotte Doyle—a lady at heart, but with the spirit to become a mutineer should the occasion arise. Millie lives in a small house on the edge of the woods, which she finds allows her to escape in the way she loves best: in the pages of a book. She loves intense alpha heroes and the women who dare to go toe-to-toe with them. Or break a slate over their heads…

DEAL FOR HIS HEIR

MICHELLE SMART

MILLIE ADAMS

MILLS & BOON

First published in Great Britain 2024
by Mills & Boon, an imprint of HarperCollins*Publishers* Ltd,
1 London Bridge Street, London, SE1 9GF

www.harpercollins.co.uk

HarperCollins*Publishers*, Macken House, 39/40 Mayor Street Upper,
Dublin 1, D01 C9W8, Ireland

Deal for His Heir © 2024 Harlequin Enterprises ULC

Heir Ultimatum © 2024 Michelle Smart

Greek's Forbidden Temptation © 2024 Millie Adams

ISBN: 978-0-263-32016-9

07/24

MIX
Paper | Supporting responsible forestry
FSC
www.fsc.org   FSC™ C007454

This book contains FSC™ certified paper
and other controlled sources to ensure responsible forest management.

For more information visit www.harpercollins.co.uk/green.

Printed and Bound in the UK using 100% Renewable Electricity
at CPI Group (UK) Ltd, Croydon, CR0 4YY

HEIR ULTIMATUM

MICHELLE SMART

MILLS & BOON

To Laurie.

Thank you for being such a great support
and for putting up with me. xxx

CHAPTER ONE

LONDON'S SKYLINE, Sebastiano Russo grudgingly admitted, looked spectacular that evening with the soft glow of the setting sun creating a shimmering golden haze around its iconic rooftops. The helicopter he was travelling from Edinburgh in swooped down and landed on one of the most magnificent London buildings of all, the elegant home to the world's most exclusive private members' club.

As usual Lazlo, the unobtrusive manager of the Diamond Club, was there to greet him on the roof and whisk him inside.

Being in no mood for small talk and with no inclination to seek the company of the other club members in residence that evening, Sebastiano headed straight to his private suite. Losing a billion euros of his fortune in one fell swoop had a way of making a man not want company, especially when the reasons for losing said billion euros was down to your own mindlessness.

At least here he could switch the world off. The Diamond Club's facilities and services along with its innate alluring ambience gave him everything he needed when wanting to let off steam during his business trips in London. As the face of Russo Banca Internazionale, image was everything so any potentially scandalous behaviour was kept strictly behind closed doors. For centuries, the

Russo family had owned and steered the glamorous private banking institution with discretion and a touch of glamour. Its high-end customers—clients had to deposit a minimum five million euros to open an account—valued the high returns paid out even during world economic turbulence and the faultless, personalised service. Since Sebastiano had taken the helm, he'd prioritised expanding its wealth management arm and enhancing its digital services without losing any of the little touches that made their clients feel so valued. Under Sebastiano's stewardship, RBI's profits had doubled in five years. If Sebastiano's loss should be made public then his reputation and his bank's reputation would be decimated. Who would trust a man to take care of their wealth if that same man couldn't take care of his own?

For this one night he would allow himself to brood in solitude. Come the morning, he would summon his core team and talk damage limitation strategies.

It had been three months since he'd last visited the Diamond Club. Three months since he'd thrown that spontaneous party in his suite which had ended in the most unexpected way. It was the longest he'd spent between visits since Raj Belanger had invited him to join the club.

There would be no partying that night. The only company Sebastiano wanted was the bottom of a bottle of bourbon and someone prepared to fade into the background pouring it for him.

Lazlo remained silent until they arrived at the double doors of Sebastiano's suite. With a respectful nod, a bow of his head and a murmured wish for Sebastiano to have a peaceful evening, he disappeared with his usual unobtrusiveness. This was one of the many things Sebastiano liked about the Diamond Club. It wasn't just that the staff were all highly trained with discretion practically embedded in their DNA, it was that they all had the ability to judge their guests' moods with nothing more than a look and adapt their own personas to suit what they intuited was wanted from them. In all his years as a member there, the staff had always intuited his mood perfectly.

Having given pre-instructions that only a bar tender was required that evening, Sebastiano shrugged off his suit jacket in the small reception area of his suite and slung it on the back of an armchair, then ripped off his tie and chucked it on the jacket. The cufflinks were the next to be removed before he headed into the suite's main living area rolling the sleeves of his shirt up, only to take one look at the bar tender and come to an abrupt halt.

A long beat passed before the willowy dark blonde woman greeted him with a respectful smile. 'Good evening, Mr Russo.'

Chest tightening, eyes narrowing, he bypassed the pool table and football table that never failed to make a billionaire of any age light up like a child, and pulled up a stool at the long, dark redwood bar. 'Layla,' he acknowledged with a taut nod to match the tautness in his voice. 'I thought you were moving on.'

If he'd known her notice period hadn't ended, he would have made sure to notify Lazlo of his wish for a different dedicated bar tender.

The last thing he'd wanted was to be confronted by the one member of the Diamond Club's staff that he'd spent the night with.

She flashed the smile that accentuated her high cheekbones. 'Still here, just,' she confirmed lightly, in exactly the same tone with which she always served him. 'Bourbon, one cube of ice?'

He narrowed his stare again, searching her beautiful features for even a hint of reproach or peevishness but found nothing. Nothing to suggest Layla would behave with anything less than the intuitive professionalism that had led to him requesting she always serve his bar when he was in residence.

'Forget the ice,' he said gruffly, 'and make it a large one.'

Her brief smile this time was sympathetic, as if she'd peeped into his mind and seen the colossal mistake that had blighted his day and had the potential to blight the rest of his life.

She poured his drink and placed the crystal tumbler before him.

He drank it in one swallow. 'Another.'

The process was repeated. Only once he felt the liquid start to work its soothing magic did he slow his pace and sip his third glass. Rolling his taut neck, he said, 'Music. Anything of your choice but no jazz.' A cousin had once bored him for an entire Sunday afternoon with a lecture on jazz appreciation. If there was anything to appreciate about it, Roberto's monotonous, droning voice had put Sebastiano off for life.

'Something upbeat?'

Layla's musical voice could never be described as monotonous or droning, he thought, taking another large sip.

He nodded.

She tapped on a tablet and within moments rhythmic beats pulsed lowly through the vast room.

In the two years Layla had worked at the club she'd proved herself the most intuitive of all the staff to his needs and wants, and as the bourbon, helped by the music, continued to soothe the edges of his angst, the tightness in his chest that had formed at seeing her manning his bar loosened a little too.

Post-coital promises were never meant in the way real promises were, he told himself. Everyone knew that. Layla was an adult and there was nothing in her body language to suggest she was upset at his failure to call her. Now that he was a little more settled and a bit more clear in his thinking, the only impression he was receiving was that of a woman pleased to see him.

Well, it *had* been a great night that they'd shared together. The kind of night that lingered.

Relaxing even more, he raised his glass at her. 'Join me?'

Something sparkled in her forget-me-not-blue eyes. Pretty white teeth grazed the bottom lip of a wide mouth with a cupid's bow in the top lip and which three months ago had trailed kisses over every inch of his skin. 'Maybe later.'

He raised an eyebrow at the suggestiveness in her tone and the sweep of her long eyelashes.

She didn't miss a beat, arching her own eyebrows in return.

A frisson raced through his veins.

He recognised that look. It was one they'd shared three months ago in the hours before he'd thrown his guests out of the suite.

Maybe he wouldn't have to forget his troubles in a bottle or two of bourbon after all, he mused as anticipation roused. There were other, far more pleasurable ways to shake off a bad mood and if there was a pleasure greater than Layla wrapping her long legs around his waist and scraping her nails down his back while he plunged deep inside her, he was yet to experience it.

The sparkle deepened into a gleam and she leaned over the bar to top up his glass. For a moment her smart black, V-necked top gaped open, giving him a glimpse of the small, high breasts that had fitted perfectly into his mouth.

As she saw the direction of his stare, her mouth quirked in the corner. When she leaned over the bar again, this time resting her chin on her closed fist, and murmured, 'Can I get you anything else?' there was no doubt in Sebastiano's mind that the gape allowing him to see her black lace bra was deliberate.

The frisson deepened. He was close enough to smell her soft, subtle perfume, his mouth filling with the remembered taste of those perfect breasts, tongue tingling to remember the texture of her large raspberry-coloured nipples. Gazing into her eyes, he murmured back, 'Maybe later.'

Her lips widened into the lopsided smile that was her only flaw. And it wasn't even a flaw. Without it, her face would just be jaw-droppingly beautiful. Her smile turned her beauty into something spectacular. And sexy. It was a smile that promised erotic, hedonistic nights and by God had the reality matched up to the promise. To breathe in her perfume and the heat of her skin and to know that very soon those long legs could be wrapped around him again...

'How come you're still working here?' he asked after taking another long sip of his bourbon.

She gave the lightest shrug. 'My plans changed.'

'So you're staying?'

'No.' Another lopsided smile and sweep of the long lashes. 'This is my last shift.'

Now he was the one to sweep his gaze, taking another open peek at the small breasts wrapped in black lace before meeting her stare again and raising his glass. 'Then fortune is shining in my favour.'

Her elbow inched a little closer to him. 'It didn't look as though you thought fortune was on your side when you walked in here,' she observed.

Her intuition really was exceptional.

'Trust me,' he said ruefully. 'Today has been the day from hell.'

Sympathy brimmed. 'Want to talk about it?'

'No.' In his next breath he said, completely unbidden, 'I lost a billion euros.'

The Diamond Club's staff were the best in the business, from the level of service they provided, to their discretion, to showing no reaction whatsoever at any of the snippets of gossip or state secrets they became privy to in the course of their work, but even Layla's forget-me-not eyes widened at this.

He swallowed what was left in his glass and wiped his mouth with his thumb. 'Want to know how?'

Straightening, she reached for the bottle. 'Only if you want to tell me.'

What the hell? Layla had proved herself an excellent sounding board over the years. The best sounding board. What he told her went in one ear and out of the other. 'A company I'm the majority shareholder of in a personal capacity went into administration last night. On paper, I am now one billion euros poorer.'

She made an 'ouch' face and refilled his glass.

He drank with a grimace. 'I should have sold. The warning signs were there.'

After a day spent berating and raging at himself for his idiocy, he was still none the wiser as to where the lethargy in his brain that had prevented him acting on his instincts had come from. Anyone with an ounce of nous had known to sell and dissociate from a company that had turned toxic.

'I'm not used to screwing up,' he added after another drink.

'You're human,' she said softly. 'Screwing up happens to the best of us.'

'Not to me.'

She stared at him meditatively then put her elbow back on the bar and her chin back on her fist. 'Want to know what I think?'

Surprised—Layla rarely commented on the stuff he confided in her—he stared back and then shrugged. He supposed there was a slim possibility that a bar tender who doubled as a waitress was capable of an insight into his psyche that he hadn't considered. 'Sure.'

'I think you work too hard.'

'I have a lot of responsibility.' An understatement.

'I know, but when did you last take a break?' she challenged, eyeballing him in the sexiest manner imaginable.

'I take plenty of time off,' he said eyeballing her right back.

She leaned a little closer. 'I mean a proper break. A holiday, something like a trip around the Med on your yacht but without your PA, lawyer and accountant in attendance… I bet if you were to call them and order them here, they'd be knocking on the door within minutes.'

He couldn't help grinning at how on-the-nail her observation was, and was rewarded with another of her sexy lopsided smiles.

'I doubt you ever fully switch off,' she continued, her musical voice pitched low and sensuous. 'I bet you even check your emails on Christmas Day.'

'Think how much more money I'd lose if I didn't check them every day,' he riposted.

'You could afford to lose a billion euros a day for a month and still have billions left over.'

'I'd like to keep *all* my billions, not be left with scraps.'

'Then take my advice and take a break. A proper break. Recharge your batteries.' Their faces were now only inches apart. 'You know another thing that's good for stress?'

'Bourbon?'

She gave a short, soft laugh and leaned closer still. A lock of her silky hair tickled against his cheek as she whispered, 'A deep tissue massage.'

'Hmm... Now that sounds like something I'd be up for.'

'I just bet you would,' she said knowingly before another gleam lit her eyes. 'Shall I call the spa?'

He tilted his face. Their lips were a whisper away from brushing together. The sweetness of her breath filling his senses only added to the intoxication firing through his veins. Spearing his hand into the mass of thick, wavy tresses, he murmured, 'I can think of someone else I'd rather do it.'

Her lips parted against his. The sweet tongue that had explored him with the same passion as her mouth flickered against his lips but before he could mould his mouth to hers, she'd slithered back and out of reach. The hair he'd been holding fell like a waterfall around her shoulders.

Eyes full of cat-like sensuality, she gave her lopsided, oh, so sexy smile. 'I'll get some massage oil. Go and make yourself comfortable in your bedroom.'

Sebastiano stripped his clothes down to his briefs, hot blood pumping hard through him.

This was not an outcome he'd anticipated when he'd decided to end his day from hell by drowning his sorrows at his private club. The only outcome he'd anticipated was a banging hangover.

The last time his blood had pumped this hard was that night three months ago.

He'd fantasised about Layla for two years.

Her beauty had blown his mind from the first look. The tall, willowy blonde who could have graced the cover of any glossy magazine had entered his suite carrying a box of champagne for a small party he'd been hosting, and when she'd smiled at him all he'd been able to think was that there could be no sexier creature on the planet.

But she was staff. Not *his* staff, but still staff, paid to serve and cater to his every whim, part of his world but not of it. To seduce her would have been an abuse of his power. That didn't mean he couldn't request that she always tend his bar when he was in residence and enjoy feasting his eyes on her. Enjoy her company. Enjoy being able to unwind and confide things about his life with her and enjoy the sensation that she was listening because she was genuinely interested and not just because she was being paid. It helped that he doubted she retained much of what he confided.

The frisson that accompanied their talks when they were alone together was, he'd long been certain, mutual. And then she'd told him while lining up the glasses in preparation for the party he'd been throwing three months ago that it would probably be the last of his parties she worked at because she'd handed her resignation in.

The look that had flowed between them at those words...

Sebastiano's intention to party until the sun came up had been thrown out of the window, as had all his guests when midnight struck and he'd sent them home. He'd sent all the staff out too. Everyone except Layla.

There had been no doubt about what would happen the moment they were alone together. The last of the guests couldn't have left the corridor before she was locked in his arms. It had been the most thrillingly sensuous night of his thirty-five years, so thrilling that he'd taken her number and promised to call after his meeting and arrange a proper date. At the time he'd even meant it.

Which was why seeing her behind his bar had at first been such an unwelcome surprise.

Enough time had passed that he'd thought it right to assume he would never see her again and now, with anticipation burning so brightly inside him, he could barely remember why he'd changed his mind about calling her.

One more night with the woman who'd spent two years weaving through his fantasies...

He was sitting on his bed propped against the headboard wearing only his black briefs when she appeared in his open doorway holding a small bottle of massage oil.

Pressing her cheek against the door's frame, she slowly, unashamedly, swept her stare over his naked torso, all the while grazing her bottom lip with her teeth. It was enough to send the blood straight into his loins and relight his arousal.

With the face of a Hollywood siren in its golden age and the body of a supermodel, Layla wasn't hot, she was scorching and when she moved from the frame and stepped out of her heels, moisture filled his mouth.

Honey-blonde hair spilled around her shoulders, she walked seductively towards him, her short black skirt displaying her long, toned golden legs for his delectation, hips gently swaying. When she reached the foot of his bed she lightly ran her fingers over his calf.

'Turn over,' she murmured.

He obeyed, resting his cheek on a pillow. Anticipation thudded through him.

Why the hell hadn't he called her?

The light was dimmed. The mattress dipped. Air moved as she made herself comfortable beside him. The shock of cold oil poured down his spine. His flinch was automatic. Her musical laughter was soft.

It was the single most erotic moment of his life.

Her knees pressed against his side, she spread her palms and smoothed the oil over his back and shoulders, and then she got to work, kneading at his muscles with the whole of her hands, gripping the bicep closest to her and stretching his arm out so she could work her magic on his forearm too. So damn good did it all feel that if her breasts hadn't made the occasional brush against his back when she stretched herself to massage his other bicep, he might have relaxed enough to fall asleep. As it was, Sebastiano found himself caught on the cusp between pleasure and pain: the pleasure coming from her clever hands, the pain from his unrelenting arousal.

The deepening of Layla's breaths as she worked on him told Sebastiano that he wasn't the only one aroused.

Lips brushed the nape of his neck.

He groaned, would have twisted round onto his back if she hadn't pressed the tips of her fingers into his skull and kissed the rim of his ear before whispering, 'Close your eyes and don't move.'

Used to being the seducer, he found the novelty of being the seduced heightened the eroticism, heightened the thrums of desire pulsing through him.

He'd had no clue that the worst day of his life would end in such glorious eroticism. It was almost worth losing a billion euros for.

He heard a rustling beneath him but there was no time to wonder what she was doing for now she was straddling his lower back, mouth hot in the arch of his neck.

'Keep your eyes closed,' she commanded seductively. 'No moving.'

With her incredible body draped over him and the heat of her breath dancing sensation over his skin, Sebastiano had no wish to do anything but continue to obey.

Hands smoothed up his right arm. A breast covered in too many layers whispered against his cheek. He groaned again, resisting the compulsion to open his mouth and—

A shock of cold metal wrapped around his wrist. In the split second it took for him to open his eyes, Layla had leapt off him and parked herself at the foot of the bed.

It took another split second for him to register that she'd handcuffed him to the bed post.

CHAPTER TWO

LAYLA'S HEART WAS beating so hard she feared the force of it would make her sick.

She was shaking. Shaking from the desire that had welled in her during her seduction and shaking from the nerve it had taken to follow through with her plans.

She couldn't believe she'd gone through with it. The only time she'd faltered had been when Sebastiano first walked into the suite and her heart had exploded into her ribs.

Since receiving the call three hours ago that Sebastiano Russo was coming in that evening, she'd focused her mind solely on what needed to be done. The worst of it was over but the thought of what came next made her shake even harder.

'I didn't have you pegged for liking the kinky stuff,' Sebastiano said in the heavily accented Sicilian voice that shouldn't still soak into her skin like melted butter.

She'd left enough give in the handcuffs so he could twist himself round but not enough for him to slip out of the metal restraining him to the bed, and now he was lying on his back, head up against the headboard, staring at her with that lascivious gleam in his green eyes that had got her into this whole mess.

Okay, it was the whole Sebastiano Russo package that had got her into this mess. Tall, dark and handsome men were the stuff of romance novels for a reason and it turned out she was just as susceptible to their sexy promise as the next woman. And Sebastiano was incredibly sexy. She'd felt his magnetism from the first moment she'd set eyes on him.

Being five foot seven, Layla rarely had to look up to meet a man's eyes, but with Sebastiano she did, and when she locked onto them, it was a deep pool of green that captured her. That he had a chiselled face that could make a nun swoon and a lean yet muscular body to die for were secondary. It was his eyes that did it for her. His way of making her feel that she was the only woman he'd ever looked at before.

However he made her feel, she'd slept with him without any illusions as to the kind of man he was. She still didn't know what had possessed her. In all her twenty-four years, she'd been with only with one man, a long-term relationship that had ended after graduation when he'd taken a job two hundred miles from London and they'd both agreed the distance meant it would be too much work to keep the relationship going. She'd had plenty of offers since but had far too much self-respect to sleep with anyone on a first date. Once the few men she'd dated had realised they wouldn't be getting her into bed any time soon, they'd quickly moved on.

Turned out that all she'd needed for her so-called self-respect to desert her at the first opportunity was a man her hormones jumped to attention to and waved the bunting for.

Even now, even after the night they'd shared and the weeks spent clutching her phone, her heart skipping every time it rang, her desire for Sebastiano was as unrestrained as it had been the night she'd succumbed.

She'd had no illusions before they'd made love but in the morning she'd believed him when he'd said he wanted to see her again. Maybe if she hadn't been caught in the euphoric haze of their lovemaking she would have had the sense to realise they were just words. That he didn't mean it. She would have reminded herself that for all his devastating looks and undeniable charm, Sebastiano was, at heart, a spoilt, selfish, entitled billionaire.

How she hated that he could still affect her so physically and so deeply. There had been moments when she'd been massaging the oil over his smooth back and breathing in his cologne and the heat of his skin that the ache to turn him around and fuse her mouth to his and fuse their groins together and lose herself in their passion all over again had been close to overwhelming.

That sexy, knowing anticipatory gleam in his eyes as he waited for her to make her next move was enough to liquidise her insides and she had to pull air deep into her lungs to make her body move counter to what it ached to do.

What game was she playing? Sebastiano wondered when Layla climbed off the bed. She didn't look at him until she reached the door.

The look in her eyes turned his blood to ice. 'Layla?'

There was a tremor in her voice as she said, 'Stay where you are.' Like he could actually go anywhere restrained as he was. 'I've got something to show you.'

What the hell?

'Layla?' he called after her retreating body, tugging at the restraint on his wrist, then shouted, 'Layla!'

She was gone only moments but it was enough time for

him to realise the impossibility of freeing himself without a key or a chainsaw.

When she returned she was carrying a large handbag. There was nothing seductive about the graze of her teeth when her fearful eyes fell back on him.

'You need to release me,' he warned her. Whatever this game was, he no longer wanted to play it. 'Unlock this cuff.'

Her beautiful face scrunched up, eyes closing for a few beats before they snapped back open, her composure regained. 'I will. Soon.'

'Release me, *now*.'

From her handbag she produced a small brown envelope, which she extended to him. 'Business first.'

'What is that? A ransom demand?'

Her laugh was morose. 'In a way.'

He stared at her in disbelief, hardly able to believe what was happening. Layla had cuffed him to the bed and it was no kinky sex game. 'Have you lost your mind?'

Her smile was as morose as her laugh. 'Probably. Pregnancy can do that to a woman.'

For the second time in minutes his blood turned to ice.

Her shoulders rose jerkily and her face scrunched again. 'I'm three months pregnant. That envelope has the scan picture in it with our baby's due date and other pertinent information. You're good at figures. You'll be able to work back and see that the dates prove you're the father.' Her shoulders gave another jerky rise. 'Not that there's any other contender for it as you're the only man I've been with in years, but I knew you'd want proof. I also have a letter from my midwife confirming the window of the conception date.'

Layla squeezed her eyes shut. She'd had to beg the midwife to write the letter.

She'd thought long and hard about begging Sebastiano too but ultimately this had been the only way forward that protected her and, more importantly, protected their child.

It had been two months since she'd taken the pregnancy test. She'd almost passed out from the rush of blood to her head at seeing the positive sign on the stick.

'You've chained me up just to tell me that you're pregnant?' he asked incredulously.

'No, I've cuffed you to the bed because I need money and this was the only way I figured I could get it without you dismissing me as a fantasist and kicking me out of your suite.'

It would have been different if he hadn't ghosted her. Different too, if Sebastiano were an ordinary man. They'd have been coming at things from an even playing field but there was no chance of an even playing field between a young, ordinary woman and one of the richest, most powerful men in the world. Layla knew from the bitter experience of her own father how rich men used their wealth as a tool, and her father's wealth was a fraction of Sebastiano's. Her mother had stood no chance against her father. Layla, even with all her street-smarts and legal training, stood no chance against Sebastiano.

She pulled his phone out of her bag—she'd removed it from his jacket pocket—and dropped it on the bed within his reach. 'Five million.'

He looked at his phone, looked back at her, and laughed… except it wasn't the same timbre as his usual laughter. This was a laughter that chilled.

Fear laced her spine but she shrugged it off. She was

doing this for the child growing in her belly and so long as she remembered that, she could do this. She had to.

'I'm not joking and I didn't pluck that number from thin air,' she said. 'I'm having your child and, considering your vast wealth, it's only right that our child live in a decent home. London's an expensive city.' And Layla lived in what had become one of its roughest parts. Raising a child there was unthinkable. 'I've looked at properties and there's a nice four-bed in the suburbs with a big garden that would suit us perfectly. I've also factored in the cost of raising a child until the age of eighteen and then the cost of supporting their university education if that's the route they choose to take.'

He'd sat up a little straighter against the headboard and now crossed the non-cuffed arm over his chest. 'And you think that all comes to five million?' he mocked.

'No, it comes in at much less than that, but I'm also factoring in inflation and potential unforeseen emergencies. Anything that's left over when our child finishes their education will be all theirs.'

'You have such a selfless heart,' he said in that same mocking tone before flashing his perfect teeth. It was like being smiled at by a hungry shark and made her heart clatter frantically against her ribs. 'You seriously think I'm going to give you five million euros?'

'No, five million *pounds*, and if you want me to give you the key to unlock those cuffs then yes, I seriously think you're going to give it to me. In return, I've drafted a legal document stating that the five million is the extent of your financial obligations towards me and our child and that I have no recourse to come back to you asking for more. Once the money's in my account, that's it.'

'*You've* drafted it?'

'Yes, Sebastiano, *I've* drafted it.' She pulled it out of her bag, unfolded it and held it out for him to see, making sure not to get too close.

Other than his initial anger when the penny had dropped that cuffing him to the bed wasn't a sex game, he seemed to be treating the whole situation as one big joke. She'd much prefer anger. This jovial mood was unnerving simply because of the danger underlying it. Trapping Sebastiano was like trapping a big cat. Getting within arm's reach would give him the opportunity to bite. She had little doubt that when she released him he would pounce, but by then she would have the money. Any scars that followed would be worth it for her growing child's financial security.

'I've already signed it,' she added, dropping it on the bed when he made no effort to reach for it. 'A colleague witnessed it. I covered it so all they witnessed was me signing it. Once you've transferred the money, I'll leave it with you so you can sign your part too. I've also drafted a document regarding custody of our child. It makes it nice and easy for you—sole custody is mine and you are under no obligation whatsoever to have any involvement. I hope you don't sign that one because I want our child to know you and have a proper relationship with you but I understand the world you come from, and I hope you understand when you've calmed down and think about this that I'm just trying to do right by our child. All you have to do is transfer the money and then I'll let you go and you can forget all about me again and get on with your life.'

Head shaking, he laughed loudly. 'You use physical restraints to force me into giving you money, tell me you're pregnant with my child and think I'm going to let you walk out of this suite and forget about you? Were you dropped on the head as a baby?'

'I'm not a good Sicilian woman, am I? The only thing you want from me is my body.'

Sebastiano, she'd learned from the late nights in this suite when he'd confided much about his life to her, was putting off marriage for as long as he could, something that was causing consternation amongst the rest of the Russo family. They needed him to produce an heir and set it on the same path Sebastiano, his father, grandfather, great-grandfather and countless generations of other Russos had travelled, the final destination being head of Russo Banca Internazionale. The heir they were starting to get itchy about needed to be of 'good stock' from both sides. When Sebastiano married it would be to a respectable society woman, ideally Sicilian, of independent wealth who would fit in his monied lifestyle with aplomb. Love and passion were not required.

Whenever those of his trusted peers who'd already taken the marital plunge joined him at the Diamond club, it was their mistresses hanging on their arms and no one even commented on it. It was just the way things were. Wives were for duty and breeding, mistresses for fun, and everyone knew their place. Layla had heard enough snippets of conversations to know how mistresses and lovers who fell pregnant—and that was the attitude; that it was the woman whose body was entirely to blame for conception—were to be treated with suspicion, the subsequent child hidden away like a dirty little secret. Having been abandoned by her own father, Layla had no intention of letting her child be a dirty little secret, and that was if Sebastiano even acknowledged paternity. She longed for her child's sake for him to acknowledge it but had to be realistic and accept it was unlikely. Dirty little secrets were the children of mistresses, not the children of one-night stands you'd blocked all contact with.

He looked her up and down with a smug arrogance that made her fingers itch to slap off his face. 'I don't know, I've always rated the way you pour drinks.'

Hurt and loathing filling her veins like poison, Layla folded her arms across her chest. 'You only requested that I tend your bar because you like to look at me.' Long, lingering looks that had made her all hot and fizzy inside. 'If I looked like a goblin you would never have given me a second glance, now transfer the money.'

'It's Friday evening.'

'And? Personal transfers can be made at any time.'

'I can't just transfer five million euros in one sitting. There are procedures.'

'Sebastiano, you own your own bank. You, personally, dragged it into the digital age. I *know* you can transfer the money so that it hits my account immediately, so do it because, I promise you, you won't be leaving that bed until it's done. And it's five million *pounds*.'

The satisfaction at Sebastiano's latest flash of incredulity was almost worth the danger that came with cuffing one of the richest men in the world to a bed and demanding money from him. Layla had long suspected his assumption that because she had a pretty face and worked in a role of subservience, it meant she didn't have two brain cells to rub together. Having it confirmed carried a bitter tinge though, more proof that he thought nothing of her other than as a body he desired. What lay between her ears was dismissed. Arrogant and spoilt he might be but, over the last two years, Layla had grown to like him as more than just sex on legs. She'd grown to like *him*.

Sebastiano had always thought Layla the most chame-

leon-like of all the Diamond Club staff but this was a side
to her he would never have guessed she possessed. For two
years she'd played the role of attentive bar tender to him
with barely a hint to her lurking intelligence. He happily
admitted to himself that this was a side to her he found
very sexy. As incredible as it was to believe, the whole
situation was sexy.

But she couldn't seriously think she would get away
with this?

'Aren't you worried about the repercussions?'

She pulled a face. 'If you want to call the police and tell
them the great Sebastiano Russo was arrogant enough to
think a woman he'd bedded and then ghosted would willingly go to bed with him again and that he was arrogant
enough to fall into her trap then be my guest. You won't
have a shred of evidence to support your allegations and
I'll deny everything.'

'I never said anything about involving the police,' he
refuted silkily. 'I prefer to deal with situations in my own
way, and it wasn't arrogance that made me think you
wanted me again, it was experience. You might have seduced me for revenge and monetary gain but I know damn
well that you were as turned on when giving me that massage as I was.' And he would use her desire to his advantage when he took his revenge. Already a multitude of
scenarios were percolating in his head.

Colour flamed her cheeks but she didn't back down. 'If
you think I still want you then I have to question whether
you were dropped on your head.'

He flared his nostrils. 'I can still smell your arousal,
cara.'

Skin still aflame, she tightened her folded arms. 'Stop
with the mind games. None of this is for me, it's for our

child, so transfer the money because I'm getting sick of your procrastination.'

He pretended to consider it. As if there were a child! They'd used protection! This was one elaborate hoax by a woman he'd scorned and severely underestimated.

She sighed into the silence. 'Okay, if you won't give me the money for our child...' She shook her head, the expression on her beautiful face morphing into one of deep regret. 'It would be a real shame if the press were tipped off that the owner of the famed international banking group Russo Banca was so careless with his own money that he lost a billion euros overnight on an investment he knew was going bad. Imagine what that would do to your reputation. Imagine what your fellow billionaires who entrust their wealth with you would think if they learned you can't be trusted to manage your own wealth.'

Layla had no idea where this threat had come from—it had reeled off her tongue before her brain could catch up and stop it—and was having to fight hard to stop the fear gripping her heart from showing on her face.

This was going way too far and now she was digging herself a massive hole by antagonising and threatening him. Baiting the big cat that was already biding its time to pounce and sink its teeth into her neck was the height of idiocy.

None of this was going how she'd envisaged. Call her naive but she'd talked herself into believing Sebastiano would take one look at the scan picture of their baby and immediately transfer the money just to get rid of her. He'd made it patently clear he wanted nothing more to do with her. She was a warm body to him, nothing else.

Once she'd accepted she was pregnant, she'd bitten the bullet and dialled his number. She'd dialled into fresh air.

He'd either blocked her or got rid of his phone. A text message that failed to deliver proved it was the former. He'd blocked her.

Trying to get hold of him through his bank had been a nightmare of comic proportions. It had taken a week of near-constant calls and emails before she reached the heady heights of his personal office. She'd left numerous messages for him to call her. At her wits' end, she'd gone as far as to tell a snooty woman that she needed to speak to Sebastiano because she was pregnant with his child. The woman had sighed and said in the most condescending voice imaginable that this was a business line and any calls of a personal nature should be made to Mr Russo's personal phone, and that if she called the business number again a restraining order would be sought, before hanging up on her.

Terrified, knowing that to hack the Diamond Club's computer system to get Sebastiano's personal details was not only impossible but that to even attempt it would end in her imprisonment, Layla knew she had to keep her employment at the club going until he made his next visit there, and so had called Lazlo asking if she could extend her notice period. As the Diamond Club's recruitment procedure was intricate and lengthy—all staff were vetted so heavily they made the security services seem lax— he still hadn't found a replacement for her and had been happy to agree.

All she had to do was wait.

And wait.

And wait.

Before their night together, Sebastiano had been a regular visitor, gracing the club at least once a month. Since that night, so much time had passed without his presence that whispers circulated amongst the staff that he was going to resign his membership.

Layla couldn't even contemplate that happening. She *had* to believe he would show again.

In the weeks and weeks of waiting, her plans on how to tell him had shifted like sand, but it wasn't until the scan the week before that the route she had to take had solidified in her mind. It was listening to her baby's heartbeat that had done it. The clutch of her own heart followed by the explosion that had rippled into every cell in her body, an explosion of love that had turned Layla into a big cat herself whose only purpose in life was to protect her unborn child.

Sebastiano would never accept her child. Her child would be worse than a dirty secret to him. He didn't want Layla. Even with proof he would likely disbelieve her and throw her out of his suite and probably out of the entire club too, and she would be left to raise a child in a part of London only the foolish or desperate ventured into at night. And so she'd brought the handcuffs. Just to stop him from throwing her out. To force him to give her the money she needed before he hid himself in a cloak of expensive lawyers like her own father had done twenty-four years ago.

Darkness flashed in the green pools holding her gaze before he gave another chilling smile. 'You signed a watertight confidentiality agreement, Layla. Break it and you won't just lose the money you're blackmailing out of me. I will personally see that you lose everything.'

As frightened as she was, she'd dug this hole and now she had no choice but to stand in it and hold her nerve. 'I can't be the only person who knows about the loss so you'd have to prove that it was me who tipped the press off. You must know that journalists always protect their sources.'

'Everyone has a price,' he said sardonically.

'And mine is five million pounds. For you, that's loose change.'

The smile back on his face, he contemplated her lazily for a few nerve-wracking moments too long then gave a brisk nod of his head and stretched his uncuffed hand for his phone. 'I can see you will not accept no as an answer so let's get this done.'

CHAPTER THREE

'YOUR BANK DETAILS,' Sebastiano commanded once he'd opened his banking app.

She recited the sort code and account number off the top of her head.

'And your surname?'

Her forget-me-not eyes flashed. 'Sansom.'

He tapped it in, uncertain why he would feel disconcertment for not knowing this. There had been no need for him to know Layla's surname before. It was good that he knew it now though. It would make it easier to track her down when the time came to take his revenge. He didn't want to involve Raj or the staff here at the Diamond Club. This was between him and Layla, no one else.

Being Sicilian, revenge came as naturally to him as loving his family. Unlike the majority of his compatriots though, Sebastiano was of the opinion that revenge was better served cold. In truth, he'd had little need to act out in vengeance before. He came from an enormously wealthy, respected family. Slights of the kind that required vengeance were few and far between. When issues that angered or irritated him arose he dealt with them immediately, time being too short to waste on fools or incompetents.

Layla was neither a fool nor an incompetent. For two

years she'd played him like the finest violin and tonight was her virtuoso performance.

She would realise in his own time what a mistake she'd made targeting him for that performance.

His revenge would take a much different flavour from the media's portrayal of Sicilian vengeance.

Confirmation of the transfer flashed on his screen. He held it up for her. 'Done.'

Not looking at him, she swiped at her phone, read what was on the screen and took a visible breath of relief.

Enjoy the relief. Enjoy those breaths. Soon, you will be begging to breathe easy. 'You won't get away with this. You know that, right?'

She seemed to shrink before lifting her chin and bravely saying, 'If you hurt me, you hurt our baby.'

He laughed, enjoying how the sound of his laughter made her shrink into herself again. 'I *will* hurt you, Layla, but you can sleep safe—I was raised to never lift a hand to a woman and I'm not going to start with a hustler like you. There is no baby. I applaud you on a job well done. Go and spend your ill-gotten money while you can.'

She dropped her stare. Hands shaking, she put her phone into her bag and then unzipped a pocket in it and produced a small key. Fixing her eyes back on him, she grazed so hard on her bottom lip that when she spoke he could see the indentation made by her teeth.

'I *am* pregnant, Sebastiano. I didn't want it to be like this but you ghosted me and made it impossible for me to contact you. I am giving you a way out. I *do* want you to be involved in our child's life but if you can't commit to that then please, for our baby's sake, leave me alone.'

He shook his head with faux disappointment. 'As deeply

touching as that little speech was, it is time for you to release me.'

Backing away from him, she threw the key but her aim was off and it landed on the floor beside his bed on the other side from the post he was chained to.

Seeing the uncertainty cloud her beautiful face, he raised his eyebrows. 'I can't reach it, *cara*.'

The uncertainty deepened.

'I fulfilled my side of your demands,' he pointed out. 'Time to fulfil yours.'

She gave the slightest nod before tentatively moving to the side of the bed and bending down to scoop the key up.

Sebastiano waited until precisely the right moment to pounce.

Layla had never truly appreciated Sebastiano's agility or the wingspan of his muscular arms, not until she was straightening with the key in her hand and a much larger hand suddenly whipped through the air and clasped her wrist. Caught off guard, the key dropped onto the mattress as she was half pulled and half stumbled onto the bed. In the blink of an eye she found herself sprawled on top of him, her breasts crushed against his hard chest and her face in his neck, only the tips of her toes still making any contact with the thick carpet.

She was winded more through shock at the unexpected than anything physical, long stunned beats passing before she found anything approaching sense and tried to scramble off him. Tried because the arm of the hand that had captured her wrist was now wrapped around her back, trapping her to him. Trapping her against Sebastiano's mostly naked body...

Panic shot through her and she dug her hands into the mattress for the purchase needed to lift her face out of his neck then wriggled urgently…except the way she instinctively twisted to pull her face away to stop herself breathing in his scent meant she was trying to escape to the opposite side of the bed from where her feet were. Before she could demand he let her go, Sebastiano clasped her bottom and shifted beneath her, pulling her further onto the bed so she was no longer on top of him but facing him with her head in the crook of his chained arm and her legs draped over his thighs.

His gleaming green eyes captured hers. A seductive, knowing smile tugged on lips that were so close she could feel the warmth of his breath on her mouth.

It was no longer an effort to hold her breath. Layla's lungs had closed up, and when he slid his hand under her top and over her bare skin, the sensation that followed was so intense that the ache between her legs, a dull burn since she'd tortured herself by touching him so intimately, deepened into a painful throb.

This was why she'd succumbed to her desires and given herself to him. The intensity of her feelings. The depth of her desire. Lust like she'd never imagined existed, growing with each of his visits to the club, deepening with each lock of their eyes until she'd found herself fantasising about him strolling into his suite, taking one look at her and throwing her over his shoulders and carrying her to this very bed and doing whatever he wanted to her. When she'd handed her notice in, she'd known her resignation meant the unspoken, invisible physical barrier they had both erected would be torn down.

One night. That was all she'd wanted, all she'd thought she needed. But it hadn't been enough, not for either of them. The reality of their lovemaking had been headier than even her wildest fantasies. Only Sebastiano's meeting with the Bank of England the next morning had compelled them to drag themselves out of bed to shower and dress, and even then they didn't make it out of the bedroom before he had her back up against the wall.

'*Dio*, how am I going to get my head straight to discuss regulations when I can still taste your sex on my tongue?' he'd murmured, spearing her hair as he kissed her deeply. 'I will call you later, as soon as I'm free.'

But the call had never come. She'd waited until the next evening and sent him a breezy message that in no way matched the dread that had been thumping in her heart. *Hope your meeting went well and all's okay. Layla.* Blue ticks indicated the message had been delivered and read. His blocking of her had come later. She didn't know when. She didn't reach out to him again until after the pregnancy test.

She'd been so wrong. One night *had* been enough for him. He'd only responded to her seduction tonight because he was so highly sexed he would respond to any woman offering herself on a plate to him, and it was with that thought shouting in her brain that Layla clamped her lips together to swallow the moisture filling her mouth and tried desperately to tune out the pleas of her delirious body.

'Don't even think about it,' she said in a voice that was far huskier than she'd been aiming for.

Another knowing smile on his lips, he inched his face even closer. 'Think about what?'

If Sebastiano was agile he had nothing on Layla. Now she had her wits about her, she used her natural litheness to spring herself free. Feet connecting to the floor, she snatched up her handbag and raced to the door.

His mocking laughter hurt her ears. 'Run, little rabbit, run. Run as fast as you can and as far as you can. It doesn't matter. You know I will catch you.'

* * *

Sebastiano climbed out of the car and gazed up at the office block that had once been modern but now showed severe signs of wear and tear. Set in the stonework of the doorway, an intercom with a list of the businesses that occupied it. He pressed the button for Clayton Community Law and announced himself. The door buzzed. He was expected.

With a paper sign on the aged elevator declaring it out of order, he climbed the stairs to the third floor where Laurence Clayton, the law firm's bushy-white-bearded founder, was waiting in a rundown reception area for him.

'A pleasure to meet you. Thank you for agreeing to meet me out of business hours,' Sebastiano said as they shook hands.

'Believe me, the pleasure is all mine. My office is this way. Forgive the carpet. We keep hoping to replace it but funds never stretch that far.'

The threadbare carpet, Sebastiano was certain, was older than his father.

'I am quite sure we can do something about that,' he assured the man who'd set up a not-for-profit law firm three decades ago and dedicated his working life to providing free legal services for people who couldn't afford it, all paid for through fundraisers and charitable donations. 'I understand your computer system is in need of updating too?'

Laurence opened a door to reveal a small office heaped with legal texts and mountains of paperwork, and pulled a rueful face. 'Sending attachments to the courts and barristers is our biggest problem. The system is so dilapidated and cranky it can't always cope with the size of the files. We manage—we always manage—but it's frustrating because it's sucking time that should be spent helping our clients.'

Sebastiano took the offered hard chair and smiled.

* * *

Layla dragged herself out of bed after yet another fitful excuse for sleep, showered, dried her hair, and dressed carefully in skinny black trousers, a cream and black horizontally striped top, and a pair of black ankle boots that were on the cusp between funky and professional. After throwing a slice of toast and a cup of tea down her throat she went out into the cosy back garden to say goodbye to her mum.

Jilly Sansom was on her knees doing some early morning weeding, although that was really the wrong word to use for her mother's method of pulling out unwanted plants considering she found so many of them to be pretty that she tended to let them stay rooted and do as they pleased. Whatever her methods, the results were incredible, their back garden a tranquil oasis that blazed with year-round colour.

It was the garden that was making her mum prove so stubborn about moving to the suburbs with her. The garden was her labour of love. The cannabis farm next door and their area's recent crime rate explosion paled into insignificance in her mum's mind. Layla had fallen in love with one of the houses she'd viewed that weekend, one that had a garden she was certain her mum would love, and had already arranged a second viewing to drag her mum along to. She couldn't bear to leave her behind.

Jilly beamed to see her daughter. 'You look great. Very professional.'

Layla yawned through a smile.

Eyes so like her own brimmed with compassion. 'Another bad night?'

She gave a 'what can you do?' shrug. 'It'll get better.'

'It always does,' her mum agreed then brightened again. 'Got your passport?'

'In my handbag.' She was flying to Italy that morning to meet with a mega-rich philanthropist who wanted to set up a charitable legal firm using a similar model to the one she worked for with hints of a sizeable donation to their own firm dangling before them.

She'd been blown away at being chosen to represent the company. 'Me?' she'd said on Friday to Laurence, the firm's founder, when told about it. 'But I only qualified five minutes ago!' Well, three months ago. Three months since Layla Sansom had become a fully qualified solicitor of law.

'And that's why it has to be you,' Laurence had told her earnestly. 'You could have joined any law firm when you graduated but you chose us. I'm well aware that numerous other firms have tried to poach you since you gained your full qualifications but you have stayed loyal.'

'Only because I believe in what we do.'

'And that's why it has to be you—you are still passionate about what we do.' He'd pulled a wry face. 'You haven't been around long enough to get jaded.'

'Oh, I'm sure it'll happen at some point,' she'd assured him.

He'd laughed. 'That's the spirit. But seriously, if anyone can sell the importance of our work, it's you, so clear your diary for Monday.'

After kissing her mother goodbye and promising to let her know when she'd landed, Layla went back inside, grabbed her smart black fitted jacket and carried it to the living room to wait for the car that would be taking her to the airport.

Standing at the reinforced sash bay window, she watched a small gang of teenagers in school uniform trundle to the bus stop she would normally catch her own bus to work from. Most of them were kids she'd known since they were in their own mothers' bellies, some she'd babysat for in her own teenage years. She loved the lot of them, pains in the butt that they were, but wished every interaction with them didn't come with the argument of why she wasn't going to buy cigarettes or booze for them or why she didn't want to buy cannabis from them. Poor kids. She could only pray that they stayed strong, focused on their education, and got the hell out of this neighbourhood. Pray, too, that they stayed within the walls of their homes when the sun went down. The people who roamed these streets at night were not the kind of people you looked in the eye. At night you only left your home if you had to, and if you did have to, you kept your head down and walked as fast as you could.

A tall, dark-haired man appeared on the other side of the street. Layla's heart caught in her throat and she shrank back from the window even though her brain had already registered that it wasn't him.

It had been over two weeks since she'd fled the Diamond Club. For the first week she'd shied away from all shadows. For the first week she'd behaved like a fugitive in a film, constantly looking over her shoulder and watching out for places and spaces where someone could hide and pounce. A cricked neck had stopped the constant checking over the shoulder but even now, travelling on a crowded bus through London's rush hour, she felt exposed, which was ridiculous. As if Sebastiano would be seen dead on public transport! All the same, she felt safer on busses than the tube so that was now her favoured mode of transport. She'd also taken the precaution of adding even more locks and chains to the front and back doors at home leading her mum to complain that it took longer to lock up than to brush her teeth. Although she knew deep down that these precautionary measures were a complete waste of time when up against a man with unlimited resources, they at least allowed her to get a little sleep, if not the full night she so craved.

What was even more ridiculous was that she knew perfectly well Sebastiano wasn't going to break into her home and kidnap her from her bed and he wasn't going to snatch her from the street or drag her from a bus.

Constantly thinking and worrying about the form his revenge would take was what was stopping her from sleeping. She hoped he waited a few months longer, when hopefully the pregnancy would be visible. He wouldn't be able to deny it then. Three and a half months gone and no one would guess she had a baby growing inside her.

She wished she could stop the idle fantasies that kept creeping on her when her brain became especially woolly with lack of sleep, of Sebastiano approaching her and then stopping mid-step, his gaze dipping to her stomach and the expression on his face changing from whatever revenge looked like to rapture.

Despite everything, she wanted him to want their baby. She wanted him to love it. She wanted her child to have what she'd never had—a father.

An email from a client pinged, an impoverished woman with three small children, under threat of eviction for non-payment of rent after the children's father stopped his maintenance payments. It was for people like this client that Layla had chosen her career path, people who needed but couldn't afford decent legal representation. People like her mother.

It was as she was sending her reply of reassurance that everything was in hand that a huge car with darkened windows expertly pulled in to the small gap at the front of her house. Every person within Layla's eye line turned to gawp at it.

Only when she'd unlocked all the locks and chains on the front door and stepped outside did she realise the car was a stretched Bentley.

'Wow,' she murmured. Her years at the Diamond Club had taught her more about the societal value of cars than she could ever hope to forget, and this car was of a breed of the super-rich.

The waiting chauffeur opened the back door for her.

The interior was every bit as luxurious as she could have imagined, the cream seats made of the softest leather, all the panelling a highly buffed dark wood.

'If you open the panel in front of you, you will find cold drinks to help yourself to,' the chauffeur said via an intercom.

London's streets were heaving that busy Monday morning, and as they crawled their way through rush hour traffic, Layla had a marvellous time exploring the luxurious cabin. Such a marvellous time did she have that it wasn't until The Shard suddenly loomed in her vision that she realised she was being driven in completely the wrong direction for the airport...

Just as she was processing this, the driver entered an underground car park. A trickle of unease crawled up her spine.

The car came to a stop. The back door opened. A tall figure in a dark grey suit slid in.

'Hello, little rabbit.'

A handcuff was locked around her wrist before she even found the wits to scream.

CHAPTER FOUR

IT TOOK LAYLA approximately three seconds to regain her wits and understand that she'd guilelessly walked into Sebastiano's trap and that she was handcuffed to him. Three seconds for the instinct to escape to kick in, an instinct she knew would prove futile even as she yanked on the unyielding door handle and stabbed at the unresponsive window button, and shouted for the driver to let her out.

'He can't hear you,' Sebastiano said mildly as they drove up the ramp and back into the daylight.

Furious, Layla turned her head so she could glare directly at him, and, for the first time since she'd fled the bedroom of the suite she'd chained him in, made eye contact with the father of her baby. Her already wildly thumping heart accelerated.

He winked. 'Great to see you, Layla.'

Trying hard to catch a breath, a feat made harder as every snatch came with a dollop of his gorgeous cologne, she stared at his perfect face and debated which part of it she should punch.

She should have known. Potential benefactors didn't appear from nowhere. Their law firm wasn't fashionable enough to attract them without a lot of groundwork and pleading. Their clients were the kind of people who slipped under the radar of people's attention, mostly ordinary people without a tragic backstory who'd fallen on desperately hard times and had nowhere else to turn for help. Layla had started at Clayton's straight from university. The salary offered was so far below the market rate that she was the first graduate to approach them as a first resort and not a last. She hadn't cared about the money, and in any case the money from her part-time evening job at the Diamond Club had made up for it. The day she'd received her practising certificate, she'd received a modest pay rise to reflect that she was now a fully qualified solicitor, just enough extra money to enable her to quit the club.

Quit the club and sleep with its sexiest member.

As perverse as she knew it was to be feeling it, the primary emotion jostling for space with her fury was relief that the worst had finally happened. No more looking over her shoulder. Like watching a horror film, anticipation of the screams was always worse than the screams themselves. Whatever form Sebastiano's revenge took, it couldn't be worse than her imaginings, which had ranged from being thrown in the boot of a car and driven over every speed bump in England to Sebastiano using the cuffs currently binding her to him for an entirely different purpose that shouldn't have made her feel all hot and sticky just to think of it…

'Where are you taking me?' she asked tersely.

'Sicily.'

That made her back straighten. 'You are out of your mind.'

'Possibly. Being chained to a bed and blackmailed out of five million pounds has a way of making a man…' he widened his eyes and wiggled his fingers '…a little crazy.'

'Unhinged is the word that springs to mind if you think you can kidnap me and take me out of the country.'

'I've already kidnapped you, *cara*. You've got your passport. Getting you out of the country is the easy part.'

She snorted her derision. 'And what are you planning to do if your depraved little fantasy...delusion...of getting me to Sicily works? Lock me in a dungeon?'

His eyes gleamed. 'Now that's an idea I could run with.' He lifted the wrist chained to hers, forcing her own arm to rise. 'I already have the restraints: thank you for leaving them with me. Let us hope I don't misplace the key.'

'I can look after it if you want?'

He leaned his face into hers. 'Nice try.'

Hating the pulsing sensation in her pelvis at his closeness, close enough now that every inhalation came with the musky scent of his skin as well as the cologne covering it, she gave a sarcastic smile. 'I thought so. But if you really are planning to smuggle me onto an aeroplane then there's the little matter of security and all those pesky metal detectors to get past.'

The tip of his nose a whisker from brushing against hers, his smile made her think again of the caged big cat, except this time the cat had been freed and was selecting the choicest area to take his first hungry bite. His voice dropped to a seductive whisper. 'I am confident that you will walk willingly onto my plane, no restraints required... unless requested.'

She had to expel the breath she'd been holding to ask, 'Does Laurence know what you're doing?'

He shifted back. 'Laurence believes I am your secret lover.'

Sebastiano delighted to see the multitude of expressions that flittered over Layla's beautiful face. He was quite sure she was thinking of ways to overpower and possibly maim him. His veins buzzed just to imagine her acting out those thoughts.

It was rather incredible to think that in the weeks since being chained to a bed and blackmailed out of a substantial amount of money, he'd felt more alive than he'd ever done before.

He would never have described his life as being boring or predictable but being outwitted by the bar tender he'd bedded after two years of mild flirtation had pumped him with an adrenaline that even a hard workout in his gym couldn't match. Whereas after their night together he'd ruthlessly forbidden himself from thinking about her, since her blackmail he'd luxuriated in his plans for vengeance, the image of Layla's perfect oval face, cute nose, striking eyes and lopsided smile always there whether his eyes were open or shut.

He settled back as far as their locked cuffs would allow so he could take the whole of her in. *Dio*, she was stunning even with minimal makeup, her honey-blonde hair loose and tumbling around her shoulders accentuating her high cheekbones. Her top had slipped a little, exposing a little of her smooth shoulder. Exposing, too, the strap of her blue bra, and he idly wondered if she was wearing matching panties. 'I would feel bad about lying to him but then I learned he mentored you.' Noticing her clenched fists, he smiled sympathetically. 'Don't worry, no Laurences were hurt in the planning of my vengeance.'

Layla squeezed her eyes shut in a futile attempt to quell the rage boiling in her before flashing her fury back at him. 'You had no right dragging him into this. He's a lovely man who's spent his whole life doing his best to help others. He'll be horrified when he learns you've tricked him.' Laurence was the closest thing to a father she'd ever had, the reason she hadn't doubted for a second the validity of a trip to Italy to meet a wealthy philanthropist.

'He'll only learn the truth if you tell him, and what would you have preferred? That I used your mother to get to you?'

The mention of her mother made her chest tighten.

'I did consider it,' he mused. 'But then I paid a visit to the coffee shop she works at and…'

She almost sprang off the seat in shock. 'You stalked my *mother*?'

The musing expression on his face deepened. 'I wouldn't call it stalking, more scoping the enemy.'

'You *pig*.'

'Pigs are highly intelligent creatures and far more hygienic than we give them credit for, so thank you for the compliment.'

'My mother's no one's enemy.'

'Having met her, I understand what you mean. A beautiful woman. She could be your less shouty older sister.'

If Layla's left wrist hadn't been cuffed to Sebastiano's right wrist, she'd have swung her arm into his stomach with all her furious strength. The way the bastard was relishing every moment meant he'd probably enjoy it.

'How did she take the news that she's going to be a grandmother at the tender age of forty-four?'

It took a moment to fully understand what he'd said. 'You've investigated her?'

'Not personally. How did she take the news about the "baby"?'

'What do you mean, *not personally*?'

'I mean I employed others to do the investigating, and before you ask, yes, I had everyone with a close connection to you investigated, so now you can answer my question of how she took the news about the "baby". I am assuming you told her?'

'Of course I told her—she's my mother,' she snapped. 'And she took it much better than you did.'

'So you are still sticking to the pregnancy story then?'

'Does that mean you're still in denial?'

He laughed. '*Cara*, we both know there was no conception. Not with me. You slept with me, returned to that unsavoury street you live on—yes, I paid a little visit to it—and realised I could be your ticket out of there.'

Initially, Sebastiano had been convinced Layla had planned everything, from their initial wild coupling to the blackmail. Everything he'd learned from his investigation into her had changed his mind.

When he'd first read the full report, he'd been stunned.

He'd been unaware that in all the time he'd known her, Layla had been working for a law firm gaining the experience and qualifications needed to become a solicitor in her own right, a discovery he'd found as disconcerting as when he'd heard her surname for the first time. He'd shaken the disconcertment off, telling himself there was no reason he should have known that about her. He'd shaken off the greater disconcertment that her law firm was an entirely charitable organisation with the lowest wages for solicitors in the whole of the English capital. After all, he'd reasoned, history was littered with seemingly good people burdened with dark secrets. No one was entirely pure.

Layla's resignation from the Diamond Club coincided with her qualifying as a solicitor, which suggested her blackmail had been opportunistic rather than planned. Seeing where she lived had only reinforced this notion.

'Do you really think I would choose a man like you to

be my meal ticket?' she asked with incredulous heat. 'Deny it to yourself all you want but I *am*...'

He placed a finger firmly to her lips. 'No more baby talk, and no more Medusa looks at me. You have five million in your bank account and once we are married, I will transfer the same amount into your firm's account. One night of work will have earned you ten million pounds, so I think it is time you started showing me some gratitude.'

The shock on her face at this was as delicious as his chef's deconstructed tiramisu. He assumed it was this same shock that made her snatch hold of his finger and move it from her mouth rather than bite it off.

'What did you just say?' she whispered.

'Many things, but I assume it was the bit about marriage that you're referring to?'

Her eyes had widened so much they'd become perfect orbs. 'You really have lost your mind.'

'I have never felt saner or seen a clearer path in front of me.' To his surprise, he realised they'd just turned into the airport's dedicated area for private flyers. He hadn't noticed they'd cleared the throng of traffic. 'You and I will marry on Saturday, and you will use your excellent acting skills to put on an act of complete adoration otherwise I will not just destroy your life but I will personally see that Laurence and your entire law firm is destroyed too.' The only one he would spare was her mother.

The car came to a stop.

Sebastiano extracted his finger from Layla's tight grip and removed the key for the handcuffs from his jacket pocket and unlocked them. Freed, he rubbed his hands together and smiled at her. *Dio*, he was enjoying this. He'd known revenge would taste sweet but this tasted sweeter than a strawberry at the height of a British summer. 'It is now time for me to board my flight. You do not have to come with me. I will not force you onto the plane.' He leaned again into her ashen face and widened his smile. 'You are most welcome to take your chances and hope that I am bluffing.'

Layla parked herself on the luxurious soft leather seat facing Sebastiano.

'Strap yourself in, *cara*,' he said with the mocking tone she was coming to hate as much as she hated him. 'And that is no way to look at your fiancé. Think *complete adoration*.'

She shook her head in part fury and part bewilderment. She'd wanted to call his bluff, had had to force her feet to move one in front of the other up the steps and onto the plane. It had been the steeliness in his stare that had convinced her he wasn't bluffing. Oh, not about the marriage part—that was plainly bonkers—but about his intention to destroy her law firm if she didn't comply.

Her fury wasn't just directed at him either. A large portion of it was aimed firmly at herself for thinking she could take on Sebastiano Russo and escape with only minor injuries. For believing that, deep down, he was one of the good guys. For the longing that just wouldn't quit that he would accept the pregnancy and want to be a father. For the longing that just wouldn't quit for *him*.

Lifting her chin, she looked him square in the eye. 'What are you really planning to do to me?'

His hateful green eyes gleamed. 'Are you thinking dungeons again?'

She was close to being angry enough to cry. 'Stop it.'

'I can turn a section of my cellar into one that we can use as a play room if you want.' The gleam deepened. 'We can take it in turns to be restrained.'

The plane began to move.

Unable to look at him a moment longer, Layla stared out of the window beside her head.

'We are to be married in my private chapel at two o'clock on Saturday afternoon. All the wheels to make this happen have already been greased.'

The thumps of her heart were making it hard to hear clearly but every word penetrated. It was the lack of mockery in his voice that turned the thumps into thunder rolls that whooshed hot blood in her head and made her feel faint.

The plane lifted into the sky and the only word she could pull from her lips was, 'Why?'

'Because I need a wife.' There was a slight pause. 'Maybe not a wife, but I need a public distraction. Remember that billion-euro loss I told you about? You must do because it's the billion-euro loss you used to extort five million pounds from me. A journalist from a respected financial newspaper has been investigating it. My legal team are now out of legal avenues to prohibit publication. The temporary injunction lifts tomorrow morning. The journalist will publish immediately. As soon as the news is released, I will release my own statement announcing my wedding to a respectable English family lawyer. It is a tactic commonly known as burying bad news, and what better way to bury bad news that could bring down my whole company than with the wedding of the century? My network has dropped subtle hints to world and business leaders that Saturday is a day they should clear any plans made. Personalised invitations will be hand-delivered to them within an hour of the announcement.'

She couldn't stop her face from turning back to him

but was reeling too much to even pull one word out, never mind string a coherent sentence together.

Perfectly understanding her expression, Sebastiano pulled a sympathetic face. 'It is a lot to take in for you.'

'But *why*?' She shook her head, trying desperately to clear the blood from it. 'I can just about get my head around the marriage aspect... Sebastiano Russo getting married will make the news, that's for sure, but how you can be sure it will bury the loss beats me and I really don't get why you would want to marry me—sure, as vengeance for what you think I've done to you it makes a form of sense in a slightly psychotic way, but I'm not a society woman like you're supposed to marry and I'm—'

'You're the best thing at short notice,' he cut in. 'You are unknown in my world, which will only add to the interest. The main criterion for a wife for a man in my position is respectability and on paper you have that. You're a lawyer. That you were abandoned before birth by your father and raised solely by your mother only gives people more to admire about you because it suggests someone who is hard-working and focused.'

She had to grip the handrails to stop herself from swaying. To hear her father's abandonment thrown so casually into the conversation almost as a weapon against herself cut to the bone. Coming from the father of the life growing inside her sent the knife to the marrow.

'My investigative team looked into your entire background,' he continued. 'You have never put a foot wrong. Only I know that behind your respectable facade lies a conniving opportunist. We will marry for a short period, until any kick back from the loss has passed, and then we will announce our separation. I can already see it: *Unfortunately, with our individual work commitments, we were unable to make our marriage work but we part ways with an abundance of love and respect for each other...* I have assured Laurence you will be back in the office in a month. When that happens, we can both embrace the workaholic lifestyles that can destroy even the closest of marriages.

Her laughter had a slight tinge of hysteria to it. 'Love and respect? Now I've heard everything.'

'I have the greatest respect for you as an adversary, *cara*. It is what will make our marriage so interesting, do you not agree?'

'What, you *want* a wife who hates you?'

A frisson of desire fired through his loins. Marriage—well, the production of an heir—was something that had loomed in Sebastiano's mind since he'd taken the helm of RBI five years earlier. He wasn't just the person with overall control but its public face. His actions carried as much weight as his words. Choosing the right wife was imperative. It had to be someone respected on her own account, who could act as hostess without being fazed by the company she was keeping, who knew how to moderate her speech and steer away from controversial subjects and knew not to do anything that could bring scandal in its wake, and who was wealthy in her own right. Unfortunately, all the women he knew who fitted these criteria were as exciting as a board meeting. Layla fitted the criteria of the first two aspects. Fear of the damage he would cause would keep her in line for the second two aspects. As she'd already proved herself an opportunistic gold-digger and their marriage would only be brief, the final criterion was moot. That she was a chameleon with fire in her veins would give their brief marriage more entertainment value than all the years of the permanent marriage he would make when it was over.

Openly sweeping his gaze over her bombshell beauty, relishing the defiance in the jut of her chin and the colour slowly creeping over her high cheekbones, he said, 'In public, we will be the model of a respectable couple as befits the head of an international bank.' And then he smiled. 'Whatever war we make between ourselves and whatever form that war takes will be entirely private.'

Layla couldn't settle. Sebastiano had taken himself off to his office and she didn't have it in her to marvel that she was on a private plane with an actual office in it, or marvel at the plush living area she paced up and down in dreaming up myriad scenarios to escape this terrible trap he'd caught her in. Of course, the easiest way out of it was to simply say no and fly back home but this, as with every other scenario, was discarded because they all ended in the same way—her law firm's destruction. Hundreds of current clients with their legal representation ripped away from them. Thousands more future clients lost in the system with nowhere to go for help.

What a fool she'd been. Desperation to get out of her crime-ridden neighbourhood before her baby was born had made her reckless and now she was paying the price. There were only two brief glimmers of sunshine in the whole thing, one being that the money for her baby was already secure—at least for now. She wouldn't put it past Sebastiano to find a way to take it back from her. The other was that during their short marriage, the pregnancy would start to show and Sebastiano would have to confront the truth of it. There was a chance, slim though it was, that her baby might have its father in its life.

His office was at the tail end of the plane. Unable to bear another minute of her own thoughts, she opened the door to it without knocking and found Sebastiano perched on his desk chatting on his phone.

One look at her and he cut the conversation short.

'My beautiful fiancée,' he said, casually placing his phone on the desk without rising from it. 'Missing my company already?'

He'd removed his suit jacket and tie and rolled the sleeves up on his shirt, the muscles of his lean torso clearly delineated beneath the expensive material. Hating herself for what must be an inherent shallowness that her pulses could quicken at the mere sight of him, Layla took a step back to create more distance between them. 'I have questions.'

'And you have come here for the answers? How romantic.'

Gritting her teeth, she prayed to all the gods for strength. 'Did you mean it about donating five million to my law firm?'

'You will learn that I always mean what I say. If the wedding goes smoothly and you put on a convincing act then I will transfer it on Sunday.'

'Why would you do that?'

'Every good dog deserves a bone.'

Her outrage was so immediate that she closed the gap between them in two quick paces and pushed furiously at his chest. 'How can you *say*…?'

A large hand enveloped her wrist, cutting her off mid-outrage. In the blink of a moment, Layla found herself pulled to Sebastiano and trapped between his thighs.

'I probably deserved that reaction, but let's save the kinky stuff for the bedroom,' he murmured.

His position on the desk made them practically eye level. His face was so close to hers that the warmth of his coffee-scented breath landed on her lips. To her absolute horror, warm sensation spread through her veins, and when he speared her hair with the hand not wrapped around her wrist, she was helpless to stop the shiver of delight that zinged down her spine.

'I take back calling you a pig,' she said hoarsely, trying her hardest to wrench her stare from the hypnotic green gaze that was the cause of all this trouble. 'You're nothing but an unmitigated bastard.'

He smiled lazily…lasciviously…and released her wrist, tiptoeing his fingers up her ribcage and splaying his hand over her right breast to gently pinch the hardened nipple. He pulled her head even closer and, his voice now a seductive whisper, said, 'And what does it say about you that an unmitigated bastard like me turns you into liquid?' And then his sensuous mouth found hers.

CHAPTER FIVE

LAYLA FELL INTO the molten heat of Sebastiano's hungry kiss. For a few heady moments she returned it, winding her arms around his neck and threading her fingers into his hair as their mouths moved together in a ravenous duel of tongues and clashing teeth, her aching breasts—she hadn't even known how badly they'd been aching until he'd touched them—compressed into his hard chest.

For those few heady moments she purged herself, the angst she'd been living with all these months drowning in the feel and taste and scent of the man she'd danced into the fire with...

And who'd burnt her and reduced her to ashes.

Digging her fingernails tightly into his skull, she kissed him even harder, needing him to feel a fraction of the pain his rejection of both her and the life they'd created had caused in her heart, then wrenched her mouth away.

'Do that again and I'll bite your tongue off,' she spat.

Sebastiano tried to think of a retort but his brain was temporarily dead. All his current thinking was coming from a lower part of his anatomy.

It had been like that during their night together, he remembered dimly. A complete capitulation of his body to the sensuous pleasures of Layla. So complete had the capitulation been that his brain—his real one—had fallen too, and when he'd finally been able to drag himself away from her it had been with the sensation that if he couldn't be with her again, his life as he knew it would be over. *He* would be over.

He'd left his suite at the Diamond Club fully intending to be back in her arms by nightfall.

It had been mid-afternoon, sitting with the Governor of the Bank of England, barely able to concentrate on this most important of meetings, that sanity had pushed out the euphoric haze of their lovemaking. Or their sex as his sharpened brain had quickly renamed it.

At the end of the meeting he'd got in the back of his car and ordered his driver to take him to the airport.

The next evening a message from Layla had pinged. He'd read it with his chest so full of an emotion he couldn't discern but which every instinct in his body had recoiled against that he'd come close to throwing his phone in the swimming pool. Instead, he'd made the less extreme choice of blocking her number, then deleted it for good measure too.

He couldn't quite remember his reasoning for this other than the firm conviction that a night of great sex, especially with a bar tender, should not make a man come close to losing his head, but had felt a hell of a lot better in himself for doing it. It was quite possible that he'd sensed her opportunism, he now thought with the great benefit of hindsight. That must have been it. Some unacknowledged sixth sense had warned him Layla would bring trouble on him.

One full-blown kiss and that close-to-drugged feeling had come roaring back. The difference now was that he was going to marry her and have the luxury of revelling in the capitulation. For as long as the marriage lasted he would share a bed with the sexiest woman to walk the earth.

Gazing into her passionately furious forget-me-not eyes, he laughed softly. 'And deny yourself the pleasure you would get from it?'

That wonderful contortion of emotions played over her beautiful face again. And it was wonderful. Glorious. His fiancée was a spitfire of emotion for him.

'If you think *that* is going to happen again, you have another think coming.'

'You think you can resist this chemistry between us?'

'The only chemistry is in your head.'

'Let's see how much it's in my head when you're sharing my bed.'

'That will *never* happen,' she said with such vehemence he almost felt sorry for her.

'You will share my bed for the duration of our marriage or our deal is void.'

Angry colour enflamed her cheeks. 'No way.'

'We have to be convincing, *cara*. I have many staff in my household. I trust their discretion but only to a point—careless words cost lives…or in my case, businesses. I am marrying you to distract the world from my foolish mistake and it has to be convincing or it will backfire. To be convincing you will share my bed.' At her mutinous expression, he smiled and added, 'I will make a deal with you. As my wife you will be obliged to kiss me and show me affection in public, but if I make a move on you in the privacy of our bedroom you reserve the right to bite my tongue off. Fair?'

She managed a nod so tight he could feel the effort it took for her to make it.

'And to prove how reasonable I am and my willingness

to show good faith, when you make your move on me, I promise to let you have your way without bloodshed.'

'Never,' she whispered even as her eyes pulsed and her breathing deepened.

Sebastiano inched his face closer to hers and lowered his voice even further to match the volume of hers. 'If you're that revolted by the idea then why are your fingers still in my hair?'

It was the blood pounding in Layla's ears that delayed the horror of what Sebastiano had just pointed out from reaching her hands and enabling her to snatch them away immediately, a delay long enough for the pads of her fingers to continue their slow caress of his skull—when had she stopped digging her nails in to it?—through his soft dark hair.

In an instant she yanked them away and swiped at the hands still buried in her own hair.

Laughing, he put his hands on her waist but before she could react he'd gently steered her back and risen to his feet so she was no longer trapped between his thighs. 'We should take our seats. We'll be landing shortly.'

With the weight of Layla's outraged stare following him, Sebastiano left the office and sauntered back to his seat.

Layla had expected Sebastiano's villa to be big. He was one of the richest men in the world. It was inconceivable that he would live in anything less than grandeur and yet shortly after they'd driven the outskirts of Palermo's colourful streets and into the verdant countryside, the tall trees cleared and there before her was a stunning gold baroque palace that rose from the earth like a pair of angel wings.

'This is yours?' she practically squealed, completely forgetting the vow of silence she'd made in the wake of their kiss. She'd made a pretty good fist of it up to that point though, refusing to exchange a word or glance with him during the landing or the quick march down the plane's steps and into the waiting car. Aggravatingly, her silence and refusal to look at him hadn't perturbed him in the slightest, and she'd had his silky voice and heavy accent polluting her ears by pointing out areas of interest to her during their short drive.

'It is,' he confirmed.

'That's not a villa. It's a palace!'

He chuckled. 'Not quite. It was built in the early eighteenth century for an Italian count but it is very much a villa. It was abandoned for decades. I bought it five years ago. The renovations in the main villa are complete but a number of the guest cottages are still to be finished.'

The long drive was flanked by a sprawling landscaped lawn so thickly green and vast it reminded her of the gardens of the English palaces and castles she'd visited with her mother over the years. The closer they drove to it, the more the villa's beauty revealed itself. Soon she saw the gold was an illusion caused by the sun, the walls painted a pristine white, the tall sash windows and frames and roof a gleaming sandstone colour.

'How many bedrooms does it have?'

'Fourteen in the main villa but the guest cottages and lodges can sleep another thirty people. The staff have their own quarters.'

It made her feel quite faint. 'All this for one man?'

'One day it will be a family home filled with children.'

It should not feel like another twist of the knife to know the family he was envisaging did not include her own baby.

Determined to hide it, she airily said, 'Can I bagsy a room for our child, then?'

'If by bagsy you mean choose then of course. Choose whichever room you wish for your imaginary baby.'

'Go and buy a pregnancy test for me to take,' she said on impulse. 'You will see with your own eyes that I *am* pregnant.'

He laughed. 'You are tenacious, I will give you that. And if it does show that you are pregnant, what then? You cannot expect me to believe the child is mine.'

She could have screamed her frustration. 'You are incredible.'

'Thank you.'

'It wasn't a compliment.'

'I know.'

'I've already got the money. Why would I still need to lie?' she demanded.

'Because to admit the truth would mean admitting to the lie, and, before you start shouting at me again, we are about to go inside and be amongst staff so I need you to practise your *complete adoration* face.'

'You are going to be a father! We have created a life together! How can you expect me to walk around the home you're intending to fill with babies from another woman looking all pathetic and adoring when you're stubbornly refusing to accept that you already have a child on the way with *me*?'

A sudden warning flashed from his green eyes, all sardonic amusement vanishing. 'Do not test me, Layla. There are members of my staff I would trust with my life but we both know everyone has their price. I do not want to destroy a charitable law firm that does such good, so do not put me in a position where I have to destroy yours.'

Clenching her fists, she let out her frustration with a long, gritted-teeth scream and a stamp of her feet, then blew out a long breath of air, shook her hands loose, straightened her back and smiled. 'Lead the way, *darling*. I'm just *so* excited to finally be at the home we're going to lead a long and happy life together in.'

His eyes narrowed before a glimmer of amusement flashed back in them. 'That hurt, didn't it?'

Not dropping her smile, she nodded brightly. 'So very much.'

'Poor Layla.' He tapped on his door. It opened immediately.

Once he was out, Layla accepted his offered hand with a, 'Thank you, *darling*.'

He brought her hand to his mouth and razed his lips over her knuckles. *'Il piacere e tutto mio.'*

She gazed at him with open adoration. 'I've no idea what you just said but I'm sure it was wonderfully romantic.'

'Wonderfully,' he agreed. 'I can teach you my language, if you like?'

'I would be *thrilled*,' she cooed putting her hand to her heart.

He burst into laughter, palmed her cheek and murmured, 'Possibly turn it down a notch?'

She covered his hand and gazed into his eyes with a dreamy sigh. 'Too much?'

Amusement still writ on his face, he threaded his fingers through hers and led her through the magnificent arched entrance flanked by marble statues of men—Layla assumed Roman gods—in toga-style robes reading books.

The mid-afternoon Sicilian sun was far hotter than the sun they'd left behind in London and she welcomed the cool interior of the reception room, welcomed even more the fresh orange juice served by a smartly dressed middle-aged man with the shiniest shoes she'd ever seen as it gave her a legitimate reason to unthread her fingers from Sebastiano's.

Clutching tightly to her glass, she walked beside him through palatially sized rooms with high frescoed ceilings, the dominant colour gold, and tried to ignore the awareness zinging through her veins at his closeness by concentrating all her attention on the ornate interiors that would feel at home in any palace.

'This is nothing like I expected,' she commented as she was shown into a dining room so vast it could accommodate her entire workforce and clientele.

'What did you expect?' he asked.

She shrugged. 'Something much more modern. This feels like I've stepped back in time, and when I compare it to your suite at the Diamond Club…'

'Everything here has been renovated sympathetically. You do not buy a villa built for royalty and turn it into a play den.'

'The Diamond Club's building must be as old as this and you turned your suite there into a play den,' she pointed out.

'That's because I use it as a play den. It's a place for me to switch off and entertain my real friends, whereas this place… Just as I am the public face of my bank, this is the public face of me. It is a villa that befits my status and projects wealth, taste, capability and a serious mindset.'

She snorted.

He caught her eye and gave a wry smile. 'I run a multi-billion-euro bank, *cara*. I entertain world leaders within these walls.'

'So no table football here?'

'Image is everything in my world. Let me show you the ballroom where we'll be hosting our wedding reception and then you can freshen up before we eat.'

'I've nothing to freshen up with,' she reminded him.

'Have you not yet noticed that I think of everything?'

'Apart from effective contraception,' she riposted so sweetly that the curdling poison that infected Sebastiano's blood every time she mentioned the pregnancy was muted by the amusement threading like waves through his veins.

Layla's luminescent beauty was the first thing he'd noticed about her, the years revealing a subtle wit that came only in infrequent flashes and only ever when they were alone and she was pouring him drinks as he relaxed from the stress of his job. All those hours spent together, revealing much of himself—it was only when he looked back on those hours that he realised how much he'd given away to her—but without her revealing anything of herself. He'd never asked. Never wanted to know. Layla had been his secret pleasure, a beautiful, sexy sounding board who listened attentively without venturing her own opinions. It was her lack of opinions that had led him to believe she listened without understanding. Let him believe there was little going on in her head.

He'd made the fatal error of underestimating her. He'd forgotten that she'd been paid to serve him. Paid to blend into the background unless called to the forefront. Paid to cater to his needs and be whoever he needed her to be.

It was with not a little discomfort that he acknowledged that he'd needed her to be a decorative adornment and had revelled in her adopting that role for him. Had revelled in the sexual charge that had grown between them during their hours together. Had arrogantly assumed she'd resigned her job at the club so that unspoken sexual charge could be acted on.

Their night together had blown his mind. He'd known they'd be good together but couldn't have guessed just how good it would be. Not just the sex but the laughter that had come with it. Sex with Layla had been hot and fun and all-consuming.

It was only now with all their gloves off that he was seeing the real Layla emerge, a feisty, quick-witted beauty with hands that spoke their own language and facial expressions and eyes that told you exactly what she was thinking. He could only imagine the restraint it must have taken for her not to let her mask slip when working at the club.

'I am a man of immense wealth, *cara*,' he told her, matching the faux sweetness of her smile, 'and I can assure you I purchase only the best in contraception.' And there had been nothing during their night together to suggest it had failed for them. Nothing at all. Sure, there were a few shadows in their night together where the all-consuming nature of their coupling came to him as sensory imprints rather than concrete memories, but at no point had he failed to wear a condom.

And yet…

He blinked away the flicker of doubt that suddenly tugged at him as ruthlessly as he'd blinked it away the other times it had tugged at him.

'And I can assure you,' she said, not dropping the sweet act, 'that you need to ask for a refund.'

Layla followed Sebastiano up a wide sweeping marble staircase that belonged in a fairy tale and found herself so overwhelmed as more of the villa's majestic beauty opened itself up to her that she only listened with half an ear to him say, 'A design team is on its way. They will bring a selection of clothing to go through with you so they can learn your style, and source and create a suitable new wardrobe for you.'

'Suitable?' She craned her neck to fully take in the spectacular mezzanine the stairs led onto.

'Suitable for the wife of Sebastiano Russo.'

'Referring to yourself in the third person? Classy.'

'It often feels that the public Sebastiano Russo is his own singular persona.'

'And you expect me to create a matching persona as your wife?'

'It will be easy for you. You have already proven yourself a consummate actress. The design team will be here within the hour—I've had a room put aside for you to work with them. Once the wedding is announced, they will work with you to create a dress to marry in.' He turned his stare to her and, with a tone of the utmost regret, said, 'I know it will pain you to hear this, but we will both be kept busy before the wedding and so you will see little of me until the big day itself.'

As they were passing a room with the door open and two members of uniformed staff making up a four-poster bed, Layla made sure to look suitably crestfallen. 'Oh, that is devastating.'

His regretful expression lifted. The gleam she so loathed and yet which made her pulses soar returned to his eyes. 'Be assured you will have the pleasure of my company every night in our bed.'

Sniffing an opportunity, she put her hands to her racing heart and fluttered her eyelashes. 'Oh, darling, I wouldn't want to scandalise the staff by sharing a bed out of wedlock, so why don't I sleep in a guest room until our big day?'

They'd reached the end of the mezzanine. Leaning against a marble pillar, he caressed her cheek. 'You are so thoughtful but the staff have already prepared my room for your arrival.'

She affectionately covered the hand resting against her cheek and dug her nails in. 'Then I shall make sure to get the design team to source some all-in-one pyjamas for me.'

He tutted and murmured, 'Image, *cara*, image. What will the staff think if you wear pyjamas in bed? You will find a selection of lingerie and nightwear already unpacked in your dressing room. Come, I will show you.'

With that, he opened the door to an intensely masculine room of deep green with goldleaf etchings patterned on the walls and ceiling, and heavy deep green drapes. The furniture was all dark wood, the soft furnishings a muted olive, the bedspread of the ginormous four-poster with tied-back dark green curtains black. If the room weren't so vast in size and if light weren't pouring in through the three sash windows running from floor to ceiling, she would think it oppressive. Instead, her first impression was that it was seductive. Her first instinct was to back right away and stay behind the threshold.

He stood behind her. 'You like?'

She was having trouble taking her eyes off the bed. All she could picture was Sebastiano lying on it naked, a lascivious gleam in his eyes as he beckoned her to him…

Heated pulses fluttered low in her pelvis. Very much aware of the cleaning staff so close by, she had to swallow to huskily say, 'Bit dark for my tastes but it certainly suits you.'

However aware she was of the cleaning staff, it had nothing on her awareness for Sebastiano. Seeing the bed she would sleep beside him in for nights with no defined end to them…

Hands gently gripped her biceps. A hard, lean body pressed into her back. Hot breath swirled in her hair, then a deep inhalation as if he were breathing her in before his lips touched the rim of her ear and, his fingers kneading into her skin, knuckles brushing the sides of her breasts, he whispered, 'Tell me you're not already imagining sharing the bed with me.'

CHAPTER SIX

LAYLA WAS THRILLINGLY aware of his hardness pressing into her lower back, the fluttering pulses in her pelvis becoming molten liquid. Close to swaying, she felt her breasts tingle wildly in anticipation of Sebastiano's hands sliding from her arms to cover them, the compulsion to lean her head back onto his shoulder and into the crook of his neck...

It took a major burst of impetus to pull herself away and step into the safety of the bedroom.

Striding to a window, she fixed her gaze over the rear of the villa and what was possibly the most stunning vista she'd ever seen, and snatched as much air as she could into lungs that had lost the ability to breathe. 'Shut the door.'

The breathlessness of Layla's order tightened Sebastiano's arousal to a point.

Dio, it felt like he'd been aroused from the moment he'd opened his eyes. The knowledge he would end his day with Layla Sansom lying beside him had crowded his mind before the dreams of sleep had cleared.

And now she was here. The opportunistic hustler was going to pay her debt to him by distracting the world from the foolishness of his actions—or, to be technical, his inactions—with a marriage that would be short but in no way sweet.

She couldn't know it but she'd already repaid some of her debt. Bringing her here, all the planning that had gone into it, all the anticipation of it, had all served as the distraction he'd needed to the potential destruction of his reputation and the potential destruction of the business that had belonged to his family for half a millennia. It had stopped him thinking about it in any depth at all.

She spun around before he reached her. 'You said the bedroom would be a safe space from your wandering hands so back off.'

He held his hands up and murmured, 'I didn't put it in quite those words.'

'The intention was the same, so keep your distance.'

'What are you afraid of, *cara*? That you won't be able to restrain yourself?' The fire that blazed in those fabulous forget-me-not eyes at this... 'Has anyone told you that you're beautiful when you're angry?'

'Has anyone told you that you need to come up with some new lines because that one's so old it's beyond stale?'

'As enjoyable as it is to feel your passion for me—'

'My *what*?'

'Your passion, currently displaying itself as anger— I need you to put it on ice. Time is moving. Your design team will arrive soon and you will display all the signs of a woman excited about her new life with the love of her life. Is that clear?'

The Medusa effect of her stare didn't diminish an inch. 'You have already made that clear. Outside the walls of this bedroom, complete adoration.' She folded her arms over her breasts and spun back around to gaze out of the window.

There was something in Layla's rigid, stubborn stance,

a hint of vulnerability that, just for a moment, made Sebastiano's heart catch and throat close.

It took a longer moment to shake the unsettling reactions off.

'Who do you want to invite to the wedding?' he asked, standing beside her at the window.

Thrown at the change of subject, Layla couldn't stop herself turning her stare back to him.

'We have four full days to make the arrangements. It will look odd if you don't have anyone from your side,' he reasoned.

'We can't have that,' she muttered, knowing he was right but in no mood to let go of her anger even though Sebastiano had already called it out for what it was.

How could one man make a woman *feel* so much?

She needed to get a grip on herself and her emotions quickly because this was only the beginning.

Fixing her gaze on the deep blue sea just beyond the thick trees that served as the perimeter to his estate, she took a deep breath. 'What do we tell people about how we came to be together?'

'Exactly what I told Laurence—the truth. I met you at the Diamond Club, we were secret lovers and only once you left did I realise I had fallen in love with you.'

Well, that made her heart wrench. 'I thought you just said we'd be telling the truth.'

'Sticking to the truth as much as we can so we don't get caught out in a lie.'

'I can't lie to my mum.' She looked again at him. 'She already knows about you.'

His eyebrows drew together. 'What does she know?'

'That you're the father of my baby. That you ghosted and blocked me.' She shrugged with deliberate nonchalance.

She would never tell him of her utter desolation when she'd realised that he'd blocked her number, when her numerous calls to him had failed to connect and her desperate text message of, *I'm pregnant and frightened, please call me*, didn't even make it to delivered status. She'd found her mum curled up on the sofa watching one of her soap operas, crocheting. Her mum had looked up at her and simply said, 'Are you ready to tell me what's going on with you?'

And so she had.

'Does she know about the money you blackmailed from me?'

'Yes. I can't lie to her, Seb.'

She knew from the movement in his green eyes that he was thinking hard. 'Can she be trusted?'

'Yes, so you don't need to make any more threats—I will play my part and she will play hers. I know what's at stake if we don't make this convincing. She won't breathe a word to anyone.'

His eyes continued to bore into hers.

'You can trust her,' she reiterated into the silence.

He gave a sharp nod and looked at his watch. 'Then I shall take you at your word. Now come, let me show you your dressing room and where everything is. I have much to do.'

With Layla firmly ensconced in his home and the design team creating a wardrobe that befitted her as his wife, Sebastiano focused his attention on everything else. The press release was ready to go, all the preparations for the wedding were discreetly underway, the members of his core team working on damage limitation were readying to firefight if necessary, senior members of the bank prepared for a potentially damaging news story and spoon-fed the official line to take…everything was in hand. Everything had been considered from every angle. Everyone knew the part they had to play.

As far as his family, his directors and core team were concerned, he was sticking with the truth as he'd explained it to Layla. He would not have any of them think he'd had to threaten her and her law firm with destruction to obtain her agreement. If it turned out she really was pregnant…

Well, that would serve a purpose of its own, but he would not think about that, not with the tugging doubt in his stomach growing stronger now she was finally here with him.

It was being with her. Watching her graceful movements. Gazing into forget-me-not eyes that ranged in expression from naked desire to open loathing and fury, often within a blink.

The expression on her face when the household butler escorted her into the smaller dining room was the complete adoration he demanded of her.

He rose to greet her.

His chameleon had changed, the sexy but plain tight trousers and top replaced by a colourful halter-neck dress that fell to mid-thigh and showcased the fabulous legs he'd admired for so long. Her long hair had been scooped into a loose bun, tendrils framing her face, large, hooped gold earrings and a thick Egyptian-style bracelet adorning her skin, and he felt a stab of satisfaction that the vast range of jewellery he'd had couriered over for her use contained items that suited her so well.

She closed in on him, enveloping his senses in a cloud of sultry perfume. He'd had thirty scents brought in for her, figuring she would like at least one of them. The one she'd chosen made him hungry to breathe it directly off her skin.

It wasn't until she put a hand to his shoulder that he saw the challenge in her eyes. 'Good evening, darling,' she said breathily, before rising onto her toes and kissing him. Not a brief greeting of a kiss, but a deep, sensuous locking of mouths that caught him unprepared. When she broke it, she pouted another kiss, winked, and then slid into the chair set beside his that the butler had pulled out for her. The serenity in both her stance and her actions would have made him laugh if he weren't fighting to stop his arousal from showing.

'I think I prefer this dining room to the one you showed me earlier,' she commented brightly. 'Much more intimate.'

He cleared his throat and retook his seat. 'This one is for personal use. The other is for entertaining.'

A member of staff leaned between them to pour her wine but she covered the glass with her hand. 'Just water for me, please.'

Their food was served and then Sebastiano dismissed the staff so it was just the two of them.

Damn but he was still aroused.

Taking a drink of his wine, he passed a large envelope to her. 'Our prenuptial agreement,' he told her.

She sighed dreamily as she took it from him. 'You have romance in your soul.'

'I'm Sicilian. Romance is in my blood.'

The dreamy expression didn't drop. 'And there was me thinking it was vengeance you bled.'

'We are a people of passion in all its forms.' Just as Layla was a woman of passion, a thought that didn't help with the throbbing between his legs. He handed her a pen. 'There will be no negotiating any of the contents. All I require is your signature.'

'I'm sure the agreement is a testament to your generosity,' she riposted, peeling the envelope open and removing the document. 'However, I would be a terrible lawyer to put my signature to a document I didn't read first, plus I'm keen to learn how much of my vast fortune I need to pay you when we go our separate ways.'

Her witty irreverence made him laugh, and as he watched her read it while they dined on *pollo ai funchi*, he wondered again what it had taken to hide this side of herself when she'd worked at the club.

As she read, her serenity slowly leeched out until she put her cutlery down to look at him. 'I can't sign this. It's—'

'It is not open to negotiation,' he cut in.

'It says that if our marriage ends within a year then you'll pay me fifty million euros. Sebastiano, you're forcing me to marry you as a punishment, so why would you—?'

'I cannot be seen to give you anything less than I would in a real marriage.'

Her shoulders made a slight slump before she lifted her chin again. 'The clauses about children…'

'Again, nothing less than would be expected in a real marriage and again, nothing that is open to negotiation—none of it is. Sign it or the deal is off.'

Her eyes held his, something thoughtful flickering in the forget-me-nots before she picked up the pen and signed.

He nodded his approval and dabbed the sides of his mouth with a napkin. 'Who knew blackmail would prove so lucrative? Now you will have to excuse me—I have a video conference with Zurich. I will see you later in bed.'

Until Layla's night with Sebastiano, she'd been the soundest of sleepers. Since that night though, sleep had been erratic, morphing into full-blown insomnia after she'd blackmailed the money from him. The last thing she'd expected as she rummaged in her dressing room for something to sleep in that wouldn't make the staff suspicious and which wouldn't send 'come and get me' signals to Sebastiano was to fall asleep within moments of her head hitting the pillow.

So soundly did she sleep that when she opened her eyes she was disoriented to find the room filled with dusky light and Sebastiano standing on the other side of the bed scrolling through his phone, dressed in smart navy trousers and a pale blue shirt, different clothing than what he'd worn for dinner.

Her heart ballooned and caught in her throat.

He noticed her looking and a wry smile spread across his handsome face. 'Ah, the Sleeping Beauty awakens.'

'It's morning?' she whispered.

'Eight o'clock.'

She could hardly believe it. When she'd checked her phone after the long video call with her mother in which she'd filled her in on everything and in which her mother had been love and understanding itself, it had been ten-thirty p.m. She'd snuggled under the covers straight after saying goodnight to her.

She was almost frightened to see if the other side of the bed had been slept in.

'I assumed you'd be waiting for me with a taser in your hand when I came up but you were dead to the world,' he said, as if he'd read her mind. 'Did you know you talk in your sleep?'

If her hands weren't holding the bedsheets so tightly, she'd have clutched her burning cheeks.

'It was mostly mumbles,' he said with a wink before strolling over and perching his backside on the bed close to her.

Immediately her senses were assailed by the scent of freshly clean Sebastiano and, as their eyes clashed, for one wild moment she was overtaken by a longing for him to rip the bedsheets off her.

She tightened her grip on the sheets and cocooned herself deeper into them.

The smile that played on his lips told her he knew exactly what she was thinking, and when he opened his mouth, she braced herself, certain he would say something sexy and suggestive.

'I need you to get up and dressed.'

Well, that threw her. Sebastiano was telling her to put clothes on when she'd been anticipating him suggesting she remove what little she was wearing.

'Today is going to be a roller coaster, for all of us,' he reminded her. Reminding her of the reason he'd chosen the marriage route as his vengeance. Revenge and reputation management in one fell swoop. Not for the little life they'd created together.

'Has the article about you gone live yet?'

He shook his head. 'I have it on good authority that it will be posted before eleven. We will give it ten minutes for people to notice and share it, and then we release the news of our engagement.'

'Why wait those ten minutes?'

'So the journalist isn't tempted to retract and release it at a later date. We're burying bad news, not delaying it, so get yourself ready and, while we wait, prepare the list of guests you wish to invite with contact details for them. Your new assistant will make the arrangements to bring them here while you work with the design team on your wedding dress.'

'You've employed an assistant for me?'

'You will find it necessary. As my wife your diary will overflow with invitations which need to be managed with our individual work commitments. Your assistant will work in tandem with mine.' His phone pinged in his hand. He got up from the bed, reading it. 'My team's arrived. When you're ready, come and join us.'

The moment Sebastiano disappeared through the bedroom door, the tight control Layla had been clinging to released in a rush. Her heart and lungs exploded, blood zooming to the roots of her hair and the tips of her toes.

Hot tears prickled her eyes and she frantically blinked them away, swallowing hard while breathing equally hard through her nose. Her physical responses to Sebastiano were completely beyond her control, she already knew that. But waking from a deep sleep in the intimacy of his bedroom and him being the first thing she saw... His scent the first thing she inhaled...

It was a long while before she felt enough in control of her limbs to safely climb off the bed and pad across the room to her bathroom that adjoined her dressing room, which itself adjoined Sebastiano's dressing room, which in turn adjoined his own bathroom. No his-and-hers sinks in the master bedroom of Sebastiano's villa. Here there were his-and-hers bathrooms, and hers was the prettiest she'd ever had the pleasure of using, a retreat with a strong Japanese influence that she could lock herself away from the world in.

Lock herself away from Sebastiano and the sexual magnetism she responded so viscerally to.

She still felt shaky under the powerful spray of the shower, and as she lathered silky shampoo into her hair, her thoughts drifted to the clauses in the prenuptial agreement. What had been behind them? She hadn't misread them. They'd been translated into English as masterfully as Sebastiano spoke it.

Had they come from him or his legal team?

Custody of any child born within the marriage will be shared on an equal basis...

It was the *born within the marriage* part she couldn't wrap her head around. Why wouldn't he make the clause state any child *conceived* within the marriage? She'd sensed him doubting his own stance on the pregnancy but sensed too an entrenchment in the belief that if she was pregnant, the child could not be his. So why add that clause? Why make provisions for a child you didn't believe to be your own?

Was it a case of hedging his bets? Saving face? Or something else, something deeper?

She was still pondering it all as she went through the clothes she'd selected from the racks of clothing the design team had brought for her to choose from the day before and which had fitted her perfectly. Her mind still firmly on Sebastiano, she selected a pair of white three-quarter-length slim-fitting jeans and an elegant white silk blouse embroidered with red orchids. Dressed, pastries eaten and orange juice drunk, she was about to set off and find the man she was only four days away from marrying when she felt something she could only describe as a flutter in her belly.

Stilling, she didn't even dare to breathe, not until she felt it a second time and, with excitement coursing through her veins, she scrambled to undo her jeans and palm the still-flat surface of her belly.

The fluttering had stopped but...did her stomach feel thicker beneath her hand?

She turned on her side in front of the full-length mirror, lifted her blouse, and then slumped in dejection. Not even the semblance of a bump.

It didn't matter, she told herself, lifting her shoulders back up. She'd experienced the first real physical sign of the pregnancy since an order of barbecued ribs had made her nauseous a few weeks back.

She'd felt her baby.

Her and Sebastiano's baby.

Sebastiano sat at the desk of his home office surrounded by his core team. Everyone had crammed themselves onto the various forms of hard and soft seating, all scrolling through phones and refreshing laptops. Instead of following suit, he found his attention kept being drawn to the open door of the adjoining office, appointed to his soon-to-be wife. Layla was in there, going through her guest list and other aspects of the wedding and her working life with her new assistant.

Since she'd strolled into his office with a bright, 'This must be the war room,' before giving him a kiss that was just the right side of passionate in a working environment, the frayed edges of his nerves had soothed somewhat. Introducing her to his team and her new assistant, showing her to her office, had all helped distract from the gnawing knowledge that this could be the day he destroyed one of the world's oldest banks. And because he couldn't let that happen, he would have no choice but to resign his position. His reputation would be dust. There was no one in the Russo family lined up to take over. No one suitable. His parents had both retired from the board and as they'd been the ones to groom him into the role, they would be tainted by association. Sebastiano was an only child. With the exception of Paolo, his Russo cousins had all forged diverging careers. Sebastiano enjoyed Paolo's company immensely, trusted him to run the European branch, but that was with Sebastiano's hawk-eyed oversight. If Paolo weren't a Russo, he wouldn't have made it past customer complaints.

If Sebastiano fell, Russo Banca Internazionale would be forced to appoint a non-Russo to lead it for the first time in its long, distinguished history.

'It's live,' someone suddenly said into the silence. 'Linking it now.'

Sebastiano held his breath as he waited for the link to ping.

He'd hardly read the main headline when he felt a pair of eyes on him. Looking up from the screen, he saw Layla standing in the doorway, taking it all in.

Their eyes met.

After the longest time passed her chest rose and her neck extended, and then as she exhaled she gave a smile so soft his thumping heart flipped over.

A burst of fire zinged through his veins. Filling his lungs, Sebastiano slammed his palm on the table and said, 'Five more minutes and then we bury this.'

For the second night in a row, Layla was fast asleep before Sebastiano came to bed. This time though, she'd lain awake for an age, palming her belly, hoping with all her heart for another fluttering. Her brain had been too wired to simply switch straight off.

Sebastiano's plan seemed to be working exactly as envisaged. Once the press release about their marriage had gone out, the phones of all the people in his war room had gone berserk. Nine out of ten of the calls had been about the wedding, only ten per cent about the billion-euro loss.

Social media was ablaze, digital newspapers all leading with the wedding. Layla's phone had come close to conking out in protest at the hundreds of messages received, many from people she'd had no contact with since secondary school.

While Sebastiano and his team dealt with the media scrum, Layla had been kept busy with the wedding. Everything was already in hand but, to her surprise, she was given the final choice on canapés and the courses that would be served for their wedding banquet, and asked to approve the final colour scheme. It hadn't occurred to her that her input would be wanted. She had imagined all that would be required of her was to turn up at the appointed time and look suitably adoring.

There had been no time to wonder why this should be though, as Sebastiano had brought her a top-of-the-range laptop and liaised with Laurence about connecting it to Clayton Community Law's intranet.

She found it strangely touching that he understood how important her work was. Whether it was for show or not—he'd preordained that their respective workaholic tendencies would destroy their marriage—he'd gone out of his way to ensure she had everything needed to make working in the villa comfortable and efficient until her designated date of return to the office. As that designated date was four weeks away, Layla had spent the rest of the day liaising with colleagues—all of whom bombarded her with questions about Sebastiano—about how to manage her clients in the interim, also squeezing in the time to offer the full asking price for the suburban house. The offer was accepted in minutes. When her fake marriage to Sebastiano was over, she could move straight into it. In the meantime she would continue working on her mother to move into it from the second it was legally hers.

By the time she'd finished eating dinner with Sebastiano and his team, who'd continued discussing and strategising throughout the meal, her eyes had been gritty with exhaustion.

It had been Sebastiano who'd looked at her wan face and gently suggested she get some sleep.

Whether that gentleness was for show or not, she didn't know, but she'd lain in his huge bed for an age before drifting off, his face firmly in her mind, holding her belly in the hope of feeling his baby move again, all with the lingering taste of his light goodnight kiss on her mouth and a lingering tingle on the exact spot his stubbly cheek had brushed hers.

CHAPTER SEVEN

SEBASTIANO WAS USED to working long hours, but this was something else. Everything was proceeding as planned but pockets of fire kept flaring that all needed to be doused, and that was on top of the workload that came with running an international bank along with ensuring he was on top of his workload enough to take a week off as a sop to a honeymoon, and came with organising the wedding of the century at incredibly short notice.

He'd had the earth's sexiest creature under his roof and in his bed for three days and been too busy to spend more than snatches of time alone with her.

His current workload had him working each night until the early hours. He would climb the stairs to his room, the entirety of his being inflating to know Layla was already in there. He'd slip beneath the covers beside her sleeping form torn between making noise and movement enough to wake her and not wanting to disturb the peace of her sleep. It had to be all that fiery passion burning her energy through the day that allowed her to sleep for the dead.

Although their time alone together had come in snatches, their shared meals and adjoining offices meant he'd had much opportunity to observe her, and when he reached the dividing threshold and found her on a telephone call, he instinctively knew from the tone of her voice that she was talking to one of her clients. On the desk that formed an L with hers, Giovanna, Layla's assistant, looked up from her computer, gave a nervous smile of greeting before immediately looking back at her screen.

Layla took much longer to meet his eye, but when she did, a smile curved her cheeks and something glimmered in her eyes he was quite certain she was unaware of.

She held up a finger to indicate she'd be one minute.

Waiting was no bother, not when it meant he got a whole minute of observing his fiancée unhindered.

How was it possible for someone's beauty to grow by the day?

How was it possible for desire to turn on with the ease of a tap just to catch a glimpse of someone or catch a waft of their perfume?

Today she was wearing a dark blue maxi-dress, the buttons running its length opened to show the merest hint of cleavage, her hair in her favoured loose style. Having observed her so much, he now understood why she preferred it loose: she was always fiddling with it, whether running her fingers through it, tucking strands behind her ears or winding strands around her fingers. He could still feel the sensation of those fingers scraping through his own hair…

She ended her call and smiled at him. 'Did you need me for something?'

He had the perfect answer for that but, with Giovanna working so close to them and no doubt hearing every word exchanged, he settled for sitting on the edge of Layla's desk. Having an audience, though, gave him a legitimate excuse to lean over and stroke her cheek. 'I had a few minutes free and thought I would check in with my beautiful fiancée before she's whisked away for her dress fitting.'

The colour that enflamed her cheeks at his touch was an aphrodisiac all of its own.

The design team had moved into the villa so they could work around the clock on her wedding dress and that afternoon had been set aside for Layla's first proper fitting. Whatever direction the design of the dress took, she would be the most beautiful bride to have ever graced Sicilian soil. He traced the rim of her ear, delighting in her almost imperceptible shiver.

From the moment Sebastiano slipped into her office, Layla had been wholly aware of his presence and now, her cheek and ear aflame from his touch, she was having to fight to stop the entirety of her senses becoming consumed by him. Clearing her throat, she said in a voice she needed no effort to make sound husky, 'I'm not wanted for another half-hour.'

He pressed his cheek against hers and whispered, 'Believe me, *cara*, you are *always* wanted.'

She could do nothing to stop her breath hitching and when he pulled back and she caught the gleam in his beautiful green eyes, she knew he'd heard it, and when he reached again to stroke her cheek, the thumps of her heart were so strong she was certain he must be able to hear them too.

His desirous stare not leaving hers, he said, 'Giovanna, can you give us two minutes please?'

Layla's assistant left the office and closed the door without a murmur.

Alone with Sebastiano, her heart thumping erratically, Layla tried to wrench her stare from his, tried even harder to fight the thrills of anticipation lacing her blood at the mouth closing in on hers...

The tip of his nose brushed against her. His breath was hot on her face...

'In case I forget to mention it later, my parents and grandparents and a few other relatives will be joining us for dinner this evening,' he murmured. 'Formal dress. I will go through behavioural expectations later.'

Layla's butterfly-laden stomach turned over and she reared back.

A knowing smile played on his lips. The bastard knew exactly the effect he had on her and was positively revelling in it.

'Don't look so alarmed. They won't eat you,' he teased. 'They might *want* to eat you...' His eyes glimmered. Her pelvis clenched. 'Not in the same way as *I* want to eat you, of course, but my family are old-school courteous and they wouldn't dream of being rude to you. Not to your face.'

She had to scramble through the fog of blood roaring in her head to drag out, 'What have you told them about me?'

'What I have told everyone else.' The firm lips her mouth was tingling with need to feel compressed upon it were barely a feather away from making contact. 'That you are my lover and that there is nothing I wouldn't do to make you mine.'

Layla didn't know if it was a sob of relief or disappointment that hitched up her throat when he pulled away from her and returned to his own office.

Sebastiano had known his chameleon fiancée would charm his extremely proper, socially conscious family, and so it proved from the moment she swished into the dining room wrapped in a slinky black cocktail dress with her hair piled in a loose bun, loose tendrils and large hooped earrings framing her perfect face. Being seated opposite her meant that, though he had to forgo the pleasure of feeling the heat of her body beside him and inhaling the sultry scent of her perfume, he had the pleasure of watching her. And it was a pleasure. Not a single expression on her beautiful face or movement of her body was anything less than mesmerising. Whenever their eyes locked, he caught a shimmer in hers, a remnant of the desire that had blazed earlier and which sent a shimmer of it straight back into his loins.

Only the knowledge that the villa was overrun with hundreds of staff and external workers busy transforming it for the wedding had stopped him pressing his mouth to hers for the kiss her lips had parted for.

Layla wanted him. He knew it. And she knew he knew it.

Throughout their five-course meal, she played the part he'd given her to perfection, proving herself as graceful and elegant and learned as they could wish for a new family member, especially one who would be so prominent. His mother studied her the closest but his grandfather was smitten before the main course had been served. As for Paolo, Sebastiano's cousin and best man for the wedding, he found himself on the receiving end of death stares from his wife for his failure to remove his eyes from Layla's face, death stares he was completely oblivious to.

'Don't you drink, Layla?' Sebastiano's father asked when she poured herself another glass of iced water.

Her mesmerising forget-me-not eyes darted to Sebastiano before she bestowed his father with the lopsided smile that could break a man's heart at fifty paces. 'Not when I need to keep a clear head for my wedding,' she quipped, which made his father laugh and his mother's eyes narrow.

Sebastiano thought back to all the meals they'd shared

these last few days. She'd stuck to water in all of them. Not a drop of alcohol had passed her lips since her arrival here.

She did drink though. They'd shared a bottle of champagne the night they'd spent together.

A pulse throbbed in his temple.

Why keep up the act of being pregnant when there was nothing to be gained? Layla was smart enough to know he couldn't pull out of the wedding now. She was legally minded enough to know the prenuptial agreement was watertight and the fifty million would be hers from the moment they signed the certificate. Those of the world's press who hadn't already set up camp at the villa's gates were scurrying as fast as they could to join them. It was too late to cancel—

He suddenly noticed she had a hand resting lightly on her belly. Noticed, too, the gentle strokes of her fingers. The animation on her face as she continued charming his father suggested she wasn't even aware she was doing it.

The pulse turned into a pounding. The surrounding conversations had become distant white noise. Closing his eyes in a long blink in an effort to clear it, Sebastiano opened them to find Layla's beautiful eyes dart back on him.

His heart made a heavy thump against his ribs.

Their gazes held.

The white noise vanished into nothing.

The strangest sensation loosened in the centre of his chest. He was barely aware of it spreading to cover his lungs, not until it had squeezed the breath from them.

Layla tugged her hand out of Sebastiano's and, without saying a word, headed straight to her bathroom.

Closing the door, she rested a hand to her pounding

heart. She was struggling to breathe. For the first time since her arrival in Sicily, Sebastiano had come to bed with her.

She removed her makeup and brushed her teeth with shaking hands.

It had taken every sinew of effort to put her focus on playing the role Sebastiano demanded of her for his family. Every sinew because all her eyes had wanted to do was stare at him. Every sinew because the ache that had opened in anticipation of the kiss that had never come still burned. Just to be held in his gaze intensified it.

And now they were alone. No audience to play for. Nothing to distract her from the pulses beating in her throat and the heat between her legs.

Nothing at all to distract her from *him*.

How on earth was she going to manage their 'honeymoon' week, she wondered helplessly when she padded into her dressing room. Come Sunday morning and Sebastiano's helicopter would fly them to the tiny Mediterranean island bought by the Russo family as the perfect romantic, private getaway. With only a skeleton staff there, it would essentially be just the two of them. No work or other distractions. For a whole week.

A 'honeymoon wardrobe' had already been prepared for her by her design team. She didn't dare ask what it consisted of or hope it involved more than string bikinis and sexy lingerie.

The lingerie couldn't be worse than what she already had. The worst of it was how much her skin sang to wear it. Beautiful matching underwear for the day, delicate silk camis for the night. She had to rummage through the latter to find one that actually covered her buttocks, settling on a cream silk number that still left little to the imagination.

She felt almost sick with nerves but it was a different kind of sickness from the occasional mild nausea she'd experienced in the first few months of the pregnancy. This was a sickness of anticipation.

Desperate to have better control of herself before she joined him in the bedroom, Layla slipped her arms into a kimono-style robe and then called her mum. Just to hear her voice and know she would be joining her here in the morning, an ally in an overwhelming world, soothed a little of Layla's frayed edges.

But only a little. Once the call was finished, she was out of distractions.

She could put it off no more. She was going to have to get into bed with Sebastiano for the first time since they'd conceived their child.

Taking a deep breath, she tightened the robe and opened the dressing room door.

Sebastiano was in bed reading something on his phone. His magnificent torso was bare. She didn't dare imagine what he was—or wasn't—wearing on the lower half of his body.

He looked up from the device in his hand and, without taking his eyes from her, placed it on his bedside table.

Layla had never felt as self-conscious as she did during that walk to the bed. Not that self-conscious was the right phrasing for what she felt under the gleam of eyes that felt as if they were seeing straight through the kimono and cami to her naked skin.

Having reached her side of the bed, she sat awkwardly with her back to him and shrugged the robe off. Painfully aware that she had way more flesh on display than covered, even more aware that Sebastiano did too, she slipped under the sheets with her back to him.

The sheets rustled as Sebastiano made himself comfortable then the room was plunged into darkness.

Immediately the huge bed shrank.

She cocooned herself deeper into the sheets and fought to stop her airwaves closing up. The silence was so profound and Sebastiano so close he would surely be able to hear her erratic breaths.

His deep voice penetrated the silence. 'You did well with my family. I appreciate it must have been difficult for you.'

His voice was so close. *He* was so close.

Swallowing, she whispered, 'Your mother disapproves of me.'

His mother had been as gracious and welcoming as the rest of the Russos but there had been an underlying stiffness that went beyond the stiffness that came from belonging to one of the richest families in the world. It was a stiffness that had felt personal.

'My mother would only have been happy if I was marrying a Sicilian.'

At least he wasn't denying it.

'You do realise your family know our marriage is all for show, right?' she said.

'They might suspect but they don't know.'

'Doesn't it bother you? All this lying?' And now she was a liar because of it too, and she would be lying in two days when she made her vows and lying with every display of affection she endured throughout the day...

But that in itself was a lie, she acknowledged. How could she call it *enduring* when she was tucked under the same bedsheets as him, intensely aware that if she slid her foot back just a few inches it would make contact with warm, hard flesh? Intensely aware that if Sebastiano moved just a few inches closer his breath would fall on her skin?

'Lies based on truth. Our marriage will be real for as long as it lasts, and my family will not question it because the only thing that matters is the bank's survival.'

'That all sounds very cold,' she managed to drag out as her pelvis contracted at the remembrance of how Sebastiano's lovemaking had been the antithesis of cold.

'To someone like you, perhaps.'

She rolled onto her back and turned her face to him without even thinking about it. 'Someone like *me*? What are you implying?'

Sebastiano gazed at her with eyes adjusted to the dark. Even shadowed her beauty made his chest tighten in an echo of earlier, when he'd caught Layla's stare and lost the capacity to breathe. 'I am saying that I understand why my family and our priorities would seem cold to you. The nature of your relationship with your mother is very different from my relationship with my family.'

Her brow furrowed in question.

'I don't believe I have ever called my mother for the sake of calling her but you call yours frequently,' he explained. At least three times a day. The most recent had been only minutes ago. He'd stepped out of his bathroom and caught a hint of Layla's musical voice. It had been the softness in her tone that had been the giveaway as to who she was speaking to. It was a different kind of softness from the tone she took when speaking to her clients. With her mother, the softness had a chattier lilt; with her clients the softness was overlaid with the professionalism with which she spoke to her colleagues.

'I have an excellent relationship with my parents, but my personal life is private from them,' he continued. 'From what you've told me and what I've observed from your calls with her, you share confidences as if she was a close friend rather than your mother.'

Her gaze still locked on his, she turned her whole body to face him. Fingers appeared from beneath the sheets pulled up to her chin and her hand slid under her cheek. A long inhalation and then she quietly said, 'She's more than a mum to me. She's the closest friend I have.'

Curiosity had him ask, 'Do you think your closeness is because she raised you on her own?'

Her eyes narrowed a little in thought. 'That's definitely a factor, and her age when she had me was too. She was so young and had no one to fall back on or tell her she was doing it wrong, so she had to trust her own instincts.' She gave the smallest of smiles. 'Basically, she made it up as she went along and did parenting her own way, and it was a way that meant we were always close.'

Her little finger was poking out at the side of her cheek. Sebastiano had the strangest urge to take it in his mouth and taste it.

Dio, he could still taste *her*. It was a taste that had lingered in his memories for all those months he'd spent determinedly refusing to think about her.

As he lay in the dark, each inhalation soaking in the sweetness of her breath and the last vestiges of her perfume, heady awareness thrummed heavily through him. That the awareness was shared and thrummed through Layla's veins too only heightened the sensation.

She'd been his for the taking earlier but that moment had passed. Her guard was up but different barriers had been lowered and their lowering was starting to satisfy a different kind of hunger, one he hadn't been aware had been roused.

A hunger to know everything about her.

'What do you mean by her *own way*?'

Her lips quirked with another small smile. 'Well…she never lectured for a start. When I was little and did anything naughty or plain wrong, she didn't sit in judgement. She would get me to talk about why I'd done whatever I'd done and steer me into realising why I'd been wrong to do it.' The smile curved a little wider. 'You could confess anything and her empathy and lack of judgement made you feel absolved but also a hundred times more guilty than if she'd got angry and ranted.'

'What did you do that was so bad?'

'That's just it—I didn't, not unless you count the time she caught me and my friend Natalie smoking when we were fourteen. She didn't lecture us on the evils of smoking, just gave us this awful, disappointed smile, kissed my head and told us to dispose of the butts responsibly. I don't know why it made us both feel so terrible but whatever witchcraft she used, it worked and neither of us ever touched a cigarette again. How can you rebel against someone like that? You can't…at least, I couldn't.'

'Your upbringing was very different from mine,' he told her slowly as he digested all she'd just confided and tried not to wonder what kind of mother Layla would be to the child he was finding it increasingly difficult to deny already existed inside her.

Difficult to deny but equally difficult to accept.

'I grew up knowing I wasn't just a member of a family but an institution,' he continued, forcing his thoughts back to safer ground. 'The bank has been in my family for five hundred years. I have known my whole life that my destiny is to lead it. My father knew it and his father before him, all the way back through the generations, but every family member plays their part in upholding the Russo image because all our fortunes depend on it and we marry accordingly. That is what I meant about my family not questioning our relationship—they know a background investigation will have been conducted on you because background investigations are always made on those we wish to bring into the fold through marriage. I appreciate that it sounds cold, but to us it is a necessary evil. It's survival. I do not have the luxury of allowing emotions to dictate my actions. None of us do.'

This was nothing Layla didn't already know through all the late nights in Sebastiano's suite, pouring his favourite bourbon, acting as a smiling sounding board for him. Many confidences had been shared with her, business and personal. In Sebastiano's case, business and personal were inextricably linked.

Now she was here, in his home, thrust into the heart of his world, she understood better the enormous pressure he was under. Understood it because she'd felt it, in his office when Sebastiano and his team had been waiting for the news about his monetary loss to drop. The tension had been like nothing she'd ever experienced, so tangible that it had felt like she could wave her fingers and find resistance in the air.

It was her own resistance she was having to hold onto now. The strange intimacy of a conversation in the still darkness.

He was so close that she could feel her pores opening to breathe him in, and, as hard as she tried, she was struggling to stop her gaze focusing on the sensuous mouth that had kissed every inch of her flesh. The urge to press a finger to the indentation on his bottom lip and then replace the finger with her mouth was so strong that she squeezed the pillow beneath her cheek even tighter and half joked, 'You don't have to explain yourself to me. I'm well aware you have the emotional range of a goldfish.'

And, when it came to women, the attention span of one too, she reminded herself.

Needed to remind herself, especially as her mild insult had resulted in a growl of surprised laughter that soaked straight into her open pores.

One night of bliss and Sebastiano had cast her aside. The emotional connection she thought she'd found in his arms hadn't existed for him.

'Being compared to a goldfish is an improvement on a pig,' he said musingly.

'You took pig to be a compliment.'

'But you meant it as an insult. You like goldfish.'

'How do you know that?' Surely a childhood pet goldfish wasn't the kind of thing an investigator would pick up?

His chuckle was husky, his voice smug. 'You just told me.'

She couldn't stop the snigger that escaped. 'If you're happy to be compared to a creature that only has the brain capacity to remember the last three seconds, then you do you.'

'I'm happy to be compared to a creature that you like.' His voice lowered. 'It gives me hope.'

It was the meaningful gleam in his eyes that finally gave Layla the impetus to roll over and turn her back to him.

It would be too easy to read something in his eyes that just wasn't there and hear false meaning in his words. Too easy to let herself forget how much he'd hurt her and give him the tools to do it again.

He was talking about sex. Nothing else.

She'd allowed herself to see and hear falsehoods in the

dark of night with Sebastiano before. To him, they'd been just words. She'd been the fool for believing them.

Closing her eyes, she strove with everything she had to keep her voice light. 'Like I said, you do you. I'm going to get some sleep now, so time to stop talking.'

'Your wish is my command.'

She didn't know if she was breathing easier or harder when she felt him turn over and shift away, taking the warmth of his body with him.

There was movement as he made himself comfortable, and then he murmured her name.

She had to swallow to answer. 'Yes?'

'If I was to compare you to a creature it would be a swan. They're beautiful and elegant, just like you.'

Her chest expanded to accommodate her blooming heart, and she had to swallow even harder to speak. 'They also bite when provoked.'

His laughter rumbled through her skin. 'Kinky.'

She could have sobbed. 'Sebastiano?'

'Yes, my little rabbit?'

'Shut up and go to sleep.'

He gave one last husky chuckle and then silence finally fell.

The oblivion of sleep took many hours to claim her.

CHAPTER EIGHT

LAYLA KNEW SHE was alone in the bed before she even opened her eyes. Knew from the faint trace of cologne that Sebastiano had already showered and dressed. Knew from the all-consuming silence that he'd left the room.

She wouldn't see him again until they married. Russo family tradition dictated the bride and groom spent their day and night before a wedding apart.

A note had been placed on her bedside table. Rubbing the sleep from her eyes, she read, *I'll see you at the chapel tomorrow. Try not to miss me too much. S.*

Resting her head back on the pillow, she clutched the note to her chest and told herself the ache in her heart didn't mean she was missing him already.

Sebastiano had not expected to feel nerves. After the roller coaster of the last few weeks, he'd thought any nerves had been numbed but he stood at the altar of his chapel, colourfully dressed guests crammed into every available inch of space, his chest tight, stomach rolling, only half listening to what Paolo was chattering on about.

He had no reason to feel like this. Layla wasn't going to leave him stranded at the altar. Forget all she had to lose if she backed out, she just wouldn't do it. He knew it in his guts.

He supposed it was the twenty-four hours they'd spent apart giving time for doubt to sew its seeds.

He'd felt her absence acutely.

Five days in his home and it was like she'd imprinted into the walls. Every minute of their time apart had been spent with Layla lodged so firmly in his mind that he saw her everywhere.

She'd played her part beautifully. Everything was working out exactly as he'd intended. The fever for the wedding of the century was not just eclipsing the news about the money loss but putting it in so much shade that it was unlikely to ever see sunlight. It was the leading news story in all the Sicilian and Italian press, much of the rest of Europe's news channels including it in their coverage. An Italian television channel had set aside three hours of scheduling for an exclusive live feed of the wedding— negotiated by Sebastiano's people—which gave its crew access the press crammed at the villa gates could only dream about.

But what, he now wondered, would happen if sunlight ever did shine on the money loss? What would cause the press to dredge it back up? How long would he have to stay married to Layla for the press not to become suspicious of the timings? A few journalists were vocally doubting the veracity of the marriage but their columns and musings on the subject had been barely noticed, not when heads of state and industry had been congregating in Sicily with personal hairdressers and stylists joining them like additional baggage.

A few months of marriage would be too suspicious, he now thought. To make it completely realistic, it would have to last a few years at the very least. And if Layla really was pregnant…

For the first time since the meal with his parents, he was unable to stop his mind from conjuring her hand absently resting on her stomach and the gentle stroke of her fingers.

Layla stepped out of the guest cottage, hardly able to believe how spectacular the grounds looked with all the imported pillars wrapped in blooming red and white roses surrounding the perimeter and the beautifully adorned benches, tables and chairs artfully placed throughout. With the beautiful, winged angel villa in the distance, the whole scene was like something out of a fairy tale. Her wedding dress made her feel like she was a character from a fairy tale. The horse drawn carriage that would take her through the vast estate to the chapel topped the fairy-tale feeling off.

Three footmen appeared. One held a hand out to her mother and helped her into the carriage. When he held out his hand for Layla, the other two carefully took the train of her dress and lifted it so she could sit without becoming entangled in it.

Holding tightly to her mum's hand, she did her best to compose her features into those of a typical excited bride for the video cameras strategically placed along the route for the live feed.

As much as she knew she shouldn't feel genuine excitement, she'd woken after a fitful night's sleep with butterflies in her stomach much like the ones she'd woken with as a child on her birthday. When the horses leading them trotted along the wide pathway that cut through Sebastiano's woodlands, overhung by arched trees, the butterflies grew in strength and her grip on her mother's hand tightened.

'It will all work out for the best,' her mum said quietly without dropping her smile. 'Have faith.'

Layla bit back from saying, *What, like it worked out for the best for you with my father?*

She wouldn't hurt her mother's feelings for the world.

As her mother had gently pointed out while they were holed up in the guest cottage, fate was already taking a different course from the one she'd had to follow when she was pregnant with Layla.

Sebastiano hadn't been wrong in his observation that mother and daughter were very different. Her mother trusted fate to make things right, even when it must have felt that fate was laughing at her. Layla trusted her fate and her baby's fate only in herself. Their marriage would make it impossible for Sebastiano to walk away from their child but she would not put faith in him being an involved father once they went their separate ways. She couldn't. The only people she could trust to love and cherish her baby were herself and her mother.

None of this stopped the butterflies flying up to her throat when the beautifully renovated ancient chapel appeared in the distance, the afternoon sun shining over its domed roof.

The footmen helped her down from the carriage and her bridesmaids, all Russo cousins and Russo cousins' children, took hold of the train.

Taking her mother's hand, Layla took the deepest breath of her life and walked through the open door.

Her heart burst into song to see the man waiting at the altar for her.

Sebastiano's laughter at Paolo's whispered observation that the fascinator being worn by a royal princess looked like a piece of plasticine 'art' his six-year-old daughter would make died on his lips as the vision from heaven appeared at the door.

A hush fell.

Stomach tightening, his pulses accelerated. Blood rushed to his head.

There was a dim awareness of music striking up. The heavenly vision's eyes locked onto his and then even the music ceased to exist for him.

Slowly, she glided to him like a shimmering wingless angel. Her figure-hugging white dress with its spaghetti sleeves and scooped neckline that skimmed her cleavage was embellished with thousands of tiny crystals, around her swanlike neck a large teardrop blue-diamond necklace, smaller matching earrings on display, her hair swept into a side knot.

And then she smiled her perfect lopsided smile and the angel vanished and sexy, beautiful Layla, all warm flesh and hot blood, took her place. In an instant the blood pounding in his head fell into his expanding heart, and he took her hand from the woman beside her...her mother... and drew her to him.

Dio, he'd known she would be the most beautiful bride to have ever graced Sicily's soil but even he hadn't imagined such a magical vision.

'You are spellbinding,' he breathed into her ear, and was rewarded with another dazzling lopsided smile.

Fingers threaded, they faced the priest and the wedding mass began.

When Layla had first been told Sebastiano had organised a full Catholic wedding ceremony, she'd wondered how she would make it through a whole hour without yawning or fidgeting, but the magic of it all had seeped into her from her first look at her groom. As the ceremony went on, the music, the singing, the candles, the incense, even the Italian it was all conducted in, all commingled and slipped silently into her soul and filled it with light.

This was *her* marriage. Sebastiano was *her* groom. Her groom, looking as handsome as she'd ever seen him in a full morning suit complete with light grey waistcoat and dark grey silk cravat and handkerchief. A proper groom. A proper groom for a proper wedding.

In that moment it came to her that whatever their reasons for marrying and whatever happened in the future, their marriage for however long it lasted would be real. Everything else, from Sebastiano's reputation escaping untarnished and his ancient bank continuing with a Russo at the helm, even her law firm thriving on the money he'd be pumping into it, was a side-effect to the two most potent truths. They would be husband and wife, and their child, whatever denial Sebastiano might currently be experiencing, would have a father. A real father who, once he accepted the truth, would want it.

It was time to make their vows.

Hands clasped, they faced each other.

The priest addressed Sebastiano first. His lips moved in response but Layla's head was too full to hear.

How many brides pledged their lives to a man only to find their hearts shattered when the true nature of their loves finally came out? she wondered.

She already knew Sebastiano's true nature and because she knew it, he could never shatter her heart. He'd already done his worst. He'd lied to her. Ghosted her. Blackmailed her. Forced her into this marriage. Denied their child. She wouldn't count kidnap seeing as she'd started that part by cuffing him to a bed, but, if not for that, she could add kidnapping to her list of wrongs.

None of that meant their marriage had to be a nightmare to live through, not unless she chose to make it so.

He wouldn't make it a nightmare for her. He could. Easily. But he wouldn't. It was a certainty she felt all the way to her marrow.

The priest turned to her and recited her vows in English.

She gazed into the green depths of Sebastiano's eyes. Caught the glimmer of desire that was never far from the surface.

Caught something else too. A steadfast openness.

The little avocado-sized life in her belly stirred. Just a little fluttering before stilling again, but it was enough to make her already expanded heart bloom further as she kept her stare on the father of the little life and said, with only the slightest hitch in her voice, 'I do.'

Sebastiano stood with his new wife in the back garden of his estate shaking hands with the guests lined up to congratulate them. The train of her dress had been cleverly removed, champagne and canapés were circulating, background music playing, conversations being struck between friends and strangers alike, children running wild and letting off steam after the long service. All of this he registered on a subconscious level.

His lips still burned from the kiss they'd shared to seal their marriage. And the kiss they'd shared for the official wedding photos. His neck still burned from the cup of her hand to it when she'd leaned in for those kisses. His loins still burned from the effect of the glimmer fired at him from her forget-me-not eyes in the beat before their mouths had fused.

The line had shortened considerably when Laurence and his husband reached them. After vigorously shaking Sebastiano's hand and thanking him profusely for flying the entire firm over and putting them up in a nearby hotel for the weekend, he pulled Layla into an enormous bear hug.

'Aren't you the dark horse?' He beamed when he released her from his embrace. Holding her biceps, he stared at her with the pride of a father. 'Not even a hint that you were seeing this fine fellow.'

'We wanted to keep it private until we were both certain,' she said without missing a beat.

'Well, I'm delighted for you. We all are. And what a glorious home. You'll never drag yourself back to London.'

'Just watch me,' she said, laughing. 'I'll be back at my desk in three weeks. You'll never get rid of me.'

'Exactly what I wanted to hear!'

Once the line dwindled to nothing it was time to circulate properly with the people who most needed to be satisfied that Russo Banca Internazionale remained in safe hands. Layla remained glued to his side, holding conversations with the spouses who wanted to know all about her. The moment Layla told the spouses about her firm, the partners tuned in too, their interest piqued. Whatever their charitable public personas might say, it was beyond most of their guests' comprehension that anyone could spend all those years in education to choose a career with a law firm that barely paid a living wage.

By the time the gong rang out informing the wedding party it was time for the wedding feast, Layla had taken so much of the spotlight with their guests that he doubted any of them gave another thought about Sebastiano other than to think he must be the luckiest man in Europe to have snared such a beautiful, intelligent, compassionate wife.

He'd even overheard his mother telling a group of her society friends that, though she was of course disappointed Layla wasn't Sicilian, she was perfect in every other way.

'Nicely played,' he murmured as they headed inside to the banquet room.

She squeezed her fingers threaded through his and smiled.

'Extra nice touch pointing Laurence out to them all.' The donations would come flooding in, he was certain.

'I thought so too,' she said beatifically, then winked and added, 'I'm still holding you to that five million you promised the firm, though.'

'I will transfer it first thing in the morning,' he assured her.

She stopped walking and, eyes brimming with glee, tapped the end of his nose. 'Exactly what I wanted to hear.'

He captured her hand and kissed it. 'You seem happy.' She radiated with it, a glow emanating from her that dazzled.

She laughed softly. 'I'm an excellent actress, remember?'

If this happiness was an act then it was the performance of her life.

Slipping an arm around her waist, he pulled her flush to him. 'Can you act the role of bride who can't bear to wait another second without a kiss from her new husband?'

'Let me see…' She cupped the back of his neck and raised her face to his. He breathed in the scent of her sweet breath before her lips brushed as lightly as a feather to his. With a sigh, she tilted her head back and gazed into his eyes. 'How was that?'

He gave a soft growl. 'You call that a kiss?'

'I call it an aperitif.'

Damn it, but there was a pull in his loins, the tell-tale tugs of arousal manifesting into something physical.

Instead of doing the sane thing and letting her go, he held her even more tightly to him. 'An aperitif or a tease?'

Eyes gleaming, her teeth razed against her bottom lip. And then she kissed him properly, a deep, hungry kiss that filled his senses with her sweet taste and made him wish for a trapdoor to fall through with her and a soft mattress to land on.

He didn't know which of them broke it, but when they came apart, her cheeks were so flushed and her eyes so dazed that he knew this part, at least, was no act.

Hands still hooked around his neck, she cleared her throat and whispered, 'Better?'

Worse. Much worse. Unless he let her go right now, he'd never be able to show his face in polite society again. 'That was an upgrade on the aperitif,' he conceded.

Exhaling a sigh, she unhooked her arms, stepped back and rubbed her thumb against the side of his mouth. Then she smiled her beautiful lopsided smile and teased, 'We can't have Sebastiano Russo dining with world leaders with lipstick around his mouth, can we?'

Layla felt giddy as she danced with her new husband and swathes of their guests on the magnificent dancefloor. She kept expecting someone to pinch her and wake her from this dream where her favourite singer in the world was performing on the ballroom stage at *her* wedding.

She couldn't begin to think of the effort and cost—and headache—it had taken for Sebastiano to fly the world's most famous diva over at such short notice. And he'd done it for her. All because of a passing comment Layla had once made when selecting music for him to listen to in his suite, which made her think back to the two occasions guests at the parties he'd thrown in his suite had made drunken lewd comments to her. He'd kicked the offenders out without ceremony and with a sincere apology to her. She'd never seen those men again. Neither of them were here at the wedding.

He must have been close to them to have invited them to those parties, she now realised. All the other men who'd attended were here. One of them was dancing next to Sebastiano, shouting over the music something he clearly wasn't listening to because his gaze was fixed on her.

It was a gaze that never failed to make her heart skip and her pulses race.

Sebastiano rarely danced at social gatherings that were more public than private. He'd assumed he'd dance the traditional first dance with Layla and then network with his more distinguished guests, but nearly two hours on, he was still there. Still moving his body in beat to the music, too entranced with the graceful beauty who'd taken centre stage without even realising it to want to move away from her. The graceful beauty who was now his wife.

He'd caught the singer narrowing her eyes at the bride and was certain the diva wouldn't think twice about scratching Layla's eyes out for taking all the attention away from her. From the wide smile on his beautiful bride's face, she was oblivious to her heroine's malefi-cent thoughts, and as he watched her sing along to her heroine's lyrics with her mother, Sebastiano thought for the first time of the one person missing from the celebra-tions. Layla's father.

He thought back to her mother being the one to walk

Layla down the aisle, remembered the huge, almost familial embrace Layla and Laurence had shared earlier.

Her father had been mentioned only once between them, when Sebastiano himself had carelessly thrown his abandonment as an attribute for people to admire her overcoming.

His eyes dipped down to her stomach and that tugging sensation hit him again, stronger than it had ever done before.

A new, slower song started.

She turned to face him and without missing a beat—Layla *never* missed a beat—she hooked her arms around his neck and gazed into his eyes with an expression that vanquished the tugging sensation, a deeper, more sensuous tugging taking its place.

'Enjoying the party?' she asked softly.

'Very much.' Much more than he'd ever believed he would enjoy his own wedding. Whenever he'd envisaged it, he'd imagined the bride being one of the women who inhabited his society, a woman who didn't need to put on a performance to fit into his world. A woman who bored him to tears.

His real marriage would be as transactional as his marriage to Layla, a union much like his parents had, built on mutual respect solely to produce an heir. He'd always assumed that once the requisite heir—and preferably a few spares—had been produced, then he would follow the tradition of his world and take a mistress and his wife take a lover, any and all affairs conducted with the utmost discretion.

The transactional nature of his marriage to Layla was as different from any future marriage as night from day,

Layla herself as different from any future bride as the sun was from the moon.

If his growing conviction that she was indeed pregnant...

No. This was not the time to think of it. Not here. Not now. Not when he had her in his arms and the look in her eyes was telling him she didn't want to be anywhere else.

'You?' he added.

She pretended to consider it. 'I've been to worse.'

He grinned and, because he could, tightened his hold around her and kissed her, ignoring propriety to deepen it until she broke it with another of those breathless sighs that only fed his need for her.

CHAPTER NINE

As much as Sebastiano wanted to throw Layla over his shoulder, whisk her upstairs and lock the bedroom door, a tendril of the propriety he'd come within a breath of losing completely reasserted itself.

He was not a hormonal schoolboy. He was the head of Russo Banca Internazionale. His bank and his place in it were the whole reason he'd married her...with a dollop of revenge thrown in. When it came down to it, this marriage was a performance and though he knew damned well that Layla was as caught in the web of desire as he was, he could not say with any certainty whether she would act on it in the privacy of the bedroom or switch it off.

As he was learning, what Layla's mouth said didn't always correspond with what her eyes said. As he was also learning, it was her eyes that always told the truth. If he'd recognised the steel in the forget-me-nots the night she'd tricked five million pounds out of him, he'd have recognised that something was very wrong. Instead, he'd been too caught up in the desire that had also pulsed in them and the soft musicality of her voice and the glimpses of cleavage, too damned arrogant and confident in his own greatness to think of the hurt he'd caused her at his failure to call. At disappearing from her life.

Despite knowing it might all come to nothing, by the

time he'd taken to the stage to thank the singer and all
their guests, then fought through the crowd wanting to
wish them, again, a long and happy marriage, another
hour had passed and the heat of his desire had barely lowered by a degree.

He'd have to sleep in his bathroom. Lock the door, fill
the bath with cold water and submerge himself in it.

And so, even though Layla's hand was firmly clasped
in his as they climbed the stairs together, Sebastiano con-
centrated only on filling his lungs with air.

Their hands slipped apart at the door.

His heart beating harder and faster than it ever had before, he took a deep, deep breath, followed her inside and
rested his back against the wall.

After the noise of the ballroom, the silence in the bedroom was absolute. He had a vague awareness of rose
petals making a path to the bed and the rose-petal hearts
created on the turned-down sheets, but it was just a background blur to the main picture before him.

Layla. Staring at him with colour heightening her
cheeks, so ravishingly beautiful it made his heart hurt
to look at her, standing close enough for the scent of her
heated skin beneath the remnants of her sultry perfume
to snake into his airwaves. Close enough for him to see
the pulse beating at the base of her neck. Close enough for
him to hear the unevenness of her breaths.

Dio, he'd never known his own breaths to be so heavy.
Everything in him felt weighty, as if desire had been in-
jected into his veins.

Layla's body had forgotten how to breathe.

The dreamlike quality the day had taken since her revelation in the church and the glowing hours that had passed
since had vanished under the weight of the choice she had

to make and under the headier weight of the desire burning in every cell of her body and the blaze of Sebastiano's hunger in the depths of his eyes.

Their night together had been passionate, hedonistic perfection. Sebastiano had drawn something out of her she'd never even suspected existed, something that had destroyed all her inhibitions from the first sweep of their tongues.

When they'd parted the next morning, she'd felt the wrench of his absence a hundred times more acutely than she'd ever done for Chris. A thousand times more.

Three years she'd been with Chris and she hadn't shed a single tear when it ended. He'd been safe, she now realised. He'd been content to wait all those months for her to share his bed, something she'd only gone ahead with in the end because she'd felt she owed it to him for all his patience.

Sebastiano was the antithesis of safe. She'd known that from the moment she first set eyes on him. She'd only slept with him that night because she'd set out thinking it would only *be* for that one night. She'd thought she was safe.

She'd had no idea when she stepped into his arms that their one night together would leave in her a mark that ran deeper than the child they'd conceived. No idea that his subsequent ghosting of her would leave her desolate.

But history didn't have to repeat itself. That was something she'd told herself over and over when she'd learned she was pregnant. Her mother's path did not have to be hers. She'd taken control to stop that very thing from happening, and she'd healed and fortified her heart.

The stark truth, though, was that Sebastiano brought her to life in a way she'd never felt before. He hadn't just drawn a hidden sexuality out of her but a passionate fire that blazed in all its forms whenever she was with him. With Sebastiano, all her senses came alive.

And now her eyes were wide open.

And so were his. While electricity crackled like white noise between them, his unfaltering gaze remained steady.

She understood the silent message he was sending.

He would not touch her.

He'd made a promise that here, in the sanctity of their bedroom, it was for Layla to make the first move and he would hold himself to it. If she turned away from him he would do nothing to stop her.

Staring into his pulsing green eyes, soaking the barely contained hunger emanating from them, it came to her in a flash of wonder that just as their marriage would only be a nightmare if she made it so, Sebastiano could only hurt her again if she let him...

Her feet left the ground before the rest of her knew what she was doing.

She moved so quickly and so suddenly that Sebastiano barely had the time to register what was happening before Layla's arms wound tightly around his neck and her lips compressed to his with a soft yet wrenching moan.

The relief was almost as strong a sensation as the blood that pumped after that long heart-stopping moment when he'd detected a frisson of fear in the depths of the forget-me-nots.

Whatever doubts or fears had caught her in those moments were gone, her mouth as hot and hungry as his own, her fingers digging into his skull as urgently as his bit into her back. The need to taste and feel every inch of her swept through him like its own life force.

Deeper and harder their mouths moved together, tongues exploring ravenously, his senses feeding on the exotic, sensually sweet taste that had sat in him like a hidden memory waiting for the trigger to reawaken it. And Layla was the trigger. Layla, shedding the cloak of hurt his actions had forced her to wrap herself in for protection and embracing the desire that had flickered between them for so very long and which their night together had turned into a flame.

Why had he run from that flame in the aftermath? he wondered dimly as he buried his face in her neck and resisted the heady urge to bite down. No one made him feel like this. No one. Only Layla. No one else had ever made him ache to burrow himself into their skin. No one else had fingers that could slide down his neck and send sensation coursing to the tips of his toes.

Her breath hot and ragged in his hair, those same fingers now dragged over his chest to tug at his shirt and pull it free. His arousal deepened when she scraped her nails through the hair on his abdomen before fumbling at the button of his trousers.

In thrilling frustration at being unable to find the zip or button or whatever the hell it was holding her wedding dress together, he spun her around and pressed her against the wall to keep her steady, then clasped either side of the seam running from beneath her shoulder blades to the base of her spine, and pulled with all his strength.

Layla gasped to hear the loud rip of her beautiful dress and the shock of cold wall against fevered skin that had moments before been covered, the gasp turning into a moan when Sebastiano's mouth and teeth grazed her shoulder as he pinched the spaghetti sleeves and yanked them down her arms. The top part of the dress fell and bunched at her waist.

The fever in her was more than skin deep. It had sunk

into her veins and bones, burning even the tips of her fingers working frantically to undo the button of his trousers and release the bulging hardness trapped beneath the silky material. With the shackles of her fears finally thrown off, her desperation for Sebastiano's possession had mushroomed, all the desire she'd been suppressing unleashed and seeking the possession of the only man in the world to make her feel whole and complete.

His trousers finally unbuttoned, she yanked at the zip and reached inside the tight confines of his briefs. His groan of pleasure and biting kiss when she wrapped her fingers around his throbbing excitement only fed the burn of her own arousal.

'*Dio*, Layla,' he muttered into her mouth before scraping his stubbly cheek against hers, tugging again at her dress, trying to rip it at the waist, and mumbling something unintelligibly Italian that was an aphrodisiac all of its own whatever the words meant.

Everything about Sebastiano was an aphrodisiac to Layla, from his voice and accent to the musky taste and scent of his skin to the silkiness of his hair. She wanted to touch and taste him everywhere, feel his touch and taste everywhere, had never hated clothes more.

It was a hate frustrating Sebastiano as much as her, his efforts to rip away the multiple layers of the skirt of her dress proving impossible. With a loud growl, he lifted her into his arms and practically threw her onto the bed.

In moments he was straddling her thighs and with the same strength he'd torn the back of her dress, he pulled at his waistcoat. Buttons went flying, pinging as they landed on the hardwood floor but she barely heard them, too intent on hooking her arm around his neck for more rousing, heady kisses. Before he'd come into her life she'd never known kissing could evoke such thrills, could be so addictive.

With her free hand she yanked at the buttons of his shirt, shivering with pleasure as he undid her strapless white lace bra, then cried out loud when he covered her breast with his mouth and lathered it with such pleasure that the burn between her legs became molten. Such was her need that when the buttons of his shirt remained stubbornly unbuttoned, she found a strength she'd never known she possessed and, following his lead, ripped it open.

The moment their chests pressed together, a tiny part of the fever burning through her abated, as if her skin had been so desperate to feel his flesh upon it that it gave a little sigh of relief. The sigh lasted only a moment. The relief she so desperately sought was a wedding dress away and, lips fusing back together with his, she kicked at the thick layers entangled around her legs and feet; could have wept when Sebastiano roughly gathered together as much of it as he could and pulled it up to her waist.

His large hand ran over her thigh and he groaned into her mouth when he found the top of her white lace hold-up, and when he slid a finger into the side of her knickers and found her wet and swollen for him, his hooded eyes widened and nostrils flared. *'La mia carne brucia ti desidero da morire,'* he said raggedly before his mouth fused back to hers.

The pleasure of his fingers caressing her where she so desperately craved had her crying into his mouth and clamping her thighs together and when he slid another finger inside her she rocked into him before crying with frustration when he moved his hand and ripped her knickers apart.

Her cries of frustration became cries of anticipation

when he pushed the material of her dress up some more and yanked his trousers and briefs down to free himself properly. At the first tantalising hint of his arousal jabbing against her inner thigh she spread her legs wider and lifted her bottom, every inch of her body begging for his possession. Her breaths coming in short pants, she tightened her hold around his neck as he fought his way through the mass of material stubbornly keeping them apart until, finally, magically, he drove deep inside her.

Such was the sensation that all the air flew out of her with a moan of the deepest pleasure.

Their mouths broke apart as he lifted his head back to gaze wonderingly into her eyes. She could feel the throbs of his arousal inside her, knew he could feel the throbs of her own as her needy body adjusted to the most glorious sensation of Sebastiano filling it so completely. But it was the swirling pulses in his green eyes, which had darkened to look almost black, that had her lift her face back to him and kiss him with all the passion in her singing heart.

With a ragged groan against her lips, he clasped hold of her bottom and in moments every fibre of her being was singing in sensation.

Sebastiano was beyond thoughts. Beyond savouring the moment. They were both beyond that. They both needed relief and with Layla's long legs wrapped around him, her moans and breathless cries urging him on with the same urgency as the nails digging in his back, he drove in and out of her like a man possessed…he *was* a man possessed…possessing *her* and making her his with every hard thrust…

Dio, this was something else. Something unimaginable, something that went beyond being bare inside her. It was all he could do to hold on until her breaths shortened and she began to rock against him. Only when he felt the thickening around his arousal that had blown his mind all those months ago did he let himself go with a roar before he was pulled deep, deep into the secret place that belonged only to him and Layla.

Layla's eyes were closed, her hands gripping the pillow tightly as the sensations being evoked by Sebastiano's tongue deepened and her climax built into a crescendo.

Only when she'd finally stilled did he lift his head from between her legs and give his lascivious smile. 'Better?'

Finally too replete to speak, she smiled and held her arms out to him in answer. In response, he crawled back up and placed his head on the pillow beside her. Kissing her gently, he slung an arm over her stomach.

She gazed into his eyes and nuzzled her face closer. 'Sure you don't want me to return the favour?'

He laughed lowly and kissed her again. 'Soon. You, my insatiable little rabbit, have worn me out.'

She grinned sleepily. 'Worth it?'

Another kiss. 'Completely.'

The first filters of daylight were coming through the heavy drapes. They hadn't slept a wink. The bedroom looked like a romantic bomb had gone off. Rose petals, buttons and the tiny crystals of her wedding dress were strewn all over the floor along with puddles of their torn, ruined clothes. She didn't dare think how much money's worth of bespoke clothing they'd destroyed in their desperation to be skin on skin.

She didn't want to think, either, of how similar their wedding night had been to their first night together. Once hadn't been enough then either. Twice hadn't been enough. Three times hadn't been enough.

Sebastiano had ended up having to cut the wedding dress off her. The zip had stuck fast and the layers of the skirt were just too thick and heavy to rip through. He'd taken one look at her naked—excepting her white lace hold-ups—and she'd taken one look at him looking at her and before she knew it he'd been buried deep inside her again. Only on their third bout, after they'd shared a shower together, had they taken it more slowly. After their fourth time, this time while sharing another shower, she'd hardly been able to walk. She'd been astounded when, shortly after, back in bed, laughing about some of the fascinators their guests had worn while he'd idly encircled her breast with his fingers, desire had flamed back to life.

Finally, after her fifth orgasm of the night, Layla's desire had muted into a gentle simmer…for now.

For a long time, they just lay there, Layla on her back with her face to him, Sebastiano on his side, his eyes closed, only the gentle circles he was now making on her stomach signs he was still awake.

'Can you feel it?' she whispered. The fluttery feeling had started again, right beneath his hand.

Sebastiano's eyes flew open, the sleepiness he'd been falling into shaking off him in an instant.

Layla's open stare was glued to him.

She caught the hand frozen on her stomach and pressed it down. 'It feels like a thick fluttering. It's like no other feeling in the world. My body's changed so little that sometimes I worry I'm imagining the whole thing but it's real and it's there. That's our baby.'

Blood roared in his ears. The tugging sensation every time he looked at her belly was stronger than it had ever been, and now, with his hand splayed on it and his full concentration on the sensation beneath his skin, he could feel the strange fullness of it. The changes that came with a belly supporting the creation of a life.

'Yes,' he admitted quietly. 'I can feel it.'

He could deny it to himself no more. Layla was pregnant.

She expelled a soft breath of relief.

'But how can it be mine? We used protection the whole time.' Every time. Which only reaffirmed that, subconsciously, he'd already accepted the truth of the pregnancy because he hadn't given protection a thought earlier.

There was a helpless quality to her smile. 'I know we did and I can't explain it either but this baby is yours. There was only one man before you and that ended when I graduated.'

Just the thought of her being with anyone else punched nausea through him.

Stifling it, he rolled onto his back and gazed at the ceiling. 'I want to believe it's mine but how can I? I accept that accidents happen but nothing went wrong with the condoms.' Nothing at all. For sure, their night together had been the most intense and passionate of his life...until tonight, that was...but he'd been meticulous in his protection of them both.

At her silence, he turned his face back to her and saw the unshed tears swimming in her eyes. It was a sight that made his chest tighten immeasurably, and he found himself saying, 'It doesn't matter who the father is.'

As part of his investigation into Layla he'd had his team dig into her lovers. The only name to come up had been from her university years. He'd also got them to do a forensic account of her movements for the two months either side of their night together. Whoever the real father was, there was no proof of his existence but that didn't mean he could accept that he'd created the child with her. Sebastiano was a Catholic who didn't believe in miracles.

'The whole point of the marriage was to avoid a scandal,' he continued. 'The child will have my name and the world will see it as mine.'

Covering her breasts with the bedsheets, she sat up and stared down at him. Unshed tears still glistened but he could see her thinking hard. 'Why would you force this marriage on me if you didn't believe you were the father? I know you've been in denial but you must know it deep down else why put those clauses about children *born* within the marriage in our prenup? Why not make the clauses state conception?'

A flare of anger ignited. 'I told you, this marriage has to be believable to everyone and it's already proving to be—the wedding has eclipsed the monetary loss, and when news of the pregnancy breaks it will only add to the momentum. As for the prenup, it was drafted by the legal firm who have taken care of my family's personal business for nearly as long as Russo Banca has been operational. It is unthinkable for a man in my position to not have one and it would have been unthinkable to write conception into the clause. That is the kind of thing that makes people ask questions.'

She shook her head in disbelief. 'You accept that I'm pregnant. You've had me thoroughly investigated. You *know* there's been no one else and yet you *still* refuse to believe you're the father?'

'I don't believe in miracles, Layla,' he said tightly. 'I believe in tangible facts, but the child's paternity makes no difference to me. I set us on the path to marriage knowing there was a slim possibility that you were pregnant with another man's child—'

'It's *yours*,' she stated vehemently.

'A discreet paternity test after the birth will confirm that.'

A flash of pain lit her beautiful features at this.

'You're not worried about the imaginary father coming out of the woodwork?' she asked.

Sebastiano took a deep breath to douse the last of his anger. He didn't want what had been a spectacular day to end in an argument and bad feeling. As much as he enjoyed verbally sparring with Layla and seeing her passion roused in all its forms, this felt different from their previous sparrings. Or was his acceptance that she really was pregnant making him feel different about it?

'If it happens, he will be dismissed as a fantasist,' he said in a gentler tone, turning back to face her. 'Whatever happens, the child will be raised as mine.'

She slumped back down and held herself rigidly, chin jutted, her mouth clamped in a thin line. 'You had this all planned out, didn't you?'

Not planned but dealt with in his mind and filed away to be used only if needed.

'I never leave things to chance.' He moved closer and wrapped an arm around her. 'You should be pleased.'

Her eyes flashed, the anger he'd rid himself of transferred to her.

He kissed her smooth shoulder. 'You win whatever happens, and so does your child.' Pinching the bedsheets tucked so tightly under her arms, he pulled them down to expose her small but perfectly formed breasts, and cupped one, capturing a nipple between his fingers. 'He or she will have a recognised father and security for life. That is what you wanted for them, isn't it, when you chained me to that bed and demanded money?'

Her mutinous expression remained but her body, responding to his touch, spoke a completely different language.

Carefully sliding on top of her, he smoothed the hair from her face and watched the forget-me-nots pulse when his arousal jutted against her pubis. 'I know I forced this marriage on you, *cara*, but I don't want you to be unhappy and I don't want us to be at war. Believe me when I tell you that I will do everything in my power to be a good father to the life inside you.'

Layla gazed into the green depths and, with a deep sigh that came from her heart, palmed his cheek. He nuzzled into it, which only made the sigh in her heart deepen.

It frightened her how badly his continued denial about being the father hurt. It meant he was denying *her*. Meant he believed she was capable of passing off another man's child as his.

But he was trying to do the right thing and that counted for something. His honesty counted for something too. If she let his denial fester then the only person she hurt would be herself.

Lifting her thighs so his arousal pressed right where they both most wanted it to be, she brought her mouth up to his and whispered, 'I don't want to be at war either.'

His lips lifted at the corners. 'Then let us make peace,' he said huskily before fusing his mouth to hers and, with a long, drawn-out groan, drove deep inside her.

CHAPTER TEN

THE ISLAND SEBASTIANO flew them to for their honeymoon was everything Layla had anticipated.

Entirely private, the golden beach lapped at their villa's flowering front lawn. The skeleton staff was even more skeleton than she'd imagined, a husband-and-wife team who lived in a small cottage at the rear of the grounds and who only came to the villa when they were called for.

The honeymoon clothes that had been brought ahead for her were exactly as she'd imagined, mostly consisting of string bikinis and scraps of lace that called itself lingerie. She didn't bother with any of it, preferring to drive Sebastiano insane by wearing various skimpy, strappy little summer dresses and absolutely nothing underneath. If she wanted to swim or sunbathe, she simply threw it off and paraded around naked.

It was the most liberating feeling in the world, almost as liberating as having sex whenever and wherever she wanted. Or whenever or wherever Sebastiano wanted.

After four days, there wasn't an item of furniture in the whole villa they hadn't had sex on or against. She could no longer walk into the kitchen without her pelvis throbbing to remember how she'd been pouring herself a glass of water when he'd sneaked up behind her and bent her over the work surface. She could no longer walk past the swimming pool without seeing the sun longue he'd been laid back on, dozing, when she'd woken him by taking him in her mouth.

Sometimes it shocked her, how she had absolutely no inhibitions with Sebastiano. None at all. It didn't matter how many times she climaxed. Still she wanted more. And more. And more.

More of him. Constantly.

She was self-aware enough to know that constant love-making meant she didn't have to think too deeply about anything other than making love. It didn't change that here on this beautiful, dreamily romantic island, she was little more than a receptacle for pleasure, that her insides turned to fire just to look at him.

Wasn't all this what she'd told herself the day she'd made her vows? That their marriage only had to be a nightmare if she chose to make it so? That Sebastiano could only hurt her again if she let him? Hadn't they both agreed that they didn't want their marriage to be a war?

And so she'd chosen to push aside the wrench in her heart at his denial of paternity and concentrate on the one thing that was always good between them. After all, she'd made those vows without any illusions, and in a way he had a point, that she should be happy her baby would have the security she'd always craved.

When they parted ways, Sebastiano would already have the proof of paternity he insisted on and her child would have what she'd never had. Financial security *and* a father.

And just in case he did renege on it and found a way to overturn their prenup, she had the suburban house to fall back on.

Until they parted ways, or overdosed on lovemaking,

whichever came first, she had a lover, which was what she was training herself to see him as. Her lover.

If she kept thinking of him as her husband then she risked the danger of believing it.

Sebastiano kept expecting to wake from the dream he'd fallen into. He'd always had a high sex drive but this was something else. Five days of pure hedonism and now he was being ridden by Layla on the outside dining chair, her breast in his mouth and her hair covering them both like a sheet. The sun was setting over the sea, the sky a dark orange, the heady perfume of flowers in the air around them but losing to the sultry fragrance and taste of Layla.

He could not get enough of her. If sex was an addiction then he was rapidly becoming addicted to having sex with her. He probably already was addicted.

Who knew, he wondered, dazed after yet another powerful climax, that it was possible to become addicted to sex with your own wife?

He was still inside her when she kissed him and murmured, 'Shower, my lover?'

He laughed gruffly, thinking of the untouched plates on the table beside them. 'Food, then shower?'

She blinked as if she'd forgotten all about the meal they'd been about to share then brightened. 'Oh, yes! Food.' One last kiss and she climbed off him.

It was as she scooped her discarded dress off the patio tiles and pulled it over her head that he saw it. The slight bump of her belly.

When had *that* appeared? And had her breasts grown…?

'What's wrong?'

He met the questioning forget-me-nots and shook his head. 'Nothing. Just thinking how beautiful you are.'

She blushed and smiled and retook the rattan seat she'd been on before she'd pounced on him. Helping herself to a chip, she chewed on it then jumped back to her feet. 'Music?'

Pulling his shorts up, he laughed and reached for a chip of his own. Layla was never happier than when music was playing…apart from when making love, that was. His addiction to having sex with Layla was completely mutual. 'Sure.'

But, sitting back down and watching her fiddle with her phone to connect her playlist with the villa's outdoor speakers, he found his gaze drawn again to her stomach and breasts. His thudding heart felt colder than the chip that had stuck in his throat. Even though her short dress was floaty, he could see the delineation of a stomach that had seemingly swollen over the space of an hour. For the first time, he could *see* that she was pregnant.

Jazz music piped out. He dragged his stare away from her stomach to her face.

She tapped his nose and grinned. 'Got you.'

A moment later a band they both like replaced it and she sat back down. After she'd piled her plate with salad and a handful more of the cold chips, her forehead creased with concern. 'Are you sure there's nothing wrong?'

What could he tell her? That her pregnancy was showing and his heart had turned cold for it?

Had it turned cold? Or had that just been his chest? Was there a difference?

He wished he could erase the cynicism that stopped him from believing in anything that wasn't tangible and verifiable. When his mind refused to see Layla with another man was it because his current addiction to her had made her so entirely his or because he wanted to believe the baby could be his too much?

And that was where the danger lay. *How* could he believe? He'd thought about that night so many times and there was not a single moment when he'd been careless.

But why would she lie? What was there to gain by it when she already had the money, he'd paid Laurence the money for the firm and she'd been promised a minimum of a further fifty million? She could walk away now and he'd be obliged to give it to her.

She had no need to lie. Not now.

So why couldn't he make the leap of faith in either his head or his heart?

He opened his mouth to assure her again that nothing was wrong, then changed his mind before the words formed, instead asking, 'How did you become so good at acting?'

The crease in her forehead became one of confusion.

'You're one person one minute and someone else the next. You can turn it on like a tap.'

'But you do the same,' she protested, clearly taken aback. 'Everyone does. How we are together… When we're alone you're almost a different man from how you are in your professional life.'

'I get your point but my professional persona and who I am when it's just you and me, they are still just me. I cannot assimilate into being someone else like you can. I knew you for two years and you gave no hint that you were anything more than a bar tender.'

'You never asked.'

'I appreciate that, but you never showed a side of yourself that would make me question that there was more to you than what you were showing.'

'I was being what you wanted from a bar tender.'

'And that is *my* point. You are a chameleon. I can only

be different versions of myself but you can assimilate into being whoever you want or whatever you think someone wants you to be. You have slotted into my life and family as if you were born into Sicilian society—'

'But that's what you wanted me to do! It's partly why you made me marry you!'

He took a deep breath to keep his tone calm. 'I'm not denying that but I want to understand how you do it. I want to understand where it comes from. I want to understand *you*, Layla.'

She gave a helpless shrug. 'I don't know where it comes from. It's not something I think about.'

'What is it then? Some kind of super power?' He was only half joking. Sebastiano had met plenty of actors and actresses in his time, many of them award winning. If Layla was on a stage with them she would act them off it.

Shoving her chair back a little, she drew her knees up and wrapped her arms around her calves. 'I honestly don't know.' A short shake of her head. 'I've never thought about it.'

'Try this then—when can you first remember doing it?'

Clearly upset, she sucked her cheeks in and grazed her bottom lip. 'Primary school,' she eventually replied. 'I realised very quickly that I was different from the other children, and I didn't want to be different.'

'What made you different from them?'

'What do you think?' She shook her head. 'I was the only one without a father.'

'There must have been other children growing up in single-parent homes.'

'Yes, but I was the only one who had literally never met the other parent. I can remember, very distinctly, realising that I was the only child in my class who didn't know their father, and begging my mum to let me meet him. I thought she could magic him up for me.' Her lips pulled in and she swallowed. 'Looking back, I can only imagine how hard it must have been for her to tell me the truth—my father left before I was born and they made an agreement that I would always live with my mum and he would not be part of our lives.

'I was too young to understand. Even my friends who didn't live with their dads still saw them, so I begged and begged and begged her to let me meet him. I would not let the subject drop and in the end she agreed to reach out and ask him. I was so excited, utterly convinced he was waiting for the right moment to swing into my life.' She turned her face away and gathered her hair together, twisting it into a knot that held itself together without any means of support.

When she next spoke, all the musicality in her voice had gone. 'She got the reply on a Saturday. I only remember that because I was watching cartoons in my pyjamas. I was young enough to find post being delivered incredibly exciting and so I grabbed the envelope and gave it to her and...' He heard her swallow before she continued in the same monotone. 'When she'd read it, she picked me up and carried me into the living room and sat me on her lap and wrapped her arms tightly around me and told me that she was very sorry but that he'd said no.'

Although Sebastiano knew she'd never met her father and so had known the outcome, he still flinched. 'How old were you?'

'Five.' Her shoulders hunched up and she whispered, 'So I think that's what made me become the chameleon you think I am.'

'You were looking for love?' he asked into the silence.

Her gaze flickered back to him, surprise ringing from it. 'My mother loved me enough for two parents. She practically smothered me in it. It was rejection I became frightened of. My father didn't abandon me like you said, Sebastiano—he abandoned my mum. Me, he rejected. He rejected me before I was born and he rejected me when I was old enough to want to know him, and...' Her shoulders rose. 'It hurt. Really hurt. If I hadn't had my mum constantly telling me that it wasn't my fault, that it was all him, then God knows what I'd have become, but, even with the security of her love, I couldn't shake the fear that there was something inherently wrong with me and so I became adept at being all things to all people and being whatever I thought they wanted me to be, anything to stop them having an excuse to reject me.' A smile suddenly pulled at her cheeks but there was sadness contained in it. 'I grew out of it eventually. Funnily enough, it was my father who inadvertently gave me the tools to become comfortable in my own skin.'

At his questioning gaze, she explained, 'The letter he sent to my mum—I found it tucked in a drawer when I was fifteen. I'd always assumed he'd written it but it actually came from his solicitor, and it was a threat telling my mum that if she contacted him again, he would take legal action against her for harassment. I knew straight away that it was an empty threat but I also knew why it would have terrified her. I was old enough by then to understand.

'My mum's not academically minded—she left school at sixteen because she struggled so much. My father was a lot older than her but she had no idea he was married. She was crazy about him. As soon as he found out she was pregnant, he ran for the hills. He was rich, not by your standards of course, but rich enough to buy her a small home without his wife's knowledge and manipulative enough to get Mum to sign a document stating the house was in lieu of all future child support. He signed full custody of me over to her and she never saw him again. She was nineteen.'

Sebastiano could feel a pulse in his jaw throbbing in time to the beats of blood pounding in his head.

His investigation into Layla's background had brought to light the basics of this but to actually hear it from her and have it explained so starkly…

'She was nineteen, Sebastiano,' she repeated. 'Her parents were deeply religious and they disowned her. She was all alone in the world with a newborn baby. She had a roof over her head but no means to pay the bills for it. She relied on charity to furnish it. My earliest memory is sitting in an office with a picture book while she cleaned around me. She couldn't afford childcare so she took jobs where I could go with her, and she worked so *hard*. She worked her fingers to the bone while that bastard lived the high life with his real family, and once I understood the full picture, and once I'd stalked my father on social media— well, I stalked his wife; he doesn't use it—and saw how he lavished everything on them while letting us suffer, I found my purpose.'

'The law,' he supplied as the pieces of the jigsaw that was Layla slotted together.

She nodded. 'The money you've given the firm will do more good than you could imagine. If even just a couple of those who promised donations at the wedding keep their word, we'll be able to raise much more awareness about what we offer to those who actually need us.'

The pulse in his jaw throbbed even stronger. Years of study and training and Layla earned, by choice, the equivalent of a shop worker's salary, and all to help those too poor or too uneducated to navigate the legal system for themselves. To compare it with his own job, where he oversaw thousands of people turning up to work each day for the sole reason of making the rich even richer, made his guts clench in the most uncomfortable way. He couldn't even say he'd followed the path set for him by his parents and the generations of Russos before him out of duty because that would be a lie. He'd embraced his destiny as soon as he'd been old enough to understand what it was.

His bank and its divisions around the world played lip service to charity in a variety of ways but it was all corporate dress-up, a means of gaining social kudos and brownie points.

Layla and her firm didn't just talk the talk. They walked it in the cheapest shoes they could afford so as to leave more money in the coffers for the clients who needed it.

No one could be that selfless. Angels did not exist any more than miracles did.

Angels certainly did not handcuff people to beds and demand five million pounds from them.

'Are you going to use the law to make your father pay?' he asked. That was what he would do if his father had treated him and his mother the way Layla's father had. He would burn for revenge, and as flames licked in his chest, he understood they were flames burning for the need for vengeance for Layla.

For the second time that evening, surprise rang from the forget-me-nots. 'And destroy his children…my half-siblings? No way. They're innocent in all this.'

It wasn't just the pulse in his jaw throbbing now. All his pulses had joined in. 'They're adults.'

'Adults with families of their own who don't deserve to have their lives torn apart.'

'Surely his wife deserves to know?'

'What, like your real wife will know about the mistresses you'll take on the side?'

Breathing heavily through the swathe of rancid emotions churning in him, he stared at her. Sometimes he forgot how much Layla had learned by tending his bar at the club in the years where her every movement around him had been a performance. 'In my world, affairs are conducted discreetly but it is rare that a spouse doesn't know. It is rare for the spouse not to take a lover of their own.'

Colour suffusing her high cheekbones, her musical voice was tight as she said, 'You can fill your boots with mistresses to your heart's content with your future wife but there's no way I'll put up with it.'

His own voice equally tight, he put his arms on the table and leaned his face into hers. 'You agreed to this marriage, Layla. You knew what you were marrying into.'

The flash in her eyes this time was of pure hurt.

Getting to her feet, she said, 'It was marry you or have you destroy the firm that dedicates itself to helping vulnerable people like my mum, so that was hardly a choice, was it? And that's the difference between you and me, Sebastiano—you're happy to destroy innocents whereas I've only ever wanted to help them. I've never wanted to hurt anyone.'

'Where are you going?' he demanded as she headed towards the bifold doors back into the villa.

'To bed. I've developed a headache so feel free to sleep in a guest suite. I'm sure your staff are quite convinced enough already that this marriage is *genuine*.'

CHAPTER ELEVEN

LAYLA HAD LOCKED herself in the bathroom, showered, then thrown on the least sexy knickers she could find and the longest dress before climbing into bed. If the bedroom door had a lock on it, she'd have turned the key.

Unable to sleep…well, it wasn't particularly late, the sun still not having fully set…she scrolled through her phone and tried to convince herself it was the earliness of the evening making her feel all upset and angst-ridden. Tried to convince herself, too, that the reason she kept blinking was because she was tired and not because she was furiously trying to stop tears falling, and she didn't care if she was contradicting herself with her own thoughts.

She'd received a message from the conveyancer acting on her behalf for the purchase of the suburban house, which only added to her upset. Apparently it wasn't possible to fast-track the purchase even though there was no chain, which she knew was utter twaddle. She'd bet the whole five million pounds sitting in her bank account that if Sebastiano had asked the question the purchase would complete so quickly she'd get whiplash.

She'd just fired a message to her mum when she heard movement outside the door and almost gave herself actual whiplash by throwing herself onto her side and shoving her phone under the pillow.

She closed her eyes just as the door handle turned and played at being asleep, hoping, not for the first time, that Sebastiano was deaf to the sound of her thundering heartbeats.

She wished she'd chosen a more comfortable position to feign sleep in.

When the bed dipped, she suddenly found it impossible to feign rhythmic breaths, and when a warm, lean body pressed itself against her, an arm wrapped around her waist and a mouth kissed the top of her head, the tears she'd been fighting for the last hour filled her eyes.

'I'm sorry,' Sebastiano said heavily into her hair.

There was the slightest softening in her rigid form.

He kissed her again and sighed. He still didn't quite understand how they'd gone from bliss to poison in less than an hour but knew he'd been the driving force behind it. And all because the sight of Layla's visibly pregnant stomach had set off emotions in him he didn't know how to decipher and the starkness of her story of abandonment and rejection by her father had turned those emotions into something hot and rancid.

Layla hadn't just been rejected by her father, he thought with an ache in his chest, but her grandparents too. Rejected before she was even born.

Wrapping himself tighter around her, he pressed his palm to the small bump of her belly. 'I swear to you, on my own life, that the life growing beneath my hand will always have a father in me. They will be my heir and I will love them because they are innocent in all this. I will never abandon them and I will never reject them.' Especially not now that he knew her story and not just the facts set out as a timeline.

It was incomprehensible to him that a man could abandon their own child to poverty. His family weren't perfect—something his mother would probably disagree with—and he knew there were secret children stashed away within the family tree, but those children had not been left to suffer in poverty.

The rush of relief when Layla rolled over to face him was like a tightly coiled spring releasing.

Disconcerted at the strength of it and equally disconcerted at how deeply it cut to see the remnant of the upset he'd caused her reflecting in her eyes, he tried to lighten the tension. 'As for the taking of a mistress... What man would want a mistress if he has a Layla in his bed?'

'What about when I'm the size of a whale?' she whispered.

He rubbed the tip of his nose to hers. 'If you don't want me to take a mistress then I won't.'

Their eyes held.

He had another disconcerting feeling that she was trying to reach into his mind, and then she sighed and lifted a hand to his hair. Softly, she said, 'I entered this marriage with my eyes open and knowing exactly what I was signing up for, but I'm the product of an affair. Someone always gets hurt.'

And Layla could not explain even to herself why it felt like a knife in her heart that Sebastiano would only refrain from taking a mistress while they were married because she didn't want him to. Not because he didn't want to.

Just to imagine him with anyone else brought on instant nausea. To imagine herself with anyone else...

She couldn't. She could not imagine walking away from this marriage and being with anyone else. The thought of touching another man was as repulsive as imagining Sebastiano with another woman, which was exactly why she needed to think of him only as her lover. Because one day he would be someone else's husband. He would belong to someone else.

Layla rarely spoke about her father, had never confided the story about begging her mum to let her meet him to anyone before. Telling Sebastiano the story had been painful, the memories stirring the pain she'd experienced in those long ago days like an echo in her heart.

Fear suddenly raced like cold needles up her spine, and when he said, 'I will never do anything to hurt you, *cara,*' she dug her fingers through his hair to his skull and kissed him as hard as she'd ever kissed him before.

As he snaked his way down her body, kissing and touching her all the way down to her pelvis, she screwed her eyes shut and prayed for the pleasure to drive out the fear that the echoed memories of pain in her heart were nothing but a taster of the pain Sebastiano could inflict on her.

Her last thought before the bliss of his tongue drove her to ecstasy was that she needed to guard her heart much more tightly. Sebastiano was her lover, their marriage a performance. She must remember that. She must.

An overrunning meeting in Frankfurt meant that when Sebastiano arrived back at the villa, he waited in the car for Layla to join him.

The closest he could come to describing the feelings in his stomach on the drive home was butterflies. Whatever the feeling, when she appeared moments after the car came to a stop, the butterflies dived into his chest and extended their wings inside it.

She glided out of the front door and past the statues of scholars bathed in early-autumn sunshine, and as she stepped to the car, the backdrop of the villa and the golden glow suffusing her formed an angelic aura that dazzled him with the same strength as when she'd walked down the aisle to him.

So taken was he by the vision that he didn't notice the phone stuck to her ear until she slid beside him and mouthed, Sorry.

It was not the greeting he'd envisaged after their first night apart since their wedding.

Just one night away from her and her beauty had grown. His expert eye noted her breasts, jutting against her red maxi-dress, had grown too and that the neat little bump that would shortly be scanned at the private hospital used by generations of Russos was more prominent than he remembered.

She ended her call with a long exhale before finally bestowing her attention upon him. 'Sorry about that. Good trip?'

He bit back the churlish answer he wanted to throw at her and leaned in for a kiss that was far too brief for his liking, especially when he'd spent the journey back to her fantasising about the passionate kiss she would greet him with. 'Productive. Who were you talking to? It sounded important.'

'My conveyancer—the solicitor who's supposed to be arranging the purchase of the house for me.'

It took a moment for this to digest. 'You're buying a house?'

'I put the offer in when I first got here. I'd viewed it the weekend before you kidnapped me and it's perfect.'

Her blithe reminder of why she'd married him twisted his guts. 'Perfect for what?'

'A family.'

'And you didn't think to mention this to me?'

Surprise lit her face. 'But I did. I told you I wanted the money to buy a house for me and the baby.'

'You have a home,' he pointed out, finding himself having to swallow back his temper. 'Here with me.'

'But it won't be for ever, and besides I'm desperate to get Mum out of that hellhole.' She gritted her teeth and gave another long exhale. 'She's finally agreed to move into it but the longer it all drags on, the more I worry she'll change her mind. If she refuses to move when the purchase goes through I'll have to get you to kidnap her.'

'Good to know you have uses for me,' he said with only faint sarcasm.

Her eyebrow rose. 'What does that mean?'

He had to take a long breath of his own before he trusted himself to answer.

It was sheer arrogance that had let him assume Layla would have missed him during their first night apart in three weeks. It hadn't occurred to him that he would miss her, not until he'd found himself in his apartment contemplating flying home for a few hours and then returning to Frankfurt first thing.

From the way Layla was acting, he might as well have been gone only ten minutes.

Keeping his tone moderate, he said, 'Layla, I have just learned you are buying a home without my knowledge and that you're trying to move your mother out of the house you've just described as a hellhole. Do you not think these are things you should have discussed with me?'

She looked nonplussed.

'I'm your husband.' Did she just *flinch* at that? 'You should discuss important things with me.'

'Do you discuss important things with me?'

'If I had important things to discuss then I would.' He

took another deep breath. He didn't want an argument. That night on their honeymoon when bliss had turned to poison still lingered in him, although he had no clue why. Neither of them had mentioned it again. They'd returned home and embarked on married life, and for all that it was proving to be working well between them—better than even he'd hoped—and for all the copious amounts of sex they enjoyed together, he couldn't shake the feeling that they were building a marriage on sand. 'Tell me about this house.'

Her gaze troubled, she sighed. 'The prospectus is still online.'

After she'd recited the address, he found it.

'It's small,' he observed.

'It's huge compared to my old house.'

He scrolled for more information on it. 'It's in a good neighbourhood,' he eventually said, 'but installing adequate security will be impossible.'

'I don't need security.'

He raised an eyebrow. 'You're my wife. Your child will be a Russo. They will be a target for kidnappers. I'm sorry, Layla, but this is completely unsuitable.' He then proceeded to tell her exactly why it was unsuitable, making such a good fist of it that she'd turned quite pale by the time he'd finished.

'I have a proposition,' he told her as they turned onto the long drive that led to the hospital. 'We can look for a suitable house together which I will buy but have put in your name. We can use it as our London base.'

As of next Monday, Layla would spend her working weeks in London as had been pre-agreed. They'd only spoken about it in vague terms but it was something that had played on his mind since the honeymoon. Sebastiano's rarely used apartment in central London would work fine for a baby but not an inquisitive toddler. They needed a proper home there, and Layla had given him the perfect opening to suggest it.

'We?' she queried.

'I will arrange my schedule so I can be London-based as much as is practicable. We are newly-weds,' he reminded her. 'This is our honeymoon stage. If we spend too much time apart too soon then people will talk.'

Layla's top teeth grazed harder than normal into her bottom lip as she held herself back from reminding him that she was buying the house for her and their baby for when their marriage was over. She'd already envisaged how she would furnish it, the colour schemes, the bedroom she'd create for the little life steadily growing inside her. And as for London...

She'd assumed Sebastiano would resume his normal working life and the copious amount of travelling it involved once their honeymoon was over. So far, though, he'd taken to working from his home office with alarming frequency, only the most important meetings taking him out of their Sicilian home.

She hadn't factored in how determined he was to promote a *genuine* marriage to the world, and as a result she'd had little respite from him. She'd sit in her office and liaise with clients and colleagues and create documents and fill out paperwork entirely aware that Sebastiano was working on the other side of the door. Entirely aware. They shared all their meals together and then at night, they closed the bedroom door and fell into each other's arms.

How was she supposed to remember that this was all a performance when they were so rarely apart and when Sebastiano was treating her as if she were his real wife? It was becoming impossible.

What made it worse were the times they did spend apart. The times when she sat in her office wholly aware of his absence. And then last night she'd slept alone and it had been awful. For the first time since arriving in Sicily, her insomnia had kicked back in. She'd been unable to settle the whole night through, sleep coming only in brief snatches.

She needed some proper separation. She'd been banking on having Mondays to Fridays away from him, a chance to create physical and emotional distance. Because that was the worst thing of all. How emotionally attached she was becoming to him. The reason she daydreamed about the home that would be hers when their marriage ended was because she knew she had to.

But she was being backed into a corner. It was too soon after their wedding to start sowing the seeds of distance that would be used to explain their marriage failing. It was unthinkable that Sebastiano would let it end before the baby was born. Speculation was already rife in the press that she was pregnant, her small bump captured in a photo during an evening gala going a long way in proving their marriage was genuine.

What frightened her more than anything was what came after the baby was born and the DNA test proved beyond doubt that it was his. What if he decided this meant their marriage should continue indefinitely, something she suspected he was already thinking? What if he didn't? She didn't know which scenario frightened her the most. If he wanted them to stay together it would only be because of their child. If he let her go it would be to produce a spare to her baby's heir with another woman. Either way, Layla lost. Either way, she wouldn't be enough for him as she was, and though she knew she shouldn't care if she was enough for him, it was becoming increasingly hard to deny that she did care. Cared more than was healthy or safe.

'You don't look happy at the prospect,' he observed, cutting through her unhappy musings, his eyes narrowed with shrewdness.

For a moment, she feared she would cry.

She couldn't tell him why she looked unhappy. She knew she should be grateful that he was taking their baby's security so seriously even while doubting it was his, be grateful too at his vow that he would be a father to it whatever a DNA test might say, and grateful that he was taking the pregnancy and birth seriously enough that he wanted her to be cared for in Sicily's most eminent private hospital.

And so she swallowed back her dejection.

'I can see that it makes sense,' she said. And she *could* see it, much as she wished she couldn't, and much as she wished she could think of the perfect counterargument. 'But what about my mum?'

'She can move into the London place with us. She can live here with us too.'

Her mouth dropped open in astonishment.

He raised a nonchalant shoulder. 'We will make sure the London property has a self-contained flat or a separate dwelling on the grounds for her. Here, she can take her pick of the guest cottages.'

'Are you serious?'

Please, Sebastiano, say no. Don't do something else wonderful for me. I need to hate you more than love... like you.

He fixed her with a stare that read, 'do you have to ask?'

She had to turn her face away briefly to blink back tears without him seeing. 'You'd be happy for my *mum* to live with us?'

He tutted and folded his arms across his chest. 'I'm Sicilian. Family is everything to us, and your mother is everything to you.'

The tears pooled back, hot and brimming, and she turned away again, pretending to be transfixed with the sprawling white building their driver had come to a stop at.

In England, she'd already be out of the car and hurrying inside, afraid of being late for her appointment. Here, in this exclusive private hospital with its manicured grounds that only the ridiculously rich could afford, they would wait for her. After all, she was no longer plain Layla Sansom. She was the great Sebastiano Russo's wife.

'She won't agree,' she eventually said when she was semi-certain she could speak without choking.

'Why not?'

'I only managed to convince her to move to the suburban house by selling the garden to her—gardening's her therapy. She sits in our little garden with a cup of tea and manages to forget that the house next door is a narcotic shop and that the vampires all descend on the street at night.' She closed her eyes and laughed sadly. 'She has this amazing ability to tune out the terrible stuff and laser in on the good stuff. She turned that house into a home for us. She painted every wall and hung every curtain and it became her sanctuary from the world when she was at her most scared and vulnerable. She's frightened of leaving it. No way will she agree to move countries.'

Sebastiano digested this, breathing hard to smother the anger that had flared, not with Layla but with himself. He knew how desperate Layla had been to move out of that house before their baby was born and should have realised she'd want her mother moved out of it too. Jilly Sansom was his mother-in-law and so a part of his extended family.

Her safety was as much his responsibility as her daughter and grandchild's safety.

He gave a sharp nod. 'Will you let me talk to her?'

Her gaze moved from the window to him. 'And say what?'

He tapped her nose and forced a smile. 'Trust me to find the right words.'

She responded with a smile of her own that looked as forced as his felt. 'I know I said about you kidnapping her, but no handcuffs, okay?'

This time he smiled with his whole face, capturing her cheeks in his hand and releasing some of the angst knotted in his chest in a deep, passionate kiss. 'Believe me, my little rabbit,' he murmured, 'you are the only person I wish to use handcuffs on.'

Layla felt like she'd entered a five-star hotel rather than a hospital. The only difference was the faint trace of disinfectant that permeated the walls.

A manager escorted them down a wide, thickly carpeted corridor to the maternity wing, explaining in perfect English all the facilities they had to offer the expectant mother and the excellent care she could expect. After a full tour of the birthing wing, Layla's mind was made up. This was the hospital she would have her baby in.

By the time they entered the clinical room for her scan and she lay on the bed and lifted her top to expose her naked bump, she was filled to the brim with excitement. The first scan had been the most magical moment of her life and she'd counted down the days until she could see her baby again…

She caught the look on Sebastiano's face and her heart sank.

There was no mirroring of her excitement there.

After a beat, she turned her stare from him, smiled at the sweet-faced sonographer, and fixed her gaze on the computer screen beside her.

She would not let his lack of visible excitement ruin this moment for her.

The rapid thuds of the baby's heartbeat were much louder than Sebastiano had anticipated. They filled the room.

The beats of his own heart accelerated.

A mass appeared on the computer screen. The sonographer pressed the ultrasound probe down on the left of Layla's belly. The screen became clearer. Suddenly he could discern a head...a belly...limbs...

White noise filled his head. He could no longer distinguish the individual beats battering against his ribs.

'Is the baby the right size?' he heard Layla ask, her anxious voice distant, as if she were far away rather than right beside him.

'Let me take the measurements to be sure,' the sonographer answered. 'You are worried?'

'A little,' she confessed. 'It's only because my bump's so small.'

She was worried about that?

Still pressing the probe to Layla's stomach, the sonographer tapped at her computer's keyboard with her other hand.

Sebastiano hadn't realised he'd been holding his breath until the sonographer smiled and it escaped in a rush.

'All normal,' she said. 'Your baby's rate of growth is perfect. Everything is normal and how it should be.'

There was no mistaking the relief on Layla's face.

No mistaking, either, the relief washing through *him*.

'Would you like to know the sex?'

For the first time since she'd climbed on the medical bed, Layla turned her stare from the screen and looked at him. There was a question in her eyes. And a plea that made his still rapidly beating heart catch and his head pound.

She was pleading with him to believe her...

He cleared his throat but couldn't clear the pounding. 'Do you want to know?'

She shook her head.

'Then let it be a surprise.'

In the car on their return to the villa, Sebastiano's heart had finally decreased back to a relatively normal beat but the throbbing in his head remained. Watching Layla stare reverently at the scan photo of the baby deepened the throbs.

Keeping his voice measured, he casually said, 'I didn't know you were worried about the baby's size.'

She pressed the photo to her chest, right over her heart, then slipped it into her handbag. 'It was more a minor concern than a worry. You know, one of those things that sit in the back of your mind and niggle at you?'

He did know. Layla's behaviour was his own *niggle*. 'Why didn't you tell me?'

Her forehead furrowed. 'I never thought to. It was only a niggle.'

He held onto his temper by the skin of his teeth. That was twice in three hours he'd learned something important Layla had kept from him.

'*Cara*,' he said, taking her hand, 'you cannot keep hiding things from me. If you have worries you must share them with me.'

Although Layla knew she shouldn't feel guilty, it still stabbed at her. But if he wanted honesty from her...

'It wasn't intentional,' she said quietly. 'I think it's knowing you don't believe the baby is yours… It's making it difficult for me to open up about the pregnancy to you.' Increasingly difficult. He was doing everything an expectant father should but it all felt clinical, like he was going through the motions without his heart being in it.

She'd seen his reflection on the computer screen. While she'd been thrilling to see their baby, Sebastiano's face had been emotionless. And all because he couldn't admit to himself that the baby was his.

'Listen to me,' he said firmly. 'What I believe is irrelevant. The baby is mine. I will always be its father and I will always be there for you. Trust that, Layla, and stop shutting me out. We are in this together.'

Oh, how she *longed* to believe him.

Longed with all her heart.

CHAPTER TWELVE

SINCE LAYLA HAD cuffed Sebastiano to a bed, she'd suffered a cricked neck and virtual whiplash. Now she was close to getting real whiplash such was the speed Sebastiano had moved. One day he'd asked her to trust him to find the right words to convince her mother to move, the next he'd flown to London, returning in time for dinner with a smile of satisfaction.

Whatever he'd said to her mother to convince her to move in with them was being kept secret by them both, but convince her he had. The very next day her mother had arrived in Sicily and chosen a guest house to make herself a home in.

So much had her mother fallen in love with Sicily and the 'cosy' garden that came with it, which was three times the size of their London garden, that within weeks of moving in she was happier than Layla could ever remember. Such happiness did she radiate that Layla had felt compelled to gently remind her that it wouldn't be for ever. Her marriage came with its end already written.

'It will all work out for the best,' her mum had said with a smile. 'You'll see.'

But best for whom? That was all Layla could wonder. And because it made her heart hurt to wonder too much, she threw herself into her work, using her free time to chase up the wedding guests who'd indicated they would like to make donations to the firm.

The money came through thick and fast and accumulated so quickly that when Sebastiano suggested over a dinner with Laurence and his husband that they should think about increasing their team's salaries to make themselves more competitive to new recruits, they hadn't dismissed it with a laugh. They had laughed though, in sheer joyful disbelief, when he offered them the use of a floor of Russo Banca Internazionale's London skyscraper in the financial district. Layla had laughed too because if she'd gone with the alternative, crying, she might be crying still.

It was the most wonderful gesture from Sebastiano. The floor he gave them was three times the size of the floor they'd occupied for three decades and he was giving it rent free for a guaranteed minimum of twenty years. A week after moving into it, Clayton Community Law had a list of potential recruits wanting to join the firm when they graduated. Enquiries for placements were coming as thick and fast as the money, and now they had the difficult task of sifting the recruits for those genuinely wanting to join a philanthropic law firm rather than those wanting a fat salary and an office with a view. It was a nice but ultimately serious problem to have because the only thing they couldn't afford was to recruit someone unable to treat their clients with respect.

Layla had problems of her own with the move and all the changes, and they were entirely selfish. The move meant she had no respite from Sebastiano at all. Even when he was away travelling, she now worked from a building he owned. She walked into the lobby and was greeted by his enlarged photo flanked by photos of the heads of divisions and countries. She stepped into the elevator and knew it was an elevator he'd taken. She dined in the staff canteen that was as much a canteen as an orange was a pear. The food served was exquisite, table service given, a wine menu...she'd dined in worse award-winning restaurants and it was all because Sebastiano insisted on it. And insisted on heavily subsidising it.

She couldn't even settle at her desk without thinking of him because the very chair she sat on had been imported from Japan especially for her, a fancy ergonomic chair designed for pregnant women.

Within three months of their marriage, Sebastiano had infected her entire life and everyone in it, and all she could do was follow the lead of the character of her favourite childhood film and just keep swimming. The alternative, she very much feared, was to drown.

Layla stood in her Sicilian dressing room trying to decide which of the fresh batch of evening dresses made for her that she should wear to the evening's party. She'd needed to expand her wardrobe to accommodate her expanding belly. Now she was seven months pregnant, her bump was still small but it had grown enough that her clothes had laughed at her when she tried to make them fit.

Just as she'd settled on a floaty red dress, something caught her eye out of the window. Her heart was thrashing even before she recognised the car heading down the long driveway.

Sebastiano was home.

Five nights without him. The longest they'd ever been parted.

Enduring it had been hell.

Gripping tightly to the window sill, she fought the compulsion to go skipping down the stairs to greet him. She needed to compose herself first, couldn't bear to think of him looking into her eyes and seeing how desperately she'd missed him.

By arranging herself with a book on the chaise longue that ran beneath one of the sash windows, she hoped Sebastiano would find in her a woman enjoying a lazy Saturday afternoon. She hoped, too, that he wouldn't look too closely at her face or he'd notice the puffiness of her eyes that five nights of insomnia had caused and which gel eye patches followed by expensive concealer had barely reduced.

Sebastiano bounded up the stairs stifling the disappointment at the lack of soft lips and warm body waiting impatiently at the front door to greet his return. The butler had informed him that Layla was resting.

She was seven months pregnant, he reminded himself. Her bump might be smaller than in the average pregnancy but the effects on her body were the same. The emotional effects were the same.

It was something he had to continually remind himself of because on the surface, Sebastiano had a marriage most of the men he knew could only dream about.

Layla didn't complain about the hours he worked. She didn't complain if he had to change plans at the last minute due to issues beyond his control. She didn't ask to accompany him on overnight trips. She didn't demand a blow-by-blow account of how he spent his time when he was away from her.

He would prefer it if she did. At least it would show she cared.

His footsteps slowed as he trod the mezzanine to their

room, a tightness forming in the chest that had been pounding in anticipation of seeing her again.

For the woman who'd flushed with anger at the thought of him taking a mistress, he'd now be surprised if she'd give a damn if he did it.

The temptation was there, to take himself a lover just to see how she'd react. There were two things stopping him. One was the promise he'd made. The other was that he had no interest in anyone else. Even when alone in bed, his fantasies revolved only around Layla.

It had reached the stage where his whole world revolved around her.

Her world did not revolve around him.

On the surface, she performed as perfectly as she ever had. She was still the perfect public wife, the perfect hostess, the perfect daughter-in-law and member of the Russo empire. She was always—always—the perfect bed partner, as unable to keep her hands off him as he was unable to keep his hands off her.

She was perfect in every way and yet...

And yet when they were apart he doubted she spared him a thought. All messages and calls these last five days had been instigated by him.

He could forgive her disinterest if he thought it was the pregnancy and her job consuming her to the point of her blocking everything else out, but Layla's disinterest ran deeper than that. She'd closed a part of herself off from him and the longer their marriage went on, the more intensely he felt it and the more it ate at him.

He opened the bedroom door.

She was reclining on a chaise longue beneath a window, reading.

The light that ignited in her eyes to see him eased a little of the tightness.

'You're back,' she sang, discarding the book without saving the page and easing herself up. Padding over to him with a grace that not even seven months of pregnancy could diminish, she threw her arms around his neck.

The welcome heat of her passionate kiss overrode the rest of the tightness, and he returned it with all the hunger that had built during those interminably long days apart.

Only when the hunger had been temporarily sated enough did he break away to cup her cheeks and gaze at the face he'd missed so much that at times it had been hard to breathe.

Her cheeks were flushed, the forget-me-nots pulsing their desire.

Whatever else his wife might feel, this was the one area where the closeness between them could not be broken, and he brought his face back to hers. *'Mi sei mancata tantissimo,'* he murmured before smothering her with another deeply passionate kiss.

Layla's intention to play it cool had been forgotten the moment Sebastiano walked through the door. The joy that had careered through her had been too powerful to resist.

When, she wondered dimly as she revelled at being back in his arms and having his taste fill her senses, would she reach the point when she could look at Sebastiano and be able to breathe normally? When longing wouldn't grip her so tightly? When she wouldn't experience such a dizzying rush just to breathe his cologne?

In moments she was carefully lifted into the air and sat on the edge of the bed.

Between biting kisses, they stripped his polo shirt and her cashmere sweater, her bra swiftly following. And then he gently pushed her on her back to assault her senses, trailing hot kisses down her throat and to her breasts, kissing, licking and nipping while he slipped a hand up her short skirt and cupped her heat. Knickers yanked down her thighs and calves, she kicked them off and spread her thighs as she reached for his chinos. Expertly, she undid the button and lowered the zip, then tugged his chinos and underwear down to his thighs and took him, huge and fully erect in her hand. While his fingers pleasured her between her legs and his mouth and tongue worked their magic on her breasts, she masturbated him, bringing him closer to her heat so that when he moved his hand away from her heat, he could drive straight inside her.

She moaned loudly as he filled her and wrapped her legs tight around his waist.

This was what she missed when he was away from her, she tried desperately to tell herself. His lovemaking. The feeling of complete and utter sensory overload that she could only get from Sebastiano.

Lying back, she closed her eyes and revelled in every thrust and every burning sensation.

His fingers found hers and threaded through them.

She squeezed back.

The tempo increased. The sensory pleasure was almost more than she could endure, burning through every cell, the swell of her orgasm building and building until it exploded in a tidal wave of sensation that had her open her eyes as she cried out and lifted her head for his kiss.

Eyes dark and hooded, he kissed her hard through the grunts of his own pleasure and then, with one long final thrust, he climaxed. The pressure of his groin against hers in that final thrust set off one final wave of bliss through her and as she rode it, their mouths fused, Sebastiano so deep inside her he could be a part of her, a wave of something else, something new, broke free and rippled through her with the strength to make her cry out again, louder than she had ever done.

The wave came from her heart.

It took a long time for the thrills of his orgasm to subside. Even longer for Sebastiano to bring himself to break away from Layla and roll onto his side.

The beats of his heart echoing and pulsing through his skin, he inhaled deeply in an effort to bring himself fully back to earth.

After all this time, how could it just keep getting better and better between them?

Fingers laced with hers, he stared intently into her eyes and wished he could read what she was thinking as she gazed with equal intensity back at him.

There was a wanness to her features that he hadn't noticed earlier. Faint shadows beneath her eyes.

Had he got it all wrong about her feelings for him? Could it be that she simply respected that when he was away on business, he was working and so didn't want to bother him with frivolous calls or messages?

Was it possible that Layla really *had* missed him?

Was it possible, Layla wondered helplessly as she gazed into Sebastiano's green depths, that he'd missed her even a little bit? Missed *her*, not just the mind-blowing sex they shared?

'We should think about getting ready for the party,' he murmured. 'Especially if you want to have a bath before we leave.'

'Probably,' she whispered. She was in no rush to leave this bed.

No rush to *ever* leave this bed. To ever leave him…

A wave of emotion rushed through her, strong enough to fill her eyes with tears.

Concern filled *his* eyes. *'Cara?'*

With a sniff, she blinked the tears away and smiled. 'Our baby's kicking.'

'And that makes you cry?'

No, it's the thought of having to lose you that hurts my heart so much it makes me want to weep. 'I'm just feeling a bit emotional.'

'Can I feel?'

Her heart hitched. Sebastiano never asked to feel their baby. 'Do you want to?'

'Very much.' The sincerity in his voice and stare made her heart hitch again.

Covering his hand, she placed it on the part of her belly the kicks were coming.

Sebastiano's hand rested on her bump so long without anything happening that he thought the baby had gone back to sleep.

And then he felt it. An indentation against his palm.

Awed, he laughed at the sheer strangeness of it.

'It's something, isn't it?' she said softly, eyes now shining with something very different from the tears that had filled them only minutes ago.

There was another kick against his palm.

The ripples kicked straight into his heart then pulsed through every inch of his being.

That was his baby.

His and Layla's baby.

The bedroom was empty once Sebastiano had showered, shaved and donned the shirt and trousers of his tuxedo. He caught the scent of steamy cherry blossom and guessed Layla was in the bath.

Knocking on the door first, he poked his head around it and, despite all the emotions still careering through him, grinned to find her submerged in thick, foamy bubbles, her hair piled on top of her head, reading. 'You'll get the pages wet.'

She grinned back. 'Then invent waterproof books for me.'

'Beyond my skillset. I'm going to fix myself a drink.' As much as he would like to carry her out of the bath, lay her back on the bed and devour her all over again, Layla's daily bath was her way of dealing with the pregnancy backache she'd recently started experiencing. 'Can I get you anything?'

'I'm good, thanks.'

'Don't be too long,' he warned gently. 'The helicopter will be here in an hour.'

'I'll finish this chapter and then get out. It won't take me long to get ready.'

Blowing her a kiss, he went downstairs, poured himself a much-needed large Scotch and then headed to his office to check his upcoming schedule.

So many thoughts were crowding him, jostling with all the emotions fighting for space. He, the man who *never* allowed emotions to dictate his actions, had found himself close to being paralysed with them.

He needed to focus on something tangible, hence his decision to go through his schedule. Because he couldn't go on like this. He needed to do something about all the travelling that was keeping him apart from Layla, find a way to condense it even more than his assistant had already managed for him.

At one point he'd had the wild idea of suggesting she work remotely from Sicily for a few days each week. His headquarters were in Sicily. It meant they would be able to spend more time together. He'd rejected the idea because he'd known *she* would reject it.

It was a thought that lowered his buoyant mood a couple of degrees.

Not wanting a repeat of the poison that had started to fill his veins earlier on his walk to their bedroom, he took a drink of his Scotch and firmly reminded himself that he had a great marriage.

Wondering what Layla's schedule was like for the next few weeks, he crossed the dividing door to her now rarely used office. Giovanna, like Sebastiano's own assistant, faithfully reproduced Layla's schedule in an office planner kept on Layla's desk.

Post had been neatly piled on the desk. From the size of it, she hadn't been in here since her return from London the day before.

The franking mark on the top envelope caught his eye.

He picked it up to look more closely. Why would Layla be getting post from a London-based conveyancing firm? Any work-related post was sent to her offices in London…

His fingers had ripped the envelope open before he could stop them.

Layla checked her appearance one last time. She really loved this red dress. It was simply cut with her favoured spaghetti straps and just the right side of elegant without constricting her waist. On her feet she wore funky black shoes with a small heel. She was too pregnant for stilettos now, but not too pregnant for her favourite pair of giant hooped gold earrings. Her hair she'd left loose, her makeup a touch of black mascara and a dash of red lipstick to match her dress.

With a spritz of her favourite—and Sebastiano's favourite—perfume, she left the bedroom and set off to find him.

Strangely, she couldn't find him in any of the usual rooms. A further search proved *all* the rooms of the villa were empty of him. None of the staff had seen him.

Trying to quell her unease, she called his mobile. No answer.

A check of the security cameras showed he hadn't left the villa.

After three calls, four text messages, numerous shouts of his name and fifteen minutes of searching, she heard the sound of rotors. Their helicopter was landing. So where was Sebastiano?

About to go back upstairs and check the bedrooms again, she stopped. There was one room she hadn't looked in.

Her back now aching after all this searching, she set off again to his office. The door that adjoined her office, the one room she hadn't checked, was closed.

She opened it and her heart froze.

Sebastiano sat behind her desk, an empty crystal glass in front of him. All her drawers were open. Papers were heaped all over the desk and all over the floor.

He smiled. If a heart could freeze twice, that smile did it. 'Hello, Layla. Good of you to join me.'

The chill in her chest spreading through her veins at a rate of knots, Layla folded her arms over her stomach and absently rubbed the spot she could feel her baby's back nestled against it as it slept. 'What are you doing?'

'Me?' His smile widened and suddenly she was thrown back to the day he'd blackmailed her into their marriage.

This was the smile of the big cat before it ate its prey...

'I'm not doing anything.' If she closed her eyes she could hear the purred undertone. 'Unless you consider me going through all the paperwork in my wife's office as doing something?'

A drum was beating in her ear. She was almost too afraid to blink.

'Tell me, *wife*, when were you planning to tell me that you bought the house? You know the house I mean? The one that you agreed was an unsuitable home to raise our child in? The one you have already installed a panic room in.'

The blood in her head drained to her feet so quickly that she sagged back against the door. If it hadn't been there she would have fallen.

Eyes not leaving her face, he leaned forwards. The big cat showed its teeth. 'The house, Layla.'

CHAPTER THIRTEEN

SEBASTIANO WATCHED THE host of emotions flitter over Layla's beautiful face and, without any warning, the anger he'd been containing by the skin of his teeth erupted. 'Tell me!' he shouted, getting to his feet and slamming his palm on the desk. 'Tell me why you have gone behind my back after everything we discussed, everything we agreed, you conniving—' He bit back the curse he wanted to hurl at her and took a large lungful of air.

His instincts had been right all along.

Layla had been keeping a part of herself separate from him. A major part.

His perfect wife had gone against his wishes and behind his back to provide herself with the perfect bolt-hole to raise his child without him,

'I have given you *everything* in this marriage, Layla. Everything. And this is how you repay me. With deceit.'

'Deceit?' Eyes wide, she shook her head tremulously. 'I didn't go ahead with the house purchase because I was being deceitful or conniving—I bought it because I've spent our entire marriage terrified of the day you wake up and decide I've served my purpose, and get your big fancy lawyers on me and leave me with nothing.' Her voice caught. 'I'm sorry if you feel betrayed but that money was all I had that you couldn't touch. I needed to put it in a home that would provide safety for me and my baby if the day ever came that we needed it.'

'Safety from me?' he roared, incredulous. 'After everything I've done for you?'

'Done for your own conscience you mean,' she countered before closing her eyes. Taking a deep breath, she fixed her stare back on him and gave a helpless shrug. 'I never asked for *any* of this. All I ever wanted from you was support for my baby.'

'*Our* baby,' he corrected, unmoved.

The expression on her face at this would have made the stoniest heart laugh, but all he could manage was one laced with bitterness. 'Yes, Layla. I know the child is mine.' The truth had been knocking at him for so long…right from the start…that he couldn't pinpoint when he'd accepted it in his heart, but the emotions that had swelled in him to feel it kick against his hand earlier had blown the last of the denial out of him. 'I feel it here.' He slammed his palm onto his heart. 'Right in the place I used to feel you. And now I'm done. I'm done with trying to make you happy and fulfilled when you couldn't give a damn about me.'

Done with a marriage that had never gone beyond a performance and a wife who made promises she had no intention of keeping.

'That's not true!' she cried. 'Of course I–'

'No more lies,' he snarled before clenching his jaw and dragging air into his lungs in an effort to temper his tone. Never in the whole of his life had he felt infected by such hot, rancid emotions. 'I'm leaving. You have the night to get your stuff together—the staff will help you. I'll be back by breakfast. Make sure you're gone before I return.'

Her mouth dropped open in shock. It took an age for

anything to come out of it. 'You're ending our marriage, *now*?' she croaked.

He looked her dead in the eye.

Dio, he was having to stop himself from shaking.

'Oh, no,' he said tightly. 'Having given it some serious thought I've decided we will never divorce. I'm going to hold you to this godforsaken marriage for the rest of your miserable life. It is just that I would rather spend the night in a nest of vipers than spend another night under the same roof as you.'

Layla was trembling so hard she had to cling to the door to keep herself upright. She could hardly believe what was happening, that the man who'd made such passionate love to her such a short time ago could be looking at her with such loathing and uttering words that landed like a wound.

'I will be in touch with instructions on how we will play things from now on, and you will obey them.' He gave a smile so cold and cruel it landed like its own wound. 'Or live with the consequences... Full custody of my child.'

Her heart pounding, she stared at this stranger who'd taken possession of her lover. Of all the ways she'd imagined their marriage ending—imaginings she'd forced on herself because she'd never dared hope this day wouldn't come—she'd never dreamed it would end like this.

'Don't threaten me with our baby, Sebastiano,' she begged. 'Please, don't be that man.'

Something...a glimmer of conscience?...flashed in his eyes.

The cruel smile vanished. His voice stark, he quietly said, 'At least I never set out to make a home for it without you.'

Of all his accusations, that one landed the hardest. She threw her hands in the air, despair ripping through her. 'That's right, assume the worst of me like you always do.

The house was only ever a back-up plan for my own peace of mind, and only because I couldn't shake the fear that I'd be left alone to raise our child just like my mother was left alone to raise me.'

She snatched a moment to gather herself against the emotions battering her. 'I always knew you believed the truth about our baby but you couldn't bring yourself to admit it, could you? Because to admit it meant you'd have to accept that you'd failed, and you really can't bear to fail.'

'Do not try and deflect things back on me,' he said through gritted teeth. 'This is all you, Layla.'

'Is it really?' She shook her head. It felt like she'd sleep-walked into a nightmare she couldn't wake herself from. 'I *know* I'm scarred. Living with you has shown me just how scarred I still am, but the difference is I acknowledge it, whereas you... Life has been so gilded and effortless for you, success upon success upon success, that at the first hint of failure you take a child's default position of denial. You denied paternity when I gave you all the proof, and continued denying it. You preferred to believe I must have taken another lover straight after you than admit that at some point during our night together you screwed up. As if the great Sebastiano Russo could have got a lowly bar tender pregnant! What would polite society say about that?'

He made to speak but she wouldn't let him. She couldn't bear to hear another cruel word from his lips.

'If you hadn't discovered that I'm actually a respectable solicitor, you would never have decided to use me in your game of cover up, although what you would have done to gain vengeance against me I can only guess, and what you'd have done to cover up the money loss, again I can only guess. But you'd have thought of something because there is no way the great Sebastiano Russo would hold his hands up and admit that he'd made such a colossal mistake with those shares, or accept that his actions had backed me into such a corner that I acted in a way I should never have acted.'

She could do nothing to stop the tear that rolled down her cheek or stop her voice from breaking. 'You broke my heart, did you know that? You cut me off and acted as if that night meant nothing when you know damned well it meant *everything*.' Her voice broke again but she forced herself to continue. 'I know you'll deny it but something magical happened between us the night we made our child, but you chose to ignore it because you believed I wasn't good enough for you. I'm glad you didn't know I was a solicitor because you probably *would* have deemed me fit to pursue a relationship with and I'd have believed it was because of what you felt for me and not because I ticked the correct boxes for polite society.' She closed her eyes and clung tightly to the door. 'And then you really would have destroyed me.'

The silence that followed this was total.

Opening her eyes, Layla took in Sebastiano's ashen face. Something deep in her heart cracked.

'Do you have any idea how terrified I was when I found out I was pregnant?' she whispered. 'How alone I felt? How desperately hard I tried to reach you? And you have the nerve to act as if you're the injured party and the nerve to expect me to be *grateful*?'

Shaking her head, she took one more deep breath then looked at him for the last time. 'This is your home not mine. You stay. I'll sleep in a guest house tonight and be gone by the morning.'

Layla walked on autopilot through the sprawling rear garden breathing in the wintry air that was nothing like the wintry air she would be breathing in London come the morning. By the marble statue of the Venus de Milo, she took the path that led to the most secluded of the guest cottages. Pretty nightlights led the way.

At the door, she closed her eyes before knocking on it. It opened.

Her mother gazed at her before sympathy creased her face and she held out a hand.

Only when the door closed her in did Layla collapse with loud sobs into her mother's arms.

'Pack it all up and courier it to London. All of it.'

Those were Sebastiano's only instructions, his only hint to the staff that Layla would not be returning.

He supposed he should be thinking about loose lips but he was too numb to care. Let them talk if they wanted.

If they were talking it was not within his earshot. The villa had become as silent as a tomb.

It had become as cold as a tomb too.

On his bureau, the handwritten invitation to a Viennese Ball for the end of March. The baby would be born by then so he'd accepted it weeks ago with stray fantasies of Layla in a ball dress, waltzing in his arms. Stray fantasies, too, of making a long weekend of it, the two of them and their baby. Salzburg was a beautiful city, one he was quite certain Layla would fall in love with.

He ripped the invitation into shreds.

Sebastiano's slightly smiling photo loomed large in the Russo Banca Internazionale foyer.

Layla hunched her shoulders and blocked it out as she had every morning that week.

At her desk, she called the clerk of the court about a

case that was being heard on Tuesday. Naturally, her call was held in a queue. It felt like the majority of her time this past week had been spent on hold, and she closed her eyes and suppressed the scream that longed to come out.

It was a scream she'd been suppressing the whole week. The only thing that stopped her releasing it was the baby currently kicking at her ribs. Stress wasn't good for babies so she was doing her best to portray serenity inside and out. Her best, she was painfully aware, wasn't good enough, an awareness reinforced when a box of tissues slid beneath her.

Amelia, who'd entered her office without Layla noticing her, caught her eye and gave a rueful smile.

Smiling gratefully in return, Layla dabbed at eyes she hadn't even realised were leaking and blew her nose. She'd been suffering the most dreadful winter hay fever this past week. The main symptom was leaking eyes. They were like taps she had no control over.

Or so she'd told all her colleagues.

No one knew her marriage was over. Not that her marriage was over in name, just in actuality. She supposed the correct term to describe them was as estranged.

If Sebastiano was true to his word then she would be his legal wife for ever, consigned to live in the purgatory of his whims, brought out like an expensive doll to be draped on his arm whenever duty demanded and then be packed back in a box.

None of that would happen. She knew it in her heart.

For all his threats and the way things had been left between them, she doubted she would see him again until the baby was born. It was the only good thing about the whole sorry mess. Her child really would have a father.

And she had a few months to prepare herself emotionally for facing him again.

She was on her third tissue when her call was finally answered.

Late evening, Sebastiano strode to the dressing room that had belonged to Layla. After a day spent avoiding his family's efforts to visit him and speak to him—whispers must be spreading that his marriage was over—he'd decided to do something constructive and so had decided to turn the dressing room into a room his tailor could use for fittings when he made his three-monthly visit to the villa to measure Sebastiano up for new suits. He would not think that if he were measured today, the tailor would find he'd lost weight.

There was no point in letting the room stand empty with no purpose. It had always been intended as a room for whoever he married. Maybe one day he would marry again and his future wife could have it but until then...

An unexpected blow to his solar plexus almost doubled him over.

It took a long moment to breathe through the pain and straighten.

Where the hell had that come from?

Expelling another breath through his mouth, he turned the door handle. Already his mind was racing ahead, to bringing the master carpenter here to redesign the room. Fresh paint would be needed on the walls too. A new colour scheme. He'd also have to get the 'her' bathroom of his suite redecorated. He'd told the interior designer to go with a Japanese theme because he'd remembered Layla once saying she loved the scent of cherry blossom.

He'd never told Layla the bathroom had been created

especially for her and only finished the evening before he'd brought her to Sicily.

Kidnapped her, a voice in his head corrected.

He opened the door and stepped inside.

The emptiness hit him immediately.

He'd expected it. He'd ordered it be stripped bare.

Seeing it though… Feeling it…

This went beyond emptiness. This was absence.

A scent danced through his senses and into his airwaves and for a moment, just one solitary moment in time, he saw her. Layla. Hair tumbled around her, that perfect lopsided smile that could break a man's heart at fifty paces on her face.

His beautiful, graceful, witty Layla. The woman who'd entered this cold, palatial villa and filled it with warmth. Filled *him* with warmth.

The woman rejected before her birth by the father who should have loved and protected her. Rejected by the grandparents who should have loved and protected her too.

And now rejected by him.

God help him, he'd pushed her away. Cruelly. On top of all the other wrongs he'd done to the woman who'd dedicated her life to helping those unable to help themselves. A woman who refused to seek vengeance for fear of creating new victims from it.

A shining angel of light in a cold, dark world.

He'd pushed her away.

The image before his eyes vanished.

The pain that ripped through him was enough to bring him to his knees.

Layla exited the underground and trudged carefully through the sleet falling around her and landing like slush, and was thankful of the small mercy of having enough money in the bank to pay for decent winter boots. Thankful that her mum had a decent coat and set of boots to protect her from the elements too. Thankful for her mum full stop. It was hard to fall deep into despair when you had such unflinching love and support.

That didn't stop her heart feeling bleaker than the weather or stop her eyes from leaking. A weekend of comedy films and she'd cried silently through all of them, smiling only during the times her baby woke up to play football in her belly, then crying again to know Sebastiano wasn't there to share it with her.

She couldn't stop thinking about him and thinking about that awful, awful evening when everything had fallen apart. His ashen face at her home truths. The guilt she felt for going behind his back and buying the house even after she'd agreed not to. She hadn't made a verbal promise not to but the implication had been there.

So deeply was Sebastiano on her mind that when she walked into the skyscraper's lobby and stamped the sludge off her boots, it was no surprise that her gaze zoomed straight to his photo before she had the chance to block it.

Lowering her stare, she passed through the usual security checks and turned in the direction of the elevators. A waft of his cologne almost made her stumble but she kept walking, and—

'Layla.'

Her heart stopped before her feet did.

It took for ever to find the courage to turn around.

It was him. Standing close enough that if she reached an arm out she'd be able to touch him.

Her heart kick-started back to life and suddenly she was

clinging tightly to the large bag slung over her shoulder and struggling to breathe.

She *should* have foreseen this, she realised dimly through the blood rushing in her head. With the size of the building and the infrequency of his visits to it, there had only been a slim chance of their paths crossing here, but she should have prepared herself. After all, she knew better than anyone that the tiniest of odds could play out. Her baby was proof of that.

It had never taken so much to say two words. 'Hello, Sebastiano.'

His chest rose. It hurt to see it. It hurt to see him. Hurt to see how just eight days apart from him had distorted her memories. She didn't remember his face being so gaunt or so…pallid. Or his eyes being bloodshot.

'Can we talk?'

She gaped at him. It was hard to be certain if she'd heard him correctly through the roar in her head. She didn't remember his voice being so hoarse.

He closed his eyes and bowed his head. 'That's fair. After the way things were left between us I don't blame you for not wanting to talk to me.'

Had she said that?

'I will make it quick.' The tiniest quirk of his lips that was in no way a smile. 'I know you need to start work. I'm sorry for doing it here but I only landed an hour ago and I knew you would have left home and I would be more likely to catch you here in the lobby than anywhere else.'

Alone in the empty dressing room, everything had become clear. Hours and hours Sebastiano had sat on the hard floor, paralysed, the depths of what he'd done pounding into him. And then his loss had hit him and all the pain he'd been feeling up to that point was nothing, nothing, compared to the agony that had ripped through him.

He'd lost Layla.

But she'd never been his to lose.

Gasping for air, he'd groped for his phone. He'd called his lawyer, and then he'd called his PA. 'Get me to London,' he'd whispered to her, hardly aware that it was two in the morning.

Layla clutched her bag even tighter. She had a vague awareness of people swarming around them, hurrying to their offices, busying themselves for the start of another busy working week, all of them oblivious that her heart was smashing so loudly it had woken her sleeping baby.

He lifted a foot as if to move closer then hesitated. 'Layla…' Something that looked much like pain flashed over his beautiful face. 'I know an apology can't make up for what I've done to you but I have to try. I have to try because you deserve it. I'm…' He shook his head and ran his fingers through his ungroomed hair. 'I'm everything you said I am, and more. I am an arrogant, self-absorbed bastard. But you didn't get everything right. I didn't cut you off and ghost you because you were a bar tender but because the way you made me feel terrified the hell out of me. What I feel for you is like nothing on this earth. That magic was there from the start and I felt it as deeply as you did but I'm a coward. I don't know if it would have been different if I'd known who you really were.' Another quirk of the lips that wasn't a smile. 'I think what I felt for you would have made me run whatever I believed you to be. All those months working so hard not to think about you stopped me thinking altogether. That's the power you had over me even then. I didn't pay attention to the things that matter as much as I should have and the result…the loss of a billion euros.'

He pinched the bridge of his nose before continuing. 'I avoided the club for months until I thought it was safe to return. I thought you'd be gone. It wasn't even a conscious choice. But I couldn't run from you the second time. What you did that night—I fully deserved it. The way I cut you off was unforgivable—but it brought me to life. Everything I'd been suppressing, all the feelings I'd been hiding from, it all hit me.' He shook his head. 'I didn't know a force like that was possible. It shook my heart…shook all of me. I was obsessed by you. Unhealthily obsessed. And I schemed and plotted to make you mine and force you into my life, all the while telling myself that it was what you deserved, what you owed me.' He let out a disbelieving laugh and shook his head. 'Can you believe I told myself that *you* owed *me*? You don't owe me anything, Layla. You never did. You certainly don't owe me your trust and that's what it comes down to, isn't it? I love you and I think a part of you loves me too—or maybe that's my arrogance rearing up again—but there is no trust. I killed it when I deleted your number from my phone and everything I have done since has only proved that you were right not to trust me. I'm not surprised you went to such lengths to protect yourself. I'm only surprised that you can bear to look at me. But know this—I will go to my grave regretting my treatment of you.'

She wiped away the tears blinding her and saw the contortion of his face.

'I'm sorry for everything, Layla. And I pray that one day you can find it in your heart to forgive me.' Swallowing, he reached into his inside coat pocket. 'These are divorce papers. I've already signed my part and postdated it—we have to wait a year to lodge it but I wanted you to have this now so that you can sleep knowing your freedom is in your hands, and not in mine.'

She stared from the envelope in his hand back to his face and whispered, 'You're letting me go?'

Tears swam in his eyes. His voice was hoarse when he said, 'You were never mine to keep. Love without freedom is no love and I cannot endure another day knowing I've clipped the wings of so beautiful a spirit and tethered her to me. All I ask is that I be involved in our child's life—I do want to be a father to it.'

'Of course,' she said dazedly. 'You can be as involved as much as you want to be.'

He gave a pained laugh. 'I knew you'd say that. It's so much more than I deserve.'

'It's what our child deserves.'

'I knew you'd say that too. It's what you deserved from your father and I wish like hell that I could travel back in time and force him to meet you. If he had done...' He swallowed. 'There is not a soul on this earth who could resist falling in love with you.' And then his gaze dropped down to her belly and he sighed. 'You will keep me updated?'

'I promise.'

Another pained laugh before he put his fingers to his lips, kissed them and then pressed them against Layla's mouth. 'Goodbye, Layla.'

And then he turned around and walked away, and the swarm of workers continued to stream around her, only a few giving double takes at the tears streaming down her face.

CHAPTER FOURTEEN

LAYLA STEPPED OUT of the elevator with no memory of stepping into it.

The envelope was still clutched in her hand.

Not moving beyond the threshold, she stared around at the vast reception area where two nail-biting women were waiting nervously on the plush chairs, then gazed beyond the reception to the library where paralegals and others were reading legal texts, photocopying documents, chatting amongst themselves, and then turned her stare to the long, wide corridor. The fourth door on the left opened into her office. Like all the other solicitors, she now worked on a computer that was ultra-modern and ultra-speedy.

She gazed back at the two waiting women. They weren't her clients. She knew neither of their stories. Looking more closely, she saw the remnants of a bruise under the eye of the woman to the left. A victim of domestic abuse? Was she here because she'd heard through Clayton Community Law's growing network that this was a place she could get legal help against her abuser for free? Maybe the woman really had just walked into a door. No two people's stories were the same, the only commonality between their clients being they couldn't afford to pay for legal help or the free help they were entitled to wasn't enough for what they needed.

And now they could help more people. A lot more people. They were already looking at premises in three other cities as they sought to expand their services to other areas of the country.

None of this would have been possible without Sebastiano. He'd been under no obligation to do anything more than pay her the money. He'd given the firm this vast floor to work from because he wanted to, and if it had been to salve his conscience as she thought then it meant he *had* a conscience. And if he had a conscience then it meant he was capable of redemption…

'Layla? Are you okay?'

She blinked.

Audrey, one of her colleagues, was staring at her with concern.

Layla stepped back, her head alternating between nodding and shaking. 'I need to go. I'm sorry.'

Holding her belly, she walked as fast as her heavily pregnant body would carry her to the elevator. Outside the building, she hailed a black cab.

Maybe her mother was right about fate because the sleet had cleared. The Monday morning traffic parted for them and every single traffic light stayed on green.

When the driver pulled up outside the large suburban house on the quiet street, she paid with her phone without even listening to the price.

Inside, music played loudly above her. Holding tightly to the bannister, she climbed the stairs and followed the noise to one of the guest rooms where she found her mum on a step ladder painting the walls a soft yellow, humming along to the music.

Seeing Layla, she stepped off the ladder and hit the off button on the radio. 'What's happened?' she asked anxiously.

'Mum, what did he say to you to get you to move to Sicily? Please tell me.'

The anxiety disappeared.

After the longest time spent just staring at her, her mother sighed and smiled. 'He said that you needed me.'

Layla's heart caught and her hand fluttered to her mouth.

That had been the last thing she'd expected to hear.

What made it more unexpected was that it had been true. Layla had been thrust, pregnant, into a new world and desperately trying to swim in it whilst fighting against her feelings for her own husband. Sebastiano might not have recognised her fears but he'd recognised that she needed her mother when even Layla hadn't recognised she needed her.

He'd known enough about the Sansom mother-daughter relationship, too, to know it was a need her mother would never refuse.

Her mother had only agreed to move from the hellhole because it was what Layla had wanted.

After resting the paintbrush she was holding on the tin, her mother lanced her again with her compassionate stare. 'He isn't your father. You do know that?'

Too choked to speak, Layla nodded.

'Sebastiano loves you.'

She nodded again. He did love her.

And she loved him. Loved him with the same unhealthy obsessiveness that he loved her.

It was a love that had weaved into her veins and tightened its tendrils even as she'd kidded herself that she could guard her heart against him.

A ray of winter sunlight shone through the window and pierced Layla's heart. She closed her eyes and let its warmth fill her, and when she opened them again, it was like opening them for the very first time.

Sebastiano loved her.

'Mum, do you like this house?'

Confusion creased her mother's brow. 'You know I do.'

'More than our old house?'

'Much more.' An impish grin widened her face. 'It is nice to go into a garden and not be overcome with the fumes of cannabis plants when the wind's blowing in the wrong direction.'

Layla burst into laughter. 'I'm glad you said that, because it's yours.' Then she threw her arms around the woman who had sacrificed so much to bring Layla into the world and given her all the love and emotional security a child could wish for.

Holding her tightly, she whispered, 'Thank you for everything. If I can be half as good a mother to my child as you've been to me then I will consider myself to have done a great job, but now it's time to cut the apron strings. No more putting me first. You need to start living for *you*. Go and explore the world. Find yourself a lover. Find yourself two lovers! Whatever you want to do. Just get out there and start living.'

As she pulled apart from the embrace, tears welled in her mother's eyes. 'Oh, honey… I am so proud of you.'

'Everything I am is because of you, so be proud of yourself.'

Her mum pressed a hand to her heart and sniffed as she smiled. 'You're going to him?'

Layla nodded and smiled her first real smile in so very long. 'Yes. I'm going home.'

Home to the man she'd subconsciously found a different form of emotional security with from her very first night in his villa when she'd fallen into a deep, deep sleep.

It was late when Sebastiano returned to the villa.

He'd never felt so drained in his life. He had to force his leaden legs to climb the stairs.

He would sell the place. Find somewhere new. Somewhere Layla's ghost didn't haunt him.

He could smell her perfume, stronger than a memory, as if she'd very recently walked the mezzanine.

It was more than a man could endure.

But endure it he must. For the sake of his child.

Knowing that in a couple of months the life he and Layla had created together would be born was the one spot of brightness in a world that had turned so bleak.

He couldn't even face sleeping in the bed they'd shared together. It didn't matter how many times the sheets were changed—and he was having them changed daily for this very reason—her scent still permeated.

He dragged his legs into his bedroom. Her perfume was even stronger in here. He would brush his teeth and then get his head down in one of the guest rooms...

He came to an abrupt halt.

Closing his eyes, he counted to ten then opened them.

His lungs closed. His throat closed. His heart turned over.

Layla was on his bed.

She was naked. To her side was a pile of shredded paper.

Her left wrist was handcuffed to the bedpost.

Her beautiful forget-me-not eyes were staring at him,

an emotion filling them that filled his own eyes with tears he could do nothing to stop.

He didn't feel his legs move towards her.

Overwhelmed with the emotions swirling like a tempest inside him, he sat on the bed and gently placed his hand on her swollen belly. Movement beneath his palm turned his heart over again.

She smiled tremulously and nodded.

Wiping away a falling tear, he kissed the swell, right where his child had moved, and then reached for the tiny key she'd thrown out of her reach and unlocked the cuffs, pressing his lips to the delicate skin it had been wrapped around.

She gave another tremulous smile and palmed his cheek. 'I love you, Sebastiano Russo,' she said quietly, her forget-me-not eyes brimming with emotion. 'With every fibre of my being. I love you and I *do* trust you.'

He sucked in a breath, hardly daring to believe what she was saying.

She smiled and kissed him gently. 'You're like a wounded animal when hurt but you never lie…except to yourself…and for all the wrongs you did after our night together and in the way you forced me to marry you, you always, *always* treated me with respect.' She kissed him again then stared deep into his eyes. 'You're like a wounded animal when you're hurt but I'm like one when I'm scared. The house was never about you, it was about *me* because I was too scared and you were too stubborn to admit the truth—that I belong to you and you belong to me and our baby belongs to us both until they're old enough to belong to themselves.'

Overwhelmed, Sebastiano nuzzled his cheek against hers and breathed in the scent of Layla's skin, still hardly daring to believe that he would spend the rest of his life breathing it.

Her hand cupped the back of his neck. Her nose rubbing into his temple, she whispered, 'I'm not scared any more.'

And neither was he, Sebastiano thought dazedly as their mouths crushed together and their arms wrapped tightly around each other, and the light and warmth that came from the sexy angelic creature who loved him—Layla *loved* him!—seeped into his cold heart and brought him back to life.

It was a warmth that would fuel him for the rest of his life.

EPILOGUE

EXCLUSIVE!

Sicilian billionaire banker Sebastiano Russo and his wife, English lawyer Layla Russo, have welcomed another baby into the world!

CMB can exclusively report that the Russos, famed for their philanthropy and the hosting of parties with guest lists to make A-list celebrities weep, have added to their growing brood with a healthy baby boy. No name has yet been decided for the child, who is brother to Jilly (six), Lara (five) and Dante (two). But if tradition is anything to go by, CMB's money is on it being an Italian name!

More to follow as it comes...

* * * * *

GREEK'S FORBIDDEN TEMPTATION

MILLIE ADAMS

MILLS & BOON

CHAPTER ONE

THE EMPTY BARSTOOL next to Dionysus Katrakis was luxurious as it was tragic. It ought to be. Tragic because it was empty as the man who had once occupied it was no longer living. Luxurious because the Diamond Club was the most exclusive club on earth. With membership consisting only of nine of the world's richest men.

And one woman.

The empty chair was now for her.

And yet it wasn't.

It seemed somewhat baffling to her that there was a whole bar in this establishment that catered only to the uber elite.

You're one of them now.

But she never really would be. She wasn't the one who should be sitting here right now. And she didn't know when or if that truth would ever come forward. If there was any point to it. All she knew was that her life had changed forever. That her joy was shattered and the future they'd imagined was…

It was impossible now.

She blinked back rising tears—she really didn't want to cry right now.

And so Ariadne Katrakis took a seat on the luxury barstool next to her brother-in-law, and did not cry.

She looked at Dionysus's profile. Proud. Arrogant. Familiar. His features were arranged in the exact same order and shape her husband's had been. Stunningly handsome with a strong, square jaw, a nose that was sharp and angular. His skin was the same tawny gold, his brows heavy. His black hair was longer than his twin's, rakish, looking as if a woman had just finished running her fingers through it. Whether by design or simply because that's what had just happened, she couldn't say.

One never could with Dionysus.

Her brother-in-law was so different than her husband. Hedonistic, selfish. Unpredictable.

Horrendously likable and magnetic in spite of it all.

That was her true tragedy. She'd always felt bathed in warmth when she was in the company of Dionysus.

She imagined every woman did.

She cleared her throat.

"It's done," she said.

He turned to look at her, one dark brow raised. Yes, he was identical to Theseus. And yet he wasn't. Theseus had carried the weight of the world on his shoulders. His face had been a study in granite severity while Dionysus's was mobile. His face could cover a broad spectrum of emotion in a moment. It had always fascinated her.

"So then you've bathed in the blood of virgins and completed the requisite ritual sacrifices." The corner of his mouth curved into a smile, but she could see the exhaustion there. The grief.

"All I got was the blood of a very tired pigeon and a ritually sacrificed guinea pig, have I been misogynied?"

"I believe that is what they call *pink tax*." He picked his glass up from the bar and knocked back the remaining Scotch. "Drink? They have to get you whatever you want now. You're a member."

"Yes," she said, staring down at the marble bar-top. "I am a member."

"I apologize for everything my father said to you after the funeral."

That farce of a funeral that hadn't said a single real or deep thing about Theseus. That farce of a funeral hadn't included the people who had really mattered to him.

"Did you *hear* any of the things your father said to me?"

He tapped his glass and the bartender materialized and poured him another measure of Macallan without being asked.

The man paused and looked at her expectantly. "Just some sparkling water, please," she said.

"I didn't need to hear them," Dionysus said as her sparkling water filled the glass. "I can guess exactly what he said. I imagine he'll be fighting you for the money."

"He was thinking *you* should fight me for it."

He lifted a brow. "Because I'm so impoverished?"

"I am *slightly* richer than you now," she said.

"Amazing what hundreds of years of hoarding wealth will do." He took a drink of Scotch. "But this situation is of my father's own making, he's the one who chose to give Theseus the empire upon his marriage to you."

"Conditionally, Dionysus, which I think you know.

It wasn't to be final until he produced an heir. But you did not hear…" She curled her hands into fists. "I'm pregnant."

"Pregnant?"

She didn't know if she was imagining the shock in his voice. If she was hallucinating any sort of reaction. But that was the truth. She was pregnant with Theseus's child. And that should be good news. For *everybody*. A part of him would live on.

As far as the details of all of it… She wasn't going to share them. Not with anyone.

If the truth came out the Katrakis patriarch could still disinherit her child. And that was something Theseus had wanted to avoid at all costs. He'd shaped his whole life around the desire to see the two of them at the helm of the company and to see the legacy pass on to their children, who they would raise differently than he'd been raised.

She'd made him a promise. With her whole heart, her whole life.

She would not do anything to compromise it now.

Her eyes started to fill with tears and she blinked those tears back.

He'd given her a good life. One filled with love and laughter, even if it had been unconventional. Even if there had been times she'd struggled—who didn't struggle on occasion? Who didn't regret their choices on the odd rainy Sunday?—but mostly her life had been full.

It felt desolate now, but she could not afford to be destroyed. Not now. She had the baby to think about.

"And I assume that you told my father this?"

"Of course I did. I am carrying his precious heir. You know how he favored Theseus."

There was no point sugarcoating any of it. She didn't say it to hurt Dionysus. Though honestly, she didn't think Dionysus had feelings to hurt. Not any longer.

Her current relationship with her brother-in-law was… Uneasy at best these days.

But the bedrock of their relationship was a near lifetime of friendship. They had known one another since she was ten and the boys were twelve. They had been thick as thieves growing up, anytime their families had been on the island for the summer.

She had been drawn to Theseus's quiet, serious nature, his sly wit that had flown under the radar of anyone who didn't get close enough to really listen to him. He made her laugh. He'd made her feel understood in a way no one else ever had. He listened. Really. Deeply.

Dionysus on the other hand, had been an explosion. All she could do was watch and hope that none of them got hurt by the aftermath. There had been a cheerful sort of naughty joy that he took in his exploits and she couldn't help but let herself feel a bit of delight in it too, even if from afar.

It was only after the implosion at her eighteenth birthday party that she understood his behavior wasn't just reckless…it was dangerous.

Ten years later and that was all behind them, their shared history growing up together more important than a few moments in time.

They were bonded by deeper things.

She'd been alone before Theseus and Dionysus.

And without each other, the boys had been vulnerable to the rages of their father.

Patrocles Katrakis had a mentality as ancient as the stone walls of his home country and a cruel streak as deep as the Aegean. He had exacting expectations of what he wanted from his sons. But most especially Theseus. Who was born three minutes before Dionysus, making him the focus of their father's wrath and unreasonable nature. He was shaping the son who would take over the industry.

Because that was what mattered to him most. The legacy he had built, the billion-dollar shipping company that bore the family name.

His sons were the richest twins in the world. Evidence of his virility, of his might.

A legacy nearly as ancient as Greece itself.

So he thundered, loud and often.

As Theseus's wife, Ariadne had been under her fair share of pressure. Theseus's strengths weren't in organization or admin. Or in finance, which was what James had begun to manage—and just as well because it wasn't Ariadne's strength either. Theseus was good with people. Compassionate. Things his father didn't value. But they had done a good job holding each other up as they managed the company, and their strengths complemented one another's. Patrocles, of course, minimized Ariadne's role in the company but as she'd often told Theseus, she wasn't hungry for the recognition of an old, cruel fossil.

Thank God for James. He'd been managing everything at Katrakis Shipping for the past few weeks, which seemed unfair in many ways, but he'd told her it gave him a way to matter privately.

Since he wasn't able to publicly.

And she'd desperately needed his help.

"Yes, I am aware that my father favored my brother." He laughed, a hollow sound. "Of course being favored by my father was always a poisoned chalice. As I think you know."

"Yes. I know." She looked down into her glass. "Your father approved of me as a wife for Theseus."

Dionysus laughed, the mirth in his eyes sharp, uneasy. "I am aware of that. Even still he was terribly hard on you all this time, wasn't he?"

She blinked, and looked away from Dionysus. She was afraid they were having a shared memory. One she didn't want to have at all right now, much less share.

She needed to keep her stress managed. She'd been feeling off the last few days. Well, *off* was an understatement. She'd felt bereft since Theseus's accident. Numb. Then angry. How could the world be so cruel? They'd been ready to have their child and once they had that child…

Everything would have changed for Theseus, finally.

But her emotional exhaustion had turned into physical aches and pains that had her feeling wary.

"He doesn't want me to be in control of the company, that's for certain. He also doesn't want me being the steward of all the wealth. Sadly for him… There's nothing that he can do."

"You never struck me as someone who cared overmuch about money, Ariadne."

She wasn't. Of course, she didn't know life without it. She couldn't say how she would function, but she knew how to work. That was the thing. There were a few components to this that mattered. The first was that Theseus's legacy carry on. In the form of their child. The second was that she was able to take some of this money and put it toward causes she knew Theseus would have wanted to support.

Because there were children out there, like Theseus, who lived their lives in shadows. Who could not be themselves. Who had to hide who they were from their parents, from the world. She would...do something for them. A tribute. A charity.

She couldn't give Theseus the happy ending she'd wanted him to have, but perhaps she could take his memory and use it to make the world happier. What was the point of money if she couldn't make changes with it?

"Did he know you were pregnant?" Dionysus asked.

He'd been so happy. They all had been.

It had also started a ticking clock on the way their life was structured. She'd been excited, but nervous. Happy. Relieved.

"Yes," she said. "We found out two days before he died."

"How lucky for you that you managed to fall pregnant just before his death."

She flinched. She knew that what he said was true—if there was no baby the company wouldn't be in her care. If there was no baby none of the Katrakis money would come to her at all. But that wouldn't have been the tragedy. The tragedy was losing Theseus. The end.

"You know me better than that, and you should know I loved your brother better than that too."

His expression was contrite, which was unusual for him.

"I'm sorry," he said. "That was out of order. You didn't deserve that. The money is yours, Ariadne. My father has no right to take it from you."

"I'll be a steward of it, it will be our child's."

"You will continue to run the company. You will maintain your position at the club. Until my nephew or niece comes of age."

His voice took on a hard edge there. It was difficult to imagine Dionysus as a doting uncle. It was difficult to imagine him doing much of anything other than making flippant remarks and indulging in excess.

What had amused her when they were younger had turned into something dangerous and frightening when they had become adults.

Dionysus had always seemed insatiable. But as Theseus went further and further into himself, Dionysus seemed to explode beneath the strictures of his father. He had gone off on his own. Had made a fortune independent of the family name.

Theseus had said he envied his brother sometimes.

Wouldn't it be nice to be my brother, flaunting conquests everywhere like prizes?

Dionysus was a libertine. She wouldn't be surprised if he couldn't count the number of women that he had taken into his bed. He might even lose track of a weekend. A forty-eight-hour orgy seemed right up his alley.

Maybe she was bitter. Bitter because Theseus worked

so hard to do the right things, to stay in his father's will, to be the oldest son that fit the image.

Bitter because Dionysus seemed to have no idea. His life might be a middle finger at his father, but whether he meant it or not, also at his brother.

He was the second born.

And he was free.

Of course, Theseus could have defied his father much sooner than he'd planned. But he had spent a lifetime being conditioned to fall in line and after he'd decided that things had to change, he'd still wanted to wait until they'd had a child until the inheritance was secured, before making any drastic public moves.

"Well, given the blood rites, I *do* want to maintain my position at the club."

He chuckled. "Of course. Why would you give up all this?" He lifted up his glass and waved it around, indicating the luxurious nature of the space.

"You may not understand this, but the company actually became very meaningful to me. I know the people there. I care about them. I understand the important part our work plays in keeping the world turning. People depend on us. For their livelihoods. For survival. Under Theseus, there was quite a lot of charity work structured into the business. Employee salaries were raised, benefits packages improved. I want to keep building on what he did, and I'm the one who knows. I know it inside and out. We were a team."

"It's shocking," he said. "The suddenness of it."

"He was just going back to the office to get some paperwork. A drunk driver hit him. He wasn't speeding.

He wasn't…he was himself to the end. Taking care of his responsibilities."

"A terrible waste," said Dionysus. "If one of us was going to die young, I had always thought that it would be me."

"You certainly earned it," she said.

He smiled ruefully at her. She wondered if she had gone too far, if she had crossed the line, but he didn't seem angry at all.

In fact, he seemed amused. But it was hard to say with Dionysus. She'd known him once. Really known him. They'd been friends. They'd been in-laws for a decade and she saw him casually. For dinners, holidays. They bantered, they were good at it.

There had been whole Christmas dinners where she'd lost herself sparring with him. Like the whole room had faded away and everyone else with it. But that had always been about current events or completely inconsequential topics.

They didn't *know* each other. Not anymore.

Now she felt the ache of that.

Because here they were. Without Theseus.

"It's true," he said.

"And yet, you also built your own massive business. If you didn't care about anything the way that you pretend, including your own life, why would you have done that?"

"You underestimate just how badly I wanted to prove my father wrong. About me and about everything. I made something out of nothing. My father just managed to continue to multiply a fortune that was on that path generations before he was born. I am not belittling what

Theseus did with the company, or what you have done with it. But my father takes a disproportionate amount of pride in the little work that he has done."

It made sense. In a sick sort of way.

She took a sip of her sparkling water. "He would also take a disproportionate amount of pride in wresting the company back from me if we didn't technically fulfill the terms of the rather complex inheritance stipulations."

"Yes."

"He would want to automate. Get rid of as many employees as possible."

"A business is not a charity," Dionysus pointed out.

"Do you run yours with the same sort of ruthless precision your father would?"

He laughed. "That would require me to care about being rich or simply for the sake of it. And I don't. I have what I want. A portfolio of successful businesses running the gamut on practical delivery services. From car services to food and grocery delivery. It has been lucrative, and I no longer have to go in to work every day. I help people with their everyday lives, I'm able to take advantage of the fact that people will pay money for convenience, and in turn, my life is more convenient. I can do as I please."

For some reason, something about that hit Ariadne strangely. He could do as he pleased. She had so much money now. She had devoted so much of her life to her friendship with Theseus. And in all of that, she hadn't been truly satisfied with it.

She'd hoped to be.

But no one could see the future.

Maybe it wasn't Theseus who had envied Dionysus. Maybe she did.

She felt a sharp cramp low in her midsection, and she pressed her hand to her stomach.

"What's wrong?" he asked, grabbing her arm and looking at her fiercely.

"Nothing," she said.

She had been having these strange phantom pains for a couple of days, but her doctor had said they were nothing to worry about. Because they hadn't progressed, and there had been no bleeding.

"I'm just going to…" She slipped off the luxurious stool and stood up, and felt a rush of warm liquid escape her body. But it didn't stop. She was dizzy, and suddenly the pain was quite intense.

No.

This was what she'd been afraid of, more than anything, when she'd begun to ache a few days ago. When she'd been dealing with the shock of losing Theseus.

That the baby would be taken from her too.

No.

No.

The last thing she saw was Dionysus reaching out to take her in his strong arms as she lost consciousness and everything went dark.

CHAPTER TWO

DIONYSUS CURSED EVERY deity he didn't believe in as he held Ariadne in his arms for the first time in ten years.

This was not how that fantasy played out in his mind.

This was not a fantasy at all. She was dangerously pale, and now completely unconscious.

He signaled to the bartender. "Tell Lazlo I need a helicopter immediately. And have them call ahead to the hospital."

He would not be taking her to the kind of medical facility available to everyone.

Lazlo would know that. As manager of the Diamond Club and right-hand man to its founder Raj Belanger, the richest man in the world, Lazlo trafficked only in the elite, the discreet, and the luxurious.

There was no time to waste.

He knew that by the time he reached the top of the building the helicopter would be waiting. Picking Ariadne up, and holding her close to his chest, he rushed into the gilded elevator, the doors closing behind them. He felt something on his hand and looked, seeing streaks of red on his palm.

She was bleeding.

She was far too pale.

Ariadne...

Dionysus, for all the world to see, cared for nothing and no one.

The truth of him was much more complicated. He moved quickly in order to silence his demons, and he had a ready smile in order to keep a tight leash on his rage. Right now, his rage knew no bounds.

Because Theseus should be here. The world was cruel, but it had no right to be cruel to his brother, who had done the right things. Who had lived a life his father was proud of and married the perfect wife, who was supposed to have his perfect child.

Rage because Ariadne was now pale and limp and he couldn't even begin to think through what was happening to her, because if she didn't survive this...

There really would be nothing and no one in this whole world that he cared about.

Dionysus had thought, back when he had been younger, and he had longed for things to be different, that he would give any amount of fortune if Ariadne would look at him the way that she did Theseus.

But like most everyone, she had known that Theseus was the better bet for a life of stability.

And then this.

Theseus was meant to make her happy. It had been the one consolation he'd felt and even if he had no longer been as close to his brother...

He saw his brother. He had meals with him. They dined at the club often enough but they had never been truly close since the night of the engagement party.

How could they be?

Now Theseus was dead and there was no hope of repairing it. He might have despised himself then if he hadn't been so consumed with worry about Ariadne.

The elevator seemed to be taking far too long.

It arrived at the top floor, finally, and the doors opened. And the helicopter was there. He rushed across the space, holding her tightly, and climbed inside. The wind and the sound made her stir, but only just slightly.

"Hurry," he said when they got in.

And they were off. Careening over the city of London, the lights below twinkling. On their way to the only hospital he would trust with her.

If she lost the baby...

Of course, she was losing the baby. And that would mean his father would try to wrest control of the company back.

But all he cared about right now was that Ariadne lived.

He didn't care about much. He had long ago let go of the concept of anything sacred or divine. He had sold his soul for parts as he had worked tirelessly to prove his father wrong, and drink himself into oblivion just as tirelessly. Moved from one woman's bed to the next.

Yes. He had decided to fashion himself entirely after his namesake. The god of wine and debauchery.

Because why not?

He wasn't the oldest son.

But now his brother was gone.

They were only minutes away from the medical facility in Bath, formerly one of the buildings that had housed Roman Baths people used to flock to for healing. He didn't care how picturesque it was, only that they might find healing there.

Part of the building had been modernized, with a helipad on top, and when they landed a team came out quickly, and he deposited Ariadne onto a gurney, his arm suddenly feeling bereft. Empty. He looked down and saw blood staining his clothes.

He followed quickly.

Nobody tried to tell him not to follow. It would have been a foolish thing to do.

She was wheeled into a room that looked like a standard hospital room. But he supposed this was where they had to work to make her stable. And work they did.

She was hooked up to IVs, and monitors. Whole teams worked to revive her. "She hasn't lost enough blood to need a transfusion," one of the doctors said.

"Good," he said.

"She miscarried," said another doctor.

He wanted to growl and turn something over. Because it was obvious she had lost the baby. Was she going to lose her life?

She had lost this last piece of Theseus, and he felt that pain deep inside himself. But she'd also lost this last piece of the future she'd been hoping for.

And the last piece needed for her to secure the inheritance.

Ariadne was losing everything.

"This doesn't leave the room," he said. "None of this."

"Of course," said the doctor, looking vaguely offended that Dionysus had bothered to mention the standard nondisclosure protocol of the facility.

Patient privacy was of course protected in most cases, but there was an extralegal layer of protection here, and that was essential.

It took about fifteen minutes for her to stir. It felt like hours to him.

She looked at him, oxygen tubes covering most of her expression. "What happened?"

"I'm sorry, Ariadne. You lost the baby."

He didn't see the point in hiding it from her. Even though he wanted to. Even though he wanted to cushion her from the truth. He could not allow her to lay there in hope knowing already that hope was lost.

He wouldn't do that. In honor of the friendship they'd once had. In honor of how much his brother loved her, he wouldn't do that.

And maybe even more, in honor of how much she had loved his brother.

Tears began to track down her face. "*No*," she said.

Her pain was wordless, soundless. Yet it radiated from her. He felt it move deep inside of him and he didn't know how to shield himself from it.

She was his weakness.

She always had been.

He hadn't comforted another person in more years than he could count. He didn't have practice with connections. But she was one of the few he had.

"I'm sorry."

"This can't… There's no more… I can't have another baby."

Her eyes were red, her face streaked with tears. She was still beautiful. Another man would marry her. Another man would love her. She might not be able to imagine it now, but he knew it was true.

"You will someday."

"What about *now*?" She swallowed hard. "It was supposed to be our baby. It was supposed to be his. What about Theseus's legacy? This was his last chance. It was... It isn't just that he's lost a piece of himself wandering around in the world, he has lost all of the work that he has put into Katrakis Shipping. Everything that mattered to him. Because it did matter. This baby mattered."

"I'm sorry, Ariadne," he said.

"It was supposed to be..." She swallowed hard. "We were so happy to finally have a baby. When he died I thought the only bright spot was this baby. This... piece of him that would still live. That would walk in the world."

"If you think about it," he said, aware that he was defaulting to that shallow place inside of him that handled everything with flippancy, which had never been less appropriate than it was now, "I am a piece of him wandering in the world. We are identical. If we had planned things better, I could've assumed his identity."

The words hung heavy between them.

"You're not identical," she said.

Something about the way she said it, the disdain in her voice, made something dark twist in his chest.

"We were identical enough," he said.

Just then, the doctor came into the room. "Mrs. Katrakis, we are going to move you to a more comfortable space."

"Okay," she said.

But she looked vacant. Like she was only half there.

He lingered behind as she was wheeled away, and took out his phone. He called his PA. "Cancel my meetings for the next week. There is a pressing matter I must take care of."

He had hired Carla primarily because she was an old dragon who yelled at him when she disapproved of him, and gave him a strange sort of structure neither of his parents had ever managed. His mother had ignored him, his father had beaten him. Carla was a happy medium.

Predictably, she sighed. "Does that mean you're going on a bender?"

He looked around at the sterile space. "Yes. I am terribly sorry, but I currently have two supermodels ready to climb into my limo, and then into my bed. And I am not planning on curbing the adventure until it curbs itself."

"You're lucky that you're charming," she said. "Otherwise there's no way you could have conned investors into throwing money at a business the owner is never in the office of."

"I guess I am very lucky."

He hung up, and made his way to the recovery area that she was being installed in. He wasn't going to leave until she was discharged. He had done little for his brother in the last few years. And the feeling of failure was intense.

He could do this. He could stay with Ariadne.

And he would.

* * *

It was like a spa. Except here her grief had been compounded. Here, everything really did feel like it was crumbling around her.

The room she was staying in had a glorious whirlpool tub, but when she got into it, and let the hot water soothe her, it was soothing away lingering cramps. And the cramps were a reminder. A reminder of her loss.

A reminder that she had failed. She had failed this baby.

She hadn't ever wanted to hurt like this. Who did? But Ariadne had taken so many steps to try and avoid ever feeling pain.

As a child, she'd been like another suitcase her father had to bring any time he moved. Nothing more. Like his luggage, she would appear in his new home and then get packed away again. He was invested in his relationships.

His tempestuous love affairs and marriages were so much more interesting than the little girl he'd been left with when his first marriage dissolved. Though at least he had made sure she had a place to stay, she supposed.

Her mother had simply gone away, and Ariadne had never even missed her. Because how could you miss a vapor that had never played a substantial role in your life?

She'd vowed to be a different kind of mother. It was one of the gifts she'd known her marriage would bring. Children. Children she could love and cherish. Could be there for so they weren't lonely like she'd been.

Theseus had wanted to wait to have children. They

had always planned on using artificial insemination. They didn't have an intimate marriage, and there was no reason, with the advent of modern medicine that they had to. She wanted to rage at him now about so many things. About not doing this sooner. About not freezing embryos or banking more sperm. About not…

Not staying here with her.

He was gone. He was gone and it wasn't fair.

It was like an aching, endless pit inside of her.

Her grief might not be what everybody thought it was, but it was deep.

He was the closest friend that she had in the world. Her most constant companion.

He was gone and so was her hope. This child had been her hope. Of being happy again. Of loving again. Of having a future that didn't feel cold and dark and sad.

She picked her phone up and looked at her texts. James had sent her something and…she was going to have to tell him. She couldn't, not right now, not while things were so raw and awful.

Not while they were still tentative—with Patrocles and the inheritance.

It wasn't for her. It was for the employees. For Theseus. For James, even.

She heard footsteps in the corridor, as if the universe was reminding her that she was in fact not alone at all. Because Dionysus had not left since he had brought her here two days ago.

She set her phone back down.

"I really hate to be the one to get in the way of your preferred lifestyle," she said.

He had barely made it to Dionysus's funeral. He had rolled in hungover, and he had left with a woman on his arm.

"Believe me when I tell you, nothing gets in the way if I don't want it to. You need someone to stay with you."

"Supporting your brother a little bit late?"

That wasn't fair. His jaw went tight.

She didn't need her complicated Dionysus feelings rising to the fore right now.

Things were complicated enough.

"I'm sorry," he said. "Sorry that I… I wasn't as close with him these past years as I might have been."

Of course they hadn't been close. It had been a tangle of lies, and Dionysus didn't even know that. But how could he be close to them?

When their marriage wasn't what it seemed. When the fight they'd had at the engagement party all those years ago wasn't about what he believed it to be.

If Dionysus knew the truth, maybe he would understand. But if Dionysus knew the truth, it would…it could undermine what Theseus had deferred his own happiness and freedom to achieve and she just wouldn't do that.

She stood up, and walked out onto the terrace. It overlooked a beautiful courtyard with fruit trees, well-manicured pathways and perfect hedgerows. So beautiful it nearly felt like a mockery. She could see cars driving beyond all this, in the distance. Life carried on.

She wanted to stop time for a moment.

"I imagine you've spoken to your father about this?"

"No," he said. "Why would I do that?"

"Because he has to know eventually. And he'll decide I suppose if he's going to give the company to you or to himself."

"I have not told my father. And everybody here is under strict orders to keep things completely silent."

"But surely at work…"

"I called. I made excuses. I said that you needed some time away to grieve."

"I didn't take any time away as it happened."

"Grief is strange. It can become more intense with time. Once the shock wears away. At least, I've heard."

She turned back and looked at him speculatively. Was he talking about himself? It was so impossible to tell with him. But she knew that he wasn't unfeeling. She had known him long enough to know that he was someone who felt very deeply. At least, he had at one time. She could remember his moods, his temper, his declarations that some food or another was the best he had ever had, or that a sunset was the most beautiful.

It had changed, as he had begun to channel that into more physical pursuits. But she felt like it had to be a part of him still. Somewhere.

Which meant his grief for Theseus must be raw.

"Thank you."

The breeze caught her hair, and she closed her eyes, trying to let go. Trying to let go of the dream that she had just lost. She visualized it. She couldn't.

If you think about it, I am a piece of my brother out in the world.

She stilled. Everything in her suddenly alight. She turned and looked at Dionysus. "You are identical."

"You only recently told me that we were not."

"Not me, maybe. But genetically, you are identical."

"Yes," he said. "That is how identical twins work. We are the copy paste of the natural world."

"That means that a DNA test would not be able to determine whether a child was Theseus's or yours." Her heart started to beat harder. Faster. "Dionysus," she said. "I need to have your baby."

CHAPTER THREE

DIONYSUS LIVED HIS life in such a way that very few things had the power to shock him. But this succeeded.

Ariadne succeeded.

Wasn't that the story of his existence? Ariadne got beneath his skin where no one else ever could.

"And how exactly would that be accomplished?"

He had an idea. One that was vivid, and blasphemous given the circumstances. Given that his brother had only been dead in the ground for two weeks.

Given that she was his sister-in-law.

That she was as forbidden to him now as she had ever been.

Given that she was now frail and recovering from what had just happened.

"Insemination," she said.

His lip curled. "You expect that I will... Go into a clinical bathroom and take myself in hand."

"Of course not, you idiot. You're a billionaire. Use your imagination. You will go into your luxury bedroom and take yourself in hand."

She made eye contact with him, her expression bold, her cheeks bright red, indicating that she was not quite so unbothered by the image as she was pretending to be.

That was Ariadne.

It had always shocked him that she had been quite so infatuated with Theseus.

Dionysus loved his brother, but there was so much seriousness in him. He never had the fight that Dionysus did. He didn't carry the rage.

In the end, Dionysus often felt that it was the rage which kept him going. The rage which compelled him on when it sometimes felt as if things were hopeless.

It was also likely what had kept him and Ariadne apart. There was an intensity there that vibrated with far too much energy.

Theseus had been easy for her to get close to because of his stillness.

Though then, Ariadne had been bold.

He could remember her well as a young girl running feral about the island. When they first met, he would never have known that she was the daughter of a wealthy family who had their house built across the sandy expanse of shore. He would have imagined that she was the daughter of a cook, or perhaps a stable hand.

Their father took far too much of an interest in everything they did. He ruled them with an iron fist. Ariadne's father, by contrast, barely seemed to remember that he had a daughter. She had been raised by a series of nannies, and as she had gotten older, by no one at all.

A girl isolated and lonely in a palatial estate. Theseus and Dionysus had adopted her with vigor.

She had climbed rocks barefoot, leapt from waterfalls into deep clear pools below. Her dark hair had always been a mass of tangles.

After she had married Theseus, she had changed. They didn't have the closeness they'd had as boys, but he and Theseus had still spent holidays together, and of course both were members of the Diamond Club, as the richest pair of twins in the world.

And two of the richest men on earth in their own right.

They also often attended many of the same charity events. Where Ariadne tamed all her wildness and presented herself as a sleek socialite.

But this, this right here was the fire that he expected to see in her eyes. This was the intensity that he counted on from Ariadne. At least the Ariadne of old. Problem solving, never letting go. Clinging to something with all tenacity.

He had seen glimpses of this woman over the years. Flashes of the wild thing she'd been once and he'd always wanted to draw her all the way to the surface.

He could remember baiting her at the last gala they'd both been at.

The girl I knew once would have dared me to steal a bottle of champagne and swim in the fountain.

The girl you knew once didn't have responsibilities.

A shame then, that we've both had to grow up.

We don't live in Neverland.

A painful thought since he could have easily seen the two of them as Wendy and Peter. Perhaps he was more Captain Hook.

But now the girl with fire in her eyes was back.

He should hate that it was due to her loss. He found it hard to hate anything about the sparks in her eyes.

Her request was as a predator, tearing through his chest.

"You would have me be… A favorite uncle? To my own child?" he asked.

"Yes," she said, her tone placid. "You don't want children, do you?"

"No," he said. Simply.

If there had been a notion in him to carry on his bloodline, if he had even for a second of time entertained that he might marry, find a wife, produce children, he had given it up long ago. And he would not allow it to be revived now.

Not during this discussion. This discussion of him providing *his brother* with the heir he could no longer have.

With the woman who had been haunting his dreams since he was a boy.

"Then why should it be a problem?" she asked. "Many people donate their genetic material toward the creation of a child, it does not make them that child's mother or father. My mother, for instance, was certainly never around."

"No indeed," he said. "But a noted difference is that I would be in the child's life. Presumably. And that might complicate things."

"Is that a bad thing? Fatherhood, in a sense, without the real responsibility of it?"

She believed what the press said about him. That much was clear. She no longer saw him as the boy she'd known when they'd spent their days running free in the forest. She thought he'd become the kind of man who could father a child and pretend it hadn't happened.

The media painted his portrait in that shape. He had never minded it.

He minded it now.

"And what will you tell the child?" he asked.

She looked stunned by that. "The child has yet to come into existence, so I think I have time to figure that out."

"And what will your story be? Because you have lost this baby, which I assume must have been nearly a month along." His words sounded flat and calloused even to his own ears.

"Timing?" She blinked. "That's what you're concerned about?"

"It is not wrong to concern myself with the credibility of this."

"I will tell your father that Theseus banked his sperm. In case there were issues."

"All right." He had to admit that was possible. A man in Theseus's position would likely have put something like that in place. In fact, he was surprised his brother hadn't.

"So you'll admit that you lost a pregnancy, but claim you had artificial insemination done afterward."

"*If* questions of timing arise. And if they do, undoubtedly at that point your father will demand a DNA test. Which I will give. And it will be impossible to tell whether or not the child was fathered by you or by Theseus. And in fact, doing so would demand… I believe it's extensive genetic sequencing, which can no longer be done on your brother, since he is deceased." She swallowed hard. "I know. This is all extremely hard and mercenary. When Theseus is dead, and my baby is lost. I don't feel mercenary about it. I don't feel hard. But I cannot allow this to break me. And I cannot allow your father to win. One thing I need you to understand, is that Theseus hated your father."

That shocked him. To his core. Because as far as Dionysus was concerned, Theseus was their father's puppet. It was nearly impossible to imagine that his brother who had behaved as a performing monkey for their father all this time *hated* the man.

He knew they'd both…had complicated relationships with him but Theseus's willingness to please him had convinced Dionysus it was a Stockholm Syndrome situation.

He wasn't a psychologist but he knew well enough just how complicated things were with abusive parents.

"He never indicated as much to me."

"He wouldn't have. It was important that he kept that secret. Under control. Because he never wanted to lose his power over the shipping company. He worked to change things. You have no idea the state it was in when he took over."

"Why didn't he publicize that it was in poor condition?"

"It wasn't the company. It was the treatment of its employees. It was workplace safety. Wages. There were so many illegal things happening, and he restructured it all. He changed people's lives. Your brother was a very good man. And you might be angry at him for leaving. I know that I am sometimes. But he was a man who cared very deeply about all of these things, and it was a weight that he carried that grew heavier and heavier as time went on. One thing I know for sure is that I cannot allow your father to put his hand back into this company. I have to preserve it. I have to save it. And I want Theseus to have a legacy. That legacy will be a child that grows up to be nothing like your father. That legacy will be a child who has a father that he can be proud of, even if he isn't here."

"And for yourself?"

"Of course I'm…" She suddenly looked very small and lost. "I can't think about myself right now. Because I've lost too much. Because if I start to ponder the intensity of everything that is now gone for me I'm afraid that I'm going to collapse. I won't be able to stand back up. I can't afford it. Not right now. All I can do is keep moving forward. So will you do this for me or not?"

That actually was no choice to be made. He hated it. The very idea of it all. But…

Hearing what his brother had been carrying, work that he had done, and feeling the extreme guilt he did over not being closer to his brother these past years when their time had been limited, what else could he do?

He owed his brother. It was as simple as that. Though he would not give her confirmation just yet.

"We will need to come to an agreement on details."

"Good. I'll talk to the doctor about…" Her eyes filled with tears. "When will be best to proceed." She was so strong, even as she sat there looking devastated. Her dark hair reminded him more now of the girl she had been. No longer captured in a smooth bun, but wild curls framing her face, falling down her back.

She was pale. Strong.

She had always been slender, and petite. And always

containing an immense amount of strength. Much more than you would have ever imagined a girl her size could carry. Now a woman with slender shoulders carrying the weight of his brother's legacy.

Foregoing any thought to her own.

"Your safety is paramount," he said. "I will not allow you to sacrifice yourself upon the altar of my brother's legacy. I need to know if you're at a greater risk of hemorrhage than another woman might be. Do you understand me?"

She looked at him. "And why exactly should you have anything to say about that?"

"Because my brother appears to have sacrificed himself upon the legacy of our company. And I think it's quite enough martyring for one family, don't you?"

"It isn't martyring. It is simply doing the right thing. I know that that's antithetical to your libertine lifestyle."

"There is more than one way to throw yourself onto a pyre, Ariadne. Of this I am certain. But there isn't any reason for you to continue doing it."

"I want a child," she said, her voice getting thin. "I was… You know about my childhood. I was very lonely. My parents barely acknowledged that I existed. They still barely acknowledge my existence. And you know that. I want to be the kind of mother that I never had. That I never saw. I don't want to have a child simply for the legacy. I want to have a child so that I can love them. And if I can't have this baby, not only will I lose the staff that has become so important to me, this company that has become part of my own legacy, part of something that I have built, I will lose the future that I was planning for myself. I will be left entirely alone.

Theseus was my best friend. He was my confidant. He was the person I was closest to in all of this world. And he's gone. I can't call him and speak to him. I cannot say good morning to him. I cannot seek shelter in his arms as I try to figure out how to deal with both his loss and the loss of our child."

"And I'm very sorry," he said, hot emotion rising up in his chest. "But I am not the one who took anything from you."

"I know that. But I just hope, that because of the love you have for your brother, and because of the friendship that you and I have shared for so long, that you will... Take that into account as you make your decision."

"If you fall pregnant, you will come and stay with me. I will not allow you to be by yourself. Not after that."

"You're never home," she pointed out.

"Then I will be."

"Don't get controlling," she said.

"Is it controlling when you are an integral part of something?"

It was not a question. He would rearrange everything to make sure that Ariadne was safe. There were spare few people in his life that mattered to him. She was one of them. His brother had been the other.

She was right to say that it was his feelings for the both of them that compelled him now.

Her doctor came in after and told her that she was free to leave today. And he took it upon himself to make arrangements to get them both out of England as quickly and discreetly as possible. His private jet was outfitted and ready to go, and he had decided that he knew exactly what they needed.

She was correct, of course. They would not be conducting this pregnancy attempt in a standard clinic. They had the luxury of bringing the perfect team to them, and he fully expected to take advantage of that. Not that he knew anything about trying to help a woman get pregnant. His expertise lay in the prevention thereof, if anything.

But he intended to become an expert, and quickly.

"Are we headed back to my town house or…" she asked once they were on the road, being driven toward the airport, and, quite clearly not toward her town house.

"No," he said.

"Didn't I tell you not to get controlling?"

"You also asked for my sperm. I feel like we're living in a strange time where our boundaries are not quite as clear as they used to be."

"Dionysus…"

"We are going to Greece," he said. He paused for a moment, feeling like he was about to peel back the curtains covering his deepest heart and expose things he'd rather not. "I bought the island, you know."

She looked at him, shocked. "No. I didn't know that. Why would I know that?"

The realization she hadn't known hollowed out a space inside of him.

"I thought perhaps Theseus might've told you."

"Theseus didn't speak of that island."

"A shame then. Because there were good times there too."

"Maybe for you. Your father was hideous to him. He was—"

"Our father was with us whether we were on that island or not. Our father was with us always." He tapped on his temple. "Our father's greatest game was being in our minds. Don't you think that is true? Our father's words were the poison in his veins then. Telling him that he had no value. Telling him that he would never be good enough. Don't you agree?"

He watched as she swallowed hard. "I suppose so."

"You know it to be true. Perhaps he felt a certain measure of trauma tied to the island, but I don't. I consider it taking control back. Anyway, if I was happy anywhere, it was there."

It was perhaps a little bit more revealing than he had intended it to be. He hadn't realized until he had said the words just how true they were. He had loved his time on the island, because it was where they had met Ariadne. Because it was the only place they ever had any freedom. When they were in England they were locked away in a manor house with teachers dictating their every movement. When they were in Athens it was the same. Their father's corporation had always maintained offices in both countries, and that meant they spent a significant amount of time in both. Their father was Greek in heritage, but often more English in nationality. Their mother had been English.

Still, it had been essential that they spoke Greek. Spanish. Japanese. Chinese. Part of their rigorous education to make them superhuman. Men without flaws.

Of course, it had been an asset to Dionysus in business. And also in pleasure. Though he found words were often unnecessary when he seduced a woman, it was nice to be able to communicate at least on a rudimentary level. And the removal of language barriers certainly made things more interesting.

Dionysus wasn't certain if his father really cared about his sons being a glorious reflection of him, or if he simply liked to flex control when and as he could. And having control over their education down to the very last detail was having control over them.

Having control over their minds, as he had just said.

"I was happy on the island," Ariadne said softly.

He was surprised to hear her say that, if only because the weight of his transgression loomed large between them without Theseus here. He felt no guilt over it. He had wanted her and it had been his one chance to taste her.

He regretted that he'd damaged his closeness with his brother.

But he *never* regretted that he'd kissed her.

"I won't mind going there," she continued.

But she hadn't, he realized. Because Theseus hadn't wanted to. Theseus had known Dionysus had bought the island. He'd known about his plans for it. They had spoken about it over drinks at the Diamond Club only last year.

He had invited them to come, and Theseus had not said anything half so bold as *I hate it there*. He had been as he ever was. Diplomatic. Easy.

He had said that of course when they were able to clear their schedules both he and Ariadne would be delighted to come to the island.

But they never had. And he had decided for some reason that Ariadne was the one who did not wish to go. Perhaps because he often tied pain in his chest to

Ariadne. If he tied it to his brother, if he blamed Theseus, well, that would have been a loss he couldn't afford. He had never wanted to cut ties with his twin.

And now his twin was gone.

They pulled into the section of the airport which housed private aircraft. They were taken right to his jet. They got out of the car and he braced her.

"I'm all right," she said.

"I don't wish for you to fall. You still seem fragile."

She looked up at him, green eyes sparkling. "Does anything about me seem fragile?"

No. In spite of her frame, she had never seemed fragile. That was why it had been so terrifying to watch her fold like that in the club. To glimpse her mortality.

It all felt too raw. Too frightening. He trusted nothing. The world was cruel. It always had been. But it seemed eager to flex that cruelty now in a way that it had not for the past several decades.

"Is my father's house still there?" she asked as they boarded the plane.

"No," he said. "Both homes were leveled. I cleared them out. Built one new residence for myself. There is nothing and no one else on the island."

She looked shocked. "Really?"

"I always thought the perfect paradise would have been one without our families there. One where we were allowed to roam free and wild. I suppose I made that for myself."

"And you have massive parties there every weekend?"

"No," he said gravely. "I don't."

She looked baffled by that.

"But I would have thought…"

Anger rose up inside him, and he did not bother to hold it back.

"Do you know me, Ariadne, or do you only know now what the papers print about me?"

He didn't know why it irritated him, that she had reduced him to the headlines, the same as everybody else.

It wasn't that they weren't true, they were. He was an incorrigible libertine. All the better to numb life's pain. All the better to manage his rage.

Rage that had knit his bones together in the womb, a legacy from his father. Twisted by his upbringing.

Cemented when he'd lost the one woman he'd ever cared about.

He had changed.

But he was also still *himself.* He was still the boy that she had known. He still found solace in remote and wild places. In swimming beneath natural waterfalls and lying in the sand. He still found sanity in olive groves and solitude. He was not only the voracious monster that devoured everything in his path. Turning it all to hedonistic pleasure.

It was not *all* he was.

She was the only person left on earth who ought to know that.

He wondered then, how Theseus had spoken of him, in the privacy of their home. Because he had seemed as pleasant as ever the last time they'd seen each other, but surely, Theseus's own vision of him must have shaped hers.

"What am I supposed to think? We haven't been *close* in years, and you know that. Small talk at events and holiday dinners packed full of other business associates is hardly a relationship. It isn't as if we... Talk the way that we used to. We are not children. We have lives. You went out and started a major company, and I do applaud you for that. The success that you have, you earned yourself, and it is an amazing thing. Different, and no less amazing, was Theseus taking that empire that was rotten to the core and turning it into something that he could be proud of. But you know that there has been distance these past years. You know that. We see each other, we talk as if we are still friends. We smile. But I don't know anything about your life beyond what I read. You banter with me, you don't *talk* to me. It's different." She settled onto the leather sofa in the main portion of the private plane. And he took his seat in the chair across from her.

"Is that what you think? That I have become a stranger to you now?"

"Tell me about your life. Prove me wrong."

"Perhaps you should tell me about yours too." Because he had to question what he really knew about her life. He saw her socially, along with his brother, but right now with the loss of Theseus looming large he felt the true gap between them. The real distance.

"You first," she said.

"I'm one of the richest men in the world."

"I know," she said, her tone flat. "We're in a club dedicated to that. That is a Wikipedia entry. It isn't you. If you want me to know more than I can read on the Internet, then give me more."

He cycled through everything he had done in the past year. Finished the rebuilding of the island, that was the main thing. It was one thing that nobody knew about, likely because it wasn't interesting, and didn't further his image in the media as a break. Everybody liked to keep to their particular narratives.

It wasn't a secret, it was only that it wasn't interesting.

That was why there were no stories about it.

Then there was travel. Every city he was in a blur. Business meetings. What was there to say? That was what he didn't understand.

They had once talked about dreams. But he was in the middle of living those dreams, wasn't he? So what was there to say?

"Tell me about a typical day for you," she said.

"And how is that not some pithy newspaper interview?"

"It isn't," she said. "Because I want you to give me an honest answer, not one that would make a good pull quote."

"All right," he said. "I wake up around noon, and begin the day."

"I don't believe that."

"Why don't you believe it?"

"Because you run a successful billion-dollar business. And I find it very hard to believe that you're accomplishing that waking up so late."

"It is a global business. And that means that I'm working across time zones. It means I don't have to rise early."

That was true.

"All right. So you're a night owl. You were always like that. I remember I used to go down to the beach late and find you there."

He jerked away from her, the memory too sharp.

"Yes," he said.

"Go on."

"I have very strong coffee, ignore the hangover, begin having business meetings. I work until around nine, and then it is time to go out. Of course, going out is often tied to work. There are specific clubs and venues that I visit in order to forge relationships with investors, and partner with businesses. That shouldn't surprise you. Now the sex, that has nothing to do with business."

He watched her face. It went pink.

"Great. Thank you for sharing."

"I had thought that you might want honesty," he said.

"Of course. Nothing is more important than honesty."

"I think that you are being sarcastic. But this is what you asked for."

"I thought maybe you might tell me about a relationship that you had in the last year."

"A one-night stand is not a relationship, and I realize that you may not know that, since even my brother married very young. But there is nothing to say. I don't know their names. And if I do, I forget them soon after."

"That's what doesn't seem like you."

He lifted a brow. "How?" What he hated was that he cared about the answer. That he cared what she thought about him. That he cared whether or not she had seen this in him when he was a boy.

He shouldn't.

Because he had refashioned himself into something new, something stronger, something insulated from all of the emotions that he'd once had, as he'd needed to do it to survive. To move beyond the abuse that he had suffered at the hands of his father. To move beyond the way that Ariadne had...

"Because you used to care. You would never have treated people like they were interchangeable or disposable. Yes, you were reckless. But with yourself. Not with others. That is the part that makes you a stranger to me. It is the thing that makes me question whether or not you... I don't know what happened to you. And this is why we don't know each other. Because you pulled away from people. From us."

Anger spiked in his veins. She wasn't going to acknowledge it. And if not, then he would.

"Here's another Wikipedia entry for you, Ariadne. Ten years ago on a balcony, on my future sister-in-law's eighteenth birthday, I took her in my arms and kissed her. She kissed me back because she thought I was my brother, and I didn't care."

Her face went scarlet. "You *knew* that I thought you were Theseus."

"So you said at the time. And yet you say I've changed? If you always believed that of me, then you never truly thought me any better than this, did you?"

"We agreed to leave that in the past," she said. "I know Theseus forgave you. I did too. But you were never as close to us..."

Rage was his constant companion. Low level static in the background of his soul. Normally, keeping hold of it was easy.

But she was asking him to give her a baby. And at the same time scolding him for the way he'd carved out a life for himself. Especially when she'd believed the worst in him when he'd believed them to be friends. He would not mind if not for the naked hypocrisy of it.

"*I* wasn't? The two of you concealed yourself in that estate of yours in London. You were completely inaccessible to the outside world. There are no photos of you that are not carefully crafted to project a certain image. You don't simply go out, you go and perform. How dare you accuse me of changing? How dare you accuse me of performing for headlines or being somehow inauthentic when you and Theseus were strangers to me every time I ever saw a picture of you. I'm convinced it's why my brother called me as little as possible. Because he never wanted to have a discussion about it. Because he never wished to be called out on the fact that he was… Engaging in some masquerade for all the world to see. And for some reason you were involved in that. For some reason, the most honest, feral, forthright girl I had ever known became a woman who lived behind a mask. Perhaps explain that to me."

"Because we had a legacy. Because we were trying to repair things."

"To protect my father?"

"No. To protect Theseus. Because you know that your father would have wrenched everything back if for one moment he had been disappointed in Theseus's life. If he had been disappointed in the profits that the company was putting out. If he thought that Theseus was in there intentionally dismantling the system that your father had put in place. It was a tightrope walk. I know this is difficult for you to understand Dionysus, but sometimes people do things and it isn't about you. In fact, we didn't think of you at all."

He was past feeling wounded by such things.

"I am well aware that you didn't think of me, Ariadne. There is no need for you to draw a line beneath it."

Her rage was a living thing. Palpable.

Good. She should be angry. She should think about what he had said. He could understand that his brother was living in a different reality, but…

You shut them out as well, you know that.

Of course Theseus had said the kiss was forgotten. Forgiven. But they'd never been the same after. The twin bond, strong though they were so different, had fractured that night and it had never, ever been the same.

At the time, Dionysus hadn't even wanted it to be. He'd wanted Theseus to be scorched as he was.

"Maybe the simple truth is you don't want to know who I am now," she said. "And maybe I don't want to know you."

"Good thing then, that we don't have to in order to have a child together. Especially one that I can never claim."

"Of course we don't. There is nothing intimate about artificial insemination."

"You say that as if you know."

Her head jerked away, and she looked out the window. Her stock response to that surprised him. And it made him wonder.

But there was no reason that she and his brother would have used insemination. Unless they had trouble getting pregnant. In which case, his comments were likely very insensitive.

But that was fine. She was so disgusted with who he was now. She could be disgusted with his lack of sensitivity too.

All fine with him.

"I'm tired," she said. "I think I'll go lie down before we arrive in Greece."

"Yes. Get your rest."

And when she abandoned him to walk into the private bedroom on the plane, he found himself letting out a breath he had not been aware he'd been keeping in. Likely since she had collapsed in the club.

Nothing with Ariadne would ever be simple.

But he was committed to behaving as if it were.

Because what was the point of a well-crafted façade if it abandoned him when he needed it most?

No. He would do this for her. This favor. He would use it to wipe his conscience clean. And then...

He would forget Ariadne and the child existed.

He would have to.

CHAPTER FOUR

ARIADNE WOKE UP as the plane began its descent.

She was groggy, and fragile—in spite of what she'd said to Dionysus. Everything hurt. Her heart, and her body.

She was still in disbelief that she had asked Dionysus to father her baby. And in even greater disbelief that he had agreed. And that they were on their way back to this island where they had once been children. Where things had been simple. When they had not fought with each other, or played games.

Until they had.

She was still dressed in her clothes from yesterday, and she tried to smooth the creases out of them as she exited the bedroom, and went back into the sitting area. Dionysus was still seated in that chair. Or rather, he was back in it. There was something mysterious and powerful, she thought, in the way he maintained the exact same posture as he had when she had left.

It was by design, she was nearly certain. Because that was him.

It struck her then, the truth of that. He had curated an image. He might be angry at her for believing the press, but who had informed the press of who he was.

He had. Dionysus was not a fool. Every asset he had to his name bore witness to that truth. He had built his company from the ground up. His father's name was a blight, if anything. And yet, he had styled himself a billionaire, one of the richest men in the world. A member of the Diamond Club.

She was as well, but her entry was a collaborative effort. The same could not be said for Dionysus.

She knew exactly why Theseus had crafted an image and clung to it so dearly. She had her own opinions on whether the extent of it was necessary, but his own trauma was wrapped so tightly around his costume, the adhesive of bandages he wrapped around his wounds firmly affixing the mask to his face. She might have disagreed with that, but she did not know how to tell him it was wrong. Perhaps she should have. Yes, in hindsight, she questioned if the cost had not been worth the promised reward.

Of course there had been happiness. But it had been had in secret.

Both of them had been the staid, lovely power couple in public. Only in private did they laugh. Share secrets and stories.

Only in private could Theseus love and be loved.

She swallowed hard. "I slept well."

She moved to the couch she had been seated on prior to taking her leave.

"Good," he said, sounding supremely unconcerned either way.

"Somehow I don't think you mean that."

"I would rather have you well rested. Especially given the state of things."

"My fragility?"

"You find that word so offensive. Why?"

He was looking at her, his eyes far too keen.

"You are one of the richest men in the world," she said, doing her level best to continue to meet his challenging gaze. "But there is always something a person can't afford. No matter how wealthy."

"Is that true?"

"Yes. I cannot afford to be fragile. I have to keep moving. For some reason, Dionysus, I think that you believe you can't afford to care."

She was rewarded by a lift of his brow.

He really was astonishing to look at. She marveled at the ways in which he and Theseus were identical, and yet not. Not to her.

They never had been. Right at first, she had struggled to tell them apart. Though she had noticed quickly that Dionysus had a small scar at the bottom of his chin. The light in his eyes was different. The mischief.

Where Theseus always seemed burdened by an invisible weight, Dionysus seemed to always be fencing with an invisible enemy. And that, she realized in the moment was the difference between the two brothers' burdens.

What Theseus had tried to carry, Dionysus chose to do battle with.

"You know me so well," he said.

"I did once."

"Yes. Once." They were silent for the rest of the descent, and she looked out the window, at the familiar white sand they approached. At the crystal blue water.

Her heart began to race. She hadn't been back here since she was a teenager.

Her father had sold his home shortly after she had married Theseus, and shortly before his sixth divorce. She wasn't sure where all the homes he owned were now. He had come to Theseus's funeral, a new wife on his arm, of course. But he had not... They had never checked in on her.

She didn't need him. Even now, she didn't need him.

The landing was smooth, and she could only attribute the dread in her stomach to the memories here.

The memories were good, in part. But they were twisted around the pain of her childhood. And now around the loss of the man who had been such an integral piece of these years.

But Dionysus remained.

So when he stood and reached out his hand, she took it.

They disembarked from the plane, and the hot wind coming in from the Groves touched her skin, reviving something in her after all the damp of London.

She hadn't left England in the past year. All of her global meetings had been done via the computer. As she had tried to prepare for pregnancy, as she had worked at the company, as she had done her best to try and manage the life they had built, the façade that was so important to them both, she had found herself increasingly isolated and stagnant. She hadn't fully realized it until just now.

She closed her eyes, and let the familiar air kiss her face.

Theseus might be gone, but the island greeted her as

an old friend. And she found it did not feel so empty or lost as she had expected it to.

A tear slid down her cheek.

"Are you well?"

She turned and looked at Dionysus, and she was thrown backward. Into a memory. Or maybe not even a specific memory. But the feeling of a moment. Of running with him along the banks of their favorite swimming hole. Him grabbing her hand and pulling her in with him.

She could remember well the frame of his wiry, strong body.

Her throat ached.

She could remember his smile.

Sneaking strawberry cake and champagne.

And the moment he'd found her on a darkened balcony and taken her into his arms.

It might not be a singular moment. But a hundred pieced together.

And it was no less powerful for that. Perhaps, it was even more.

"I didn't expect to be... So happy to be back."

Another tear slid down her cheek. He reached out, and brushed his thumb over her cheekbone, capturing one of her tears. His hand was rough.

She wondered why. All she could do was stare at him, look into those dark eyes. Not familiar because they were the same shape and color as her late husband's. Because he was Dionysus. And he had once been as familiar to her as breathing. As the air here. As the feeling of the sun on her skin.

She swallowed hard, and moved away from him, breaking the contact of his touch.

"Where's the new house?"

"I will drive us there. I have a car just here."

He gestured to the garage that was nearly hidden by the side of a rock. The door slid open as they approached, and inside was a bright red sports car that was as unsubtle as its owner. And she would love to be scathing about that. She would love, absolutely, to tie that to the new, hedonistic version of Dionysus who had changed so much since their childhood. But this... This was him. In fact...

"This looks very like the car that you had when you were seventeen. I remember you sending me a photo of it."

"It is in fact the car that I had when I was seventeen," he said, grinning. "I could think of no better vehicle to serve me on the island."

It was such a strange, nostalgic sort of thing. But then, the entire purchase of the island was such a nostalgic thing for a man who seemed to fashion his life around the entire concept that he cared for nothing and no one.

It disrupted her thoughts on him. She wasn't in the mood to be disrupted. Not right now.

So she got into the car without thinking too deeply about any of it, and let him drive them both up a new road that had been cut into the island. His new house must not be on the beach.

She couldn't see where it was. The road was winding, and the grounds were no longer manicured in any fashion. It was like the island had taken control back.

And then, she could see windows, glinting through the trees. A house made of dark natural stone cut into hard angles seemingly set into the rock. It was entirely different to the ostentatious and palatial dwellings their families had had on the island.

This seemed designed to complement the surrounding environment, rather than take it over.

There was a staircase that led up to the front door, because the house was indeed seemingly melted to the side of the mountain.

"Part of the house extends back into the rock," he said. "It's very effective for cooling. And helps reduce some of the carbon footprint."

"Oh," she said.

It was a very stupid thing to say. It wasn't crisp or charged. It wasn't pithy or clever.

But she found she couldn't make fun of him for caring about something. Whether that was the environment or anything.

In some ways, she supposed he was demonstrating care in a fashion by bringing her here.

Even though she had been annoyed with him for taking her out of her life.

The trouble was, she wasn't sure what her life was at the moment.

As she and Dionysus got out of the car, she looked at him. And realized that for the foreseeable future, he was her life.

He was going to be the father of her baby.

She felt like the wind had been knocked out of her in one great gust.

Dionysus was going to be the father of her baby. And

it was easy enough for her to lean on the fact that genetically, the child would be indistinguishable from a baby that she and Theseus had made.

But it was different. It was simply different.

Theseus was her friend. The idea of having his baby, a baby that was part of both of them, had felt like the ultimate expression of their friendship. The way they'd melded their lives together. It hadn't been a conventional partnership, but it had been real. The thought of carrying his baby had not been... *Intimate*.

What a strange word. As she stood there staring at Dionysus's proud profile, the idea of his child growing in her womb felt...

It made goose bumps raise on her arms.

And she had another memory. Of when they had been young. Still teenagers. Treading water in the middle of that swimming hole. And his eyes had gone dark when he had looked at her, and when his gaze had flickered down to her mouth, she had panicked.

Because she had made a promise.

She had made a promise to Theseus, and she couldn't betray that promise.

Because she had known in that moment that if she drew closer to Dionysus, everything would be ruined.

She didn't want passion. She wanted to be cared for while caring for someone else. She wanted companionship.

She wanted stability.

She had watched her father discard women, one after the other all through her life. When they got too mouthy, too bored, too old. Passion was fleeting and selfish. She did not want to live a life governed by passion.

She had decided instead on a life without it entirely.

She loved Theseus. With her entire soul.

But Dionysus had begun calling to that wild thing within her she tried so hard to keep hidden, and when he'd kissed her on the balcony…

Of course she'd told Theseus she had thought it was him.

She wasn't sure either of them believed her.

But she'd done her best to forget it all. To put it behind her. Still…

He was Dionysus.

The only reason she hadn't felt his impact like a wrecking ball when she had seen him in the Diamond Club was that she had been in a state of shock for the past two weeks. And then she had miscarried.

Her body was wrapped in discomfort and sadness.

But right now, she didn't feel as if she had the protection of those horrible feelings. Right now, she was left with the impact of him. And memories. And honesty.

About the real reason she didn't like seeing him as much as she once had. About the real reasons the headlines about his exploits bothered her.

Yes. Right then, she was confronted with honesty, and she hated that most of all.

When he turned to face her, it was like seeing him for the first time. The sun hit the side of his face, casting a harsh light on his strong features. That proud nose, his sensual lips. His square jaw. The slight dip in his chin, a scar, not a feature. Because it was the one physical feature on his face that differed from Theseus.

And yet it was an entirely different face. The sight of it did entirely different things to her body.

Where Theseus was home and comfort, love, if faded from a red rose to a yellow one as the years had passed, Dionysus was a straight shot of whiskey.

And there was nothing comfortable about him.

There never had been.

She didn't like these feelings, because they reminded her of being seventeen. And torn violently between two truths. One being that she loved Theseus as much as she could have ever loved anyone.

And the other, she had been increasingly confronted by the pull she felt to Dionysus that was nothing like the affectionate feelings she had for his brother.

But she had made a vow when she was fifteen. To keep Theseus's secret. To marry him.

She could remember that so clearly. They had been out on the beach too late, and he had sat so close to her on the sand. And part of her had wondered if he would finally tell her that he had feelings for her like she did for him. What had come was a sobbing confession she hadn't expected. She had ended up holding him in her arms while he told her that he had tried to ignore his feelings all of his life, but recently had had a romance with the son of one of the visitors to the island, and he couldn't deny it any longer.

He was gay and he was never going to be what their father wanted him to be.

I fear he might actually kill me.

He won't. I'll protect you.

Will you? You are my dearest friend in the world. And I love you. If you marry me... If we can have chil-

dren, then I can be what my father needs me to be. And he never has to know. No one ever has to know.

She had agreed. Because she had been young, and she had loved him.

And it had been a sharp, uncomfortable thing.

By the time she married him, she had known it was never going to be romantic. Those were a foolish teenage girl's hopes and dreams. But she had accepted that in the way Theseus had given up on the idea of truly having love and passion in his life, trading it for friendship, companionship and for walking the path that he was expected to, she was also making that trade.

She did it with her eyes open. Because she had committed so hard to that life, to supporting him. Protecting him. Building a family with him.

She felt honor bound to continue doing it now.

But right now, she couldn't deny the ways that her feelings about Dionysus were different.

Utterly different.

It called to things inside of her that she had intentionally cut off. That she had intentionally decided to let go fallow.

Nuns married the church.

And she had married Theseus.

Both were an exercise in chastity and devotion.

Of course, Dionysus couldn't know that. Not now.

It would mean that she had failed at her mission. It was as simple as that.

Theseus's legacy was entirely in her hands now, and she would not falter. Otherwise what was the point of any of it? Of all these years?

He was gone, she didn't even have a child. If she lost control of the company...

Everything she had done... Starting with the moment that she had swerved away from Dionysus in the swimming hole, all of it, it would be *nothing*.

This was the last stretch. They'd been so close.

It wouldn't all fall because of her.

She could not face that. She could not turn around, look behind her and see nothing but ash. She was grieving. Grieving the loss of Theseus. Grieving the loss of her pregnancy. The loss of all that had come before, the work that she had put in, the sacrifices she had made would be too great to bear.

She simply could not.

"Come inside," he said, gesturing up the stairs.

She was grateful for the reprieve. Grateful for the break in the intensity of her thoughts. It was all too much. She could scarcely breathe past it.

So she focused on the tranquility and beauty of their surroundings. On the way the water dripped from the rocks, natural springs continuing their flow even around the house. Moss grew on the eaves. She saw the tree frog nestled in one of the deep-set windows.

"This is beautiful," she said.

"It reminded me very much of our swimming hole," he said.

It had been their swimming hole. Theseus hadn't particularly liked it. She and Dionysus had been the adventurous ones. The ones who were more independent.

Though Dionysus was far too independent. And she had taken her strength and used it to protect his brother.

She tried to let that make her angry. Except she

couldn't, with any credibility allow that to infuriate her. Not when she knew that Theseus simply hadn't confided in Dionysus.

She could think of a thousand reasons why. The largest being that if Dionysus knew something like that, and their father decided to physically hurt him, then it would be a danger to Theseus, and Dionysus.

She knew that. So there was no point letting herself rewrite things and make it seem as if Dionysus couldn't be trusted. He had simply always and ever been another victim of their father.

Dionysus entered the code, which unlocked the door. The inside was much the same as the outside, in many ways. There were plants and stones, and a small river ran through the entry with a raised wooden platform going over the water.

"Why did you do this?"

"It was like that," he said. "I didn't want to disrupt the flow of the water."

This was his sanctuary. It suddenly made sense why he didn't invite people here. Why he didn't have parties here.

His life outside this place was loud. This was his touchstone with another time.

A time they had shared.

"It's beautiful."

"Thank you.

"All of the medical records from the spa facility have been sent to your doctor. She's on her way."

"Oh," she said. "Good. Great."

"If you don't feel ready yet…"

"I don't. But there are reasons…reasons we have to move quickly."

"Of course."

Still, she was stuck on the fact that somehow being pregnant with Dionysus's baby was different.

And with that came the discomforting thought that she might not be comfortable passing his baby off as Theseus's. Because he was right, what would she tell the child?

She pushed that to the side.

She walked into the beautiful dining area, where there was a long, natural wood table with raw edges beneath an entirely glass ceiling, windows allowing small shafts of light in, mostly shaded by the foliage all around.

There was a large platter of fruit sitting out waiting.

"Sit here," he said. "Have something to eat. When your doctor arrives, I'll let you know."

"Can I have some coffee?"

She hadn't been having caffeine, and now… She might as well.

"Of course," he said.

He disappeared, and she was left feeling… A strange sort of ache in her chest. When he returned a moment later with a mug of strong espresso, she looked up at him, their eyes clashing. She was very careful not to touch his fingers as she took the mug from his hand.

"Are you in the habit of making coffee for the women that stay with you?"

"No. Because women don't stay with me. If you're going to try to make this feel less heavy by diminishing me, you might as well stop. I can't remember the last time I made a cup of coffee for another person. I normally don't even make it for myself. Of course I know how. I'm not useless."

She stared at the coffee. At the small act of kindness. Yes, she was used to having drinks made for her. She and Theseus were incredibly wealthy, and she had been raised wealthy before that. But as a child whose parents had ignored her professionally she was keenly aware of the difference between someone being paid to complete a task that served you, and somebody in your life deciding to do something for you.

They were entirely different things.

And she was almost entirely unfamiliar with one of them.

When she took a sip of the coffee, she felt a strange emotion rising in her chest.

Before she could say another word to Dionysus, he was gone.

She sat there in the silence for a long moment, eating tropical fruit and drinking coffee. Her mind completely blank, because there were no words for what she had experienced in the past three weeks. None whatsoever.

It was all just tragedy.

It was all just… Crushing. But she was not crushed. She was still here.

Back on the island, and with Dionysus, which felt entirely symbolic of something she couldn't quite grasp hold of.

She sat like that until her doctor arrived an hour later, and Dionysus directed her and her physician to a bedroom upstairs.

It was plush and comfortable, though no amount of

luxurious surroundings could make the examination, or the topic any easier.

"There's nothing physically wrong with you," she said. "Though, I would want to take precautions during labor and delivery, as I suspect you're prone to hemorrhage. But, likely there was simply something wrong with the development of the baby. These things do happen. The process of creating a human is quite complicated."

Ariadne nodded. "I know." She did. But it still felt something more than common when it was her. It still felt something more than the precariousness of life.

It felt personal. Like a dagger straight to her soul. But she imagined every woman in this position felt that way.

She wasn't a doctor. She was a woman who had lost the promise of a future that she had wanted desperately.

She could try again. She would try again. But it didn't take the sting away from this moment. From this loss. The possibility of this child was gone forever, and she felt wounded by that.

"I would like you to wait at least one cycle. And then I come back for the insemination. He explained your situation to me."

She blinked. "He doesn't know. He doesn't know that this baby… The previous pregnancy, was conceived through insemination."

Her doctor looked at her, her gaze level. "And it isn't anyone's business but yours. You know that I am committed to keeping your confidence."

"Thank you. I will need you to keep confidence with this even more so."

"I understand. He did explain the situation."

"It is very important," said Ariadne, feeling like her doctor was judging her. Even though the other woman looked entirely nonjudgmental. But maybe Ariadne judged herself.

Maybe that was the problem.

She was the one who was worried that this decision was mercenary. She was the one that was worried it was heartless.

It was just she had to protect... Everyone. She just had to protect everyone.

The workers at the company, the memory of Theseus. Everyone.

"Four weeks... You're sure?"

"I would not feel comfortable performing the procedure prior to that. It's a little bit sooner than I would like. My preference would be to give you some normal cycles, but I understand that there is urgency here."

Of course, Ariadne knew that people got pregnant sooner than advised all the time. But she also understood that didn't involve doctors going against their medical inclinations.

That would require making a baby without medical intervention.

For a moment, the thought immobilized her. She was looking into Dionysus's eyes again in her memory.

No. She had to stop.

There would be no quicker way for Dionysus to find out the truth than for him to discover that his sister-in-law was still a virgin after spending eight years being married to his brother.

Even after being pregnant. Granted, she was reasonably certain the physical evidence of her virginity was long gone. But still, it would be obvious. She had no practical knowledge of how to touch a man.

Except for the once, she had only ever kissed a man as a performance. She and Theseus had kissed often. Their only truly passionate looking kiss being the one on their wedding day.

And after that, casual kisses to make them look like an affectionate couple. It had always made her feel warm. Happy in some ways. Connected. It didn't light her on fire.

It didn't feel like drinking a shot of whiskey.

She thought of Dionysus's eyes again.

And she pushed all of it to the side.

"I understand. I do. I want everything to be as safe as possible. I don't ever… I never want to go through something like that again."

"I know it's a lot," her doctor said. "I'm very sorry for everything you've been through." She put her hand on Ariadne's. And her first instinct was to pull away. Because this care, the softness, felt dangerous. It felt like an invitation to weakness, and Ariadne did not have the luxury of weakness.

After that, her doctor left and Ariadne opened up the closet, surprised to discover an entire wardrobe hanging there. Light-colored, floating linen things, that all looked incredibly friendly to spending time on an island.

She wasn't going to be able to try to conceive again for four weeks. There was really no point in her being here.

She had her computer, though, and she had conducted

all of her meetings of late virtually. Why couldn't she do it here?

She could admit to herself, in this moment alone, that she might need to take this time to herself. That she might need to take this time to sit in some of these feelings. In grief.

She couldn't have her body being under undue stress when she was trying to prepare to conceive another baby.

Of course, there was no reason for Dionysus to stay, and as she put on a navy-blue linen jumpsuit with wide legs that were both loose and flattering, she rehearsed what she was going to tell him in her mind.

She walked downstairs, expecting to find him sitting in the dining room, but he wasn't there.

She walked back into the far reaches of the house, and there was a low doorway that seemed to go into darkness.

Her breath left her body as she made her way through the craggy corridor, realizing that it was a cave. And then she saw light.

She walked into a massive chamber, well lit. The walls were limestone, almost white. And all around were beds of pink salt, and large glowing lamps made of the same material. The light it cast into the room was warm and rosy. But the biggest shock of all, was seeing Dionysus, sitting there in the middle of it all wearing nothing but a pair of white linen pants, his chest bare.

"What is this?"

"It's a cabin that I found here when I was a boy. I always wanted to build a house centered around a natural cave. I always felt as if there was a strong energy here.

Or at least, it suited me to believe it. I used to come to this cave when I needed to heal from my father's latest beatings. Whether verbal or physical."

"Oh," she said.

She wasn't sure what to make of this. This insight into his mind. Into the fact that he believed in something... Almost metaphysical, even if he left space for the idea that it might be in his head. He had filled the place with pink sea salt, which she was sure she had read somewhere had some spiritual quality to it.

"I like it," he said. "Whether or not I believe it actually does me any good. It is a cathedral of sorts."

It was funny, how it reminded her of a large, stone cathedral in some ways.

"I can see that."

"And how was your appointment?"

"She wants me to wait until I have another period. I wanted to tell you, there is no reason for you to stay this whole time."

And then his eyes met hers, the light there immobilizing her. "I'm sorry, Ariadne. I'm afraid that you're stuck with me for the duration."

CHAPTER FIVE

SHE HAD BEEN lying low the past couple of weeks, slowly beginning to feel like her strength was coming back. Slowly shutting the symptoms of both her pregnancy and the pregnancy loss. The heaviness of everything was still there. But she felt... A sense of purpose, anyway.

She was thankful for James and his handling of things at Katrakis. Her phone call where she'd had to tell him about the miscarriage had been much harder.

I'm so sorry.

You don't have to be sorry, Ariadne.

But the baby mattered so much.

Not for the company. Not only the company. Because it had been part of Theseus.

Of course it did. But so do you.

I'm trying again but I know for you it won't be the same.

I still want to be involved.

Of course.

James was one of her best friends. How could she not love him when meeting him had changed everything for Theseus? After a lifetime of isolation James had truly brought him to life.

It was the one comfort she had. That Theseus had been in love when he'd died. That he'd had that joy. That he'd had hope.

But they should have been able to have a life together. That had been the plan.

She thought of Theseus's ashes, safely kept at their home, because right now choosing a resting place for them felt wrong when...when what would be written on the stone would have to be a lie.

When James couldn't be mentioned.

James and Theseus had met and fallen in love when James had taken a CFO position at Katrakis—as it had become clear neither Theseus nor Ariadne were a fit for the role. The connection had been instant.

Ariadne had encouraged it. She'd never seen Theseus so happy.

He'd been with James for three years when he'd told Ariadne he couldn't keep his sexuality a secret for the rest of his life.

Lavender marriages are so Victorian, Ari.

As are we, Theseus.

What if we weren't? What if after we have a baby, after the inheritance is set, we divorce. And I... I could marry James and you could marry whoever you like.

That had been the plan. And when they'd started trying to have a baby the plan had also included James coparenting that child. It was why he shared in the loss too.

Everything wasn't lost. She refused to let herself feel like it was.

Because she and Dionysus would find their way through this. They would... They would have a baby.

Well, she would.

She needed to get out of the house. She had been babying herself indoors, only venturing out to the patio at the side of her room, which was a lovely grotto with rock walls all around it, and vines growing down the sides of them.

There was a little table and chairs there, and she felt secluded within the walls.

But she felt... A restless spirit beginning to rise up inside of her. Because she had been free here once. She had been a child, filled with hope and joy.

She had found a sort of joy in her life in the time since.

But she had never been as happy as she was here. The summers that she had spent roaming around with Dionysus had been the happiest. And yet...

She had given him up.

She pushed her guilt aside.

He had never made any declarations toward her. They had been friends. He had kissed her, and she still didn't know...

He wants what I have.

Theseus had said that, angry after Dionysus had kissed her.

She wondered if that was true. Dionysus had never acted jealous of Theseus, not in her presence, but maybe he was. He was the younger brother, after all. He wasn't going to inherit anything. He had had to make it on his own, and maybe that had caused more strife between them than she had realized.

He made light of it, even now. Using it as a trinket

to hold up in front of her, to bait her. Goad her. If it had mattered to him at all he wouldn't have done that.

She felt like he'd done it...she had never understood why.

She was his friend, she always had been. And there had been moments of tension between them. But if he'd had feelings for her...he'd certainly never said. Dionysus seemed like a man who would say.

She'd wondered if it was a joke. She'd always been secretly afraid it might be. Though, she didn't know if the alternative was better.

She rummaged through the clothes and found a bathing suit. It was shockingly brief, bright orange with triangle shaped cups that had a ruffled edge. The bottoms barely covered her bottom, and she squinted at herself in the mirror. She looked... Disturbingly good. She didn't like clothes that were overly sexy, because it... It implied a desire to attract attention. And she was never comfortable using her body in that way. She liked to look nice, of course. What woman didn't?

But she tried to look classy. Not...

She was alone on an island. Well. Mostly alone. A disquieting feeling went through her, and she felt a strange sensation between her thighs.

She wasn't really alone.

She sucked her breath in through her teeth and then grabbed a white dress and put it over the top of the bikini.

It suited her skin tone, and made her eyes look even brighter green.

When she slipped outside, the air was sultry, and it made her feel... Younger. Like she belonged here.

Like a wood nymph.

As she began to walk down a path that led to where, she didn't know, she felt some of her burdens rolling off of her shoulders. She let herself forget.

Who she was. What had happened to her. She let herself forget all of her pain. Everything.

She looked at the trees, at the flowers.

And she remembered. Everything had been so beautiful here. They hadn't been carefree. No. They had been something even more poignant. More intense. They knew how difficult life could be. And they had appreciated the glory of having this place. Having friends.

That almost made her want to weep, because it was such a simple sentiment.

And yet so real. So true.

She kept on walking until sweat beaded on the back of her neck, and she was beginning to wish that she had some respite from the heat. And that was when she heard running water.

It was the waterfall. She knew it. She was thrilled that she had somehow directed herself toward that familiar place, even though it had been so long since she was here. Even though she was disoriented by the change in landmarks.

She paused for a moment and tried to orient herself. The waterfall was in front of her somewhere, which meant that her parents' house was behind her when it had stood.

But somewhere past where Dionysus had built his home.

From there, she could figure out the direction of the beach. The direction of some of their favorite caves.

A thrill went through her. She began to move more quickly, that feeling of being unencumbered moving with her.

She moved nimbly over the rocky path, and when she came to the waterfall she stripped her dress off without thinking about it. And she dove straight into the clear blue pool.

The water was cool and clear. Perfect.

This had been their place. Their blue lagoon. Where she and Dionysus had gone to get completely away from the adults. They had talked about their hopes and dreams. They had talked about what a monster his father was, and what a useless fool hers was. He had talked about his car.

It made her smile.

He had kept the car. He had bought the island.

He was an extraordinarily sentimental person for all that he pretended not to be. For all that he pretended that no one and nothing meant much of anything to him.

But then… Who had he had in his life?

He was right, he and Theseus had been distant. She didn't think that Theseus had held onto his anger over the kiss, but perhaps he had.

At the very least, he had been afraid to be too close to his brother. For fear that Dionysus would realize that the marriage wasn't everything that it seemed.

But it was so difficult to get him to open up on that topic.

She submerged underneath the water, and she let those thoughts float away. She let herself think of nothing but the moment. But the cool of the water, the sound of the waterfall. She treaded water, kicking her feet to keep herself afloat.

And then she heard a splash come from behind her.

She turned, just in time to see Dionysus surface above the water.

"How did you know I was here?" she asked.

He grinned, and her heart clenched painfully.

It was… It really was like being in the past. And she wanted to cling to that. She wanted to leave all of the baggage, all of the pain, somewhere else.

"This is where you always are," he said.

Her heart lifted.

"It's my favorite place on the island."

"Completely unspoiled," he said.

"A good thing neither of our fathers ever explored beyond the confines of their very comfortable houses. Or they might have figured out that they could monetize it, and then it never would've stayed unspoiled."

"True," he said.

"I finally felt like getting out," she said.

"Good," he said.

The sun reflected off the water, casting a glow on his face. It made him look younger. More carefree. It added to the illusion.

"Tell me about your business. Why did you decide to do… Delivery."

"I thought it was amusing. Because I thought that it was rather like shipping. But on a smaller, more personal scale. It turned out that people were ready for the convenience. It has been good for me."

"Poking at your father even while you separated yourself entirely?"

"I wouldn't be me if I didn't."

"No. I guess you wouldn't."

"My father was very hard on Theseus." His expression went remote. "He demanded absolute perfection from him. In a way he didn't for me. But if I acted up enough, I could draw fire. And if I can keep him distracted, then he left Theseus alone."

"Poor Theseus," she said, her chest clenching. "It was always hard for him."

"Yes," said Dionysus, though his voice went hard.

She swam nearer to Dionysus, but he moved away. And she couldn't help but feel as if she had missed something. As if… She had done something wrong. But she didn't want to ask. She wanted to bask in good feelings. And nostalgia. She didn't want to turn over rocks or dredge up skeletons.

They had had a rather unhappy childhood. Except for this.

"Remember when you told me that fairies lived here. And that the water was enchanted."

"Did I tell you that?"

She studied him closely. "Yes. I don't believe that you forgot it either. Because I don't believe you forget anything."

"That is possible," he said.

"More than possible."

"All right. I do remember that I made up a story. But to be fair, I heard a bit of it from the cook. It was a legend about this island. That it was enchanted. That's why it's so lush. Even though it can get dry here. It is different. Unlike any place else."

"It is," she said. "I know I was never as happy when

we were in the States. In New York I felt so lonely, even surrounded by thousands of people on every street. Here, I was often alone, and yet I never really felt by myself."

"It's the land. I feel connected to it too. I always have."

"What was it like? When you weren't here?"

"Surely Theseus must've told you."

"He told me what it was like for him. What was it like for you?"

"My father was exacting and cruel at times. He took pleasure in setting tasks he knew were relatively impossible so that he could punish us. He said that was how life was. That good enough didn't exist. And you must always strive, even knowing that there will always be a punishment waiting."

"What did he do to you."

"He particularly liked to isolate me. He tried fists, but at a certain point I hit him back." His expression went hollow. "He realized that threatening Theseus had a far greater effect on me than that. That was why I never did it again. It wasn't worth it. Because he would see Theseus punished, and I could not... I couldn't stand that. What he began to do instead was separating us. Isolating us. He made me worry for him. I don't know what he told Theseus about me."

"He told Theseus that you were away. Partying."

His face went sharp. "What?"

"That's what Theseus said. He... He was angry about that. He felt like you left and got a reprieve, and that your father was hardest on him."

"That bastard. No. I spent that time locked away

in an attic. Until I figured out how to scale down the house, but even then, I wasn't off pleasing myself. I would just go back into the woods behind the house."

"Oh, Dionysus…"

"Don't," he said. "No wonder my brother thought the worst of me."

"He didn't. Yes, he had some issues. But… He loved you."

She moved closer to him, and suddenly realized her mistake. Because he was looking at her, intent in his dark eyes.

"Do you remember when it was just us?" And she didn't know if he meant that first few moments of the conversation they were just having, or if she meant the time in the pool when he had captured her in his arms. She could remember how strong his body was. She had been laughing. He swam to her then, and she realized why he had moved away before. Because there was something powerful throbbing between them, and it was unwelcome.

But she didn't move. She stayed there like that, entranced.

"Here we find ourselves," he said, his voice filled with wonder.

"Dionysus…"

But everything, all her words, her intent, died on her lips just then.

He moved to her, and then he reached out and touched her face, moved the water droplet away from her cheek, his thumb over her lips.

"Ariadne. Don't you know if there was anything enchanted here, it was always you. Just you."

For the moment, everything stood still. There was nothing but this. Nothing but him and her. And the silence between them.

"I wasn't the only one who thought so."

His voice was rough. He moved away from her abruptly and she felt...bereft.

She knew why he wouldn't close the distance between them. And she should be grateful.

Instead she felt a kernel of something close to anger building in her chest.

Theseus wasn't here anymore. Yet she still felt...tied to him. To his legacy. To what they'd built together. How could she abandon it all now?

How could she undermine it all with Dionysus.

It was her turn to jolt.

She swam toward the bank and climbed out of the water, moving toward her clothes. She'd lost herself for a moment. She'd lost her focus.

She had let herself go too far back in time.

She'd lost herself.

She had to remember what mattered.

Theseus's legacy.

When she got back to her room she felt cold.

"Theseus is dead." She said it out loud.

Theseus was dead and she was still here. And in spite of herself, the anger she'd felt when Dionysus moved away from her continued to burn.

CHAPTER SIX

IT WASN'T HIS plan to be here with his sister-in-law for that length of time. But now that he had made his decision, he would not correct course.

Three weeks since he had come to the island with her, and the week of potential conception was closer than he'd like.

He sneered even standing in the room alone. *Conception*. With medical instruments. Things like this tempted him to believe in God. Because it seemed as if whoever ran the cosmos had quite a lot of intent.

Making a baby with her this way, passing the child off as his brother's...

He couldn't help but think Theseus was demanding his pound of flesh from beyond the grave.

In this, he and his twin were alike.

He was not a man who did things by half measures. And he was determined to make sure that Ariadne was well cared for.

The glittering, refined relationship that Ariadne and Theseus presented to the public might have been mysterious to him, but the truth was, Ariadne had always seemed well cared for by Theseus.

One thing he knew for certain, was that Theseus

would see Ariadne cared for. Because of that, Dionysus would see it done as well.

But being around her was… Its own sort of challenge.

He brought in some household staff to help make
sure that she was cared for adequately. To ensure that
she had all of the food and necessary blankets and anything else that she might require.

For his part, he spent much of his time in his office,
working. Followed by periods of strenuous outdoor ac-
tivity. Including rock-climbing, swimming laps in the
sea, and any other method he could think to thoroughly
exhaust himself.

He hadn't been lying when he'd told her that he often
felt peace when he was in the cave in the house.

There was something about this place. Something
about the nature here. Or perhaps, it was simpler than
that.

For him, there had never been a happier time than
when they had spent summers on this island.

It had been the only time they'd had freedom. He
wondered if that was why it had been difficult for Theseus. Perhaps it wasn't happy for his brother to have
moments where he felt like their childhood might be
normal. It didn't bother Dionysus to take a vacation
from the unending iron fist of their father.

Yes, it was always waiting back home for them.

But the afternoons…

They belonged to the rocks and the trees. They belonged to the water.

He could never be sorry for those moments of peace.
Of sanity.

Though, he had to admit now that perhaps some of it

was the feel of her, saturating the place. Covering each memory in a sort of golden sunshine that had never been quite the same without her.

But she was here now.

The tension it created inside of him was unexpected.

Because he had been certain he had left behind any unwanted feelings for her the night of her birthday party.

Any that had lingered, were dealt with swiftly and brutally when they popped up. He had rearranged himself entirely after that.

And yet this prolonged exposure to her…

Typically, he left her to her own devices. Typically, he had his staff care for her. But he had woken up this morning aware of the fact that it was her birthday. Her birthday, in the middle of all of this loss. And whatever conflict he felt, he was not conflicted over the fact that she deserved some sort of acknowledgment.

After all, at one time, she had been one of his only friends.

His brother was the other.

There were not two people in the world he had cared for more. Theirs had been a bond he hadn't quite understood, and he'd felt on the outside of it. He was a blunt instrument. A fighter. And while he'd wanted to find his way into that relationship, to be closer to both of them, he hadn't fully known how.

He hadn't known how to do it without breaking something.

Now Theseus wasn't here.

But Ariadne was.

He tasked the kitchen with making her favorite cake.

He remembered well from their teenage years. Her eighteenth birthday.

He had made her cake. He had intended to give it to her.

We're engaged.

He threw the cake in the trash. She never knew about it.

Instead he'd kissed her. And his brother had taken hold of him with iron in his grip. Ariadne had looked shocked.

Still, now that meant he knew exactly what she liked. He made sure to have his staff create something suitably rich for her. He made sure that there was a spread of her favorite, freshly made pastas, and salads. Along with fresh baked bread.

Perhaps an attempt to prove to himself that he'd changed. That he could acknowledge this without thinking of the kiss.

He'd had so many women since then.

That the memory of her mouth continued to haunt him seemed improbable.

A reminder, he was certain now, of all the ways he'd managed to fail in the protection of his brother. Perhaps if that had never happened, Theseus wouldn't have frozen him out. Maybe he would have called Dionysus and told him how much he was struggling.

There isn't anything to be done about it now.

When Ariadne came downstairs, wrapped in bright pink silk, he questioned his own sanity in this farcical re-creation of a time best forgotten.

She looked better than she had only a week ago. Stronger. A little bit less haunted.

"Oh," she said. "I didn't expect to see you here."

"It is your birthday," he said.

Her eyes flared. "You remembered."

It struck him as a very odd thing to say. Remembering implied that it was something he had to think of. Something he didn't simply know. And the truth was, he knew her birthday. Just as he knew his own. He felt it coming on like a change in the weather. A whisper across the wind reminding him that it was close to the time when Ariadne had first come into the world.

How could he forget, when he'd exposed his own heart so badly on her eighteenth birthday.

He'd changed since then. The lessons his father had taught him hadn't taken hold yet when he was a young man, but that moment with Ariadne had been clear.

Maybe he was insane. It had been suggested a time or two. That in his mad pursuit of wealth, and his dogged pursuit of pleasure, he had lost some piece of himself. Or some piece of civility, anyway.

Except…

He had never wanted to be his father anyway.

And while his brother had certainly taken an admirable path in life, that wasn't him either.

Maybe in order to succeed the way that he had a bit of insanity was required.

And if that meant time in the wilderness, and the feeling of Ariadne's birthday as if it was an oncoming season, then so be it.

"Yes," he said simply. And nothing at all about seasons.

"You… You decided to have dinner with me for my birthday."

"When we were on the island, I never missed it."

"Of course not. But we were all here together."

"As we are now."

He extended a hand, and only when she took it, her silken skin sliding against his, did he realize that it might've been a mistake.

Because touching her...

He had a vivid flashback then. Of a time when they had been younger. When they had very nearly...

Or perhaps she hadn't. But he certainly had.

Maybe a kiss hadn't been on her mind that moment they had made eye contact in the water. Maybe she hadn't been thinking what it would feel like for their mouths to touch. For their slick, wet skin to glide together. Maybe she hadn't wondered what it would be like if they lost their senses and claimed each other completely beneath the warmth of the sun.

But he had.

He had been a virgin then. Because of her.

He had lost his head at her eighteenth birthday, because of her and she'd been certain that he'd done it to hurt her. Trick her. Like they hadn't been friends before.

He'd had plenty of opportunity to be with someone. But he hadn't wanted anyone else. It was only when Theseus had made his announcement that Dionysus...

Of course after the engagement announcement, and after the kiss, he'd realized what a fool he was.

Ariadne had not been waiting for him.

And if in that water Ariadne had felt an attraction toward him, if she had responded to his kiss, it had likely been because he looked exactly like his brother. Because his brother was who she wanted.

He could see how the attraction between them had been a confusing thing for her. It had sure as hell confused him as a teenage boy longing for any touch, any hint she wanted him. But it was Theseus she'd loved.

He just happened to look like him.

And he would do well to remember that.

Still, it didn't change the fact that through all the years, in spite of all the other women, in spite of her marriage to his brother, the fact that she had been pregnant with his child, he wanted her.

Perhaps she remained unfinished business. For he was not foolish enough to believe in love. Not now.

He had left that childish dream behind long ago. In that sense, he was thankful. And Theseus and Ariadne had married each other.

It was Theseus who had broken her heart. Theseus who had failed her.

Had Dionysus married her, right now, he would have been the one to fail.

His father was a monster. And he was not that manner of monster. But his father had broken something in him.

When he had told her he didn't wish to be a father, he had spoken the truth.

He did not wish to impose himself upon a child.

He would not even know where to begin.

It would be as foolish as taking a wife.

Foolishness at the highest level.

But today was her birthday. And he would honor that. Because while there was no scope for forever in him, between them, or between himself or anyone else, there was this moment.

The space of time where he was dedicated to…

Martyrdom?

What a strange pursuit for a libertine.

Though, if he were honest, his self-indulgence was a form of self-denial.

He had more sex than most. More partners than he could count.

And yet, never the one that he had wanted first.

Never the one he had wanted most.

He had not anticipated having a revelation standing there before Ariadne, and that dress that clung to her curves.

Dionysus was a martyr.

Here he was, sharing a home with his brother's wife, who he wanted more than he could recall ever wanting another thing. His one experience of self-denial, and he savored and cherished that self-denial. Held it close to his heart. It was why he could never quite let go of Ariadne. And now he was considering giving her a child which she would pass off as Theseus's. Completing the metaphor, in many ways. Because he felt that she should have always been his first. And yet she had given herself to his brother. A body that had felt innately his from the moment he had begun to recognize her as a woman.

Was that perhaps why he could not let her go?

Did he get something out of that core of self-denial?

Perhaps he just didn't know how to let go of the pain he had been raised on.

"I had the chef prepare a selection of your favorites," he said, gesturing toward the dining room. The table was laden with food. All of her very favorite things, cheeses and meats, kebabs and flatbread with dips.

And that chocolate cake, marvelous, at the far end of the table.

Her eyes went round. "This is far too much."

"It is just enough, to celebrate your birthday. Given everything."

"Is this a pity banquet?" Her delicate brows knit together, but there was a small glint of humor in her eyes, and that reminded him of bygone days.

"Obviously. Nothing more than pity chocolate cake."

"Well, since you've gone to so much trouble. Or rather, your chef has."

She stepped inside, and he noted the tears sparkling in her eyes.

"Don't cry," he said.

She looked over at him. "All I've done is cry. For weeks now."

His chest went tight. He hated to see her sad.

"Well. Stop. I'm trying to give you something nice."

"It is the niceness that makes me cry. Because I don't think I have been on the receiving end of your kindness in years."

"Have I not been kind?"

"Things have not been like they were."

"We shared many meals together in the past several years."

"It isn't the same. We were real friends once."

She wouldn't allow him to trip her up or play games of any kind. It was one of the things he admired about her. But also one of the things that he found singularly irritating.

Because he did know. There was a wall between himself and Ariadne, and had been ever since she had married Theseus. Just as there had been a wall between himself and Theseus.

"I loved my brother," he said. "And I do not wish to turn your birthday dinner into a eulogy. So I will say this once, and then we will be done with the topic. I loved my brother, but I did not know how to relate to him. The way that he chose to deal with my father was entirely opposed to my own method. I don't blame him. I do not think what he did was wrong. Except that it made him miserable. It was not you, Ariadne. That we can be certain."

"It wasn't only your father either. Theseus made choices about how he wanted to live his life. He made choices about how he wanted to be seen by the public. There were... Pressures that your father put on him, yes. But he took them to heart. And no matter how much I tried... He was rigid in that. He refused to change his perspective."

"So you see, there was a wall there, you are correct. Because I wanted to tell him he did not have to be our father's puppet. And I wanted to tell you that you didn't have to be that perfect accessory to that life."

"It was complicated by the fact that your father demanded a level of compliance in order for Theseus to maintain control of the company."

"I understand that. As did you. But it didn't stop you from wishing he would change things, did it?"

She shook her head. "No. I would have had him be happier."

"Yes," he said. "Of course you would."

He looked at her, and he wondered why she thought he hadn't been *happy*. He'd had no call to not be. Theseus had Ariadne.

And weren't you just thinking only a moment ago that if you'd had Ariadne you would have found a way to ruin it?

Dionysus had a feeling his own failure would have been to burn them both out. To ruin what might have been beautiful if he were not…

Himself.

"But now that has to shift. The focus is on you," he said.

"The focus *has* been on me. Entirely, for these past weeks. Ever since… Ever since the funeral. And then the miscarriage, and now I'm here. Everything has been about me."

"No. Everything has been about the tragedy. You're sure you want to have a child? You can do whatever you wanted. You are not bound to Theseus anymore."

It seemed as if it had never occurred to her. Something like wistfulness passed over her face, and a deeper, more complex emotion that rocked him down to his soul.

Made him feel adrift. And he didn't do adrift. He filled that restless void. With drink. With sex. Overindulgence.

And here he was sitting at a banquet, and yet in the land of self-denial.

Because what he truly wanted, he could not have.

What he truly wanted, he would destroy.

"I committed myself to him," she said.

"I would like to have a conversation with you that

has nothing to do with him." It wasn't fair. It bordered on cruel. But he hated that even after he'd died, his brother still stood between them.

"I don't know that it's possible," she said. "Not now. Although… It may be hard to understand, but I really do believe in what he was doing. It matters to me. I like the work that I do."

"And running the company, that is your dream?"

"Yes."

"And a baby?"

She nodded slowly. "My parents have never had anything to do with me. My mother went back to modeling and traveling when she divorced my father and I never lived with her. My father was always more interested in his newest lover. If I am ever going to have a family. If I am ever going to have that connection, it will have to come from me."

"And if you meet another man? And fall in love?"

"I will never forget my marriage to your brother. He will always be one of the most important people who has ever been in my life. I won't wish it away, any more than I would wish away a child that represented that union."

"But you'll know the child isn't his," he said, unable to stop himself from poking.

"I know a lot of things," she said.

But she didn't elaborate. Instead she began to fill her plate with food, and he realized that they had no small talk between them. They had simply known one another for too long. And yet there was distance there. Distance could not be bridged by talking about favorite movies and the weather. And they would both know that it was a counterfeit attempt at filling the silence if they attempted it. So instead he reached into memory. One that had nothing to do with Theseus.

"Do you remember when we stole champagne from your father's party."

Her eyes lit up and for a moment he felt like he'd conquered the world. For a moment, Ariadne didn't look sad. "And strawberry cake."

What a rare thing to share a memory with her that didn't have teeth.

"Yes. We hid out in the back in the darkness and overindulged."

She laughed. "I had forgotten about that. We were... Perhaps fifteen and seventeen?"

"Something like that," he said. He shook his head. "Theseus was of course far too strict with himself to engage in such activities."

She laughed. "It would never have occurred to him."

"But it did occur to us."

"Yes," she said. "It did."

"We were incorrigible at times."

"But our parents were terrible all the time. And we were always trying to figure out how to make some joy out of what we were given. That was my favorite thing about you," she said. "You taught me how to have fun. Otherwise, I was just alone in my father's house, rattling around, feeling isolated. But you showed me that I could make fun out of anything. More and less responsibly, depending on the moment in time, I grant you. But... The most important thing was that we laughed. We created things to smile about, even when there was nothing."

He had never once seen himself that way. He'd done his best to protect Theseus. He'd misbehaved as a matter of distraction. That was all. He'd seen himself as something dark and unwieldy not...

Not as a source of joy for her.

Of happiness.

It rocked him for a moment. He wouldn't let it be two.

"That is why I love this place," he said, as close as he could ever get to revealing his own deep wounds. "Because for me it is not the site of pain. But of joy. Of the ways that we found to make a bit of happiness. Before we went off into the real world."

"Do you find joy out there?" she asked. "You took a very different path than I did."

She didn't mention Theseus. But then, he wondered if she looked at him and saw herself. Because they had been alike then.

"I have decided that the concept of finding joy is far too nebulous. I have decided instead to embrace all forms of momentary, fleeting pleasure that I can find, because happiness is temporary, and false besides. You think that I'm different. That I've changed. The truth is, I think it does harden you to live as I have. But I never possessed the ability to be self-contained. And now that I've changed in this way, now that I have decided to seek my own pleasure, to put my own desires above anything else, I have found a lot more joy in isolation. A birthday party for one, if you will."

"But you don't understand," she said, her face suddenly grave. "That Theseus never had that option."

"There is always an option, Ariadne. Always. I chose the life I live. But Theseus chose his."

"It wasn't so simple for him. Your father built a cage around him when he was a child. He spent his life fighting. To have what he deserved in spite of your father, and to try and make joy where he could."

"You make it sound like it was such a battle for him," he said, the words acidic. "He had the company. He had our father's approval. He had *you*. He had a baby on the way. He had everything."

"He didn't," she said, her voice clipped. "He…he lived in fear most of his life. It was only in the past few years… Dionysus." She looked up at him, tears sliding down her cheek. "Did you really never guess?"

"What?"

There was something in her eyes, something haunted and hopeless, something that tore at his gut and made him question everything. Her. Himself.

And most of all Theseus.

"Theseus and I had a marriage in name only, Dionysus. I swore to him that I would marry him. I promised. When I was fifteen I promised him, because I held him as he told me he could never be what your father needed him to be. Because he was gay, Dionysus. And he spent his whole life trying to make it go away, trying to hide it. Until he fell in love. And then he decided he was going to *live*. He meant to live. For his child, but most of all for himself. He was finally going to be true to himself and now he's gone, and he never can be. He didn't have it all. He spent his life living a lie and not even you ever guessed the truth."

CHAPTER SEVEN

SHE PRAYED FOR FORGIVENESS. Wherever Theseus was, she could only pray that he could forgive her. And she prayed for forgiveness from her own self, because even as the words hung there in the air between them, her lips cold, she felt anger at her own weakness.

She hoped James would forgive her. For saying this now when it was never out in the open while Theseus was with him.

She felt like a failure for saying it out loud when Theseus hadn't been able to.

For telling Dionysus when she knew full well Theseus had hoped to tell his brother himself one day.

But she couldn't stand it anymore. She couldn't stand walking on eggshells. She couldn't stand making the wrong apologies for her husband. For herself. She couldn't stand his idea that Theseus had an easy, perfect life without pain, when she knew that he had suffered.

And in that moment, one thing was clear enough. Theseus's pain deserved to be acknowledged. Not erased.

So did his love. The love he'd shown her as a friend. The love he'd found with James. A testament to his resilence and strength and to the enduring power of hope that could live inside a person.

Theseus wasn't his suffering. He was more than that. But she also couldn't stand Dionysus writing his life off as easy.

He had no idea.

"That is *impossible*," he said, his expression one of utter shock.

"It isn't only *possible*, it's *true*."

He said nothing for a long moment. "You've known, all this time?"

She exhaled slowly. "I was his wife. Of course I knew."

"For how long?"

"Always," she said softly.

He shook his head. "How?"

"He told me," she whispered. "When we were teenagers. You have no idea… He was so ashamed of it. He wasn't… You. He wanted to be you, Dionysus. You were more what your father wanted."

It was Dionysus's turn to laugh, though it was humorless. "I was not what my father wanted. I never have been. My father hated us both. Perhaps for different reasons, but… I will always believe what he hated was that he could not inject himself into us and live life over again. What he hates is his own mortality. Watching us walk around, young, with our lives ahead, and his mostly behind him. And so he set out to try and mold us exactly how he wanted. I refused. But it had the side effect of drawing fire away from Theseus."

"Theseus saw you as the masculine ideal. He wanted

to be like you. Everything would've been easier for him if he could have been. He was quieter, and he was… He lived so much inside of himself, and I don't know if that was because of his secret, or if it was because it was simply who he was. It took a toll on him. Of course it did. He didn't want to live in secret, he wanted to be like anyone else. He wanted a partner and a family. And I know that I don't have to explain to you why he had to keep it a secret."

"Why did he keep it a secret from me?" Dionysus asked, his eyes blazing.

"He…"

"He didn't trust me," said Dionysus.

She was silent for a moment. "Do you blame him?"

"Because of your birthday party," he asked.

"Yes."

"If he wasn't in love with you, why was it such a betrayal?"

She looked at him, his dark eyes piercing her. And it forced her memory back.

She remembered Dionysus sweeping across the expanse and taking her in his arms. She hadn't thought. She couldn't remember actually applying a name to that lean, hungry face. The expression in his eyes nothing like Theseus's. They weren't identical. They never had been.

It was only after Theseus had come out and seen them. And she had… She had panicked. She had pushed him away. She'd sworn to Theseus she'd been disoriented and had been convinced it was him.

She had wanted so badly to forget it, to forget the way

that it had lit her skin on fire. Her first kiss. Her first kiss had been from her brother-in-law, and it had been the passion she had dreamed of finding with Theseus. It had been confusing. And she had been trapped anyway.

"You knew we were together. That we intended to marry and you kissed me anyway. I was his life raft."

"What a flattering designation."

She ignored that. "It was more complicated than that …we were best friends. He was like a brother to me in so many ways."

"I actually was his brother. His twin."

"Yes. And he didn't want you to…see him as less."

"I wouldn't have," Dionysus said.

"I know. I do know that but you have to understand he hated himself so much, for so many years, and I was the only person he trusted. In many ways we were more than friends because for years I was the only one who really got to know him. I was the only one he let know him." She paused. "It changed. He met someone and it changed. He started to be himself with a grow-ing group of people."

"Still not me."

"He needed it to be…a new life. A new thing. It was too hard for him to try and revisit old wounds."

"Why was I a wound?"

"Because he associated you too much with your father. With his own…failures, I think. But isn't that the real tragedy of your father? He chose Theseus as his favored son, which put him under a pressure he could never live up to and you, you who would have been much more able to be the alpha heir he wanted, were his chosen second."

"Are you saying I'm more like my father?"

She shook her head. "No. But he would see himself more in you. What man wouldn't? Adventurous. Successful with women."

"So flattering, Ariadne."

"I'm not trying to flatter you. I'm trying to make you see. Your father styled you both as players in a game neither of you could win, partly because of the roles he cast you in. It was easier for Theseus when he was removed from the game. When we had the power to make Katrakis what we saw it could be. When he met James. Who is just…the most wonderful man, he truly is. He helped Theseus find himself." She blinked back tears. "I'll love him for that forever."

Dionysus looked pained, but it passed quickly. "And where is James now?"

"He's the CFO of Katrakis, he's covering for me in my absence and in general keeping all of my secrets, still. I had to tell him about the baby. He…" She blinked.

"He wanted the child too."

She nodded, grateful that at least Dionysus could understand that. "Theseus and I were going to divorce. Once all of the inheritance was set in stone for us and our baby we were going to divorce and he was going to marry James. With my blessing."

"You didn't love him?"

"I did. Desperately. I will mourn Theseus for the rest of my life. But I didn't love him as a wife. He was a kind of soulmate, but it wasn't a romance. Not ever."

"The child…"

"I was artificially inseminated. I never slept with your brother."

There were so many bombs now laying on the table between them. So many twisted, tangled truths.

Because if you pulled that one thread in the tapestry it threatened to unravel them all.

It frightened her, because these were all things she had never voiced before.

"You have to walk me through everything. From the beginning. From the day that he told you, to your eighteenth birthday." He let out a hard breath. "To now."

"Okay," she said, nodding slowly. "I always felt protective of him. It felt like falling in love. I wanted to keep him safe. You and I could run across the island together, we were fools together. Theseus…"

"He was more reserved," he said.

"Yes. But then I discovered that it was more than that. He wasn't just reserved. He was frightened. He was angry."

"He never seemed angry."

"He was. At himself. For so many years, Dionysus."

"Why didn't you tell me? When you asked to have a baby with me?"

"An element of it is the inheritance, I won't lie. Because of course your father could still take that away."

"And you don't trust me either."

"No. That isn't it. I just think the less said out loud the better. But also…it is his story. And I wanted to honor that this story, his story, was very personal and painful for him. And then he found James, and that means there is another person involved who is still very much alive. Who is…grieving and who loved him and who can't acknowledge that love right now and when the truth comes out—because he wanted it to—James has to be part of that decision."

She couldn't read his face. She wished, not for the first time, that they'd stayed as close as they had when they were younger. But it had been impossible. She was keeping secrets—some Theseus's and some her own.

She wanted to comfort him. She wanted, right then, for things to be different, but the distance between them hadn't been down to Theseus entirely. It had been her.

The memory of the kiss, and the knowing the kiss had brought.

Because after that she could never pretend to be ignorant of why she felt a pull toward him that was so very different than the one she felt for Theseus.

She had wanted to get rid of the imprint of his lips on hers, the heat of it all.

When she thought of it, she did her best only ever to think of her upset. How angry she had been.

How betrayed.

Because thinking about anything else was… Even now, as he looked at her, her skin burned.

And it wasn't shame that she felt.

Regrettably.

How could she? Talking about Theseus's pain at the same time she was looking at Dionysus and remembering what it had been like when he had claimed her mouth with his?

How dare she, when she had just lost Theseus's baby?

Maybe she was like her father after all. Perhaps she

would have found it easy to find new lovers and then discard them.

Except, you never touched Theseus. And Dionysus has always been a problem.

Even worse. She would be the discarded.

Because she knew how that kind of thing works. One thing that he had said to her when they had sat down to dinner stuck with her. Her life did not have to be about Theseus anymore.

She needed space. Time. That didn't mean she wasn't ready to make the decision about the baby, she knew that was the right thing to do. But thinking about anything physical with anyone, let alone Dionysus was... Absolutely not.

She had been bound by vows since she was fifteen years old.

The last thing she would ever do is jump into something so complicated. As if having a baby with him, no matter the method wouldn't be complicated.

She had told herself that it could be the same, but when had Dionysus and Theseus ever been the same?

She had told herself she could ignore Dionysus, but when had she ever been able to do that?

For one fleeting moment she imagined running away. Leaving behind the company. Leaving behind everything. And for a moment, it felt freeing. For a moment, it felt exhilarating. But then she imagined herself, alone, falling through space.

With nothing and nobody. Without the found family she had made at the shipping company. Without any lingering connection even to Dionysus.

She couldn't bear it.

She couldn't bear it.

"Even if you can't understand," she said, reinforcing all of it within herself as much as she was doing anything else, "it's what I have worked for. I care about Katrakis Shipping. I have put my heart and soul into it. As much as I put my heart and soul into trying to make Theseus happy. Again, you might not understand. But he was my best friend. We might not have been in love, not romantically, but I did love him. Were your parents happy?"

"Of course not," the Dionysus. "Nobody could ever have been happy with my father."

"And you know all about my parents. My father traded in wives like they were cars. Every couple of years he wanted a new model with better features.

"That is my expectation of romance. That it's fleeting. At best. The friendship that I had with Theseus, that wasn't fleeting. It was real. A real commitment to being a family."

"And that's all you think you want?"

"That's all I really want to invest in. Even if you can't understand it, you must… You must be able to get it. I want to build something that lasts. Something where…"

"Where people need you?"

His words might as well have been a blade.

"What's wrong with that? At least people can depend on me. You're out there alone, caring for nothing and no one."

"I also run a company that benefits thousands of employees worldwide, do you not think in that sense I take care of people in the same way you do?"

"It's different."

"Why? You fancy that it's different because you know their names? Because you have taken something that was bad and made it better? I am not denigrating the achievement, but it seems rather hypocritical that it matters when you do it, but doesn't matter when I do."

"It's only that... I gave you the opportunity to tell me about your life. You make it sound like you don't have any connections."

"I don't. You're correct about that. But I suppose my conclusion has been the opposite to yours. There are no connections in life that last. Look at you and Theseus. Theseus is gone. And while you might want to honor him with this... Commitment, that's about you. He isn't here. And my relationship with him fractured years before his death. Nothing lasts forever, Ariadne."

"So what? I should just accept the inherent loneliness of the human condition and wallow in misery? Sounds like fun."

"No. Just accept that it's all an illusion."

"Then what are we doing here? If all of this, if connection, if care of any kind is an *illusion*, then why are you here with me?"

He went remote then, his eyes going hard, shutting her out completely. Then he laughed. "I don't know. Perhaps there is something in me that doesn't fully believe my own creed. Or perhaps I'm just like so many other devotees of a religion who follow it imperfectly. I believe in making your own way. But apparently I can't entirely let go of the past."

Her breath left her body, her heart pounding hard.

He was admitting to something. To that connection between them, and to the fact that it had never truly been broken, not by years. Not by that one, heated moment.

She felt undone with it.

She wanted to deny it. Wanted to turn away from it.

But if it was so easy to turn away from Dionysus, she wouldn't have held the memory of the kiss so close. But maybe that was part of her problem. Maybe part of the problem was that no matter how much she might want it to, her passion couldn't entirely be extinguished. When she had been younger, it had been expressed in the way she had loved to explore the island. And she had connected with Dionysus that way. Then when she'd been sixteen in the water, she had felt it change to something different. Growth. And that frightened her. Because she had already made her bargain. Before she had understood what desire was. And once she did understand, she feared it. Then when she'd been eighteen, he had turned the key that he'd put in the lock two years earlier. He had showed her exactly what she could want. Exactly what she could feel.

And it had changed her. Utterly and completely.

And terrified her. She had doubled down on the decision that she had made.

Because the idea of wanting somebody that way, of trying to build stability that way, was foolish. And she well knew it. Because she had seen the way that her father…

To try and make herself matter to a man by using her body was to make herself disposable.

That brought her back to the moment. To reality.

It underlined the importance of staying on the path. Because as long as she had the company, if she was going to be a mother, then there was security coming from many places.

She was… Useful. She mattered.

And when she looked at Dionysus everything zeroed in on him. Only him. She couldn't allow that.

"I don't know how to look at you now," he said. His words were rough, and she didn't quite understand the note in his voice.

"What do you mean?"

"When I kissed you on the balcony, I thought that I was fighting against the passion you felt for my brother. When you acted shock, as if I might've been Theseus, I assumed that the two of you must have an incendiary connection, and that is how I have always looked at you. I wanted you, Ariadne. But I thought you were giving your body to my brother. With the enthusiasm that you returned my kiss, but you weren't. You felt something for him, but not what I imagine, and now you're telling me… Are you a virgin, Ariadne?"

She felt pinned to the spot. Because exposing Theseus's secrets had meant exposing her own. And perhaps the impossibility of tearing apart Theseus and his secrets was simply too much for Dionysus to bear, and that brought the spotlight straight back to her. She hadn't fully considered that. She felt foolish for that.

And now he was asking…

What did it matter? She had chosen to make sex a non-event in her life. She had chosen to make herself more than desire. So what did it matter?

"Yes," she said.

"God in heaven. That is a travesty."

"It's my choice. If I had wanted to find lovers and make them sign nondisclosure agreements I could've done so. I chose to live my life the way that I have. I have other things that matter more."

"Because you never wanted him," said Dionysus. "Clearly."

"When I thought that I was in love with your brother, I was too young to know what desire felt like. And yes, as I got older, and… No. I didn't want him. Not really."

"Did you want me?"

"I cannot have this conversation with you, Dionysus. I can't. I closed the door on that years ago. And I did it on purpose. I chose a life of stability. A life of safety." And suddenly she felt the dam inside of her beginning to crack, beginning to break. Because she had chosen that life of safety and now it was gone. She had chosen him because it was love in a way she could manage. Could contain it all within her and never wonder if it would betray her.

She had suppressed all of her passion, because she had chosen safety over it. She had… She had allowed herself to feel nothing but shame because of that kiss she had shared with Dionysus, because of what it had made her feel.

She had allowed herself to feel crushed by it.

Because she had wanted that emotional safety he represented above all else.

Now it was gone.

It was gone and she was left with this, this raw, unfiltered emotion. This temptation that had never truly gone away.

What a fool she had been.

The world wasn't safe. Her choices hadn't kept her safe because how could they? Her friendship, her marriage had insulated her but now that it was gone everything she'd never dealt with had been dragged out into the light. Exposed.

It was all still there, unhealed and unmanaged. And she was angry. At herself most of all for not seeing that someday a reckoning would come. Even if Theseus had lived it would have come. They would have divorced and she would no longer have had their marriage to shield her from the choices she'd tried to stop herself from ever having to make.

They were still there.

And so was Dionysus.

She stood then, and so did he.

"I didn't want to be disposable. I don't want to be… out here unsafe and unprotected in the world without…him." She finished that on a fierce whisper. She looked at him, and suddenly, it was like the veil had been ripped away. Like that crumbling dam had let forth not just the grief, but the need that she had been suppressing every time she looked at him, not just these past weeks, but every time she had looked at him since she was sixteen years old.

That gala where he'd goaded her about stealing champagne and swimming in fountains.

Christmas, three years ago, when they'd found themselves alone at the bar adjacent to the dining room at her and Theseus's stately London home.

I won't ask if you're getting champagne.

He was teasing her and it was welcome. It had been a long time. She tried to ignore the tangle of feelings in her heart.

She wasn't supposed to have feelings for him at all.

That kiss wasn't supposed to be the first thing she thought of when she saw his face.

It had been years.

They had never spoken of it again.

They didn't have to.

I like champagne, she said.

These days I prefer something harder, but perhaps you can toast to our youth.

Or four years ago, when they'd both gone to a political event in London and had been forced to sit through droning speeches. Their eyes had caught across the room and held.

He didn't smile, but the light in his eyes reminded her of when he was younger. And by the time it was over her guard was down and she found herself standing in a corridor with him, hiding from everyone else as they talked about nothing as substantial even as the weather, but she felt consumed by it. Cocooned.

She forgot she was married until she saw her ring flashing in the light.

Then she'd had to leave. She'd barely said goodbye. She'd needed space. To think. To breathe.

Then she thought back to six years ago at Easter Brunch when he'd wound up all the small children with sweets and had turned them feral before the egg hunt had begun.

She'd admonished him—but none of the children were hers so it had been amusing more than anything.

Don't you wish we'd had that sort of fun as kids?

We did.

Her breath froze in her chest. She thought he might be remembering the kiss.

Not when we were this small.

Or at her wedding, when she'd avoided him entirely. He'd been the best man, but the tension had been thick. She'd blamed the anger between him and Theseus over the kiss. And not her own feelings.

Then there was ten years ago…

He'd been coming right to her. And she'd let him.

He wrapped his arms around her, his hold strong. And when he lowered his head and claimed her mouth, it was like she had been dipped in the living flame.

She wanted to be burned.

She wanted to forget.

It was like jumping from high rocks into the sea. It was like climbing to the top of a mountain.

It was like running, barefoot and without a care across the sand.

It was the full expression of all the wildness that lived in her soul. And for a brief, shining moment she embraced it as she let him embrace her. As she felt the slide of his tongue against hers. And then echo of salvation rang throughout her body.

What the hell is going on?

And then she was back. Back in the moment. Looking at the man seated before her. And she wanted... She wanted to go back. She wanted to have that kiss. She wanted to feel passion. Because turning away from it hadn't protected her.

She had devoted herself to someone else's life.

She had promised her body to that marriage, like a nun to the church, as she'd often thought.

Even though she hadn't ever had sex. She had traded that part of herself away, and she had done it for a reason, but that reason had turned out to mean nothing.

Nothing. She had been left anyway.

She hadn't been enough anyway.

And there she was, staring at the man that she had wanted. Oh, he would've broken her several times over by now.

He would never love her. He didn't believe in that sort of love, and neither did she. Why should they? Why should they? They had never been shown an ounce of it in their own lives.

But she wanted him.

She wanted him, and the real reason that she had to keep her distance from him was that it had never gone away.

She wanted to weep. But she wasn't going to. Because she wasn't going to collapse.

"Yes," she said again, stronger this time. "I am a virgin."

"A shame," he said.

His words were casual, but his tone wasn't. He sounded harsh. Hoarse. As if speaking them had been a struggle.

And suddenly, she felt like she was being weighed down by the burden of her virginity. And she had kept it all these years and for what?

She had turned off that part of herself for what?

Dionysus had wanted her once. And rather than diving into it headfirst, she had turned away from it. She had never spoken of it, she hadn't even allowed herself to think of it. Not honestly. Yes, she had decided internally, that she had thought it was Theseus, but not to absolve herself so much as to protect herself. From the truth of it. From the deep, resonant reality of it all.

The fact that she wasn't effortlessly free of the temptations of her father or the women who got themselves tangled up with him. The sins of her mother, no.

She was simply very, very good at hiding. Very good at being afraid. And she had still ended up alone.

So it was all for nothing.

She had stolen it from herself for nothing.

Theseus had stood between herself and Dionysus all these years. And now he was gone.

It was an entanglement she didn't need.

It was one she didn't want.

It was one she should turn away from.

"Dionysus," she said. "Kiss me."

CHAPTER EIGHT

EVERYTHING IN HIM went still. The revelations of the past twenty minutes had taken everything he believed and turned them on its head.

His brother hadn't been in love with Ariadne. And he had married her all the same.

His brother hadn't *wanted* Ariadne, and he had claimed her nonetheless.

But he had never touched her.

Dionysus had waited for her.

He could still remember the agony of realization that she hadn't done the same for him.

That he had never given in to any sort of sexual temptation because there was nothing greater than his desire for her. But he had simply been waiting for her to be ready. For her to want him.

And then… And then he had found out they were engaged. Nothing matched that. The anger that he had felt. The brutality of it.

The realization that Ariadne had given her body to Theseus.

A man identical to him in every way physically.

He had not been rejected because of his body, but because of who he was. And that was like dying.

And yet, it hadn't been that. Not ever.

But he would not give her what she wanted just because she demanded it. Because she tried to absolve herself here. To make it so the move had to be his.

He burned with anger. At himself, at his brother. At her. He ached with grief. Fresh and new, because his brother had lived in a hell that he hadn't even realized he was in. Because he wanted to shake Theseus and tell him there was no shame in who he had been made to be. And he had never been given that chance. Because of his forbidden desire for Ariadne.

But it was all a circle, because if Theseus hadn't lied to him, then…

They could have figured something else out.

But he had lied. He had shown all the world that Ariadne belonged to him, when all she had been was a shield. His protection.

He knew his brother had experienced pain. He knew Ariadne had been more than a shield, but a dear friend, but they were both still left with all this. This shattered, ruined world.

And now she was alone.

But he had been soft with her all these weeks.

And her grief was not even that which he had thought. It was something else.

The loss of a friendship, the loss of her stability. The potential loss of her inheritance, but not the loss of her lover.

She had never had a lover.

Mine.

And that was when he realized, there was no question about any of this going forward.

There would be no artificial insemination. He would make her his. In every way. And, however she wanted to pass the baby off… Whatever lies she wanted to tell his father, she could do so. But the child would know the truth, and so would he.

She would be his. There was no question.

Possibility was a roaring beast inside of him. A possibility that hadn't existed only moments ago.

And all the dangers remained.

He couldn't love her, not in the way she deserved. But neither had Theseus. So why couldn't he have her, imperfectly.

Why not?

"Tell me," he said. "Did you really believe that I was my brother?"

"No," she said.

"And why did you lie?"

"Because… Because I was afraid. I was afraid of what that meant."

"When you were sixteen, and we went swimming together. You wanted to kiss me," he said.

"Yes," she whispered.

"You were afraid."

"Yes. I was afraid. Because you could have made me go back on my word. You could've made me… I'm not a fool, Dionysus. I knew that it wasn't love. I have never seen any evidence in my life that romantic love exists or means anything. And all I wanted was something stable. Something safe. I knew that with you it could be… Mad and passionate and dangerous."

"It still could be," he said. "I've wanted you for a long time. Don't you understand that something like this could set us both on fire?"

"Yes," she said, her voice a hushed whisper.

"And?"

"I tried the other way. I tried, and what did I get for it? *Nothing*. I am left here fighting by myself. I am left with the awful realization that whatever I've tried has never been sufficient enough to protect me. I would rather have what I want and damn the consequences."

"Little girl, don't you know that I will devour you?" Need roared in his veins, his whole body on high alert.

"Yes," she whispered.

"Then so be it."

He moved toward her, his heart thundering hard. She sat there, looking up at him, and then she stood, moving down the table, the dress poured over her curves like liquid. Her eyes glittered, and he growled.

Because he had wanted her, and he had kept himself on this leash. Had martyred himself to this desire for so long, and now she was offering herself to him.

"How many men have you kissed?"

"You and Theseus," she said.

"Did you ever kiss him because you wanted him?"

She shook her head. "It was a performance. Every time." She swallowed. "I admit that I felt attraction to him, but…" She looked down. "It was a shadow of what I felt for you. And that was why I liked it. Theseus needed me. I was his support, his confidante. You…

You didn't need me at all. You were wild and untamed, and you whipped up the wildness in me. I was afraid of that. It was much better to be needed. It was much better to be the one who was necessary."

"You wanted me?"

"I didn't know what it was at first. I didn't understand. I was too young. But when you kissed me I did. And I knew that I couldn't... I knew that I couldn't. And he would never have married me if he knew that I wanted you."

"I don't think that's true. He was desperate from the sounds of things."

"Yes, but so was I. To feel secure and he offered me...he offered me stability. A commitment to our friendship that was so deep and I wanted it. It was my choice."

"As you said. A choice you made when you were a girl. So you tell me now, what choice is it that you make as a woman?"

She understood. But it was up to her. That she was going to have to close the distance between them. Because he had done it once already. And he had paid for it.

She moved toward him, and something like a fist tightened in his chest. She was so beautiful. Her dark hair, her glittering eyes. And the woman standing in front of him right now, she was the one who ran over the island with him. She was the one who made everything brighter.

She was the one he desired. Above all else.

She wrapped her arms around his neck, their mouths a whisper apart.

An echo of the swim they had taken the other day. An echo of the desire they felt in their youth.

And then finally, she pressed her soft lips against his. And that was all the invitation he needed. He growled, crushing her lips to his, and forcing them apart, because he was starving, and he had waited enough time.

His heart was raging, his body hard as steel.

He wanted her. Desperately.

Needed her. With a strength that transcended anything else.

He felt nothing but desire. And it was like the past decade had burned away. Like he was twenty years old again, claiming her mouth finally. His body untried, preserved for her. Only for her.

He wanted this woman. With everything in him. He wanted her.

And she would be his. Because Theseus hadn't touched her.

Untouched.

His.

His arousal surged, his whole body alight with need.

"I aim to have you in every way possible," he said. "I would've had you that night, you know."

She shivered. Her need apparent as she did so.

Yes. She needed this just as badly as he did.

He cupped her face, letting his fingers drift over her lovely, familiar features. She had been there, within arm's reach for all these years, and yet utterly untouchable. Behind glass. And that was how his brother had kept her. A doll that he had put in a box, treated like a collector's item and placed on the shelf. Untouched. Virginal.

In pristine condition.

He intended to ruin her. Utterly. In the way that she had ruined him all those years ago. It wasn't vengeance, no. It was a reckoning.

For the unutterable need within him demanded satisfaction, and it would have it now.

And she would burn the way that he had.

She trembled. He relished it.

He thought of how he had been the first time he kissed her. Trembling himself. Wild with the risk he was taking, and with all the need in his veins.

He had been eager, untried like a horse.

And now, he knew exactly how to touch a woman. Exactly how to prolong pleasure. To turn it into agony.

He intended to do so with her. Tonight.

On her birthday.

He moved his hands down her neck, let his fingertips drift along her collarbone, flicking the strap of her dress away from her shoulder. He could see her nipples bead beneath the thin fabric. She couldn't be wearing a bra with this dress. Her breasts were perfect. He already knew they would fill his palms just so. Round and firm. His mouth watered. He wanted them in his mouth. He wanted to taste her. Yes. He wanted her.

He did his best to hold his need at bay. To keep control. He had practice restraining himself, as long as he wasn't touching her. But now that he was…

He drew the front of her dress down, exposing one perfectly rounded breast, and a dusky colored nipple.

She was beautiful. Beyond. A goddess.

He had seen countless women naked. But it had never been Ariadne, so it didn't matter.

Mine.

Her breath left her body in a gust, and he savored the reaction. The obvious need on her face.

"Take your clothes off for me," he said.

Would she fight against him or would she obey. He wasn't certain. But then with trembling hands she unzipped her dress, and let it fall to her hips, then she slipped out of it, her eyes round, her lips parted, her breath escaping in short bursts. She was standing there in only a pair of very brief underwear the same color as the dress. And a pair of shocking pink heels.

"Beautiful," he said. "I want to see everything."

She took her shoes off, and he thought about demanding she leave them on, but decided he didn't need that kind of performance. He just needed Ariadne. Soft and pliant and his.

Then she took her underwear off, and his eyes zeroed in on the dark thatch of curls between her legs.

He felt like his skin was being flayed away from his bones.

He had never felt desire this sharp. This acute. It had never mattered so much who he was looking at. It was Ariadne's skin.

Ariadne's secrets.

All for him.

He was never possessive, not with anyone but her.

And living with the agony of not possessing that which he wanted to be only his was something he had become accustomed to living with. A wound he knew would never heal, but was his all the same.

And now…

It was like healing and being cut all at the same time.

He moved to her, and lifted her up, gripping her thighs and encouraging her to wrap her legs around his waist. He claimed her mouth, holding the back of her head as he did so, feeling her breasts crushed against his chest.

He wrenched his mouth away from her, his arm around her waist as he walked them both out of the dining room and up the stairs.

He took her into his room.

It was dark, nearly empty. With windows that gave them a view of the sea. But that didn't matter. The only view he needed was her.

She gasped as he threw her down on the bed, gazing at her as she lay there with her legs slightly parted.

"Yes," he growled. "Open your legs for me."

Color flooded her cheeks.

Yes. She was a virgin. It was so hard for him to remember that.

And yet, that stamp of possessiveness had branded itself upon his soul.

She was his. Only his, and while he knew it, he could also scarcely believe that a woman so beautiful was untouched. But it was there, written in that flush on her cheeks, and her hesitance now.

"I think you're beautiful," he said. "And I want to see all of you."

"I… I don't think I can."

"Let me help," he said.

He moved onto the bed, and pressed his palms to the insides of both thighs, parting her legs and giving himself a perfect view of her glistening, pink flesh.

She was wet. For him.

"Yes," he growled. He moved his hand, up the inside of her thigh, just to the edge of that tempting glory there. And he paused. To say a prayer. Because he was about to tread on holy ground. He had dreamed of this. Of her. Before he could even imagine how glorious it would be.

But now he knew.

He slid his finger through her slick folds, before moving down to push one inside of her.

She gasped, her hips lifting up off the bed.

"I'll take it slow," he said.

She bit her lip, moving her hips in a sinuous rhythm. "I… I've had… I doubt there's a barrier still."

Of course. She had medical procedures that would've probably dealt with that.

"But you are still a virgin," he said.

The word echoed inside of him. He had known that it mattered to him back then. Because it had mattered in the way that he had deferred his own pleasure for her.

He hadn't realized it could possibly matter now.

It did.

He moved his thumb over that sensitive bundle of nerves there, as he pushed one finger in and out of her body, before adding another, watching as her expression transformed into one of pleasure. Feeling her thighs relax, as she began to lose track of her shame.

Then he bent down, and replaced his thumb with his tongue, tasting her sweetness. Ariadne.

He withdrew his fingers and gripped her hips, pulling her forward, claiming her with his mouth. He growled against her, lapping at her skin, unable to stop himself from devouring her entirely. This was his fantasy. Her. This.

And when she shattered beneath his touch, he consumed every drop of her desire, his body pulsing with need.

But he wanted it to last.

He had waited for ten years.

And this night would take as long as he wanted it to.

Ariadne was undone.

She was boneless, panting. And Dionysus was above her like a dark god, lord of the underworld, staring down at her with sharp eyes. He was still fully clothed, and it made her ashamed of just how hard she had shattered.

But he was… He was not unaffected.

Sweat beaded on his brow, and he breathed heavily.

And the hunger in his eyes was unmatched. Undeniable.

"Take your clothes off," she said, repetition of what he had said to her.

A look of triumph crossed his face as he got off the bed and began to unbutton his shirt.

Her mouth dried as he exposed that gorgeous chest, those beautiful muscles. She had seen him shirtless only recently, but not like this. Not knowing that she was going to be able to touch him. To taste him like he had tasted her, if she wanted to.

And she did.

She had tried so hard to suppress this part of herself. Had been ashamed of it.

But she refused to be ashamed of it now.

She wanted him.

She wanted Dionysus.

She always had.

And she was going to have him.

He had just licked her like she was ice cream, and it left her shaken.

But in the best way.

And the only thing she could think, as he shrugged his shirt off his shoulders, and his hand went to his belt, was that the one good thing about being alone in life as she was, was that no one was around to be ashamed of her. There was no one to perform for. Nobody to please. It was all about pleasing herself. Keeping herself safe.

But no one else would ever even have to know about this.

It was all for her. All her need. All her desire.

He removed the rest of his clothes, and then she was looking at a naked man in person for the first time in her life.

She was very afraid that what she had done was open Pandora's box. Because the need inside of her was as keen as if she hadn't just experienced a shattering climax.

She'd had orgasms before, of course.

She was familiar with her own body. But there was

always regret attached to it. She wished she didn't need the release. She wished that she could be as free of temptation as she pretended that she was.

And if she saw Dionysus's face sometimes when she reached climax, she had told herself that it was more Theseus, because it had to do with her familiarity with him. He was the man she knew best after all.

But if she was honest, she knew that it was Dionysus she was thinking about all this time.

As ever.

She let her gaze drop to his arousal. Bronzed and hard, standing out proud from his body. Thick and glorious. She chased that feeling of knowing that there was nobody to disappoint. That the only person she would ever be accountable to for this was herself.

And if she didn't enjoy it to the fullest, she would have herself to answer to. And so, she pushed aside any virginal nerves and got up onto her knees, moving toward him. She tentatively wrapped her hand around his arousal, squeezing him.

"You're beautiful," she said. Just as he had said to her. His teeth were pressed tight together, his breath exiting his mouth on a hard hiss. Her mouth watered when she looked at him, and she leaned in, flicking her tongue over the crown of him. Then she wrapped her lips around him and took him as deep as she could.

His response was nearly violent. He reached back and grabbed a handful of her hair, tugging hard.

She looked up at him. "Did I do something wrong?"

"No," he growled. "Don't stop."

She moved back to him, taking him in deeper, sliding her tongue over that hot, satiny flesh.

He tasted incredible. Dionysus.

The one man she had ever wanted like this. With a burning passion that would have left her ashamed at one time.

It had left her ashamed.

But not now.

She pleasured him like that until he gripped her hair again, moving her away. "I don't want to finish like that."

The image that painted was erotic.

She did want him to finish like that.

She wanted to swallow him down. To have all of him. To feel wanted. Suddenly, she felt a surge in her chest, power like she had never known.

She had imagined that desire left women weak. But she had never fully understood how powerful it could make a woman feel. She felt powerful. Because he wanted her. Wanted her so badly he was shaking with it. Wanted her so badly that he could no longer allow her to pleasure him with her mouth. Because he would lose control. Utterly.

He wanted her. And that mattered.

He wanted her, and that made her powerful.

Still, she obeyed him, patiently waiting to find out what would happen next. She ached for him. And when he moved back to her, and kissed her mouth, taking her deep and long, she sighed against him, her hands on his broad chest, moving over his muscles, the hair on his chest was crisp and enticing, his skin hot. She marveled at the difference in texture touching him versus touching herself.

He was so masculine. Absolute perfection. Large where she was small. Hard where she was soft.

He held her tightly, her breasts crushed to his chest, his hard abdomen like steel against her much softer body.

And then she felt that ridge of his arousal, and she wanted to guide him where she needed him most. She ached for him. She felt empty.

She was so wet it would've been embarrassing, if it hadn't felt so good. Her body was ready for him.

"Please," she whispered.

"I'm not going to wear a condom," he said against her mouth.

They were close. Close to the time when her doctor had said they could try to conceive.

It made her want to weep. The idea that their baby could be conceived tonight. This way.

She felt like she wasn't entirely prepared for that. Like it made it more real. How could she ask him to release his claim on a child that they had made in bed together?

She wanted to ask him that. But she couldn't make the words come out. Because she wanted him. Bare and without a barrier inside of her.

So she pushed all of her reservations away.

"Yes," she said.

He pushed her down onto her back and hooked her leg up over his hip. Then he guided himself toward the entrance of her body, sliding in slowly. He was so big, she felt her body stretch to accommodate him. She might not have a barrier remaining, but she had still never been tested like this. It felt good. So good, to have him fill her like this, even as it almost felt like too much.

"Dionysus," she said, his name a prayer on her lips.

And then he began to move, hard and intense, a feral growl on his lips every time he thrust back home within her. She came alive. Like she had never truly known joy until this moment. Like she hadn't been a whole person. How had she walked on this earth for twenty-eight years without knowing what it was like to have a man inside of her. Without knowing what it was like to have Dionysus inside of her. She had thought to give this away. To give it up for safety, and safety was an illusion.

This was worth all the risks. This was worth everything.

She said his name like an incantation, over and over again as he claimed her. She looked up at his face, they really weren't identical. It was always so clear who was who. Dionysus was wild. And never more so than now. His dark eyes gleamed, his lip curled, his teeth like those of a predator, glinting in the dark light.

She wanted him. She had him, and yet she felt like it wasn't enough. He was deep within her, and yet she wanted to be closer. She moved her hands over his shoulders, let her fingernails dig into his flesh. She cried out with her need, her need to be filled, her need for release. Her need for this to never end. Never.

She wrapped her legs around his waist, trying to

take him deeper, deeper still. Arching her hips against his. Their skin was slick with sweat, the sounds they made untamed.

Finally. Finally.

She didn't feel virginal, not now.

Because she felt as if she had been building to this moment all of her life. Like everything had been waiting for this. Poised on the edge.

And when he found his release, she went right over the edge with him, shattering as he spilled himself within her, his hardness pulsing inside. She gripped him, taking him deeper, deeper as she cried out his name.

And then it was done. Except… With her heart beating hard, lying there exhausted but not sated, she knew that it wasn't done. She knew that it couldn't be. It would take more than once. More than a night.

This need couldn't be satisfied quite so easily.

"Ariadne."

He leaned in and kissed her. It was tender. So different than everything else had been. And she let her need to embrace that tenderness wash through her.

His lips were like home.

And it made her want to weep.

This moment… This was all she had ever wanted. The way that he held her was so strong and firm and sure.

It was everything. And so was he.

He moved away from her then, rolling onto his back. "You realize this changes things."

It was like being doused with cold water. "Does it?"

"Of course it does. There is no question now of artificial insemination. You and I don't need the intervention of a doctor in order to conceive a child."

She put her hand on her stomach.

She felt... Wounded. Confused by the abrupt shift.

"Is that all you wanted?" she asked, "the chance to avoid having to do it into a cup?"

"Of course not," he said. "But there is nothing standing between us now. I wasn't going to touch you out of deference to my brother, and out of deference to your loss. But now that I know the truth of it... You're mine, Ariadne. I will allow you to pass my baby off as my brother's. But only to my father. And when he dies, the world will know the truth. But by then it won't matter anyway. Because you will be my wife."

"What?"

"You're going to marry me, Ariadne. Because you're mine. And I'm going to make sure that everyone knows that."

CHAPTER NINE

EVERYTHING HAD BECOME clear to him the moment he had buried himself deep inside of her.

She was his.

There was no question, there was no hesitation. Once he had claimed her, he would never go back to not having her.

"Your father will appreciate that," she said, turning away from him.

He gripped her arm, and didn't let her scamper across the room. "Are you implying that I only did this to try and secure access to the company? To try and secure some sort of approval from my father? Have you listened to nothing that I've said to you." Rage was a living flame in his chest. But then, it always was.

"I don't know," she said.

"Understand one thing, Ariadne. I have wanted you from the first moment I knew how a man could be with a woman. As certain as my brother ever was about his desires, mine were just as fixed. It was you. Why do you think I kissed you even knowing you were engaged to my brother? Why do you think I risked the spectacle? Because there was no risk. I either had you or I didn't, and everything else was collateral damage. The only reason I didn't steal you away is that you didn't seem as if you wanted to go. I want you. I am also realistic enough to know that I would have destroyed us at least seven hundred different ways by now. I do not regret the way of things. I can't. But you are mine now. After all this time, and if you think that has anything to do with money, or pleasing anyone but myself, then you are a fool."

He released his hold on her.

"If you want me so much then why can't you be civil for five blessed seconds?"

"Because there is nothing simple about desire like this. It has teeth. If you don't understand that…"

She stood up, and he was overwhelmed by the sight of her naked body. He had seen countless women. They didn't matter. Nothing mattered but her.

His sexuality had belonged to her from the first. He had not been lying or exaggerating when he'd said that.

But he also wanted her to be clear not to confuse that with softer, more refined feelings.

Theseus hadn't felt passion for her, apparently. He felt nothing but passion for her.

And when he said that it was painful, he did not lie.

If he was a better man it might bother him that she didn't feel the same. Or it might deter him. He wished that she did. He wished that she would burn right along with him.

"I have never been free, Dionysus. I married your brother when I was so young. And I committed myself to it long before we walked down the aisle. You're asking me to chain myself to another man."

"And one who looks just like the other one. People will think you have no imagination."

"Stop it. You're nothing like him. You've never been identical, not to me. I lied. I lied the night that you kissed me. Not just to Theseus, but to myself. I wanted to think that I imagined it was him. I didn't. I knew that it was you, and I hated it. It terrified me. I never wanted... I don't want this," she said. "It hurts, you're right."

The beast within him was gratified to hear her say that.

"I have pushed it down, and pushed down all this time. All this time, Dionysus, because I was afraid that if I let it out I would... Am I my father? Or am I his endless succession of lovers, who can say? And I don't like either one. I have never seen lust dressed up as romantic love become anything other than a weapon. You either destroy people with it or are destroyed by it, and I don't want it. I chose what I thought was safer. I chose what felt...you just can't be safe in this world, can you?"

"Perhaps not," he said. "But I won't leave. You have my word on that. If I could have let go of my need for you, then I would have done it a long time ago."

"You sleep with women interchangeably. How could you possibly say that just because you're attracted to me, and that attraction has endured, that you have experienced any kind of..."

"I was a virgin the night that I kissed you," he said. "I wanted you. I didn't want sex. When it became clear that I would never have you I gorged myself on sex. To prove to myself that it didn't need to be you, to prove to myself that it didn't have to mean anything. I have had all the partners that I could ever care to have. It didn't take it away, Ariadne. Nothing did. I wanted you all the same, every time I saw you."

It was his turn to stand, and he began to pace the length of the room. "You, my brother's perfect wife. So buttoned up, so demure. You have any idea how badly I wanted to wreck that façade? Do you have any idea how badly I wanted to... I thought about it. Kissing you, in your own home. With your husband in the very next room, I thought about it. I thought about violating your marriage vows in a hundred different ways, because I wanted to rid myself of that demon. Don't tell me what I want. Don't tell me what will fade. Do not try to minimize what I have felt for you because I chose a way to handle my solitude in a fashion you can't quite understand."

She shifted, her breasts moving along with her, and he couldn't help but let his eyes drop down to their perfection.

"We don't know each other," she said. "Not anymore. I'm not certain we ever did. You thought all this time that I was in love with your brother. That I was... His lover, and I wasn't. And I thought... I thought the kiss was a game to you."

"Then you're right," he said. "We never knew each other. I thought we did. I thought here, in this place, you knew me in a way that nobody else did."

"Did you love me, Dionysus?"

The words cut him like a knife.

"I thought I did. Yes. I got over it."

"You just never got over the desire to see me naked?"

"What I got over was the idea that life might be a fairy tale. I was tempted to believe it when I met you. Because you were… Something bright in what had been darkness until that very moment. So yes, I thought it was love. It was the first blush of lust, and I didn't know better. I stayed a virgin until I was twenty years old because of how badly I wanted you. I told myself that had to be true love, because what else could it be? But you are right. I also have never seen any evidence of romantic love being anything other than painful. Anything other than a shifting tide. Lust, that's honest. The things that our body say that we want, that's real. But it is a hunger like any other. And perhaps like your love of chocolate cake, my desire for you is simply innate. A preference. One that I couldn't change if I tried. It will always be the thing that I want the most. But that is not love."

"You don't believe in love?"

"No. Not in any fashion. Life is a series of bonds that can be broken always. Depending on which angle you come at them from. I was a twin, Ariadne, there is no longer bond. I was formed in the womb with my brother, and in the end, we didn't trust one another. I felt betrayed by him when he took you, even though he could not have known that I wanted you for myself. I didn't tell him. I held back. Then I kissed you, and he felt like that was a betrayal, when to me it felt like being true to myself. But he was harboring his own secrets, and he didn't tell me the truth. I would have said that bond was the closest thing to love, but was it? To have been given a brother that close, so close we even share facial features. And to not even be able to maintain that, that says more about Theseus and myself than anything else ever could."

She was silent then, staring at him. "How do you see the marriage, then?"

"I will support you. As you run the business. I will be a role model to our child. You can tell my father whatever you need to. It doesn't matter to me. As long as we know. You had a marriage based on friendship with Theseus, why should we be different?"

Because they were never really friends. They had been something different. He knew that. But maybe she didn't feel it. And maybe she wouldn't admit it now.

Even if she had.

"You will be faithful to me?"

"Of course. Have you listened to nothing that I've said?"

"I just find it hard to believe. You have seemed utterly uninterested in me these past years, and now you're telling me... I don't know how to look at you." She repeated his own words back to him.

"You and I are both filled with secrets. We will have to start over."

She nodded. "Yes. I would... I feel that we should wait to marry. An appropriate amount of time. We should wait until after the baby is born."

"The baby we have yet to conceive?"

In spite of himself, he felt his body begin to harden again, at the mention of working to conceive a baby.

She was ruinous to him.

"You think in that way we can create a narrative that will make it appear as if we simply… Fell for one another in the absence of your husband?"

"Well, it's better than making it look as if I jumped into your bed immediately following his death."

"You did, though."

"But I was never in his bed. Which you now know."

"I don't understand why the two of you didn't carry on affairs," he said.

She blinked. "I told you. What I wanted was to be safe. I wanted security. I didn't want all of the dangerous things that came with passion. Not in the least. What I wanted was to have… I wanted to have safety. He was my safety. He was… He was meant to be everything. He would give me a home, he would give me a family, he would give me a baby. And he was my friend."

"And that was enough for you."

"It was. It was until it wasn't enough for him anymore. It was hard to watch him struggle but he did find love. It wasn't going to be forever but at that point I trusted that I wouldn't lose him even if we divorced. We were making a family together. I was supposed to have that."

"And now you have me," he said, somewhat ruefully.

She met his gaze. "I knew exactly what being married to Theseus would look like. He was very clear on it. There was not going to be any sex. In private we were best friends and in public we played our roles expertly. I knew exactly what it would look like, I could imagine it clearly even when I was younger. But I can't imagine marriage to you."

"More of this," he said.

She looked away, her cheeks turning pink. "I'm having a hard time embracing this is something... Something it's okay for me to want."

"Here is what I can promise you. And don't dismiss me this time. I will never trade you in for anyone or anything else. When I make vows I keep them. And I protect what's mine. There is no greater truth than that."

She moved closer to him, and his heart froze in his chest. Then she reached out and put her hand just there, over where his heart had ceased beating. And it started again.

"I'm tired of being lonely."

Her words hit him strangely. Loneliness was simply part of life. At least, as far as he could see. As far as he could understand it. He didn't know if there was any real way to fix that. Except when she touched him, he felt something quiet inside of him. He felt like he could breathe.

As if he was drawing a full breath for the first time in many years.

She leaned in and pressed her mouth to his. It was slow, achingly deliberate. There was no mistaking that she had chosen this. No mistaking that she meant to kiss him.

And when she pulled away, her green eyes were shining. "Yes, Dionysus. I'll marry you."

CHAPTER TEN

SHE WAS WRUNG OUT. She was… On the edge of herself. But the truth was, she was bound to Dionysus whether she married him or not. If they had a baby… He was right. She had been fooling herself. Thinking that it would be so simple as to have his baby and pretend… And pretend. Even when she had first thought of carrying his child instead of Theseus's she had felt the weight of that intimacy. Even before they had made love.

And now… She knew that she would never be able to pretend the child belonged to Theseus. Not forever.

She could lie to her father-in-law, but she could never lie to the child. She would never be able to cut Dionysus out of this.

She suddenly felt… Overcome with shame. What she had asked of him was deeply selfish. It had been on behalf of Theseus, but… Had it been?

Had she only been trying to justify her own decisions?

That was entirely possible.

Trying to prove that she had been relevant in some way. Was that what all of this was about? She wondered. She really did.

And the truth was, she wanted him.

If she hadn't, she wouldn't have been able to give herself to him like this. She had always wanted him. She had been scared. And then a few moments ago she had managed to be angry enough to push that fear aside. And now she was...

Ashamed. Of her own behavior. Ashamed of how she had used Dionysus as a convenient object.

In a bid to avoid seeing him as a man.

There was no denying he was a man now. He sat there next to her, a perfect sculpture. His well muscled shoulders and arms a testament to his strength. His chest was broad, his waist tapered and solid. His thighs were thick and well defined, and that most masculine part of him was beginning to rouse again, so quickly after they had already come together.

She was sore, but she would take him again.

All these years...

It was tempting to believe that this was fate. But... None of this felt like fate. Because it had taken the death of Theseus, and the loss of her pregnancy for her to be here.

And those things could simply never feel meant to be. Perhaps that was what people told themselves when they were desperate to dress their lust up to something other than that basest of needs.

Perhaps that was why.

She couldn't readily untangle what they were. But she felt good when she kissed him.

And she wanted more.

"Why do you want to marry me?"

"You asked. Or rather, you told me to."

He chuckled. "Is that all, sweet Ariadne? Is that all I ever had to do? Crook my finger and make demands of you and you would come?"

He let the double entendre linger between them, she was certain that he meant it.

"I don't want to be without you," she said.

And that was true.

Real enough at least.

"Do you want me, or do you want the connection to my family?"

"I already have Katrakis Shipping. I have a connection to your family."

But she couldn't deny that his words got under her skin like the edge of a knife's blade.

"And you're right. About the baby. I wanted to give Theseus something that he didn't get the chance to have. I don't need to do that. Life can be cruel in some ways, but… I can't right that wrong by enacting another wrong. Our child will know his father. And that will be you."

"Good."

"You said, though, that you didn't want a child."

"I never have. It turns out, though, that I would love to make one with you."

"There is the making, but then there's the raising."

"I don't know how to do that," he said. "But you don't either."

"No. I don't. We can learn. Together. Our child will be…" She lost herself then, because Theseus and Dionysus were not the same man. She knew it. But she had been lying to herself while she tried desperately to repair the situation she found herself in. And part of that life had been that because they were genetically indistinguishable from one another, the child would be the same as if he had come from Theseus.

But Dionysus was an entirely different man.

Dionysus called to the wildness in her. Together they were something different. Entirely.

"I will need you to help me raise that child," she said. "Because you and I…"

She felt it again, that sensation she had when they had first arrived here on the island. That tapestry of memory. Not a single moment, but a feeling. The essence of what they were. The freedom they had found together.

Their first time together just now had been intense. Of course it had been. But suddenly she wanted more.

"Take me swimming," she said.

He stood up off the bed and held his hand out toward hers, and she took it wordlessly. Slipping off into the night with him.

He knew the path by heart, and she trusted him.

He held her against his body, and then jumped. Then both of them went into the water, and they surfaced again, breathless, clinging to each other.

He kissed her, deep and long, wildly. They had nearly done this all those years ago. They had nearly done this yesterday.

And now, it was like the culmination of that need, of those moments, all coming together.

They were fire.

They were inevitable.

Except, they very nearly hadn't been at all.

Because she had been afraid.

She had very nearly sacrificed everything to that fear.

Their skin was slick, and he moved his hands over her curves, driving her forward in a frenzy.

To be touched like this, held like this, it was the single most incredible feeling that she could possibly think of.

To be held. To be wanted.

She let layers of her fear fall away.

She had never let herself want this. But she did.

She wanted it down to the very depths of her soul.

She wanted this and him and everything.

Her heart beat fiercely, desperately. Dionysus.

She would never mistake him.

"Dionysus," she said it out loud. Like a prayer, an incantation. A plea for him to never disappear.

And he devoured her. Just as he had promised. Consumed her, left her aching and needy down to her very core. To her essence.

She clung to him, wrapping her legs around his hips, as he hauled them both up out of the water, and laid her down on the sandy shore.

"I always knew you were the enchanted thing here," he said. "When I bought the island, I tried to recapture the magic. I did my very best. And it… It suits me. But it has never been magic. Not since we were here."

Suddenly, she felt overwhelmed. By the truth between them. The reality of what they could've been.

She had asked him if he loved her.

He had.

Had she loved him too? Had she clung to Theseus because he was easier.

Because he represented safety, while Dionysus was the unknown. He still was.

But she had tried safety, and it had gotten her nothing.

And now she was wholly consumed by him.

She wrapped her legs around his hips and canted them upward, urging him to claim her. To take her.

"Good girl," he whispered against her mouth as he thrust his hips forward, in one slick glide, claiming her with his mouth, his hands, his iron masculinity.

She moved against him, chasing release. But chasing something even more dear, that connection that she had felt only ever with him.

And as he moved, the years fell away. As they clung to one another, they were all there was.

And she let him drive them both over the edge.

Their cries filled the night air. He was right.

They were the magic.

And this place was theirs.

She sat up afterward, brushed at some of the sand on her skin. Leaned in and kissed his shoulder before leaning her head against it. They sat like that, saying nothing. She moved her fingertips over his chest, relishing the feel of him. The way that she could touch him. She was trembling. Because the enormity of this moment was blooming inside of her and growing larger and larger, a chasm of desire that she could not entirely rationalize.

She had been dishonest with herself, that was the

thing. For so much of this time, she hadn't allowed herself to fully see, to fully know exactly what he meant to her. She had suppressed it, pushed it aside.

And now she wanted to mourn for entirely different reasons.

For the fact that they could have known each other, and hadn't. For the fact they had wasted all these years.

Maybe it wasn't love. Maybe he was right.

But then what was it? She couldn't rightly say.

It was far too difficult to know.

"I will buy you a ring as soon as possible."

"It can't be public," she said, hating herself for saying it, because this was supposed to be their moment. Because it was supposed to be them, only them, here in this sacred place. And not logistics and machinations, and all the things they had to do because of his father.

His father.

All of this was because of him.

This whole mess.

No. Much of it is because of you.

The realization stung. But it was true. Her own cowardice was not a small part of the mess that had been made here.

"I'm going to buy you a ring and you can wear it in private. But you will know that you're mine."

"I won't forget," she said.

She was branded with it. All the way down to the bone.

"Let's go back."

She almost didn't want to. She wanted to stay here. Naked outside, wild and free.

She felt tender. Like a shield of protection had been stripped away from her, revealing her vulnerabilities, not to him as much as to herself.

But it was confronting.

And she felt quite strongly that she had been through enough recently. She'd had enough character development.

Or maybe she hadn't.

The world had changed around her, but perhaps she had changed herself sufficiently.

"All right," she said. "Let's go back."

They went back to the house and showered. He ended up taking her again when they landed in a heap of tangled limbs in his bed.

She clung to him all night.

She didn't sleep.

When the sun rose the next morning she was still in Dionysus's arms. And she knew that it was the first day for everything would be different.

CHAPTER ELEVEN

HE HAD WON. It was really that simple, and that complicated. His brother was dead, and he had claimed the woman that he had always wanted.

A victory. And not a Pyrrhic one. A complicated one, yes. One that mixed grief and regret with no small amount of triumph. But it was the single greatest achievement of his thirty years.

Ariadne was his.

He woke up each morning holding her in his arms, and he relished it.

When she would walk out of their shared room entirely nude to eat breakfast in the courtyard with the sun shining down on her skin, he gave thanks.

Like a wood nymph. An incredibly sexy one.

He had her.

And you don't know what to do with her.

He shut off that voice inside of himself. He absolutely knew what to do with her. He kept her panting and crying out his name as often as possible. If they had lives at jobs outside of this place, they had both done a good job of forgetting. Yes, they devoted a bit of time to making sure that things weren't on fire. But mostly, they were dedicating themselves to conceiving a baby.

At least, that was how they framed it. In truth, he felt as if they were making up for the lost years. Her, for her virginity which had overstayed its welcome, and him for all the years he had everyone but her.

In this place, it was easy though, to forget that any years had passed at all. It was like that kiss on the balcony had led to this moment, instead of the ten years after, which had been...

He had been dead, basically.

It was why it had been so easy to put everything into starting his company. To put everything into defying his father, and perhaps trying to prove that he was a better man than his brother.

That thought hit him especially hard as he sat there, drinking his coffee and looking at Ariadne's beautiful profile as she sat with her face upturned toward the sun and her eyes closed.

Yes. Maybe a not insignificant part of himself had wanted to prove that the way he had done things was better.

She said Theseus had hated himself.

But Dionysus couldn't say he was an avid fan of his own behavior.

Everything he did came from a place of rage. Anger.

Everything he did was about... Her.

Her eyes fluttered open, and she looked at him. "What?"

"I didn't say anything," he said.

"You were thinking. Loudly."

"You can hear my thoughts now?"

"I've always been able to hear your thoughts."

He shook his head. "No. If that were true, then you would have run away from me back then."

"I did run away from you," she said, her words soft. They hit him in a particularly vulnerable place. And the truth they carried had implications that echoed in parts of him he didn't want to examine.

"And now you have nowhere to run to."

"I chose this," she said.

She stood from her chair and came to him, sitting on his lap. He was instantly hard, the feel of her soft, lush body pressed against his more than he could bear.

"Then you are a fool," he said.

"Don't be like that. You want me."

The certainty in her eyes hit him low in the chest.

"You know I do."

He was tangled up in this. In her. What a strange thing to finally have what he craved.

To have what he had wanted all this time.

And still feel like there was something... Missing. Something that he couldn't quite grasp.

"In some respects these past weeks have been the saddest of my life. How could they not be." She looked down, and then, back up at him. "And in other ways, they have been the best. And I don't know how to un-tangle those things from one another."

His heart did something shattering. Something he didn't want to name.

"Why?" He couldn't stop himself from asking. Even if it was selfish. Even if it was a betrayal.

"I have spent my life taking care of myself. Taking care of other people. I loved Theseus. But I see now that I loved him like a sister. I protected him. I was his shield. And I didn't do it because I'm so good, because I'm so altruistic. Far from it. I did it because by building a safe place for him, I built one for myself too. I did it because it made me indispensable in a way that no other relationship could have. By protecting him, I thought I was protecting myself. By protecting him, I thought that I was making sure that I would never end up alone." He watched as tears welled up in her eyes. He found himself angry again at his brother for putting them there. "But since I collapsed at the Diamond Club, you have taken care of me. No one has ever taken care of me before."

He moved toward her. And put his hand on her cheek, just in time to catch a tear that spilled from her eye and tracked downward. "I'm very sorry that I'm your only option for care, Ariadne. You deserve better than that."

Because when had his care ever accomplished much? Historically, it hadn't.

It hadn't been enough to protect Theseus from their father. Hadn't been enough to protect him from the feeling that something was wrong with him. It hadn't been enough to make him want to trust Dionysus with the truth.

"I don't want anyone else."

He would have argued with her, but he didn't have the strength. Because he had wanted her all this time, all these years, and he had never been able to have her. And he did now. It felt selfish, and yet, he couldn't fathom releasing hold on her now.

This was complicated. But he'd lived simply for a very long time. Had pleased no one and nothing but himself.

Part of him had always craved this. The chance to care for her.

He had told her that he had wanted her without end all of this time, and it was true.

But the desire to care for her was even more pronounced. Even more driving than the lust, and that was saying something, because it was quite simply the most powerful need he had ever experienced.

But there was no point discussing that. Because he didn't know how to define these feelings, and the only thing he knew for sure was that if she married him, he would have her. If they had a child together, she would stay.

She had stayed with Theseus all that time out of loyalty to him. She would stay for the loyalty to their child. Of that he was certain.

And in this way, she would hold onto him.

He would have her.

And if he felt a strange sense of disquiet over the truth that Ariadne had been kept for far too long by a man who couldn't give her everything she deserved, he pushed that to the side. She had made her choice. She wanted certain things that pushed him toward demanding this.

She knew what she was getting into.

She was wild like he was. And she had made her choices. She might deserve more than him, but she herself had said she didn't especially want it.

Of course, she had also thought that she didn't need passion.

But there, he was giving her that at least.

He could give her freedom.

That determination bloomed inside of him. "You know that with me you don't need to present the façade of the perfect wife. With me, you get to be the girl you were here."

A smile curved her lips. "Why do you think I'm out here in the sun and nothing else?"

"You are not beholden to those old rules anymore."

She sighed. "I always will be until your father dies. He can always revoke my position at the company."

"And it means that much to you?"

For the first time, a small crease appeared between her brows, and she looked just slightly like she might not know the answer for certain. When before she had been so... Ruthlessly direct. He could see now, though, that she had spent these past years as Theseus's personal Joan of Arc. And with his actions, he had fundamentally tied her to a stake, and put her at risk for being burned alive.

Because she was right. Their father would hold her hostage, endlessly. And to release hold of it would be to let go of all her work. It would be to lay her sword down after all these years in battle.

He could see why she couldn't do that easily. But he wanted her to. But that was where he had to acknowledge the limitation of what he offered her.

If he could be everything, then he would demand everything in return.

But he couldn't.

He didn't deserve to ask for everything.

"As long as I have a place where I can be myself, then I'll be all right. I haven't had that."

That realization broke him. "You said my brother

was your best friend. But you... You couldn't be yourself with him?"

"I couldn't be everything with him, no. Because of course we didn't share this. This part of myself was pushed down so far, and it wasn't him. Not only him. He can't shoulder the blame for the decisions that I made. For my fears. I let myself get bogged down in what I saw as my own flaws."

"You thought your passion was a flaw?"

"Yes. So I buried it."

He saw again the image of her in full armor, with a sword.

And he saw her clearly.

"You never repressed your passion, you just channeled it into a different place. You were a warrior for him, all this time. You kept everybody away from the thing he was most ashamed of. You stood between him and all of the enemies that he saw around him."

"Some protector," she said. "He's still gone."

He gripped her chin. "You were the fiercest of protectors. That it ended in a way no one would have wished doesn't change that. Your passion shines too brightly to have ever been suppressed entirely. And passion is more than one thing. Your passion was never dangerous." He leaned toward her, his mouth a whisper from hers. "I envy that. I wanted your passion for myself. Of course, I wanted to use it differently, even if I didn't realize. But you could never have suppressed that. It was what I saw from the beginning. Whether you express it by running freely here, or putting on a suit and going to work, and advocating for the people that you employ, you are all passion, Ariadne Katrakis. And it has served you well. It's what makes you strong." He kissed her then, lightly. "Never forget that."

Ariadne thought about what Dionysus had said to her all day. She thought about her own core beliefs, the way that she thought she had successfully taken her passion and extinguished it. He was right. She had simply channeled it into something else. Relentlessly.

It was why protecting Theseus had become her everything. Because it had become her sole mission. Because she had taken that part of herself that had a constellation of dreams and built the dam, so that it was all contained into one pool. She had done it to protect him. She had done it to protect herself.

And she recognized that it wasn't serving her.

Yes, she wanted to continue her work. But she was going to have to allow her passion to be multifaceted again.

Because she was going to have a husband who...

She looked out at the ocean, feeling the sand between her toes as she walked. It was warm. Perfect. She paused, and relished the feeling of the breeze moving over her skin. The way that it made her dress flutter around her ankles.

She and Dionysus had both declined to label what they were.

But he needed more than protection. So did she. That was one way to keep somebody with you.

But it wasn't them.

When they talked, they were always trying to get beneath the surface of each other's skin. When they touched, it was like they were trying to find a way to melt into one.

He had said he imagined her in armor. That was accurate. Because she had found a way to make sure that nothing much hit her. She couldn't feel it. It bounced right off. That was how she lived in a house with a man who she...

She had cared for him more than he cared for her. It might not have been romantic love, but the realization that the investment had been largely hers was a painful one. So of course, she had learned to walk through the world protected. To make sure that she was keeping herself safe. But she couldn't do that with Dionysus.

That wasn't the relationship they were having. It wasn't one where they lived separate lives with walls both inside and out between them. It wasn't the role of protector and protected.

She couldn't have armor, because she needed to be able to be changed by what they were. By what they were finding with each other. And she found she wanted that. She wanted caring for him, being with him, to change her.

Because of course, she wanted to have a child with him. And if she wanted to have a child, she had to be willing to shift and change for that child as well.

It was hard. To try and shift things that had kept her protected for so long. That had protected her from crumbling.

She had wrapped herself in purpose. And that purpose was protecting Theseus. It had kept her from having to deal with anything too multifaceted, anything too difficult.

It had kept her from having to reckon with that shift and feelings she had experienced with Dionysus.

Dionysus had been her friend. Purely. When they had been younger, that had been all it was.

But as they had gotten older, it had changed. And if Theseus hadn't been there to stand between them, the reckoning would have been...

Well, she was afraid of that reckoning. At least, she had been. Until she had lost her safety, until she had lost her comfort, until it had felt in the moment like she'd had nothing left to lose.

And in that bravery, she had found something brilliant. Something beautiful.

She could feel that there were other steps to take. Steps beyond the ones she had already accomplished.

There was further to go.

But it was just... Even if she could fix her own issues, she couldn't fix his.

No. You can't fix his. He has to do that himself.

Well. That left her with very little in the way of reassurance.

Except that she had been trying to fix other people's problems for a very long time. Or at the very least, act as a Band-Aid for them.

She was struggling. With the realization that there was no safe love.

But without love...what was it?

So if she let go of that. She hadn't been able to protect Theseus from that accident. How could she have?

She couldn't heal Dionysus either.

And if she tried, she would only be back in the exact same situation.

She took a long, solid breath and stopped walking. She thought about who she had been. Before she had been taught to be different. Before she had been shown how disposable women were to her father. Before she had been taught that she was easy to abandon, by her mother. With Theseus she'd flung herself into earning her place. She'd loved him, he'd loved her. Their friendship had been deep and real and yet she'd had a role to play within that and in many ways she'd found it comforting. It had been a way to make herself useful.

Dionysus had simply existed with her.

They had run together. Swam together. Smiled together. Laughed together.

Somewhere, in that time with him, he had shown her that she was just fine as she was. And yet it was a lesson that she hadn't wanted to learn. A lesson she had been afraid to learn that, for some strange reason or another.

It scared her even now.

She couldn't say why.

She was still enough for him.

Even in the state he was in. He wanted to marry her. He wanted to be with her. And even if that didn't mean love to him, it meant something. Because he didn't have to do that.

What was love, then?

She wished that she had an answer to that. For her, it had meant a lot more giving than receiving.

She thought about what she knew about Dionysus. He loved being outdoors. He was sentimental. He had that car that he had gotten at seventeen. He had this island that had belonged to them. He had that cave, a sanctuary that was quite literally at the heart of the island, and he had built his house around it.

And yet he was alone. So often in his life, he was alone. She wondered if that was why he took so much care with his surroundings. Maybe it was his way of not feeling so alone.

She had been alone too. She understood. The ways that you went about trying to build community. She had done it through the business. She had tried to make her friendship with Theseus enough.

For him it was sex. And solitude.

Two things that didn't go together, not when you were actually trying to foster intimacy. But he wasn't. Because he was afraid of it. With her, he touched the surface of it. As she did with him.

They were like two wary creatures, cautiously circling each other. Wanting to get closer. Not knowing how.

She had an idea. She knew how to cook, she enjoyed it, in fact. It had been a way that she connected with Theseus, when things were good. They would cook a meal together, and share stories about their day.

She gave the household staff the rest of the day off, and drew on her memory of him. Of what they used to eat together when they were young. She found fresh strawberries, and champagne. And she smiled, thinking of that memory of when they had been so reckless together.

She made fish—his favorite, locally caught from around the island—and risotto, which was more to please her. She set out a fruit platter, similar to the one he had made for her when she had first arrived.

She could remember that night well.

And she knew that he was a nostalgic man. So she just had a feeling. She had a feeling that if she looked in her closet, there would be a white dress, similar to the one she had worn on her eighteenth birthday.

She looked through all the dresses, and found the one. Whether he intended it or not—but knowing him he had, it was strikingly like the one she had on that night.

She wanted to find the words. Inside of herself, between them, to express what she wanted. To express what he meant to her. Right now, this wordless seduction would have to do. This digging in to what mattered to him.

And as she put that white dress on, she mentally imagined taking her armor off. She had been working on that. On being unguarded. On being herself, with nothing between them. But tonight, she was doing it deliberately. Tonight, she was reaching for vulnerability, not just accepting it. Because her armor did a good job at keeping wounds at bay. But it also did a good job of keeping everything else out too. And she didn't want that. Not now.

She left her hair loose, just as she had that night.

She and Theseus had announced their engagement that night.

It was a memory she didn't allow herself to have often. She stood there, in front of the mirror, and let it play out.

CHAPTER TWELVE

Ten years ago...

THE ROOM WAS decorated beautifully. It was the most amazing birthday party she had ever had. And the only reason it was happening was because of Theseus. Because Patrocles so approved of their future union, that he had given his home and resources over to the celebration.

It was beautiful, but it could've been for anyone. It wasn't for her specifically. But for any girl her age. That was fine with her.

She didn't know why she felt like grieving.

She didn't know why she felt like her life was ending.

She was resolved in her friendship with Theseus. She loved him. More than anything.

But as she stood there, watching the room filled with people, it wasn't Theseus's face she saw. She knew that most people would think that was insane. Because they were identical.

But they weren't. They simply weren't.

She didn't see Dionysus. Not when the party started. And not when Theseus took her hand and led her to the front of the room, holding her left hand up, the diamond sparkling there. Not when he announced their engagement.

It would be a long engagement. They wouldn't marry until she was twenty.

She felt like she was spiraling out of control. Because what difference did it make? They could get married tomorrow. It wouldn't change anything. They weren't ever going to kiss, not really. They were never going to make love.

When he did kiss her, there in front of the room, it was dry. And she had to fight to keep from pushing him away, which made her feel instantly guilty. She had agreed to this. Happily. She hadn't been coerced. Not in any fashion.

Afterward, she went out to the balcony.

She walked over to the railing, and put her hands on it. She looked out into the darkness, squinted to see if she could find the sea. Or maybe she was looking to see if she could find Dionysus. She wondered if he was angry.

She hadn't told him about Theseus. He didn't know anything. He would be the one person most likely not to believe it at all. Unless he could really believe that she had kept such an elaborate secret from him. A secret liaison with his brother.

This was the best thing to do. Friendship meant something. It lasted.

It was the only way.

"Ariadne."

She turned sharply, and saw him striding toward her. The look in his eyes was fierce. On fire. He was wearing a white shirt and black pants, just the same as

Theseus, but it was so patently not Theseus. And when he moved to her, and caught her up in his arms, there could never have been any doubt.

His mouth was a wildfire. Setting every part of her on fire. His hands moved over her body. And she wanted to weep. She wanted to run, and she wanted to cling to him for as long as she could. To claim this one taste of passion.

"What the hell is going on?"

She heard Theseus. And she pulled away. Sharply.

And then she separated herself from Dionysus, and went to Theseus.

She let herself come back to the present.

She had run away then. Because it had been too much.

It had been too strong.

It had been everything that she wanted. But she had been just… She wanted to be angry at that girl, but mostly she just felt sorry for her.

What a terrible, awful situation to be in. Because what she wanted more than anything was for somebody to be true to her. To honor the promises they had made to her. So she wouldn't have been able to respect herself if she would have broken her word to Theseus. But also, it left her… So much more alone than she had realized. She just hadn't known men. She just hadn't known.

Her heart beat painfully as she walked downstairs, and set the scene on the terrace. It was a different terrace. Just like it was a different night.

It was different, and yet so much the same.

She texted Dionysus to let him know dinner was

ready, and then she went to stand with her back to the door, her hands on the railing, her focus out toward the sea.

She heard footsteps behind her.

"Ariadne."

She turned, and it was like those moments melted together. The man he had been, filled with anger and passion and need, right there with the man he was now.

And there was nothing between them.

He took her in his arms and he kissed her. And she kissed him back. With all of the passion and need that she had tried to suppress then.

"Dionysus," she whispered against his mouth, because she would let there be no doubt that she knew exactly who he was.

Exactly what she was doing.

She knew. Of course she did.

The kiss was a burning wildfire, and it was like she had a second chance. To burn because she chose to. To burn because she wanted this, and wanted him more than anything.

The reason that she was here was lost.

All the sadness, all the grief, all the years apart lost in that moment.

She clung to him, and kissed him from the depths of her very soul.

Because she wouldn't run away. Not this time. She had a chance to do it differently. She had a chance to make a different choice.

"Dinner is lovely," he growled against her mouth. "But I have to have you."

"Yes."

Because this was how that night should have ended. She should have chosen him then. She should have.

As he picked her up, sweeping her off her feet and carrying her in the house, up the stairs, she felt like she was living in those two moments. And what might've been and what was.

At least he was here now.

He was here holding her now.

He felt it too, she knew that he did. Knew that this was more than just another coming together. It was a reclamation. A reckoning.

It was their chance to start again. To explore what might've been.

It is. It isn't just what might've been. You get to make a different choice.

You get to choose him.

Her heart felt like it had wings, lifting her chest. He stripped her dress from her body, and cast it to the floor. And she took her time baring his body to her own hungry gaze.

He was everything.

She said his name like an incantation, over and over again. It had always been him.

The moment that she had met him, it had been like all the pieces of her life had fallen into place. Theseus had been by his side, and Theseus had been vulnerable. He appealed to her, because he needed her. She had turned away from her clear and obvious fate because she had been too afraid. And when he had been the braver of the two of them, when he had pulled her into his arms, she had walked away. She had run away. Because she had been too frightened to do anything else.

Because Dionysus could truly hurt her.

With Theseus, she had chosen a clear path that she could see the end of.

And he had never had the power to shatter her.

It was devastating to admit that. Even to herself. She had cared for him, but what she had chosen was safety. Not in the way that she had imagined. It wasn't just about a sense of physical security, or even companionship. It was that there were two paths in front of her. And one had the potential to be wild and glorious. But she had chosen safety, not over potential heartbreak, but over potential joy. Because she hadn't felt like she was worthy.

Had she always felt like she wasn't enough?

And then she had been grappling with it all over again while life had taken Theseus from her. Had taken the first pregnancy from her. But she was still here. And so was Dionysus. And just like that, she felt like she was enough. She felt like she deserved everything.

Truly.

She took a great gasp of air, trying to do something about the sharp pain in her chest. Because this hurt as much as it healed.

But then Dionysus kissed her again, his firm mouth grounding her to the spot, making her feel breathless. Weightless. And wholly secure all at the same time.

She ran her hands over his muscular body. Committed every inch of him to memory.

He was hers. He was hers and she wanted him so very badly.

What was love?

He wanted her just like she was.

He was the only one. Who seemed to want every part of her. Who seemed to think that she was enough, just as she was.

He loved her.

She knew it. As sure and certain as she knew where the sea was just beyond the courtyard. As sure as she knew the path to the oasis that they loved to swim in. He loved her.

And she loved him too.

It was why she had run away from him. Because that terrified her. The real truth was she was afraid of being in love alone. So she had chosen a man that she could never truly fall in love with, who could never fall in love with her, so that she could never be blindsided by what she was lacking. She had chosen half, because she didn't want to try to carry the whole of it and fail.

She had chosen it.

She was done. She wanted all. She wanted everything. She wanted him.

And everything that meant.

She kissed her way down his body, found herself on her knees before him, and encircled his hard, masculine length in her hand. She moved her head forward, and took the head of him between her lips, tasting him, but more than that, telling him how she felt. How much she loved him. How much she wanted him.

"Only you," she whispered as she slid her tongue along his shaft.

She pleasured him like that until he gripped her hair. Until he hauled her to her feet and kissed her. Driving her back against the wall, where he thrust into her hard, holding her thigh up over his hip as he took her over and over again.

As he reminded her that they were the only ones that were like this.

This was passion.

And for the two of them, this was the only passion there can ever be.

She felt replete with it. Bursting with it.

It was absolutely everything.

And she gave herself up to the joy of it, clinging to his shoulders and crying out his name as she found her release. As he roared out his own, clinging to her, pulsing deep within her.

"I love you," she whispered.

But then he let go of her. And he took a step back.

The look in his eyes was wild. Confused. And she knew that she had done something wrong. She knew that... She had made a misstep.

No. You didn't.

She had to say it. She'd had to tell the truth, even if he couldn't handle it. Even if it would end badly.

She had to, because she was done living with half. Done living in the darkness.

"Dionysus, I love you."

He turned away from her, the muscles on his broad back shifting as he put his face in his hands for a moment.

"Did I say something wrong? Because I thought that between us there was no wrong thing to say."

"Ariadne." He turned to face her, his eyes wild, haunted. "You don't have to say that. You don't have to do this, just because you agreed to marry me."

"Why do you think the marriage has anything to do with this?"

"I don't think that you want to get married again for any reason other than love. And… You're right. I shouldn't have made demands of you. Not when I wasn't ready to give you everything. I can't do that to you again."

"You love me," she said, the words coming from a deep, convicted place inside of her.

"It isn't enough."

"Of course it's enough. You are enough for me."

"That isn't what I mean," he said, his face suddenly going cold and remote. "I couldn't give you what you wanted back then, if I could have you wouldn't have married him. Not even to protect him."

"I didn't choose him over you," she said, pain lancing her chest. "Not like that. You know that. I chose fear over you. That is true. But I'm done with that now. I'm not choosing fear anymore."

"It's already done. And it can't ever be that way between us. And the fact that you think it can is why this has to be over. You chose him. And that's all there is to it."

"I am choosing you now," she said. "I'm choosing you because this was what I was too afraid to take then."

"If my brother hadn't died we never would've had this."

"I don't think that's true."

Her chest felt like it had been caved in. "I don't think it's true. Because I really do believe that we would've found a way to each other eventually. You're my fate,

Dionysus. I really believe that. I have been… Untangling this for weeks now. Maybe even for years. Spinning it all out inside of me. There's a reason that you were the person that I went to that day at the club."

"You were joining the club. It wasn't as if it was magic that you were there."

"You were my touchstone. You were the only way forward that I could see. You were the only person that I wanted to be with. Don't you understand that? You terrified me then. Not just passion, but you. Because if I couldn't have you, then I was afraid that life wouldn't be worth living for me. And I was happier to take half and feel safe."

"And what changed?"

He was challenging her. Like she didn't actually know what had changed. She did.

"I did. I changed. I realized what I was doing to myself. I realized that I was letting all of the bad things in my life decide how good my life was going to be, and I don't want that anymore. I realized that I was happier loving the people around me more than they loved me, and I don't want that anymore." She looked at him directly. "So if you can't love me as much as I love you, then I will walk away, because I'm not going to live like that anymore."

"Why are you risking everything now?"

Because everything was different. They were different. And the same. Far too much the same and it had to change. It needed to. She had been too afraid of risk ten years ago. She had been afraid of being hurt.

But she'd lost her best friend. He had died right before he'd gotten to step into his truth.

What tribute would it be if she didn't learn from him? What good would it do?

She had to live in her truth. Just as Dionysus needed to learn to live in his.

They had the kind of love that could easily live in the light, why be afraid? Why hide?

For Theseus, for all the love she still felt for him, she couldn't hide.

She should have been honest with him. She should have been honest with herself.

She'd never go back to lying. Not now.

"Because. Because I matter. I do. And you have only yourself to blame for that realization. Because you treated me like I was a whole person from the moment that we met. You were waiting for me to do something interesting. You didn't need me to do you a favor. You didn't need me to rescue you. You loved me the way that I was. Even if it was just as a friend, Dionysus, though I don't think that's the case. Realizing that, looking back at everything with clear focus, that showed me what I want. I want to find my way back to that. I want… I want for us to be together. Really. But I can't heal you. You have to heal you. The reason that I didn't feel like I was enough for Theseus was that I thought it was my job to love him in a way he couldn't love himself. I thought that I was holding him together, but you simply cannot do that for another person. I can't. You can't."

She took a deep, shuddering breath. "I have to let you find your own way in this. And I'm brave enough to do it. Because I would rather risk everything to get what we're both worth, than go along with half. Ever again. That night… That night when you kissed me on my birthday, I ran away from you. I wish that I hadn't. I wanted to give you a night where I didn't run. So I want to make it very clear that I am not running away from you. I'm giving you space. So that you can decide what you're going to do next. So that you can decide if you want to heal, because one thing I know for sure, I cannot sit there in hope that I will be enough to heal someone ever again. I need you to do it. I need you to find that in yourself."

She felt shattered. She felt… Devastated. But she had to do this.

"I love you, Dionysus. And that's why I have to leave you. Even if you don't understand that, it's the truth." She blinked back tears. "I'm going to go pack. And then I'm going to call my pilot and have him come and get me."

"Oh, yes. Of course you have a pilot now as well."

"I'm one of the richest people in the world," she said. She blinked hard. "But right now I feel like I don't have anything. It's terrifying. But I would rather be terrified and know that I was demanding nothing less than what I deserve."

She turned and she left him. It was the hardest thing that she had ever done.

Her chest felt like it was caving in, as she made the phone call. As she waited.

Finally, she walked down to the beach, with her one bag of belongings, and boarded the plane.

She was leaving the island. She was leaving Dionysus.

She was leaving behind her hopes and dreams.

This was bravery. And it was terrible.

But she knew that it was the only way that things could ever be all right in the end. The only way they could ever be more than all right.

She knew what happened when you sit in an old wound and let it fester. She knew what happened when you didn't do the hard work of healing.

And she loved Dionysus too much to consign him to that fate.

She loved herself too much.

She cried all the way back to England.

Life had been especially unkind to her recently.

And this had been her choice.

She could only hope that in the end everything worked out as best it could.

She could only hope, that in the end, she had his love.

Because if not, she knew that nothing would ever be the way that it was supposed to be.

Dionysus was her fate.

But he was going to have to do the work so that they could both claim it.

CHAPTER THIRTEEN

HE SAT IN the grotto at the back of his house. He looked at the soft glow of the salt lamp in the corner. And then he stood up and turned it on its side. The salt shattered into millions of pieces.

He did the same with the other and watched it go to pieces. A spray of rose-colored failure all around the floor.

Where was the healing? He hadn't seen it yet. He hadn't even come close.

Nothing in him was healed. Everything was broken. Fractured and ruined.

She loved him. She claimed that she loved him.

But no one had ever... No one had ever stayed with him. No professions of love had ever been enough. Why would this one?

She had chosen his brother over him. But that wasn't what he was truly afraid of. He had been a bastard, and he knew that.

He had been unnecessarily cruel to her. But he had done it to protect himself.

Because...

Because he had taken his father's fists for Theseus. He had stood in between the two of them. He had been a target so that Theseus could remain unscathed. And it hadn't been enough.

Theseus had stolen Ariadne from him.

He hadn't even loved her. Not like Dionysus had. But there was something about him that made what he wanted unimportant. He had thought that he and Ariadne had connected, but she had chosen Theseus.

Nothing that he did, no part of him, had ever been sufficient. She said that he loved her as she was, but when had she done the same for him?

She said that she was afraid.

Yes, she had. She had said that. But she had… She had utterly destroyed him. When what he had endured losing her had been unthinkable. He…

And you're losing her again. To what end?

If he didn't lose her now, he would eventually. He would lose her over and over again. Because that was how it was with everyone.

He had never seen love in his life that had lasted. He had never seen love in a way that endured. There was not a single connection, not blood or water that seemed to stand up in his life.

What was he supposed to think. He had no example of love lasting. He had no example of him being worthy.

Ariadne had just taken a risk. She had laid everything down for him.

And still…

Still.

He had his island. He had his cave.

That would be enough.

All of this has been a replacement of her. And you know it.

All of it. He had built this house, he had built this cave, where he used to go to hide from his father's violent moods.

He had structured this entire place around finding some sanity without her. Finding something that held him to the earth.

And now he was left with only this place, and it felt utterly insufficient. It was nothing, and so was he.

Without her.

She took a risk. Why can't you?

It wasn't enough.

No. So far, it hadn't been enough. But neither had this place. Neither had his salt lamps. He laughed, bitterly. Because everything had been a bandage, on a mortal wound. Everything had been a pointless, useless exercise, trying to piece together a life that felt like something without Ariadne in it, and now he could have her, and he wasn't claiming her.

Now he was being a coward.

She had said that she wanted to re-create that kiss. Re-create the moment where she had chosen to walk away, and stay instead.

But the truth of it was, he hadn't gone after her then. He had never said everything that was in his heart.

He had been a coward.

At the first sign that she might not feel the same, he had fallen back.

Rather than ripping himself open.

She had done it over again. He had to do the same.

He stood there, frozen, in the middle of his ruined grotto.

Because the grotto had only ever been a mirror of his soul. Hollow and lonely. And now broken.

He would have her.

He would.

He would go after her, and he would tell her how he felt. Because of course he loved her.

Thinking that fixed something inside of him. Something he hadn't fully realized was broken. Oh, he knew that much was broken inside of him. But he hadn't realized that what he truly needed was her love. And to love her in return.

But she was right. He already did.

Railing against it was futile.

He loved her.

And if he didn't claim her, then he would be the author of his own misery. He would finally have to blame himself, like he should have done years ago.

Because she might have walked away, but he had let her go.

And he wouldn't make that mistake again.

He loved Ariadne.

And she would be his wife.

She would be his love.

Because she was everything. And he was finally willing to admit it.

When her period failed to come, she wasn't shocked, so much as resigned.

She was pregnant. With Dionysus's baby. And she

could carry on the way that she had intended to. She could carry on the way that they had started.

But she wasn't going to do that.

She had lost Dionysus, so nothing else really mattered. She was going to have to be billed.

All she had was herself, and she was… She was embracing it. The terror of it. The beauty.

She had no other choice. This was what living bravely felt like. This was what being true to herself felt like. It was hard.

But this was what she needed to do. This was the only way she was ever going to become the kind of mother that her child deserved. The best mother that she could be.

She wasn't afraid. She wasn't afraid anymore that she wouldn't know how.

Because she knew that she could grow. And change. She knew she could be braver and better.

She was proud, and she was happy in some ways for the girl that she had been.

Even if she was wretchedly sad for the woman she was now in other ways.

But she had a meeting scheduled with Patrocles. And she was ready.

He still kept an office in the main building of Katrakis Shipping. And she was ushered in immediately. Where he sat behind the desk. He was small now. Shrunken with age. And it amazed her just how much trouble this one, small, shriveled man had caused. Once, he had been feared. And now… He had lost his oldest son. A son he had never truly known, because he was such a horrible man. And she could throw that back in his face now. But he would never understand. He would never see it. Because he would never grow. That he would never change.

He would never do the work he needed to do to become a decent human being.

"Ariadne. You have been off the radar for some time."

"I've been dealing with some things. I have to tell you. I had a miscarriage."

He looked up at her, his eyes sharp. "That is a shame."

"Yes. But I am pregnant again."

"Good. I had thought that Theseus might have left behind insurance."

She shook her head. "No. It isn't Theseus's child. It's Dionysus's."

Because she would never deny who the father of this baby was, no matter what happened between them. She was going to tell him next. It didn't matter that they couldn't be together, she would give him a chance to be a father. She knew that he would be a wonderful father.

"*Dionysus,*" said Patrocles. "That changes things."

"I thought it might. And it's all right if it does. If you take everything from me, I don't care. I'm not playing your games anymore. Theseus and I lived our lives trying to please you. It was so important to him. I'm not going to do that anymore. I don't care about you. I care about this company. And I care about the people in it. I think you should let me continue to run it because I do a great job. I could've lied to you. And I could've told you that this was Theseus's baby. You would never have known. Science wouldn't have been able to prove otherwise. But that would just be giving you more power than you deserve. You don't deserve any."

"Then you will not keep this company."

"I thought you might say that. But know this, I have a plan to expand things over the next few years, and if you keep things going the way that you were running them before Theseus took over, the company is going to die. You are welcome to cut me off as a sop to your pride. You lose your legacy. You'll lose everything. So it's up to you. Be spiteful, and cold, as we all know you are. Cut off your own legacy to spite your face. Or let me have it. Let me continue on in the work Theseus was going to do. The work that I planned to do. After all, we will still be connected by a child. Whether either of us want that to be true or not."

She turned and walked out of the office, but stopped. "I hope you know, that your sons are two of the finest men ever to be born into the world. I love Theseus. But all he really cared about was being good enough, and he never thought he was. He was. He was good enough just like he was. And so is Dionysus. He has always been my friend. He has always been... You don't give him any credit. But he built a life for himself completely apart from you. And that must be why you dislike him so much. He set out to prove that he didn't need you. And he did it. Spectacularly. As much as I love Theseus, in the end, it's Dionysus that I want to be. Because he proves just how useless you are."

And then she did walk out, her breath leaving her body in a painful gust.

She had done it. She had potentially cut everything

off. And it was a gamble. One that terrified her. Because maybe it wouldn't pay off. Maybe she had just condemned all the workers in that company.

She would start again. She would hire all of them. That was exactly what she would do. She didn't need to lean on anybody.

She would make her own legacy.

Her own Katrakis legacy.

In honor of everything Theseus could have been.

In honor of everything Dionysus was.

Because her child would know about both of them.

When her child learned about the heritage of being a Katrakis, she would make sure that it meant something good.

And she would be a part of that.

She swept out of the building, and walked back toward her townhouse.

She didn't know how she was going to hold herself together. She was shaking. She wanted to call Dionysus. Well. She had to. She had to tell him about the baby.

She walked into the lobby of her building. And she saw him. His back turned away from her.

It was just like that night, on the balcony.

When she was eighteen.

Except their positions were reversed.

And she found herself striding toward him, all of her need, all of her passion, rising up inside of her. "Dionysus."

He turned, and she grabbed him, kissing him, for all the world to see. And she knew that they still had so many things left to be said between them.

She knew that she shouldn't be doing this, that she had taken a firm stance on love, or nothing. But she needed to touch him. This was honest.

And she had vowed not to turn away from these kinds of moments.

So she didn't.

"Ariadne," he said, his voice hoarse.

"You're here."

"Of course I am. I had to come for you. I had to. Ariadne, I love you."

Her heart hit her breastbone hard. "You love me?"

"Yes. I was a fool, and I was a coward. I was so... I didn't know what love was, Ariadne. I had no idea what it looks like. I knew that what I felt for you was real, but I didn't know what it could be.

"I was afraid. I was afraid of what it would look like to lose you. But then I did. And... I have never felt like I was enough for anyone."

"Please," she said, holding his hands. "I need you to understand. It wasn't that you weren't enough. You were too much. You were so much that I was overwhelmed with it, overflowing with it. So I ran away. But I'm not running anymore. I'm not." She took a deep breath. "I'm pregnant. And I told your father. I told him it was your baby. I think I've lost everything."

He stood there, looking stunned. "You... You're pregnant?"

"Yes."

"You little fool. Why did you tell him that I was the father?"

"Because you are. Because I'm proud that you're the

father of my baby. And I'm proud that you're the love of my life. Because I wanted him to know. Because I wanted everyone to know. Because... Because I was committed. To being brave. To being honest. I am not hiding away parts of myself to stay safe anymore. So I am very, very not safe and I'm so glad that you're here."

He gathered her up in his arms. "You're not running. But I came after you. To tell you that I loved you, even then. To tell you that I have done everything in the intervening years to try and convince myself that I didn't need you. But I did. You were always what was missing. You are my fate, Ariadne. You are right about that. Because nothing was ever quite so perfect as it was when we were together. And we didn't find this as soon as we might have. But we have it now. We have it now."

"I love you."

"And I love you. Always."

It had started in the Diamond Club, with that empty chair. Or perhaps it had truly started here, all those years ago. But one thing she knew for certain was that she loved Dionysus Katrakis with all of her soul.

And there was no room at all for fear.

EPILOGUE

WHEN ARIADNE FOUND out that she was pregnant with triplets, she had some strong words for her husband. Only the Katrakis genes could be blamed for such a thing.

They had married quickly. They didn't care about what the world thought, not anymore.

And there were rumors, of course there were. But she didn't care.

The pregnancy with the triplets was surprisingly uneventful, though she did have to stay in bed for most of it. And it wasn't until Androcles, Adonis and Achilles were eight, that she was back to being a rightful member of the Diamond Club, on her own merit.

Her new shipping empire had absolutely smashed Katrakis. She had hired all the employees from Katrakis and given them raises.

In the end, she had bought the struggling company from Patrocles. The payoff that she gave him was nothing compared to what the company had been worth at one time.

It felt like justice.

As did making James godfather to the triplets, and

ensuring he was the beneficiary of most of Theseus's wealth. They also brought him on as CFO of their company.

When he joined the Diamond Club some years on, it created the most delightful ripple in the staid institution.

It was also a particularly bittersweet joy to finally inter Theseus's ashes with a grave marker that truly honored him.

Beloved partner to James
Dearest friend of Ariadne
Most loved brother of Dionysus

James and Dionysus had become very fast friends, and though part of her would always mourn that Dionysus hadn't known Theseus fully, in the way she had, she loved that he got to know him through James.

And when James found love again ten years later they and the triplets were in the wedding.

Identical boys, and all menaces.

She loved them.

As she loved her husband. They were busy, of course, but they always found time for each other. They always took time out on the island.

They brought their children, who ran around and swam and played.

And one night, they snuck down to swim, just the two of them. Like they were young, and like they were themselves. She swam up to her husband, and wrapped her arms around his neck, kissing him. "Do you know," she said. "I'm the richest woman in the world."

"I had heard that," he said.

"It isn't the money," she said. "It's us."

"Ah," he said. "Something we can agree on."

* * * * *

COMING SOON!

We really hope you enjoyed reading this book.
If you're looking for more romance
be sure to head to the shops when
new books are available on

Thursday 15th August

To see which titles are coming soon, please visit
millsandboon.co.uk/nextmonth

MILLS & BOON

MILLS & BOON®

Coming next month

GREEK PREGNANCY CLAUSE
Maya Blake

'You have thirty seconds. Then I walk out,' Ares warned in a soft, dangerous murmur.

Odessa believed him. After all, hadn't he done that once, this man who was a world removed from the younger version she'd known. Or was he?

Hadn't he possessed this overwhelming presence even back then, only caged it better?

Now the full force of it bore down on her, Odessa was at once wary of and drawn to it, like a hapless moth dancing towards a destroying flame.

She watched, mesmerized despite herself as his folded arms slowly dropped, his large, masculine hands drawing attention to his lean hips, the dangerously evocative image he made simply by...*being*.

At what felt like the last second, she took a deep breath and took the boldest leap. 'Before my father's memorial is over, Vincenzo Bartorelli will announce our engagement.' Acid flooded her mouth at the very thought. 'I would rather jump naked into Mount Etna than marry him. So, I'd...I'd like you to say that I'm marrying you instead. And in return...' *Dio*, was she really doing this? 'And in return I'll give you whatever you want.'

Continue reading
GREEK PREGNANCY CLAUSE
Maya Blake

Available next month
millsandboon.co.uk

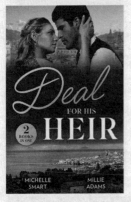
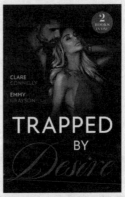

Afterglow Books is a trend-led, trope-filled list of books with diverse, authentic and relatable characters, a wide array of voices and representations, plus real world trials and tribulations. Featuring all the tropes you could possibly want (think small-town settings, fake relationships, grumpy vs sunshine, enemies to lovers) and all with a generous dose of spice in every story.

♪ @millsandboonuk
⊙ @millsandboonuk
afterglowbooks.co.uk
#AfterglowBooks

For all the latest book news, exclusive content and giveaways scan the QR code below to sign up to the Afterglow newsletter:

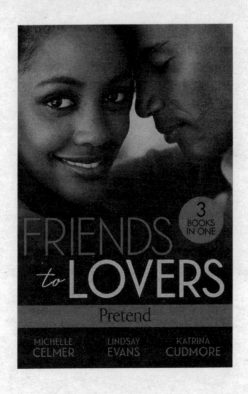